Nine Lives

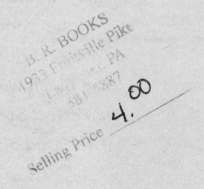

Also available by
Wendy Corsi Staub

Blue Moon

Blood Red

The Black Widow

The Perfect Stranger

The Good Sister

For a full list of titles, visit
www.wendycorsistaub.com

Nine Lives

A Lily Dale Mystery

Wendy Corsi Staub

CROOKED
LANE

NEW YORK

Copyright © 2015 by Wendy Corsi Staub.

All rights reserved.

Published in the United States by Crooked Lane Books, an imprint of The Quick Brown Fox & Company LLC.

Crooked Lane Books and its logo are trademarks of The Quick Brown Fox & Company LLC.

Library of Congress Catalog-in-Publication data available upon request.

ISBN (mass market): 978-1-68331-086-0
ISBN (hardcover): 978-1-62953-248-6
ISBN (paperback): 978-1-62953-825-9
ISBN (ePub): 978-1-62953-249-3
ISBN (Kindle): 978-1-62953-648-4
ISBN (ePDF): 978-1-62953-649-1

Cover design by Lori Palmer
Book design by Jennifer Canzone

Printed in the United States.

www.crookedlanebooks.com

Crooked Lane Books
34 West 27th St., 10th Floor
New York, NY 10001

Hardcover Edition: October 2015
Paperback Edition: September 2016
Mass Market Edition: November 2016

10 9 8 7 6 5 4 3 2 1

For the real Lily Dale and the spirited people who live there—always close to my heart, if no longer to my home.

For the real Chance the Cat, who showed up as a pregnant stray on our doorstep on a warm June evening and now contentedly snoozes away her days in a chair beside my desk.

And, as always, for my sons, Morgan and Brody, and for my husband, Mark, on our twenty-fourth wedding anniversary. Cent'anni!

Prologue

June 18
Lily Dale, New York

Less than two weeks from now, when Lily Dale's official summer season is under way, Leona Gatto's guesthouse will be teeming with overnight visitors. But on this cool and gusty June night, she and Chance the Cat have the place all to themselves.

The mackerel tabby is lounging on the bay window seat downstairs in the front parlor, watching the world go by on Cottage Row. At this time of year, the world mainly consists of fireflies and the occasional flitting moth, though tonight, the breeze has sent all sorts of fascinating things—to a cat, anyway—skittering past the window.

Soon, however, the annual human parade will begin. Lily Dale might be the tiniest of tiny towns, but as the birthplace of the Spiritualist religion well over a century ago, it remains populated almost entirely by psychic mediums. A handful, including Leona, are in residence year-round. Most prefer to spend the rigorous western New York winter elsewhere. They return just ahead of the throng of summer visitors who find their way to the Dale because they're seeking something: a connection to a lost loved one, psychic counseling, physical or spiritual healing . . .

No exception, Leona arrived fifteen years ago, middle-aged and newly widowed, paralyzed by grief and hoping somebody here could connect her to her late husband.

Inevitably, somebody did. Her husband's message: that she should stay for a while instead of hurrying back home to Wyoming.

"Are you sure Edgar said that?" Leona asked the medium in surprise. They'd built a wonderful life together out west, and she couldn't imagine that he'd want her to abandon it. "Maybe it's not him."

"He's wearing a black cowboy hat and he's very insistent," Patsy Metcalf said with a smile. "He wants me to tell you that it's about time you've come to your senses and put on a practical pair of shoes."

"That's Edgar! He was always yelling at me for wearing heels when I travel. But I can't believe he wants me to stay out east. He was born and raised on a ranch, and so was I. Wyoming will always be home."

"Remember, my dear, I'm not here to tell you what you expect or even want to hear. I'm here to relay what your loved one wants you to know."

Truer words were never spoken. Little did Leona realize then that she herself would eventually be capable of parting the delicate veil that separates this world from the next. She knows now that Edgar did, indeed, want her to sell their dude ranch to the hotel chain that had been sniffing around it for years. He'd always said they'd get the place over his dead body. In the end, that was what had happened—but with his blessing.

Wyoming was her old home. Lily Dale is her forever one.

This house had a long history as an inn but had been turned into a private residence when she bought it. She reclaimed its roots and transformed it into a guesthouse very much like the one she'd left behind, only with a Victorian theme instead of a Western one.

She's always enjoyed welcoming new people into her home, getting to know them, and making them feel comfortable.

But that isn't the only reason the terrible loneliness is behind her.

After years of mediumship training, she remains in touch with her late husband, along with countless other folks. Some are old friends, and some are just plain old. Centuries old. She's grown quite accustomed to having them around. Most of the time, the spirits coexist with her just as seamlessly as Chance the Cat does.

Tonight, however, one of her regular spirit guides is as twitchy as the weather. Typically a benign presence, Nadine has been wreaking havoc around the house. At first, Leona attributed the flickering lights and random creaks and thumps to the night wind.

And she attributed her missing laptop—which she hasn't seen since this morning—to good old-fashioned old age. But now that it's failed to turn up in any of the usual spots where she might have misplaced it, Leona isn't so sure Nadine is to blame. This wouldn't be the first time Nadine or the others have played hide-and-seek with her belongings, but it should have resurfaced by now.

Then the usual drip from the upstairs sink faucet turned into a gush that overflowed onto the floor. While Leona was wiping that up, the downstairs faucet mysteriously turned on and flooded the kitchen sink and then the floor.

"That's enough!" Leona said sharply after slipping and nearly falling.

Harmless little pranks are one thing, but she could have been hurt. And water damage in an old house is no picnic.

This just isn't like Nadine.

The last straw was when, minutes ago, a fuse blew with a popping, sizzling sound, plunging the whole house into darkness.

"Oh, for the love of . . ." Leona stood with her hands on her hips. "What's going on? Are you trying to get rid of me? You'll have to try a whole lot harder than that."

After a grueling trip to the ancient fuse box in the spidery cellar, she decided that a snack would settle her nerves. But when she opened the fridge and started rooting around, she discovered that the full carton of half-and-half she bought this afternoon was somehow empty.

Nadine again. Leona hasn't touched a drop—the carton is still sealed—and cats can't open refrigerator doors.

Some might argue the same about Spirit. Funny how even that particular word—*Spirit*, as the energy is called here in the Dale—had sounded awkward to Leona's ears when she first arrived. Funnier still to think that she, like so many newcomers, was steeped in skepticism.

If you spend enough time here, the extraordinary becomes ordinary.

Now, thanks to Nadine's antics, she stands in the bathroom mirror trying to make herself presentable for a late-night trip to the closest store a few miles down the road. She takes her morning coffee with plenty of cream, and Chance the Cat, unlike most felines, isn't exactly lactose intolerant. She laps it up, especially in her current state, which—

Hearing a creaking sound downstairs, Leona frowns at her reflection.

"Oh, Nadine, now what are you up to?" she asks, and she is startled to see the spirit guide fleetingly take filmy female form in the room behind her.

That's unusual. Nadine rarely materializes. Like the others, she is usually merely a presence Leona can feel but not see or hear, other than inside her own head.

Framed in the doorway, the apparition holds up a transparent hand, her palm facing Leona as if to stop her from leaving the room.

Leona scowls. "Make up your mind. I thought you wanted me out of the house, thanks to your Houdini act with my half-and-half. Now you want me to stay put? I don't . . ."

She trails off, realizing that Nadine is no merry prankster. Nadine's shaking her head, and her glittering eyes are wide with concern.

"What is it? What's wrong? Are you trying to warn me about something?"

But the spirit has already faded, leaving Leona alone.

The silence in the bathroom is punctuated by wind chimes tinkling below the window. That's not unusual. Wind chimes are as common as porches in the Dale.

But to Leona's ear, they've drastically multiplied: a tintinnabulation as ominous as the alarm down at the old firehouse. The clanging grows to a fever pitch and is abruptly curtailed.

Silence again.

Unsettled, Leona goes back to brushing her hair.

Her strokes slow as she hears another creaking sound, this time in the hallway outside the door.

She isn't alone after all.

She uneasily attempts to tune into the energy, wondering if one of her other guides has come to pay her a visit. But the presence doesn't feel familiar, and it certainly isn't Edgar, whose proximity always fills her with light and warmth. This energy is dark and oppressive. Maybe it's not Spirit at all.

Maybe it's a living person: a stranger, a prowler.

Wielding the hairbrush in one hand like a weapon, she uses the other to painstakingly turn the knob and pull.

She was right about one thing. She isn't alone. But she doesn't find a stranger on the other side of the door.

Her eyes widen in shock at the sight of a familiar face. "What are *you* doing here?"

Chapter 1

"If one more thing goes wrong today . . ." Bella Jordan steps over the broken vase on the floor and grabs the broom propped in a corner of her tiny kitchen. She's been tripping over it all morning, but there's no other spot amid the clutter, and it doesn't make sense to store it back where it belongs: jammed into the usually overcrowded pantry cupboard that triples as a linen and broom closet.

Her goal today is to *empty* that closet, transferring its contents to the cardboard moving boxes she also keeps tripping over, along with the big black trash bags stuffed with household items that are, like all their furniture, destined to be tossed or given away.

Most of it is perfectly useful. She'd keep it if she only knew where she and her son Max will wind up living. But she can't fit much into her small car, she can't afford a moving van or storage unit, and she refuses to borrow money from her mother-in-law, to whom she's plenty beholden as it is. So the Salvation Army will get the lamps, books, decorative glassware . . .

Minus one vase.

With a sigh, she begins sweeping the shards of crystal into the dustpan she'd tossed onto the already crowded countertop following a previous mishap with a glass—which was how she'd then knocked over the vase.

Maybe I should go around with a dustpan hanging from my belt like some klutzy handyman. Or rather, nonhandy nonman.

She's never been the most graceful gal in town, but the move-out process has produced more mishaps than usual. Earlier, she'd chipped a plate and broken the handle off a coffee mug. Neither had value, sentimental or otherwise. But this latest casualty was an expensive one.

Not as expensive, by any stretch of the imagination, as the collection of vintage Carnival glass pieces she'd inherited from her godmother and sold off over the past few desperate months to pay the rent and bills.

There may not be hordes of antique dealers lining up to buy a fancy vase like the one she'd just broken, but it had been a wedding present from . . .

Who was it? A friend? One of her coworkers? Sam's late great-aunt Doris?

Funny how easy it is to forget things you probably should remember and remember things you'd rather forget.

Oh, Sam . . .

Bella doesn't want to forget *him*. Just the illness that had stolen him away late last year after long, dark months of suffering.

As if mustered by the mere thought of Sam, a breeze slips through the screen. It's slightly cool, fragranced by the blooming mock orange shrubs her husband always loved and silvery with tinkling wind chimes he gave her for her last birthday.

She was charmed by the strings of pretty stained-glass angels cascading from delicate chains, but he kept apologizing.

"I wanted to get you something more, but . . ." But he was sick, and money was growing tighter by the day.

"I don't want anything more. I don't need anything but these." *And you. I need you, Sam . . .*

"Your Christmas present is going to be great," he promised her. "I already know what I'm getting for you, so don't worry."

She did worry. Not about Christmas presents. About Sam.

She can hear his voice amid the swaying wind chimes, calling her his "Bella Angelo—my beautiful angel," the literal translation of her name. His version of it, anyway.

Her ancestors were from Sicily, and her maiden name was Angelo. Her given name is Isabella, but Sam never called her that.

To him, she was Bella Angelo—that, or Bella Blue, she remembers, staring at the gently fluttering curtains he said exactly matched the cobalt color of her eyes. She'd made them from fabric remnants, using a sewing machine in the domestic arts classroom at the middle school where she taught science.

"Why are you so good at everything you do, Bella Blue?" Sam was so impressed, you'd have thought she'd just hand-stitched a designer gown.

"Oh, please. You're the only one who thinks so."

"Not true." He ticked on his fingers the people he felt were equally enamored of her: their friends, her colleagues and students, and, of course, Frank Angelo, her own doting, widowed dad, still alive at the time.

Conspicuously missing from the list: Sam's mother.

Millicent Jordan had made up her mind long before Bella even met her that no woman could ever be good enough for her son. The fact that she lives almost a thousand miles away in Chicago was a blessing throughout Bella and Sam's marriage. Sam loved his mother, but Bella privately called her Maleficent—after the villainess in *Sleeping Beauty*.

Now, however, life would be easier if she were nearby. For all her faults, Millicent's the only family they have left. She's a lousy mother-in-law, but she was a good mom and would probably be a decent grandmother, given the opportunity.

Which I'm about to give to her.

Sam was young and brash enough not to have made life insurance a priority and had accidentally let his meager policy lapse. Even with health insurance coverage, expensive treatments for his illness had consumed the money they'd been saving to buy a home of their own one day. On the heels of losing him, Bella lost her teaching position to budget cuts. As she began a futile job hunt, the landlord decided to put the house on the market. A wealthy buyer snapped it up, planning to turn it into a majestic private home.

Her lease expires at the end of June. Which is tomorrow. With nowhere else to turn, she and Max are driving out to visit Millicent for the summer and figure out their next step.

If only she didn't have to uproot Max after all he's been through. This is the only home he's ever known, the only home that's ever mattered to her.

She'd grown up in rental apartments all over New York City. She was a new bride when she moved into the first-floor apartment of this Victorian triplex in Bedford, just eight short tree-lined suburban blocks from her first teaching job and three to the commuter railroad that carried Sam to his Manhattan office.

Even now, whenever she hears the rumble and whistle of an evening train, her heart stirs with expectant joy: *He's coming home!*

But he isn't, ever again.

She and Max are alone now.

With a wistful sigh, Bella steps out the screen door to deposit the broken glass into the garbage pail—and trips over a lump of gray fur with black ticking. Somehow, she manages not to fall and even keeps the shards from flying through the air.

"Well, we meet again," she tells the fat tabby cat perched in a patch of dappled doormat sunlight. He was here yesterday morning, too, but darted into the bushes as she stepped out the door, scaring the heck out of her. Later in the day, she glimpsed him stalking chipmunks in the yard, and last night around dusk, he was snoozing under a shrub.

"Are you lost?"

He seems quite certain that he isn't, looking up at her as if he belongs here.

He doesn't, of course. The landlord has a strict no-pets policy. That's always been fine with Bella, whose last apartment came with a neighbor's dog that barked twenty-four-seven. Besides, Sam is severely allergic to dander.

She expects the cat to bolt as she steps around him and dumps the broken glass into the metal garbage can, but he doesn't even flinch at the clattering din. Impulsively bending to pet him, she's rewarded with loud purring.

Hmm. He's wearing a red collar, so he's not a stray.

"Mommy?" Max calls from the kitchen.

"Out here."

"Can I watch TV?"

"Nope. You know the rule." Only an hour a day, and only in the early morning or before bed, unless it's raining.

"Then can we play Candyland?" he asks.

She sighs. Playing the interminable game is questionable anytime. But now?

Sam would have dropped everything to play Candyland with Max.

"I was an only child, too. I get it," he'd say.

Bella had been an only child as well, and of course, she got it, too. But she and Sam each had their forte when it came to occupying their son. Books and puzzles were her department; board games and anything involving wheels or a ball were Sam's.

Now it's all up to me, and how the heck am I supposed to squeeze playtime into this crazy day?

"Maybe we can play later," she tells Max as he appears in the doorway with the Candyland box and a hopeful expression.

He's still barefoot and wearing the pajamas she'd told him to change earlier this morning. A five-year-old version of his late father, he has the same sandy brown cowlick above his forehead and the same solemn brown eyes behind his glasses. Now they widen when he sees the cat.

"Where did he come from?"

"I'm not sure. You have to get dressed, Max. It's almost noon."

"I will." He crouches beside the kitty. "Can we keep him?"

The timing of the question is so ludicrous, it's a wonder Bella manages to keep from blurting, *Are you nuts?*

Instead, she counts to three before gently reminding her son, "We're leaving tomorrow, and I'm sure he already has a home." *Lucky him.*

"But Doctor Lex said that I should get a pet, remember? And the only reason we couldn't was because it was against the rules. Now that we're moving, we don't have any rules."

"Oh, sweetie." She stands and wraps her arms around him. "I'm sorry."

Doctor Lex is the child psychologist Max started seeing last winter. The kindly man did, indeed, mention that a pet might provide effective grief therapy for a child who's too shy—around other kids, anyway—to have made any kindergarten friends of his own. His teacher had suggested that Bella set up some play dates for him, but Sam's illness enveloped her. She didn't have the heart, or the time or energy, to reach out to other parents who would ask painful questions. She'd distanced herself from even her own friends during those dark days.

In the aftermath, she realized too late that Max wasn't the only one who was lonely and isolated. Doctor Lex was right. Her grieving son sorely needed companionship. The landlord's zero-tolerance no-pet policy was the only thing that stopped Bella from acting on the suggestion to at least get him a parakeet or goldfish. But now . . .

"He can come with us to Grandma's," Max says as the cat brushes against their bare legs, purring to show them how darned lovable he is. "Please?"

Again, Bella chooses her words carefully: "Grandma is allergic, just like Daddy was."

She doesn't know that for a fact, but as it is, her mother-in-law probably isn't thrilled about welcoming into her perfect household her son's imperfect widow and a child prone to scattering crumbs, Matchbox cars, and Lego pieces. There's no way they can add an animal to the mix.

Still purring, the cat stretches and takes a leisurely stroll down the back steps. Bella admires his markings aloud to Max, pointing out the angled stripes that form an *M* above his eyes, the hallmark of a mackerel tabby. Even his tail is striped, standing straight up with the tip curved over.

"If it was red and white, it would look just like a candy cane," Max observes. "I love him. We have to keep him, Mom."

"He already has a home," she repeats.

"But how do you know that?"

"Because stray cats don't wear collars, so he's someone's pet and he—"

She breaks off as the cat stops walking, lies down on the walkway, and rolls over onto his back, arching to expose his belly as if inviting them to rub it.

"And he what?" Max prompts as she raises an eyebrow.

"And he isn't a he; he's a she," Bella informs her son with a smile, "and *she's* about to become a mommy."

"How do you know *that?*"

She indicates the parallel rows of exposed pink nipples like buttons on a double-breasted suit and offers a simplified explanation of how mother nature is preparing the cat to nurse her impending litter—a sizable one and due any second, judging by her bulging stomach.

She rests a hand on Max's shoulder to steer him back into the house as the mother-to-be stretches lazily in the sun.

"Come on, kiddo. Let's let her rest. She's going to need it."

* * *

A little over twenty-four hours later, Bella's sneakered footsteps echo across the hardwood floors of the home where fate catapulted her from bride to wife to mother to widow.

Ever since she realized she'd have to move, she's been trying to focus on what lies ahead, not behind. Now, however, she allows herself one last look to make sure she didn't forget anything. There are plenty of nooks and cubbies to check: closets within closets and cabinets within cabinets, cupboards beside the fireplace, compartments under the stairs and concealed beneath window seats . . .

Sam's voice echoes back over the years. "I don't want to live in a boring box in the city," he said when they were apartment hunting before the wedding. "Promise me that we'll find a cozy place that has character, and a backyard with lots of trees."

They did. These sun-flooded rooms radiate old-fashioned charm, with high ceilings and original wood-work. A leafy backyard beckons beyond the paned windows.

Too bad her mother-in-law's Chicago neighborhood is a boring old maze of monochromatic rectangles in the sky.

"Don't worry, Sam," she whispers around a lump in her throat. "Wherever Max and I wind up after we get back on our feet, I promise you it will be just like this— cozy with character, in a real house with a yard. And I promise you . . . I promise . . ."

Those same two words were the last she ever said to him, holding both his hands in a hospital room. Her sturdy husband had grown so frail and exhausted, but he wouldn't let go. Not until she'd promised to move on with-out him.

"You've always been so strong."

"Because I have you. We're strong together."

He shook his head. "You can do anything."

"Not this. Not alone."

"You have Max. You have . . . *me*." He was fading; every word was labored. "I'll be with you, even when . . ."

"Sam . . ."

"Promise me you'll . . . stay . . . strong . . ."

"I promise."

Swallowing hard, she pushes away the memory. It's time to go.

There's just one more place for her to check: the hid-den compartment under the second to the bottom tread on an old servant's staircase that leads to nowhere. The top was boarded over years ago, probably when the house was transformed to apartments.

This is where Sam always left little gifts for her. He'd send her an e-mail or text telling her to check "our spot," and when she did, she'd find something sweet: a box of her favorite chocolates, a book she'd been wanting to read, a piece of jewelry . . .

"I wanted to give you that pendant for Christmas," he told her, near the end, and she didn't have to ask what he meant.

She thinks about the pendant they'd found browsing in a jewelry store last spring, when they'd spent a glorious sunny Saturday in quaint Port Jefferson. Max was exhilarated by the ferry ride across the Long Island Sound, and Sam was still healthy then, not a care in the world other than the hefty price tag on the delicate blue tourmaline pendant. He said the gemstone matched her eyes exactly and wanted to buy it for her on the spot, but she wouldn't let him.

"That's a crazy amount of money to spend on a piece of jewelry, Sam. We have a million other things we need to buy right now."

"Maybe right now," he agreed, before adding with his dark eyes twinkling, "but you just wait. The necklace was meant to be yours, and it will be—when you least expect it."

In December, near the end, he told her he'd planned on buying it for her for Christmas. "I really . . . wanted you to have it." His voice was weak, his pale face clenched in pain.

"Next Christmas," she said fervently, clasping his hand. "You can get it for me next Christmas."

But she knew. They both knew. There would be no *next Christmas* for Sam—or even *this Christmas*. He passed away just a few days before.

The necklace was meant to be yours, and it will be— when you least expect it.

Those words haunt her now as she opens the stairway compartment. It's empty, of course. She knew it would be. She checked it countless times since Sam passed away, hoping irrationally that she might discover some forgotten gift he'd left there for her—the tourmaline pendant, perhaps. But there are no miracles even today, the last day.

She closes the hinged stair tread and walks slowly to the door. As she steps over the threshold for the final time, she remembers how Sam carried her in the opposite direction a decade ago, champagne-giddy and tripping over the train of her wedding gown.

Oh, Sam. I never thought I'd be leaving here without you. I never thought we'd be leaving here at all.

She wipes her eyes, locks the door, and leaves the keys under the mat for the new owner.

As she crosses the grass to the waiting car, its passenger seat stacked high with everything that wouldn't fit into the trunk, Max waves at her from the back seat.

When she sees the tears that have slid past the frames of his glasses to trickle down his little boy cheeks, a monstrous sob wells in her throat.

No. No, she can't let herself cry in front of her son. She has to stay strong for him, for Sam. She promised.

She pastes on a smile, jauntily jangling the car keys as she slides behind the wheel.

"Here we go," she says gaily, as if they've just lowered the lap bar on a ride at Disney World. "All set?"

For a moment, there's only silence from the back seat.

Then Max pipes up: "Yes."

Just one word—one tiny, tremendously brave word.

"Good." She turns the ignition key with a trembling hand, shifts the car, and presses the gas pedal.

Too late, she realizes that she forgot to take one last look at the house before it fell away in the rearview mirror.

Chapter 2

The drive across New York State was surprisingly pleasant, carrying Bella and Max past majestic mountains, endless acres of farms and pastures, old industrial cities, and picturesque villages.

Seven hours into the journey, though, she detects a faint rattling sound coming from the engine. It isn't steady, but every once in a while, it kicks in. Maybe she should get the car checked out at a service station—and pray it's nothing she can't afford to fix.

Which is pretty much everything.

Who cares about a car? Who cares about things? All that matters is the people you love.

People? There's only one person left who matters in Bella's world.

And I'm going to make sure he has a cozy, happy home again, she vows fiercely.

She swallows hard and clears her throat. "Should we find a place to spend the night now, Max?"

Surprised, he asks, "We're already in Ohio?"

"No, I thought we'd stop earlier than we planned. I can't wait to camp out. How about you?"

She packed sleeping bags and the two-man tent she and Sam used only once, when they discovered they hated camping.

But this is a fresh start. Maybe it'll be better this time around.

Come on. Nothing is better without Sam.

"I guess," Max says. "I wish we could sleep inside, though."

So do I.

But she can't even afford a budget motel. Not with gas prices as high as they are and the car acting up. She doesn't have a choice about the camping—or the fresh start—so she might as well make the best of things for Max's sake.

And really, after what she's been through, this is nothing. Camping out? Driving halfway across the country to visit Maleficent with a messy kid and all their worldly belongings on board?

I've totally got this.

Or does she? The sky, now rapidly gathering purple-black clouds, was sunny and blue until five minutes ago. She'd expected it to stay that way until dusk, which—this far west and on the cusp the summer solstice—shouldn't descend until after nine o'clock. But she recognizes an impending thunderstorm when she sees one.

"How are we going to camp if it rains, Mommy?" Max wants to know.

"I'm sure we'll stay dry in the tent." She isn't at all sure about that, and a glance into the rearview mirror reveals that Max isn't either. He sits pensively wiggling his loose bottom tooth with his thumb.

"I don't really want to sleep in the tent anymore."

"It'll be okay, sweetie. Besides, maybe the storm will pass." The remark is underscored by a rumble of thunder, and she continues almost without missing a beat, "Then again, maybe it won't. Let's look for an exit with a campsite."

The response is a high-pitched, "I really think we should just get a hotel!"

Oh, Max. Hang in there, kiddo.

"I really wish we could," she manages to say evenly, "but we just can't."

Max wants to know why not and where they'll camp, and he's worried about mud and lightning and bears and a host of other potential nature-related calamities that he catalogs for her as she nervously listens to the engine rattle.

Then—*yes!*—she spots a billboard.

Summer Pines Campground: Next Exit.

Wow. Talk about luck.

"That looks nice, doesn't it?" She points at the enormous photo of tents pitched on the grassy shore of a sapphire lake beneath a picture perfect summer sky that has nothing in common with the one looming ahead. "Should we check it out?"

"I guess," he says gamely.

As they rattle north onto Route 60, she checks the odometer. According to that billboard, the turnoff for the campground is ten miles up the road.

She keeps an eye out for a service station. But the two-lane highway runs through hilly, rural farmland. Pastures, livestock, silos—there are few other cars even traveling this stretch. To occupy Max—and keep him from asking more questions she doesn't want to answer—she challenges him to count the grazing cows on either side of the road and promises him an ice cream cone for dessert later if he can count twenty.

"Can it be chocolate chip?"

"Sure."

"Can it be two scoops? With sprinkles?"

"Sure—if you can count twenty-five cows."

That he accomplishes in short order, noting that most of them are lying down.

"That's because they know it's going to rain."

"How do they know?"

"I guess they're psychic," she says absently, checking the odometer and then the mile marker at the side of the highway. Six more to go.

Rattle . . . rattle . . .

"What's psychic?"

"It's . . . when you can predict the future."

"Cows can predict the future?"

She smiles, imagining a Guernsey with a crystal ball. "Well, I wouldn't put it that way. But some animals can be superintuitive."

"What's intuitive?"

"It's knowing something that you can't really know."

"That doesn't make sense. If you can't know it, then how do you know it?"

"Because you don't just rely on your five senses to—" She hits the brakes, spotting something ahead in the road as they round a curve.

The car stops just inches from a small animal. For a moment, she assumes that it's roadkill—a dead possum or raccoon. Then she realizes that it's a cat—a gray tabby—and it's very much alive, staring at the car. She waits for it to scuttle off into the tall purple wildflowers along the narrow shoulder, but it doesn't move.

"Look, Mom! He followed us all the way here!"

"What?"

"The kitty from home! The one with the candy cane tail!"

Indeed, this cat's tail is similarly striped, standing straight up and hooked into a curve, and its markings are strikingly similar to the one who showed up on their door-step yesterday.

"Max, he didn't follow us. And he was a she, by the way, remember? And this cat isn't the same—"

"Oh, yeah!" In the rearview mirror, she sees him slap his cheek. "He was a she because she was going to have babies, and she didn't follow us because she got here first. She's the leader. *We* followed her."

Bella can't help but laugh. "Whatever you say, kiddo. But she—or he—had better move, because she's going to get hurt if she stays there."

"I don't think she wants to move."

Max is right. The cat just sits calmly staring at the car.

Bella rolls down the window and leans her head out, noticing the chill in the air. Suddenly, the tank top and cut-off denim shorts she donned this morning feel as though they belong to a different season.

"Hey, kitty!" she calls. "You have to get out of the road!"

Nope.

Bella may never have owned a cat, but she knows enough about them to be aware that they like to do things on their own terms. Which is fine when you're talking about when to use the litter box and whether to eat your kibble. But when it comes to personal safety . . .

"Look out!" she shouts as an eighteen-wheeler comes barreling around a curve in the opposite lane.

The cat doesn't budge, nor does it blink as the truck hurtles past just a few feet from where it's sitting.

"Crazy cat," Bella mutters. She beeps the horn. "Move! You're going to get run over!"

"No! Don't run her over, Mom!"

"*I'm* not going to run her over. But somebody else will if she doesn't get out of the way. Besides, it's dangerous for us to be stalled in this lane," she adds, glancing in the rearview mirror. The road is sharply curved behind them. If another car—or, God forbid, a truck—comes along, it might not be able to stop in time.

Frustrated, she honks again.

The cat stays put.

"This is ridiculous," she grumbles, pulling the car off the road onto the narrow shoulder. She shifts into park, turns on the hazards, and climbs out of the car. "I'll be right back."

"Where are you going?" Max asks worriedly.

"To move our friend. We can't just leave him there. He's a sitting duck."

"He's not a duck. He's a cat. And he's a she, remember?"

She grins, leaving Mr. Literal-Minded securely strapped into the back seat. She darts a look to the left to make sure there are no cars coming before stepping into the road and wonders what she'd do if she did see one. And what would the cat do?

Surely it would run away—unless it's injured. Maybe that's why it's not moving. Maybe it can't.

"It's okay, kitty," Bella says, hurrying toward it and noticing that it certainly looks like the doorstep cat from yesterday. But gray tabbies are a dime a dozen, she reminds herself. They all look alike: tiger ticking; wide, green eyes; even that M-shaped marking on their furry foreheads, and . . .

And plenty of cats have red collars, too, she decides, noticing that this one happens to be wearing one, just like the doorstep kitty.

"What's the matter, fella? Are you hurt?" Casting another glance at the highway, reassured to see that it's still empty behind them, she bends over to give the cat a pat.

No sooner does her hand graze its furry head than it promptly falls backward.

For a moment, she's certain she's going to see blood, a broken leg, something, something . . .

She sees *something* all right.

The cat isn't hurt; she's purring and rolling languidly onto her back, stretching and arching her neck and then her belly to be rubbed.

"You're not a fella, are you?" she asks dryly.

This cat, like its candy-cane-tailed counterpart, is decidedly female—and equally pregnant.

* * *

Ten minutes later, the first fat raindrop splats onto the windshield as she turns off Route 60 onto a tree-lined country road.

"Is this where the kitty doctor is, Mom?" Max asks from the back seat.

"Somewhere around here, yes."

After manhandling the cat off the road and into the back seat, she was glad to see that her phone got Internet reception even in the middle of nowhere. She was going to search for local animal control but then thought better of it. Kill shelters still exist in some areas, and she doesn't want their pregnant furry friend to end up in one. Instead, she looked up veterinarians, which seemed like the most humane option.

She heard after-hours recordings on the first three numbers she called and wasn't sure what she'd do if the fourth and final one resulted in the same. But a harried-sounding man picked up.

"Lakeview Animal Hospital."

"Hi, I . . . I found a pregnant cat in the middle of the road and I—"

"Is she injured?"

"I don't think so. She wasn't moving, so I picked her up and she seems—"

"And she's a stray?"

"She's wearing a collar, but it doesn't have identification. I don't know where—"

"Bring her in. I'll scan her. Do you know where we are?"

I don't even know where I am, Bella thought.

She glances from the road ahead to the ever-darkening western sky through the driver's side window to the back seat. Somewhere along the way, the cat wound up curled in her son's lap, its loud purring punctuated by the occasional rumble of thunder.

Max remains convinced that this is the same cat from their yard back home, and she gave up trying to argue with him. In five-year-old logic, it makes about as much sense that a cat would find its way on foot across the state and wind up precisely in their path—well off the beaten one—as it does that there would be identical pregnant cats living four hundred miles apart.

Bella hits the brakes as the navigational system's robotic voice announces, "Arriving . . . at . . . destination."

Looking around for a medical facility, she sees nothing but woods. "Where is it?" she wonders aloud.

"We don't know," Max replies, and she notes that somehow, in the space of fifteen minutes, he and the cat seem to have transformed into a "we."

Off to the side of the road, she spots a tiny wooden sign alongside a barely discernible dirt lane leading through the trees.

Lakeview Animal Hospital and Rescue

After a moment's hesitation, she turns the car in that direction and they bump-rattle along until they reach a small clapboard structure. It's not a house, exactly, though it has a pitched roof and a low concrete stoop with a silver wrought iron railing. It's more like a cross between a cottage and a shed.

Getting out of the car, she notes that the air feels markedly cooler, and the maple leaves overhead are stirring, turning over. She'd better make this quick, then find the campsite before the sky opens up. The service station can wait until morning.

She grabs a hoodie from the front seat. Emblazoned with a New York Yankees logo, it was Sam's. He left it on the bed before his final trip to the hospital.

Even now, her husband's familiar scent seems to envelop her as she throws it on.

It's going to be okay, she reminds herself. *You've got this. One thing at a time: cat, then campsite, then car . . .*

She cautiously opens the back door. "Don't you run away, kitty. We don't have time to chase you down."

Lounging across Max's lap as he strokes her fat, furry belly with its double row of fat pink nipples, the cat offers Bella a languid stare as if to say, *Don't worry, darling. I wouldn't dream of it.*

No amount of coaxing will get the animal out of the car. Bella is forced to gently drag her across the seat and carry her onto the small porch, trailed by Max.

He tries to open the door for them as she shifts the squirming cat in her arms. "It's locked."

"Turn the knob harder. Maybe the other direction."

He tries. Nope. "What does that sign say, Mommy?"

"It says they closed at five. But there's a light on in there, and the vet answered the phone when we called. Can you knock, please, sweetie?"

He does, timidly and then louder, at her urging, as the cat somersaults in her arms.

At last, movement from within. A man in a lab coat opens the door. He's tall, with brown hair, broad shoulders, and brown eyes behind a pair of glasses.

"I . . . I'm Isabella Jordan." Her voice cracks a bit. "I called a few minutes ago. Are you the person I talked to?"

"Yes. I'm Doctor Bailey." His scrutiny flicks from her to Max to the cat and settles on Max again. "And you are?"

"I'm Max, and this is—"

"No need for animal introductions, Max," he cuts in brusquely. "I see you've brought your pet pig, Penelope, for her daily weigh-in."

Startled, Bella double-takes on the man's gaze and spots a gleam amid the sternness.

"She isn't a pig," Max contradicts, "and she isn't a duck either, even though my mom thought she was."

"Young man, I don't know who you're trying to fool, but I believe *I'm* the animal expert here, and I know a pig when I see one." Doctor Bailey is deadpan.

"She's a *cat!*"

"Are you sure?"

"Yes! Plus she's got more cats in her belly."

"Is that so? Then it appears *you're* the expert here. What should we do next? Have a look at her?"

"Yes!"

"All right, come on in, and can you please be sure to lock the door behind you, Max? Otherwise, we'll have all kinds of critters trying to sneak past reception now that my assistant is gone for the day. I hate when that happens."

"Does that really happen?" Max whispers to Bella, wide-eyed, as they follow Doctor Bailey over the threshold.

He answers the question before Bella can: "All the time, Max. I used to leave a clipboard on the desk overnight with the paperwork so that they could sign themselves in properly. The cats were very efficient, as were the unicorns, but the kangaroos were too jumpy, and the skunks . . . don't even get me started on the skunks." He pinches his nose with his fingers, and Max laughs. Bella finds herself smiling, too.

The waiting room is small, with a creaky wooden floor covered in a threadbare runner. The reception desk is slightly battered, with papers stacked tidily on its top and a wooden chair neatly rolled beneath it. The only other furniture in the room is a park bench with a wooden slatted seat and wrought iron arms. Above it is a bulletin board topped by a sign that reads, *Happy Tails,* and is covered in photos of smiling people clutching furry creatures.

Definitely not a sophisticated operation, but a friendly one.

Doctor Bailey flips on the light in an exam room the size of a small walk-in closet. All business again, he looks at his watch and then at Bella, gesturing at a chair. "Here, sit and hold her. I only have a couple of minutes. I've got a puppy in the next room about to wake up from anesthesia after emergency surgery, and I can't leave her alone for long."

"What happened to the puppy?" Max wants to know.

"Someone found him in the woods and brought him to me a little while ago. His leg was badly hurt."

"How?"

"I'm not sure."

"Whose puppy is it?"

"I'm not sure," Doctor Bailey says again, unperturbed by the questions but clearly focused on the cat now.

He kneels beside Bella—so close she can smell his soapy scent—and gives the cat a brief once-over, which mostly seems to consist of patting her here and there and letting her nuzzle his hand.

"She's pregnant all right."

"How many kittens are in there?" Max asks.

"Quite a few. And they're due pretty soon."

"How soon?"

"I'd say within the next week or so. But other than that, she seems perfectly fine. Here, I'll scan her."

"We'll leave the room," Bella says quickly. The word *scan* brings to mind futile, difficult days seeing specialists with Sam. He endured endless CAT scans and PET scans and bone scans, with progressively bleak results.

"No, you can stay. It only takes a few seconds." He picks up an electronic wand and waves it along the cat's head. "See? All done. She has a chip."

"A chip?" Bella echoes. "A bone chip?"

"Maybe a chocolate chip," Max suggests. "I like chocolate chip ice cream."

Doctor Bailey smiles at him and then, for the first time, directly at Bella. "She has a *micro*chip. In her ear. That's what I was scanning for. Whenever someone brings in a stray, I check for one. Most pet owners have them implanted in their pets' ears so that they can be traced if they wander. Which is what our gal here must have done." He reaches into a plastic container, grabs a handful of kibble, and holds it out to the cat, who nibbles greedily from his hand.

"So you know who the owner is?"

"I have the microchip number. I'll see where it traces. Be right back. You can be on treat duty, Max." He hands over the container and disappears.

Max looks at Bella. "Should I feed her some of these?"

"Sure. She's eating for two. Or maybe for five or six . . . or more."

"How many babies do cats have at once time?"

"A lot."

"Like a hundred?"

She laughs. "No, not that many."

"Twenty seven?"

"Not that many either," she says, sensing that they're on the cusp of a conversation where he'll throw out arbitrary numbers until she agrees with one of them.

She changes the subject back to ice cream until Doctor Bailey returns a few minutes later, harried. "I have to get back to the dog. She's regaining consciousness."

"What about—"

"Here you go." He holds out a piece of paper. "Her name is Chance."

"Chance the Cat," Max says.

"Exactly." Doctor Bailey flicks a glance at Max and hesitates, as though he wants to say something, but doesn't. "She belongs to someone named Leona Gatto. I tried to call her, but it bounced into an electronic recording that the voicemail box is full. That's her address—she's over in the Dale—so you can just bring the cat there."

"To . . . the Dale, did you say?"

"Lily Dale."

"Is that a town?"

Something flickers in his eyes. "You've never heard of it? *Where* did you say you live?"

She didn't. He never asked.

"We don't live anywhere anymore," Max informs him. "We have to sleep in a tent because my dad is dead and my mom lost her job and we don't have a house and we don't have any money and we—"

"Max!"

"Is that true?" Doctor Bailey asks Bella.

It is, but . . .

"We're in the process of moving," she explains, avoiding his gaze, "and we're making a little vacation out of it, so we're going to camp out tonight over at Summer Pines. That reminds me—"

"Where?"

"What?"

"*Where* are you camping?"

"Oh. Summer Pines. The campground. It's right near here."

"It can't be."

"Why can't it?"

"Because I've never heard of it."

Resisting the urge to remind him that he can't possibly know everything about . . . well, *everything,* she plucks the piece of paper from his hand. She was about to ask him about service stations, but forget it. She'll ask Leona Gatto.

"How far is Lily Dale from here?"

"Only about twenty, twenty-five minutes. I'd take her myself, but I don't like the looks of my puppy pal in the next room." He rakes a worried hand through his hair, leaving it standing on end above his forehead much like Max's cowlick, and Bella forgives his arrogance.

"I'm sorry," he adds. "But I'm pretty sure I'm not going to be leaving here tonight."

"It's okay. We'll take her. Let's go, Max."

"Can I carry Chance the Cat?"

"Sure, but be gentle."

Max hoists her into his arms. "Come on, Chance the Cat. You get to go home now."

His wistful tone tugs at Bella's heart. Is he wishing he could keep the cat or wishing he, too, were going home?

Following him to the door, she turns back belatedly to ask Doctor Bailey, "How much do we owe you?"

"Not a cent. You did a good thing. Most people would have driven right by her."

Bella gives a tight laugh. "Yeah, well, she kind of wouldn't let us. Thank you, Doctor. Good luck with the puppy."

"You, too. Good luck with . . . everything."

Chapter 3

The rain started falling twenty minutes after they left the animal hospital. This little detour to drop off Chance the Cat, as Max insists on calling her, means they'll be pitching a tent on muddy ground tonight. But at least the car sounds better after its brief rest, and according to a sign, Lily Dale is just a mile ahead.

The road winds past rustic homes to the right and Cassadaga Lake to the left, bordered by a narrow grassy strip with an occasional weathered private pier. The opposite shore, hilly and wooded, isn't far off.

In the back seat, Chance is curled up on Max's lap again. They're such a contented pair that Bella aches every time she glances into the rearview mirror.

Maybe she'll be able to get a cat for Max when they're settled. She only wishes it could have been this one.

There's something special about Chance. She's dignified yet affectionate, and though she's delicate in her fragile feminine state, she radiates a quiet strength. Bella is reluctant to part ways with her, but when she thinks of her mother-in-law's sterile apartment, she knows there's no other option.

Maybe if the campsite is affordable, they can put off getting to Chicago for another day or two. This is such a picturesque area, and she wouldn't mind exploring a bit—as long as they're at Millicent's before the weekend, so that Max can see the fireworks at Navy Pier . . .

Sam used tell Max and Bella about the incredible Independence Day displays over Lake Michigan. He promised they'd make the trip now that Max was older.

"There are so many things I want to show him," he told Bella last spring, when he first started feeling sick. "I think we should do a road trip this summer."

He wanted to take his son to a Cubs game and the Lincoln Park Zoo. He wanted him to taste deep-dish pizza. He wanted to sit him high on his shoulders at the crowded Navy Pier beneath the rockets' red glare on the Fourth of July . . .

The only thing that stopped them was the prospect of spending a precious holiday in his mother's company. Bella wanted to go anyway and not tell her, but Sam pointed out she'd be hurt if she ever found out.

"I don't know why she insists on our staying with her when she obviously doesn't enjoy company," Bella grumbled.

Max had been a toddler on their last Chicago visit. She and Sam spent the entire time worrying that he'd hurt himself in the apartment Millicent refused to childproof. Millicent fretted about the disruption and scolded her grandson every time he tried to touch—well, anything.

We thought there'd be plenty of time for a road trip when Max got older, Bella remembers, swallowing another bittersweet lump. *We thought it would be easier in a year or two—on him, on Millicent, on us . . .*

Tears well in her eyes. She reaches over to turn on the radio, needing a pleasant distraction. After scanning past enough static to let her know they really are in the middle of nowhere, she finds a music station.

Elton John is singing about the Circle of Life.

Terrific.

Abruptly, she silences the radio and swipes at her eyes with a fast food napkin from the console.

From the back seat: "Are you okay, Mommy?"

"I'm fine, sweetie."

The highway blurs, and she wipes again with the soggy napkin.

If you don't snap out of this, you'll need to pull off the road for a good cry.

Saved by the GPS: "Turn . . . right . . . in . . . one . . . hundred . . . feet."

Chance, whose reverberations of contentment have punctuated the drive from the animal hospital, is purring even more loudly now.

"Listen to her, Max. Maybe she knows she's going home."

"You said animals are psychic. And the cows were right about the rain."

"They were. I wish they'd tell us it's going to stop soon."

"I don't see any cows. All I see is a tiny house. What does that sign say?" he asks as the road opens up to reveal a little hut flanked by stone pillars, topped by an arched sign.

She reads it aloud: "Lily Dale Assembly."

"What's 'assembly'?"

"I'm not sure."

She hears a loud meow from the back seat and turns to see that the cat is up on her hind feet, paws on the window as she peers out.

"She knows she's home!" Max exclaims, and Bella smiles as she turns right and drives slowly between the pillars, past the unmanned guardhouse.

Branches of ancient trees sway high overhead as she bears left at the fork toward Cottage Row, following the GPS instructions. The wipers sweep away the raindrops, and she gazes through the windshield, wondering whether she made the wrong turn. This gated community looks like none she's ever seen back in the New York City suburbs, or anywhere else, for that matter. There are no sidewalks, the pavement is rutted, and the houses . . .

The houses are more like cottages, really. Victorian gingerbread cottages with shutters and porches and gables, crowded into a network of narrow lakeside lanes. Some are shabbier than others, and all exude an unconventional charm. One is painted purple, another has bright turquoise trim, and nearly all are surrounded by bright flowers spilling from pots, planters, and beds. Tiny patches of yard are well-tended and host more than the usual share of birdhouses and birdbaths, seating areas and garden statuary.

"What kind of town *is* this?" Max asks.

"Just . . . you know . . . a regular town."

"It doesn't look like a regular town."

"It's just smaller than the ones where we live because it's rural. We live—*lived*—in the suburbs. Oh, look, there's a library." She points at a stately, pillared red-brick building as they pass. A library is always a good sign. Libraries remind her of her bookworm childhood and well-worn books with happy endings.

She rolls down her window to lean her head out slightly, squinting into the gloaming. "Can you see the numbers on the houses, Max?"

"I see seven . . . and there's nine . . . and that house has a sign, and so does that one. What do they say?"

"I can't tell. Just look at the numbers. We're looking for sixteen." Thunder rumbles in the distance, and she resists the urge to drive faster. There isn't another car on the road, and there are no pedestrians, but there are people scattered here and there, sitting on porches and in a small gazebo on the park-like green. The air is damp and heavy with woodsy greens and bark mulch.

"I see it! Sixteen!"

"You . . . have . . . arrived," the GPS informs them simultaneously.

She slows to a stop in front of a three-story lavender-gray house with white trim and a wide porch. It, too, bears a wooden sign hanging from a post beside the front walk. This one she can read, and she does so aloud: "'Valley View Manor Guesthouse.'"

"Where's the valley?" Max asks.

"Good question."

"What's a manor?"

"It's a big, fancy house."

He surveys the place. "It's big, but it's not fancy at all. What's a guesthouse?"

"It's . . . like an inn. A hotel."

"It doesn't look like a hotel."

"No," she agrees, "it doesn't."

"Can we stay here?"

"We don't have any money for hotels. We're going camping, remember?"

"Oh. Yeah."

Chance meows loudly, gazing so fondly through the back window that Bella laughs. "I guess that means we're in the right place. Stay here with her, Max, while I go see if anyone's there. It seems a little deserted."

A gust of wet wind rustles leaves in the towering canopy of branches and stirs wind chimes that hang here, there, everywhere.

Wind chimes.

Home.

Sam . . .

Bella shivers, grateful for his warm sweatshirt and wishing she'd worn jeans instead of shorts. They haven't even crossed a state line and it's as though they've traveled to another climate.

A sign beside the car warns her that this is a no parking zone, for loading and unloading only. That's fine. That's all she's doing, unloading a feline foundling, and then she'll be on her way.

Thunder, closer this time, rolls off the lake as she hurries up the creaky steps onto the shadowy porch.

Along with a cushioned glider and a couple of chairs, she spots a well-used scratching post and a pair of empty feeding bowls. Okay, so this is must be the place.

She presses the old-fashioned bell and hears it reverberate inside. Then there's no sound but the rain falling beyond the porch. The damp air is heavy with a strikingly familiar floral scent. It takes her a moment to pinpoint the source: just beneath the side railing lies a mock orange shrub in full bloom.

Just like at home.

Maybe it's a sign.

Oh, come on . . . a sign of what?

It's not like you could run down to the garden center a hundred years ago to buy exotic plant specimens. Lots of houses from that era have identical landscaping: lilacs, peonies, hydrangea, mock orange . . .

So really, this isn't much of a coincidence.

And neither is the cat, she reminds herself as she rings the bell again and then knocks on the door. No answer. The house has a deserted air about it.

"Can I help you with something?"

The voice is so close Bella jumps. Turning, she sees a female figure standing behind a leafy trellis on the porch next door. She presses a hand against her galloping heart, spooked even though the woman sounds perfectly pleasant.

"Yes, I'm looking for the people who live here," she calls. "I found their cat, and—"

"You found Chance the Cat?"

Chance the Cat. How funny that she phrased it that way. That's exactly what Max has been calling her. On the drive over, when Bella asked why, he said, "Because it's her name."

"I know Chance is her name, but why do you add on 'the Cat'?"

"Because she's a cat," he said reasonably.

"I'm so relieved!" the neighbor tells Bella. "We've all been beside ourselves worrying about her."

Wondering who "we've all" entails, she asks her when the owners will return and is met by a long pause.

Then the woman says, "I'm afraid Leona isn't coming back."

That explains at least part of the situation. Chance's owner must have just taken off and abandoned her pet.

A loud clap of thunder explodes so nearby that Bella gasps.

Max opens the car door. "Mommy!"

"It's okay, sweetie, I'm right here."

As she hurries down the steps toward the car, Max cries out, "No! Chance the Cat, no!"

The cat has leapt through the open door. Moving with astonishing speed for an expectant mama, she zips past Bella and disappears into a clump of bushes.

"Oh, dear." The plump, older woman next door emerges from the shadows, standing on the top step of her own porch. Her right foot is in a walking cast.

Max, too, is out of the car, hurrying after the cat. Bella stops him, seeing a flash of lightning in the sky.

"Come on over here," the woman calls from next door.

"But what about Chance the Cat?"

"Oh, she's under the porch," the woman tells him. "She likes it back there. Don't worry."

"She'll be okay," Bella assures Max and pulls him along as the rain turns to a downpour.

"Hurry—this is going to be a doozy of a storm." The neighbor waves them up the steps, holding the door open for them.

"What's a doozy, Mommy?"

Bella opens her mouth to answer her son, but the woman beats her to it. "A doozy is a *really* big storm."

"Is it dangerous?" Max asks anxiously.

"No, that would be a humdinger, which is a really, really, *really* big storm. Don't worry, we're not due for one of those for at least a hundred years or so." She hobbles along, chattering on as she ushers them into a small foyer cluttered with decorative knickknacks. "With a doozy, you have nothing to fear except getting wet. I don't know about you, but I'm terrified of that. The rain does terrible things to my hair. How about yours?"

Her hair happens to be bright orange, which clashes with her purple cargo pants and the lime-green high-top sneaker on her left foot. Bella notes with interest that she's also—somewhat fittingly, given the circumstances—wearing red cat-eye glasses and a tiger-striped T-shirt.

After assuring her that his hair is just fine and proudly adding that he's not afraid of rain, Max asks what happened to her leg.

"Oh, this? I tripped and fell and sprained my ankle."

"My mom's a klutz, too."

The woman bursts out laughing.

"Max! Sorry," Bella tells the woman. "I'm always calling myself a klutz, and he didn't mean—"

"Oh, believe you me, he's a perceptive boy. I'm as clumsy as they come. By the way, my name is Odelia Lauder, and that," she points at a fat tabby cat dozing in a cushioned basket at the foot of the stairs, "is Gert. Leona's Chance the Cat is her granddaughter."

After introducing herself and Max, Bella says, "I've noticed that you call her Chance the Cat, and not just Chance. Why is that?"

"I told you, Mommy," Max says, "it's because she's a cat! She isn't Chance the Dog!"

Odelia laughs. "You're right about that, Max. And her full name is Chance the Cat, because she was born in the garden in the spring, smack dab in the middle of a bed of Wood Hyacinths that just happened to be in full bloom that day. Those are Leona's favorite flowers."

"So why was she named Chance the Cat?" Bella asks, not following the reasoning. "Why not . . . I don't know, Woody?"

"Oh, Leona doesn't care for Woody Allen at all."

Bella blinks. "No, I meant because you said Wood Hyacinths are—"

"But she adores Peter Sellers," Odelia goes on. "She's kept in touch with him quite regularly."

"Isn't Peter Sellers dead?"

"Oh, yes, for years. Anyway, *Being There* was her favorite of all his movies, so that's where it came from."

Bella's head is spinning. "That's where *what* came from?"

"The name! Chance the Cat!"

Bella, who never saw *Being There,* is no stranger to Sellers's *Pink Panther* movies and can't help feeling a little like Inspector Clouseau right now. "I'm sorry," she says. "I just don't get it."

"She's named after Chance the Gardener, Peter Sellers's character in *Being There*," Odelia explains patiently. "Because she was born in a *garden*. Do you see?"

Bella, who doesn't see at all, assures her that she does. She gets the feeling that Odelia subscribes to a peculiar brand of logic—one that was apparently shared by Leona. And what about Max? She's pretty sure her son has never seen a Peter Sellers movie in his life. So why would he have known to call Chance the cat *Chance the Cat?*

She makes a mental note to ask him again later, though she suspects she already knows the answer. "Because she's a cat."

Max, too, has his own unique brand of logic.

Odelia wants to know where they found the animal, and Bella explains how Chance was perched in the road not far from the exit and refused to budge.

"I knew it!" Odelia nods triumphantly. "My guides were pointing me to the south. In her condition, I'm impressed that Chance the Cat could travel that far in . . . let's see, she's been missing for over a week now."

"Your guides?"

"Spirit guides," Odelia cheerfully tells Bella over another thunderous boom and rain drumming on the porch roof. "I'm with the Assembly . . . you know, a psychic medium."

"You're psychic? Like a cow?" That comes from Max; Bella is at a sudden loss for words.

"A cow? Young man, I'll have you know I've lost ten pounds since Christmas," Odelia informs him with a grin.

"What?" Max looks at Bella.

Before she can explain, Odelia says, "I'm guessing you've never met a psychic medium before. Or even a psychic *large* medium—that's my new dress size."

"What's a psychic large medium?"

"Forget the large," Odelia grins at him. "A psychic medium is an intuitive, which means," she adds before he can ask the next question, "that I tune into the energy all around us in order to interpret the past, present, and future."

After allowing a moment to let that settle, she gives a case-closed nod and moves on—conversationally and physically.

Leading them toward the back of the small house, she says, "I'm impressed that you went out of your way to bring Chance the Cat back where she belongs. Leona will be so pleased."

Hmm . . . that's interesting. Bella had assumed Leona had abandoned the cat. *Everything* about this conversation—and this woman and this place—is bizarre. So many questions fill her head that she can barely manage to articulate even one: "So Leona . . . she's . . . um, she didn't . . . um, where, exactly, is she?"

"She's on the Other Side." In the cluttered, fragrant kitchen, Odelia lifts the lid from a simmering pot on the stove.

"You mean she's dead? A *ghost?*"

In response to Bella's blurted query and Max's raised eyebrows, Odelia turns to offer a faint smile. "We prefer to say *in Spirit.*"

We as in Odelia and the late Leona? *We* as in Odelia and Gert the cat? Or does she simply refer to herself using the royal *we?*

It's hard to tell. Odelia is undeniably dotty, yet she radiates such good-natured warmth that Bella finds herself smiling back despite what should be a somber topic.

But Odelia seems perfectly chipper as she stirs whatever's in the steaming pot and explains that her elderly neighbor transitioned to the spirit world more than a week ago, the same day the cat went missing.

"She's been so restless, the poor dear, and I know it's because she was worried about what had become of the cat. Leona really loved her." Odelia lifts the spoon to her lips and tastes the red, saucy concoction, tilting her head as if contemplating the flavor.

"What is that?" Max asks.

"Chili." She opens a glass canister on the countertop and takes a handful of whatever's inside, tosses it into the pot, and resumes stirring.

"What did you put in there?"

"Chocolate chips, what else?" she replies with a grin.

"In chili?" Bella raises her eyebrows.

"Sure. I can't think of many things that don't taste better with chocolate chips, can you?"

A few. Chili is one of them, Bella decides with a smile, but it fades when Max asks Odelia yet another question: "How did she die?"

"Leona? She had an accident."

"Was she a klutz, too?"

"I suppose we all have our moments, don't we?" Odelia says with a touch of wistfulness, setting the spoon aside and covering the pot with a decisive clatter.

"What about Chance the Cat? Who's going to take care of her? And her babies, when she has them?"

"I'll have to find a new home for them. Leona only has one relative, and I'm planning to ask him to take them, but he's not very fond of animals—which is mutual," she adds with a meaningful nod at Bella.

"Why don't you keep Chance the Cat yourself?" Max wants to know.

"Because my Gert doesn't do well with other cats here."

"But she's her grandma!"

"Cats aren't like humans," Odelia says. "Once family members have lived apart, they don't take to each other very easily. They're very territorial and set in their ways."

Bella can't help but think of her mother-in-law. Sam had always claimed she'd been different when he was growing up, before widowhood, age, and isolation had hardened her. She never got over his moving away and held out hope for years that he'd come back home. That hope had been crushed when he married Bella.

"I'd keep her if I could," Odelia goes on. "I don't suppose *you'd* like to—"

"We can't," Bella cuts in quickly, before Odelia gives Max any ideas. "We're—"

She breaks off at a deafening clap of thunder.

"Mommy? I don't want to go camping," Max says in a small voice.

"Camping! On a night like this?" Odelia looks from Max to Bella.

"We're just going to Summer Pines. It's not far."

"Where?"

"Summer Pines," she repeats, noting the woman's blank expression.

"Never heard of it."

Hmm. Struck by déjà vu, Bella elaborates, "We saw a billboard back on the highway. It said it was ten miles north of the exit, on Route 60. So it has to be around here someplace."

Odelia fixes her with a strange, long look. "If you need a place to stay tonight, you can have your pick of rooms in the guesthouse."

"We don't have any money," Max informs her, and Bella cringes.

"Oh, it would be free of charge, of course. Leona would want it that way. And you can keep an eye on the cat in case those kittens come. I have the keys, and I've been trying to look after the place, but you can imagine what a tizzy I've been in with the season starting tomorrow."

"Season?"

"The official season. The Dale welcomes visitors from all over the world every summer. We have a daily schedule of events from now through Labor Day."

Nodding as if she understands, Bella asks, "What kind of events?"

"Oh, the usual. Lectures, demonstrations, readings, healings . . ."

"What kind of healings? You mean like . . . doctors?"

"There's physical healing, yes. And spiritual, emotional healing. You'll see. Tomorrow morning when the gates open, this place will be jammed."

"Jammed with what?" asks Max the Constantly Curious Kid.

"People."

"Who are they?"

"Tourists and curiosity seekers, newbies and regulars, summer staff, and, of course, those of us who live here. Some—like me—are here year-round, but most of the mediums are just in residence for the season."

"Mediums . . . you mean there are others? Is that what the assembly is? An assembly of . . ."

"Spiritualists. That's right." Odelia smiles at Bella. "So you weren't familiar with the Dale before you got here?"

"No, we had no idea what it was." She still doesn't know what it is, though she's guessing it's some kind of new age summer resort. "We were just stopping by to drop off the cat."

"I'd say it's a little off the beaten path to the Midwest to qualify as just stopping by."

Bella blinks. Had she mentioned their destination to Odelia? She must have.

"We're not in all that big a hurry, but—"

"We have to go stay with my grandma because we don't have any place else to go," Max interrupts. "We don't really want to because she's fancy. But my mom lost her job, and we had to move out of our house, and my dad—"

"Max," Bella interrupts gently, "Ms. Lauder doesn't need to know all that."

Yet even as she says it, she comprehends that the woman already knows far more about them than they've told her.

Noticing that Odelia's fixated on something just over their shoulders, Bella spins around quickly, expecting to find someone standing there, but the spot is empty.

When she turns back, she sees Odelia nodding as if in silent agreement with the imaginary person whose presence even Bella could have sworn she felt.

"It's time for dinner," she says abruptly, opening a cupboard. "Are you two hungry?"

"I am. I love chocolate chips. We had a picnic at the rest stop, but that was a long time ago. Mom said we'd eat dinner after we dropped off Chance the Cat."

"We will, Max. I'm sure we can find a place—"

"Nonsense, you've already found it. I was just about to sit down, and I always cook extra."

"Why?"

"Because you never know who might drop in," Odelia tells Max with a twinkle in her eye. "Although, sometimes, you do. *I* do, anyway."

"Did you know about us?"

She shakes her head.

Meeting her gaze, Bella isn't so sure about that. Nor is she so sure she's hungry enough—despite being famished—to try chocolate chip chili.

Odelia turns away, taking out a stack of bowls. "After we eat, we'll head next door and you can pick out the room where you want to spend the night."

"We can't possibly do that."

"Why not, Mommy?"

"Yes, why not?" Odelia asks.

She isn't quite sure about that, either. Maybe it is a good idea. After all, if neither Odelia nor Doctor Bailey has heard of Summer Pines, it might be farther away than she thought. Driving around at night with Max in an unfamiliar remote area—in a storm—with the engine clattering precariously . . . well, that definitely doesn't seem like a good idea.

"You really have to stay. There's a house filled with empty beds next door, Bella, and in this weather, you can't sleep in a tent with a young child."

Having introduced herself as Isabella, she's startled to hear her nickname—the one only Sam called her—from a stranger's lips. Most people who shorten her name just call her Izzy.

"Is it supposed to rain all night?" she asks. "I haven't checked the forecast."

"We don't bother much with forecasts around here. This is lake-effect country. In the winter, we get blizzards that pop up in a matter of minutes; in the summer, we've had twisters tear through. You never can tell what might blow in off the Great Lakes."

That's all Bella needs to hear. "Maybe just one night. But that's it."

Odelia nods, looking pleased.

So does Max. "Now if my tooth falls out, the tooth fairy can find me!"

"She'd find you no matter where you are, Max," Bella reminds him for the umpteenth time.

"But tents don't have addresses. Houses do."

She smiles. "So the tooth fairy needs an address?"

He nods. "That's how people find things."

Bella looks at Odelia. "We've been plugging addresses into our GPS all day."

"I see. But the tooth fairy knows this neighborhood really well. The boy next door to me on the other side just lost his front tooth the other day. Of course, he knocked his out by accident."

"Did the tooth fairy come?"

"She did." Odelia tells Max, handing a fistful of silverware to him and the bowls to Bella as though they've shared countless meals together. "And he and his mom have only been here a few weeks."

"Is that a guesthouse, too?" Bella asks as she and Max begin setting the small, round table.

"No, it's a private home. My friend Ramona has owned it for years. She raised her orphaned niece and nephew there. Now they're grown and she's married and living up in Buffalo with her husband, Jeff, so she rents the house for the season."

"Why?" Max asks, predictably.

"Because rooms are in demand. There's only a handful of guesthouses in the area, and they're filled to capacity beginning tomorrow. People make their reservations a year in advance."

"Why?"

"Because everyone wants to come to Lily Dale for the summer," Odelia says easily, smiling at Max. "Leona's place is booked solid through August. I cleared my calendar for check-in day tomorrow, but I have back-to-back appointments beginning the next day. I've been wondering how I was going to manage everything, especially with my foot in a cast. Leona only had one living relative, her nephew Grant, and he's taking his sweet time getting here. I've been looking for someone to help out and now . . . here you are."

"Just for tonight," Bella reminds her.

"Those kittens will be born any moment, and someone will need to keep an eye on them, too. This really is just perfect." Odelia has a way of responding to things that makes you wonder whether she even heard you in the first place.

For now, Bella decides to let it go. A hot meal and a warm, dry bed for Max—and not having to drive out into the storm or say good-bye to Chance the Cat just yet—are more than enough incentive to stay put.

Just for tonight . . .

Chapter 4

Stepping over the threshold of Valley View Manor, Bella flips the light switch beside the door and inhales a scent as familiar as the mock orange still wafting in the air outside.

Home.

The place smells of old wood and lavender and that imperceptible *something* that always enveloped her like a warm hug whenever she walked into the apartment.

Until Sam was gone.

The homey smell went with him, though she didn't realize it until this moment. Now here it is, wafting in her nostrils, filling her with nostalgia, making her feel as though . . .

No. This isn't home.

This is a guesthouse that belongs to a total stranger in a peculiar little town in the middle of nowhere. A dead stranger, at that.

Well beyond Max's earshot, Odelia told Bella that Leona Gatto, a fellow medium, had drowned in the lake.

"She's always been leery of the water. She said it's because Wyoming—that's where she's from—is land-locked. Now I know the real reason."

"What is it?" Conversation with Odelia, Bella noted over their surprisingly delicious dinner, seems to have plenty of gaps that can be quite challenging to bridge.

"You know—because of what was going to happen to her."

"You mean she had a . . . premonition?" Bella asked needlessly.

"You could say that."

"How did it happen, exactly? Was she swimming?"

"Leona can't swim. She keeps a couple of kayaks and an old rowboat on that rickety pier behind the guesthouse for guests who like to fish. The rowboat wound up drifting out into the lake a couple of times last spring, and she wasn't sure whether kids were playing around with it or it came loose. Anyway, it was windy that night, so she must have gone out to make sure the boat was tied up tightly. It looks like she bumped her head on a piling, and she fell into the water. The next morning, the boat was found floating again—but this time, so was Leona."

Bella shuddered, as disturbed by the image as by the woman's matter-of-fact delivery. But as Odelia talked on, she noted the affectionate tone and the way she referred to Leona in the present tense.

Clearly, Odelia views premature death more as transition than tragedy.

I wish I could see it that way, Bella thinks as wipes her wet sneakers on the mat and reaches back to close the front door. The wind grabs it, slamming it behind her and Max.

"Mommy?" He reaches nervously for her.

"It's okay, Max." She pockets the big key ring Odelia gave her. In addition to the modern metal key that opens both the front and back deadbolts, it also holds a set of numbered, old-fashioned skeleton-style keys to unlock each of the guestrooms.

"Mommy?" Max says again, and everything about him, including his voice, seems smaller as he shrinks against her side. "I don't want to stay here anymore."

She grasps his hand. "Sure you do. We're warm and dry here. Let's check out this place and decide where we're going to sleep, okay?"

"I wish you'd let Odelia come with us."

The woman had offered to get them settled, but Bella could tell her leg was hurting and assured her they'd be just fine on their own.

Of course they will. They'll get a good night's sleep, and in the morning, she'll ask Odelia where she can get her car checked, and then they'll be on their way.

Listening to the rain on the roof, inhaling the familiar old house scent, she feels oddly calm.

Calm and exhausted. Weariness began to leach into her bones as they finished washing Leona's dishes, and now she can't stop yawning. The challenges of the past few days—the past year, really—have finally taken a toll.

The front hall is wallpapered in a period brocade of amber and brown, warmly bathed in the glow of vintage fixtures—a gaslight globe atop the newel post and a pendant suspended from a creamy plaster medallion, both in a milky ocher etched glass. The floors, staircase, and moldings are honeyed oak, as is the tall table that holds a guest book open to tomorrow's date. A pen rests in the crease, and there's a covered crystal bowl of M&M's alongside the book.

"Go ahead, Max—you can grab a handful," she says, knowing a treat—sugar and all—will work wonders on his jittery nerves.

Leona was all set for her first visitors to check in, she thinks sadly, looking over the annotated list of reservations she'd left on the desk. *She couldn't have had much premonition that she wouldn't be here. Or maybe she was trying to make things easier for whoever takes over.*

Their footsteps tap across hardwoods and area rugs as they make their way through the first floor. It's cluttered with furniture and a bit dusty, but otherwise neat and orderly. Everything about the Victorian cottage seems familiar, from the irregularly shaped rooms to the woodwork to the nooks and crannies, many of them concealed at first glance.

In the kitchen, she opens a door to a steep flight into a dank basement.

"I don't want to go down there!" Max tells her.

"Don't worry. Neither do I." She hastily closes the door and slides the old-fashioned lock across it.

They make their way back to the front of the house. In the parlor, Max feels around beneath the cushioned bench in a parlor bay window and finds a hidden latch. "It opens just like at home."

"This house was probably built around the same time."

Together, they stare into the cluttered compartment beneath the seat. Paper—books, photos, catalogues, sheet music—mingles with stray shoes and garments and a hopeless tangle of electrical cords and cables.

"Looks like Leona wasn't such a neatnik after all," Bella says with a laugh. "I guess she had to hide the clutter when the guests arrived."

"Just like you."

"Right." Only her clutter has been reduced to whatever was able to fit into the back seat and car trunk.

Remembering that this is a mere way station on their journey to Millicent's, she tries to keep the sinking feeling from creeping into her voice as she tells Max it's time to go upstairs.

"Already?" Wiggling his bottom tooth with his thumb, he appears to be sucking it, which makes him once again appear younger and more vulnerable than he is.

But it'll be okay. She's doing the right thing, staying here with him tonight.

And even if it isn't right, there's really nothing else you can do, so make the best of it.

"Come on, I'll let you have first pick of bedrooms."

Unable to find a light switch at the bottom of the stairs, they're forced to ascend into shadows, past a round window on the landing with a leaded stained-glass pane.

"It looks like a creepy eye, watching us," Max says in a small voice. "Can I sleep with you?"

"Sure you can, if you want. But remember how Odelia told you about the room with the antique trains?"

"Yes. I want to sleep in there."

"I think she said it only has a single bed."

"We can squeeze in."

Rubbing the ache between her shoulders and holding back another deep yawn, Bella agrees that they can. Yes, she is looking forward to the first decent night's sleep in a while—and it promises to be the last for a while, too, given her memories of Millicent's uncomfortable pull-out couch.

But if Max is anxious, she'll wrap herself around him and cradle him in her arms all night, just like she did when he was plagued with nightmares when Sam was in the hospital and after Sam was gone.

At least she won't be lonely. It'll be better than having an entire king-sized bed—the one she used to share with her husband—all to herself.

She finds a light switch at the top of the stairs. It's the old-fashioned kind with round buttons rather than a flip toggle. Pressing one, she illuminates a hallway lined with closed doors.

Old-fashioned keys protrude from every knob lock. They're attached to small rings that also contain a heart-shaped disc imprinted with the letters VVM—Valley View

Manor—and a separate key that opens the deadbolts on both the front and back doors. They'll be given to the guests when they check in.

Odelia had mentioned that Leona had just recently ordered the engraved key rings for the upcoming season along with sets of similarly monogrammed towels for each bathroom. "She was always adding homey little touches to make her guests feel more welcome," she told Bella.

Staring at the murkily lit hallway, Max swallows audibly. "Is this a haunted house?"

Oh, kiddo, this is a haunted town.

"Of course not. Come on, let's find the Train Room."

One by one, they peek into the Rose Room, the Teacup Room, and the Apple Room—all easily identifiable based on Odelia's descriptions. The Train Room is at the end of the hall, its door slightly ajar.

Max takes in the railroad-themed drapes, bedding, and framed prints on the walls. "Daddy used to ride the train to work in the city."

Bella looks at Max in surprise. "Do you remember that?" Sam had been too ill to commute for quite some time before he passed away.

Max shrugs. "I just thought of it in my head when I saw the trains. Can we sleep in here?"

"Sure." Bella tries to sound enthusiastic, eyeing the twin bed. Seeing something poke out onto the floor from beneath the quilt's denim hem, she instinctively steps back and presses a hand against Max's midsection. The house has been empty. Are there rodents?

"What's wrong?"

Before Bella can answer, the quilt moves again—and she sees a large, furry paw emerge, followed by a familiar gray feline head imprinted with an *M* above the brow.

"Chance the Cat!" Max shouts.

Sure enough, the red-collared cat comes out from under the bed, pressing her front paws into the rug and arching her back into a hump as she gives a leisurely stretch.

"How did you get in here?" Bella asks as the animal rubs against first Max's legs and then her own, purring loudly and butting her head against their shins.

"She must have a secret passageway."

"She must."

"Can she sleep in here with me, Mommy? Then you can have the Rose Room, like you wanted."

"I didn't say I wanted that one."

"I could tell."

Max is right about that. The moment she glimpsed the room at the top of the stairs, with its creamy bedding and floral wallpaper, she longed to crawl beneath the coverlet and sink her tired body into that pretty four-poster bed.

* * *

Bella had intended to retire to the Rose Room after double-checking to make sure the outside doors are all locked. Yet long after Max and Chance have drifted to sleep beneath the denim comforter, she finds herself lingering on the first floor, contentedly drifting from one inviting room to the next.

Maybe she should be more uneasy about finding herself alone in a big old house on a stormy night—especially in a town where ghostly visitors are allegedly as commonplace as gamblers in Vegas or actors in LA. But for the first time all day—the first time in how long?—she feels as though she can breathe a little more easily.

The thing she'd been dreading for months is behind her at last. Leaving home had been traumatic, but in a sense, staying there without Sam, wondering what lay ahead, had been even more so.

See? We're moving on, just like you wanted us to do, she tells him as she investigates the windowed breakfast room with its whitewashed wainscoting, ruffled blue curtains, and well-stocked morning beverage station.

For the first time, she isn't worried about where they'll wind up. Less than twenty-four hours into the unknown, she's already found a soft landing spot—albeit a temporary one. There will be others.

We've made new friends, Sam. Odelia is a hoot, and the cat just loves Max, and even Doctor Bailey turned out to be one of the good guys.

Not that we'll ever see any of them again after today, but . . .

For a few hours, the world seemed a lot less lonely.

With a sigh, she crosses the threshold into the dining room, where fine china and crystal stemware fill the built-in cabinetry. She recognizes many distinctive iridescent Carnival glass pieces among them. They're similar to the much smaller collection Aunt Sophie had left to her, but these are red and thus rare and far more valuable.

Walking into the elegant parlor, she hesitates before a closed French door off to one side. The glass panels are veiled in opaque maroon curtains. Turning the knob, she finds it locked.

Curiosity aroused, she pulls the key ring from her pocket. All but one of the skeleton-style keys has a stickered number on it. She inserts that one into the lock on the French door and sure enough, it turns.

Behind the door is a small study. Its lone window, with a cushioned built-in bench beneath, is covered by drawn blinds. A trio of blue-and-white floral pillows with ruffled hems form a backrest. The walls, painted a buttery golden shade that reminds Bella of corn on the cob, are unadorned. A couple of framed prints lean in one corner as if waiting to be hung.

The only furnishings in the room are a pair of easy chairs facing each other and a round table covered in a blue tablecloth. It holds a telephone, a large candle with a burned wick, a box of tissues, a notepad and pen, and a spiral-bound appointment book.

This, she presumes, is where Leona gave her psychic readings. There's an almost identical room next door in Odelia's house, similarly devoid of decorative touches like the fringed tablecloths, velvet draperies, Ouija boards, and crystal balls Bella had envisioned.

She idly picks up the appointment book. It's laid out week by week and appears to be a log of client readings. The first half of the book contains many of the same names week after week, most in the same time slot on the same day of the week, with a smattering of aberrations. Some are preceded by an asterisk, she notices: a woman named Mary Brightman on January 1 (New Year's Day) and another named Helen Adabner on February 14 (Valentine's Day). She wonders if the asterisks denote holidays, but the theory is quickly blown when sees asterisks on random dates as well.

As she flips through the pages, she notices that Leona's schedule shows plenty of prescheduled appointments and very few open slots during the summer months but that the final quarter of the book is nearly blank. That makes sense, given Odelia's mention that the season ends on Labor Day.

Giving in to morbid curiosity, she finds herself flipping back to June, looking for the week Leona died. Did she have some inkling? Is there some clue that she saw it coming?

Like what? An appointment to meet her maker?

Disgusted with herself, she starts to close the book when she notices something odd.

When the page is open to the first half of the first week in June on the left, the opposite side shows the second half of the second week in June.

There's a page missing between the two.

Someone must have ripped it out. Usually, when you tear a sheet from a spiral notebook, at least a partial scallop-edged strip is left behind inside the wire coil, but not here. If she hadn't noticed the jump in dates, she never would have realized a page is missing.

That bothers her for some reason.

Probably because you're being nosy.

Guiltily aware that she's violated Leona's private sanctuary, she closes the appointment book, returns it to the table, closes the door, and locks it securely behind her.

Back in the parlor, she notices a stack of leather-bound albums.

Since they're sitting right there on the marble coffee table in a public room, she wouldn't be snooping if she looked at them, right?

Right. She settles onto the sofa and reaches for the first one.

Its pages, like the others, are filled with vintage photographs of the house dating back at least a century. The exterior remains remarkably consistent through several eras, as seen in the pictures. She notices that the formal turn-of-the-century furnishings are intact but looking threadbare by the Depression, only to be replaced by exceedingly modern décor before finally reverting to the current, classic style.

The occupants, too, are perpetually made over to reflect changing times. Pouf-haired Gibson Girls trade shirtwaists and suffrage banners for carefree grins and flapper fringe, then Depression-era cloches perched atop gaunt faces etched in worry lines. Argyle-clad Jazz Age dandies with slicked, parted hair become uniformed soldiers and then proud husbands and fathers in overcoats and fedoras. Gradually, the posed black-and-white portraits give way to Kodachrome candids featuring bobby-soxers and beatniks, hippies and yuppies.

Fascinated by the window into the past, Bella can't help but marvel that generation after generation of inhabitants couldn't appear more . . .

Well, *normal*.

In this supposedly extraordinary setting, ordinary people seem to lead largely ordinary lives. The photos depict everyday folks engaged in everyday activities. They pose on porch steps, row boats on the lake, show off bicycles that have giant front wheels, and wave from Studebaker touring cars or fifties convertibles with enormous fins. They swing croquet mallets on summer lawns and pile atop sleds on wintry hills.

There are no floating tables or filmy specters, and again, certainly no Ouija boards or crystal balls.

Did Odelia exaggerate her claim that Lily Dale is populated by mediums? Bella decides she must have—until she decides to help herself to some herbal tea and stumbles across the daily summer schedule posted on the breakfast-room wall. Perusing the schedule while microwaving a mug of water, she finds it packed with mystical activities. There are daily message and healing services, classes on astrology and numerology, and workshops on astral projection and spoon bending. The guest speakers' lineup features a few household names: a best-selling author, a celebrity psychic who stars on a cable television show, and a self-help guru.

Okay, so Odelia wasn't exaggerating.

Perhaps she should find it all disturbing, but there doesn't seem to be anything dark or exploitative about what goes on here. The daily offerings, more detailed in the brochures and catalogues stacked on one of the café tables, proclaim peace and enlightenment.

Steeped in serenity, she sips steaming chamomile and browses the floor-to-ceiling bookshelves in an alcove off the dining room. The steady rain beats a pleasant rhythm beyond the windows as the antique clock ticks away the minutes. When it chimes midnight, she rinses her mug in the kitchen sink and selects a couple of local history books to read in bed, turning off lights as she goes up the stairs. Peeking into the Train Room, she sees that Max and Chance are still in deep, snuggly slumber. She marvels that the cat stayed put.

Back down the corridor, she notices light glowing in the crack beneath the closed door of the Rose Room.

That's strange. She doesn't remember leaving a lamp on earlier. She hesitates, then knocks, feeling slightly foolish.

There's no reply.

Of course there's no reply. You and Max are the only people in the house, remember?

Frowning, she opens the door and peeks in.

Flooded with cozy lamplight, the room is decidedly empty, and yet . . .

Somehow, Bella was expecting to find someone there.

Odelia? A ghost? Leona's or Sam's?

Even the prospect of an otherworldly visitor doesn't frighten her much. Not in this particular moment, in this particular place.

"I wish we could stay here forever," was the last thing Max said to her earlier, before she turned off his lamp.

Maybe not forever, she finds herself thinking sleepily as she sinks into a mound of downy pillows, *but tonight is good. Really good.*

She listens to the soft patter of the rain on the turreted roof high above her head, grateful that it's not falling on thin canvas within arm's reach.

Then, remembering something, she sits up and reaches for her phone, plugged into the charger beneath the bedside table.

The small screen glows in the dark as she types into the search engine: S-U-M-M-E-R P-I-N-E-S C-A-M-P-G-R-O-U-N-D.

Hmm. Not a single hit. Nothing that fits, anyway.

Taking a different tactic, she looks up a list of campgrounds located in Chautauqua County.

There are quite a few. None contain the words *Summer* or *Pines* and none are located off Route 60 ten miles north of the interstate exit.

There are also quite a few quaint cottage colonies in the area. Bear Lake, Van Buren Point, Sunset Bay—they all seem like regular waterfront resort communities frequented by regular people.

There is even, just a few miles away from Lily Dale, another century-old summer colony that happens to be gated and filled with charming Victorian homes. It, too, sits on the grassy shores of a picturesque country lake. It, too, is more than a mere resort. Similarly populated by like-minded souls devoted to a singular purpose—the arts—Chautauqua Institution has its own world-class symphony orchestra, ballet, opera, and theater company.

Why didn't I find my way there, instead? Why did I wind up in the one that's filled with Spiritualists?

Oh, well. She's going to find her way right back out of here as soon as the sun comes up. But for now, she's bent on locating the elusive Summer Pines Campground.

She expands the search to neighboring western New York counties—Erie, Cattaraugus, even over the

Pennsylvania border, in case there was a typo on the bill-board. In case it should have said *fifty* miles instead of *ten* or *south* instead of *north* . . .

No.

Even if the billboard was outdated and the place is long gone, there would still be an Internet trail. And someone—Odelia or Doctor Bailey—would have heard of it.

Okay, so what does that mean?

That Summer Pines Campground doesn't exist and never did?

That the billboard didn't exist, either?

Putting the phone aside and closing her eyes, Bella can still see it, clear as day, with its simple directions and photo of a picturesque lake not unlike the one behind the guesthouse.

The billboard was there. Of course it was there, because if it hadn't been there, I wouldn't be here. *Max and I would be shivering in a damp tent somewhere instead of tucked into warm, dry beds.*

As drowsiness overtakes her, that's all that matters.

Chapter 5

Bella brushes her hair.

Beyond the bathroom window, the night sky is dark, and a stiff breeze tinkles Sam's wind chimes, and something, something . . .

Something isn't right.

Gradually, it dawns on her: nothing is right. It's all wrong—the bathroom, the sound of the wind chimes, the length of the hair, and the face—dear God, even the face in the mirror above the sink is wrong.

Wrinkled, topped by cropped silver hair, it's the face of an old woman.

But she must be me, because I'm brushing my hair and . . .

And she's brushing her hair and . . .

It doesn't make sense, but the reflected woman's movements exactly mimic Bella's. The trepidation in her eyes—eyes that are the wrong shade of blue and fringed by crow's-feet—echoes the trepidation in Bella's gut.

She's me.

I'm her.

The wind chimes have gone from melodious to garish. Their deafening peal fills her head, drowning out her thoughts and . . .

Drowning . . .

Drowning?

Something about drowning.

What is it?

There's something she's supposed to remember.

But she can't think clearly amid the noise, and now the wind chimes meld with a ringing doorbell, and . . .

And I was dreaming, she realizes, opening her eyes to bright morning sunlight.

Or maybe she's still dreaming, because this isn't right.

She stares up at the wavy crack in the plaster ceiling that leads from an unfamiliar light fixture medallion to the crown molding. Struggling to get her bearings, she looks over at the lace curtains fluttering in a windowed nook, the floral wallpaper in shades of vibrant reddish pink, the heavy antique furniture.

Slowly, it all comes back to her: The road trip. The cat. The guesthouse.

Downstairs, the doorbell rings again, this time followed by a sharp knock.

"Hello?" she hears a faint voice calling from outside, below the closed window. "Leona?"

Leona . . .

Leona died.

Leona . . . *drowned.*

Unsettled by that thought, Bella gets out of bed, throws on Sam's sweatshirt, and hurries out into the hall.

The door to the room where Max was sleeping is ajar.

"Max?" she calls, hurrying down the stairs. "Max!"

From the landing, she can see a pair of human silhouettes through the frosted glass panel in the door. The bell rings again as she reaches the first floor. She opens the door to a pleasant-looking couple standing on the front porch with suitcases and a bag of golf clubs.

Their healthy tans, the woman's gold jewelry and designer handbag, and the emblems stitched onto both their polo shirts signify that they're solidly upper-middle class. Upper-middle aged, too—probably late fifties, early sixties. The man's blond hair is graying at the temples, and while his brunette wife's chic, short cut is highlighted to perfection, a faint network of wrinkles extends from the corners of her eyes and mouth.

"I'm sorry—did we wake you?" she asks apologetically, eying Bella's disheveled state.

"I—what time is it?"

"It's only ten forty-five . . ."

Ten forty-five? What? She slept almost twelve hours? She'd been planning to be on the road right after sun-up.

". . . and I know check-in isn't until two," the woman talks on, as Bella tries to gather her scrambled thoughts, "but we spent last night in the Falls, and Steve thought we might as well drive down and see if our room is ready early."

"The Falls?" she echoes, even as she darts a look over her shoulder, hoping Max is still up in bed. He probably opened the door when he used the restroom in the night, or maybe the cat managed to open it and slip out.

"Niagara Falls," the man clarifies.

The Falls . . . The Dale . . .

She really needs to get the hang of this local shorthand. Then again, why bother? As soon as she finds her son, who is safely upstairs—of course he is!—they're out of here.

"Is Niagara Falls pretty close by?" she asks, weighing the prospect of a budget-friendly sightseeing detour. It can't cost anything to look at a waterfall, right?

"It's a little over an hour away," the wife informs her. "Although the way Steve drives, about forty-five minutes."

Her husband chuckles good-naturedly. "And if I let you drive the car, Eleanor, it would've taken us all day to get here."

They're obviously from the Boston area, judging by the way he pronounces *car—cah*. Sure enough, Bella can see Massachusetts plates on the silver sedan parked at the curb in the unloading zone.

"Are you staying at the guesthouse?" the woman asks.

"Me? Oh, I'm . . . we just stayed last night, but we're about to hit the road. Max!" she calls again, then says, "I'm sorry, I need to find my son."

"And we need to find Leona," the man returns. "Is she around?"

She hesitates, wondering how to phrase it. "Leona is . . . I'm afraid she . . ."

Saved by the sound of running footsteps outside, Bella is even more relieved to see Max burst into view on the small patch of grass in front of the house.

"Hey, Mom, look what Odelia made for us!"

"Max! You went outside barefoot, in pajamas, all *alone?*"

"Not alone. Chance the Cat was with me. We were talking to Odelia through the window screen. She invited us over for breakfast and we were hungry, so we went."

"Without telling me?"

"You were sleeping. She made us kittycakes! See? And she sent some for you!" Bounding onto the porch, Max holds out a plastic-wrapped plate.

Kittycakes, at a glance, consist of a large pancake with chocolate chip eyes and bacon whiskers topped by French toast triangle ears.

"Isn't that clever!" The woman—Eleanor—peers at the plate. "Leave it to Odelia. She's quite the creative cook."

"That's the understatement of the year," her husband mutters.

"You know her, then?" Good. Bella can send the couple next door, and Odelia can break the sad news about Leona while she and Max pack up and get ready to leave.

"Eleanor knows everyone in Lily Dale," Steve informs her. "She's been coming here for years. Now she's roped me in, too."

"Only because he likes to attend the productions over at Chautauqua Institution," Eleanor clarifies. "He's a theater buff."

"The summer arts colony? I just read about that last night," Bella remembers.

"You really should visit while you're here," Steve tells her. "Do you like plays? The theater company is kicking off the season with *Our Town*. I'm hoping to see it tonight."

"I thought you were coming with me to the opening message service!" his wife protests, and he sighs.

"I said I would if you insist."

"You have all week to see the show."

"But you know how I feel about *Our Town*. It's one of my all-time favorites."

"They're *all* his all-time favorites," she tells Bella, rolling her eyes. "Especially when the alternative is to hang around with me here in 'Silly Dale.'"

"I don't call it that anymore," he protests.

"No, but plenty of people do. And sometimes I think you're as skeptical as they are."

Who can blame him? Bella wants to say, relieved to have found a kindred spirit among . . . well, the spirits and the spirit whisperers.

But now isn't the time to engage in a debate about the dubious nature of the local industry. Instead, she asks the logical question.

"What, exactly, is a message service?"

"It's a very large group reading, really. The mediums face the audience and take turns standing up and delivering messages."

"From?" she asks, though she has a pretty good idea.

"From loved ones."

"And they give messages to everyone in the room right there in public?"

"Well, not to *everyone.* Just to a few people. It's basically the ones whose loved ones are the pushiest."

"Which is why I'm shocked that your mother doesn't come through to you every single time," Steve says with a laugh.

On that note, Max thrusts the plate into Bella's hands. "I have to go get dressed. Jiffy's waiting."

"Jiffy . . . what?" *Great. Now even Max is speaking the inscrutable localese.*

"Jiffy. He's my friend. He came over for breakfast, too, and we're going to play Candyland. He lives next door to Odelia on the other side."

For a moment, Bella is so taken aback by the realization that Max made a friend—a friend at last!—that she forgets the rest.

Then it comes back to her: *we're leaving, and these people are waiting, and they need to be told that Leona is dead, and . . .*

Wait a minute. What if . . .

What if Jiffy isn't real? What if he's an imaginary friend, or even . . .

A ghost?

"Max, listen . . ."

He's already on his way up the stairs, taking them two at a time. "I'll be right back! I have to get dressed, Mom!"

Feeling helpless, she turns back to the strangers on the doorstep. "I'm sorry," she says. "I kind of have my hands full here and I'm just a guest myself, but I think that Odelia can—"

"Steve! Eleanor!"

Odelia comes limping across the lawn as if summoned by the mere mention of her name—and who knows, maybe that's precisely the case, considering the circumstances. Chance trails behind her, belly swaying just above the grass.

"Odelia! What happened to your leg?" Eleanor asks as Steve descends the steps to take the older woman's arm.

"Oh, it's nothing. I just took a spill." She brushes off the help, gripping the railing tightly and joking about her clumsiness as she makes her way up the porch steps to greet Eleanor with a warm hug.

"I can see that you've all already met, but I'll do the formal introductions. Stephen and Eleanor Pierson, meet Bella Jordan."

Noticing that Odelia has once again used her nickname, Bella shakes their hands. She's about to excuse herself to go find Max when Odelia asks if she's told the Piersons about Leona.

"No, I was about to . . ." *About to send them over to Odelia's so that I wouldn't have to break the bad news myself.*

"Tell us what?" Eleanor asks.

"What about Leona?" Steve looks from Odelia to Bella and back again.

Odelia sighs. "There's no easy way to say this. I'm afraid she's passed on."

Eleanor gasps, clasping her hands to her mouth with a jangle of gold bracelets. "But I just talked to her last week!"

"It was very sudden."

Steve settles a protective arm around Eleanor. "What happened?"

As Odelia explains quickly about the freak accident, he shakes his head grimly.

Tears fill Eleanor's eyes. "She was always afraid of the water. She couldn't swim."

"How do you know that?" Steve asks.

Odelia answers for his wife. "I'm guessing everyone does."

Even I *know it,* Bella thinks.

"It's a good thing we got here so early in the day." Steve takes the car keys out of his pocket, and Bella notices a keychain imprinted with the comedy and tragedy masks dangling from the ring.

That makes her think of her own key ring, still safely tucked under her pillow upstairs. She hopes.

"We can go over and see if we can get a room near Chautauqua and see the play tonight," Steve tells his wife, "and then head back to Boston first thing in the morning."

"What do you mean?" Eleanor asks.

"We'll go to the Cape, like we had talked about. It's been years since we've been there, and you said yourself you miss it."

"We can't get a place on the Cape at the eleventh hour on a holiday weekend. And probably not tonight near Chautauqua, either."

"Maybe there will be a last-minute cancellation. If we can't find a place to stay, we'll just go home and do some day trips."

"You have a place to stay," Odelia speaks up. "Right here."

Steve blinks. "But we can't stay here if Leona isn't . . . if she's . . ."

"Of course you can. She would have wanted business to go on as usual, and you know how meticulous she was about keeping notes. I know exactly which room you prefer and it's all set for you. No feathers. Allergies," she adds for Bella's benefit.

"Leona always took such good care of us." Eleanor smiles through her tears. "Thank you, Odelia."

Leaving them to get checked in and settled, Bella heads upstairs to find Max in the train room. He's wearing only underpants and fishing through his open duffle bag on the floor. "Do I have a purple shirt, mom?"

"Purple? I don't think so, no. Why?"

"That's Jiffy's favorite color."

Jiffy again. The ghost kid.

She doesn't really believe that, of course.

"Listen, Max . . . I don't think we're going to have time for Candyland this morning."

He looks up, crestfallen. "But I told Jiffy I'd be right back!"

"I'm sorry, sweetie."

"I don't want to go!"

"I know, but we have to."

"Why?"

"Because this isn't . . . this is just . . . it's a place where we stopped to spend the night, that's all. I'm sure the next place we stop will be just as much fun."

"Where? The tent? Grandma's? Those aren't fun places."

"You don't know that. You've never been camping, and you haven't been to Grandma's in years."

"I don't want to go, ever! I want to stay here."

"I know you do." She kneels beside him, touches his bony, pale little shoulder and finds it trembling. "I wish we could stay."

"Odelia said we can."

Odelia.

A crazy thought materializes in Bella's brain. She tries to push it right back out, but it's as persistent as Odelia herself.

"I'll make a deal with you," she tells Max.

"Can we stay forever?"

"No, not forever, or even for another night. But let me talk to Odelia, and maybe we can figure out a way to stay long enough for you to play Candyland. Okay?"

"But—"

"Candyland is better than nothing, right?" she reminds him, hating that it's all she can offer. He's been through so much and has so little.

He looks up at her with sad, brown eyes. "I guess so."

"Good. Now get dressed and let's go see what we can work out."

* * *

An hour later, Bella finds herself in the cramped waiting room of Valeri and Son Service Station a few miles from Lily Dale, listening in dismay to the mechanic's verdict.

"Is that the best you can do?" she asks, clutching a half-finished white foam cup of bad coffee, courtesy of a filmy carafe on a nearby counter.

"You mean the best I can do on the cost or on the time it'll take to finish the repair?"

"Both."

"'Fraid so." He shakes his head, eyes apologetic beneath the blue brim of his Buffalo Bills cap. "It'll take me at least a couple of days to track down the part, and with the holiday, I probably won't have it here until after the weekend. And it'll be expensive because it's old. But I'll give you a break on the labor, seeing as how you're stuck and outa luck."

Stuck and outa luck.

"You've pretty much just described the last year of my life," she says wryly.

"Yeah? Sorry." He offers a brief smile and a complicated explanation about how something in the engine isn't functioning the way it should. The technical details escape her; car maintenance was—like playing board games with Max—Sam's department.

Now, however, like everything else, it's solely her responsibility. She has no choice but to spend money she doesn't have and time she . . .

Well, she *has* time, she supposes. And a place to stay for another four or five days.

Earlier, when she asked Odelia to recommend a service station, Odelia reminded Bella that she's welcome to stick around the guesthouse as long as she'd like.

"I thought it was sold out starting today."

"The public rooms are, yes. But the Rose Room is Leona's private quarters—the closet and bureau are still full of her things, but I'll clean them out for you tomorrow."

"No need to do that. We're not—"

"Oh, it's no problem. I've been meaning to get to it. And Max can sleep in one of the smaller rooms with a twin bed. Leona always keeps one open just in case her nephew shows up to visit. He never gives her any notice, but she adores him." Odelia's tone indicated that she herself had little affection for the nephew, Grant Everard. "He's supposedly trying to get here this week, but who knows if he'll really come?"

The mechanic—who's around Bella's age and whose name is Troy, according to the patch sewn on his coveralls—asks if she needs a ride somewhere.

"Can I keep my car with me until the part comes in?"

"You can if you like hitchhiking, because you're already on borrowed time. I can't believe you managed to drive it this far without breaking down."

Bella sighs. "All right, then, I guess I'll get a cab back and—"

"A cab? Around here?" His laugh isn't unkind, but it's yet another reminder that she's a stranger in a strange land. "You'd have better luck flagging down a flying carpet."

"Yeah, well, with any luck, there's a magical genie on board, because I could really use three wishes right about now."

"If you find him, send him my way. I have a couple of wishes of my own. Come on, I'll drive you. Where are you going?"

Most people—where she comes from, anyway—would have asked that question before offering the ride. Around here, she's noticed, people are so friendly that they don't seem to balk at being inconvenienced by total strangers.

First Doctor Bailey, in the midst of an after-hours emergency, helped her with a stray cat. And Odelia—well, she's a godsend. After settling the Piersons into their third-floor room, she turned her attention back to helping Bella. She called the service station, talked to Troy the mechanic, and offered to lead Bella over there in her own car.

"That's all right, I'm sure I'll make it," she said— naïvely, as it turns out. "But Max is talking about a boy named Jiffy—"

"Jiffy Arden."

Okay. So he was a real kid and not . . . imaginary. Or . . .

There's no such thing as ghosts, Bella reminded herself as Odelia went on to explain that Jiffy's real name is Michael.

"But there are two other Michaels in the Dale, and he loves peanut butter, and the nickname stuck."

Jiffy. It could have been worse, Bella thought. *Skippy . . . Peter Pan . . .*

But it sure could have been better.

"He's a sweet boy. His mom is renting the house next door to me for the season," Odelia went on, limping briskly around the Rose Room, opening all the windows to let fresh air billow through the screens, "and I thought it would be nice for Max to meet him, so I invited him to breakfast. They hit it off, just like I thought."

Bella didn't know what to say to that. Should she be grateful that Odelia is looking out for her son or infuriated that Max has yet another reason to beg to linger in Lily Dale?

Moot point now. She agreed to leave Max and Jiffy playing Candyland on the porch at Valley View Manor while Odelia kept an eye on them and waited for additional guests to check in.

"We'll be hitting the road as soon as I get back," she reminded her son before she left.

Engrossed in navigating toward Gum Drop Mountain, Max merely shrugged.

He's going to be thrilled when he finds out we aren't going anywhere for the next couple of days.

Maybe she's just a tiny bit relieved herself. She was so emotionally drained after leaving home that she isn't yet prepared to see Millicent again. Their previous encounter—at the funeral—was a blur of grief and her mother-in-law's usual histrionics. Lily Dale will provide a convenient reprieve so that she can get herself together before the next phase of their fresh start.

"Do you know where Lily Dale is?" she asks Troy.

"Sure, it's only a few miles down the road. I have a pickup truck, so we can load everything into the back."

"Everything?"

"I noticed your car's pretty full."

"Oh, right." Somehow, she'd forgotten about all her worldly belongings stashed in the car. "I'm in the middle of a move."

"I figured. You probably don't want to leave your stuff here for a few days . . . or do you?" he asks, seeing the look on her face.

Hmm. Her overnight bag and Max's are back at the guesthouse.

"I'll leave it," she decides. "It's only a few days, right? And I'll be close by, so if I need something"—*like a tent or a vase?*—"I can always come get it."

"Sounds good." Troy grabs a set of keys from a wall hook. "Are you staying with Odelia Lauder?"

"No, next door."

"At the Taggarts'? Or Leona Gatto's guesthouse?"

"The guesthouse. So you . . . know it?" *And do you know about Leona?*

"I do odd jobs during the slow season, so I get around. I did some painting for Leona last month. I read in the paper that she drowned a few days ago. I was sorry to hear it. She was a nice lady—and she was terrified of water. She couldn't swim."

Bella wonders if there's anyone in a fifty-mile radius who isn't aware of that fact.

Troy moves the hands of the cardboard clock sign hanging in the window, indicating that he'll be back in an hour. "It won't take me that long to drop you," he says as he locks the door after them, "but I might as well grab lunch while I'm out."

"Are you the only one working here?"

"Now I am. It's a family business, but my dad passed away last year."

"I'm sorry."

"Yeah. It's lonely without him. I miss him every day."

Those words resonate as Troy leads her around behind the concrete block building, past a padlocked restroom door, a Dumpster, and an old bicycle pump. A red pickup truck sits in a sunny patch of tall grasses and orange wildflowers.

He opens the passenger's side door and gestures for her to climb in. "I asked Odelia if she could put me in touch with him—you know, through a reading," he says casually, before going around to the driver's side.

Bella is intrigued. Troy doesn't seem like the kind of guy who would buy into talking to the spirit world.

Climbing behind the wheel, he starts the engine.

As they begin bumping along a dirt path toward the road, Bella waits for him to pick up the story where he left off, but he doesn't. He seems lost in thought.

"So did Odelia do the reading for you?" she asks after a minute.

"She did."

"How did it go?"

He hesitates. "You know, I never believed in that stuff. Neither did Dad. But then you lose someone you love and you miss them like crazy and you figure . . . well, you hope there's something to it."

"Did she get through to him, then?"

"Nah. She said she was tapping into a bunch of other dead relatives I've never heard of, but not my dad. She offered to try again sometime."

"Did she?"

He shakes his head. "I said thanks, but no thanks."

"Why?"

"Because I don't want to get my hopes up. Right after Dad died, all I wanted was to connect with him one more time. Now . . . well, I wouldn't say I'm over it, exactly. But it's been more than a year, and . . . time really does heal, you know?"

No. She still endures moments when grief stabs at her like a freshly honed blade. Will that subside in six months? A year? *Ever?*

What if she could connect with Sam one more time?

She never even considered that possibility until now.

Because it's not *a possibility,* she reminds herself.

Like Troy, she never believed in that stuff. She's not going to start now just because she's stumbled across a strange little town filled with people who not only believe in ghosts but also are convinced they can communicate with them.

And now you're stuck there for a few days. Terrific.

Troy pulls out onto the rural highway, heading south toward Lily Dale. She leans back in the seat, gazing at the bucolic countryside until he cuts into her melancholy thoughts with a question.

"Where's your husband?"

Startled, she glances over at him. He's looking straight ahead, at the road, one hand on the wheel, the other thoughtfully rubbing his razor stubble.

"My . . . husband?"

"You're wearing a wedding ring, so I figured . . ."

"Oh." She instinctively twists the gold band on her left hand. After Sam died, she'd put away his ring to give to Max someday but couldn't bear to take off her own.

She takes a deep breath and musters the dreaded word. "I'm a widow."

"I'm sorry." He's silent for a moment.

She stares out the passenger's window at acres of lush, green grapevines trailing over perpendicular fencerows as far as she can see, broken only by the occasional weathered barn.

Then Troy asks, "Is that why you're in Lily Dale? To try to connect to your husband?"

"No! We were just passing through to drop off a stray cat we found on the road. I never even heard of it until now."

Maybe he doesn't believe her. His gray eyes are pensive beneath the brim of his hat. "Well, as long as you're here, you should see if Odelia will do a reading for you."

"Why?"

Troy shrugs. "Why not? It can't hurt. Maybe you'll hear from your husband."

Those words stay with her long after he's left her at Valley View Manor and driven away.

Chapter 6

By midafternoon, with the guesthouse filled up and the sun beating down, Bella and Odelia settle into a pair of Adirondack chairs on the lawn behind the guesthouse. The yard is fragrant with flowers and the lake blue and inviting on this first July day.

Chance lies nearby in a shady patch of grass beneath a sprawling apple tree, watching Max and Jiffy climb it.

Rather, Max is watching Jiffy climb to a towering branch that Odelia assures Bella is perfectly safe. "He does it all the time," she says when he effortlessly hoists himself to that height in a matter of seconds and then casually perches there, legs dangling. "Don't worry."

Jiffy is a scrappy kid with wiry ginger hair, a smattering of freckles across the bridge of his nose, and—in addition to the front tooth Odelia mentioned he'd knocked out—an array of bruises and wounds he catalogued for a reverent Max earlier.

"I got this one falling off my scooter into a pothole on East Street—"

"You ride your scooter in the *street?*" Max wouldn't have looked more astounded if Jiffy had just announced he skydives without a parachute.

"Uh-huh, and I got this one from a fish hook, and this one from a poisonous snake . . ." He pointed to a mosquito bite he'd scratched open.

"A poisonous snake? Wow!"

"Well, I *think* it was poisonous. And I think it was a snake. I didn't 'xactly see it, by the way. But it bit me right here, and I was bleeding a lot, see?"

Max saw.

And now Bella's son—who's never climbed a tree in his life—is eager to keep up with his gutsy new friend. Well, not keep up, exactly.

He cautiously clings to the lowest-hanging bough just a few feet off the ground. His knees are dirty and his face is scratched courtesy of a thorny patch of shrubs between this yard and Odelia's. But he's happier than Bella has seen him since . . .

Since Sam was alive.

Sam always wanted Max to be a carefree kid playing outside. He didn't experience that in his own high-rise urban childhood, nor did Bella in hers. They hoped things would be different for their son, but in this day and age, you don't let kids wander too far beyond their own suburban backyards. Not even in bucolic Bedford.

Here in Lily Dale, she's already noticed that things are different. Unaccompanied kids of all ages have been strolling or riding by the house on bikes, scooters, and skateboards all afternoon. A few are swimming off a small pier down the way, well outside the perimeter of the small lifeguarded beach.

Odelia mentions that Jiffy's dad is overseas with the military and his mom is busy with appointments until dinnertime.

"Appointments? Is she . . . ?"

"She's doing readings."

That Jiffy's mother is a medium shouldn't be surprising, yet somehow it catches Bella off guard. Maybe it's narrow-minded of her, but she can't seem to reconcile the image of mundane maternal life with . . . well, special powers, real or imagined.

Imagined. Of course imagined.

As Odelia forewarned, crowds of visitors have arrived in Lily Dale this afternoon. Bella was amazed that so many of them appear to be . . . normal. There's an inordinate ratio of women, and they come in all shapes and sizes, with a range of socioeconomic backgrounds and encompassing every racial and age group. There are even a few teenage girls.

"They always want to know who they're going to marry," Odelia commented earlier, as they watched a giggly gaggle pass the front porch.

"Do you know?"

"Sometimes. But I guarantee you that it's never the name they want to hear."

"Do you tell them anyway?"

"I deliver whatever message Spirit wants them to have."

"I wonder if that has an impact on their relationship, then. If you tell someone young and impressionable that she's not meant to be with the person she loves."

"Most people shouldn't marry the person they love at fourteen or fifteen," Odelia responded with a shrug.

"My parents were high school sweethearts."

"It's lovely that it worked out for them. But most people aren't the person they're going to be a decade later, much less forty or fifty years later. My husband and I weren't."

"I'm sorry."

"Don't be. I wouldn't trade my life now for anything."

It must be nice to be so content.

Bella was, back when she was living her cozy little life with Sam and Max. Back when she knew exactly where she belonged.

Now . . .

Now, as she and Odelia sit with chicken salad sandwiches and cold lemonade, she's doing her best to stop thinking about the past.

She asks Odelia about Jiffy's mother: "So you babysit him while she's busy, then?"

"Well, she hasn't been very busy until today. But now that the season is under way, I'll keep an eye on him. We all will." At Bella's dubious look, she adds, "It's safe here. We trust each other."

When Bella opts to drop that subject, Odelia promptly introduces an equally disquieting one: she wants Bella to temporarily manage the guesthouse—for pay.

"But I can't take your money."

"It's not *my* money," Odelia assures her, after popping the last bite of her sandwich into her mouth. "It's Leona's. Well technically, it's her nephew's, now. But Grant told me to hire someone to take care of things."

Attempting to rephrase her protest, Bella sips the lemonade Odelia had poured from a large mason jar she brought from her kitchen. She'd mentioned that several newcomers had arrived in Bella's absence—a young couple and a single man—and that Leona always liked to greet guests with a glass of freshly squeezed lemonade.

"I don't mind helping out while I'm here," Bella says carefully, "but that's only for a couple of days. And if you won't charge me for the rooms—"

"Out of the question," Odelia inserts, shaking her head. Her frizzy orange hair is topped by a lime-green sun visor the same shade as her ruffled sundress, and she's traded her red cat-eye bifocals for white cat-eye sunglasses. "The beds are vacant. You need a place to stay."

"Then I guess the least I can do is keep an eye on the place in return." She adds the most blatant lie she's ever told in her life: "But I don't need money."

"Don't be silly. Everyone needs money. And you'll earn every penny. This is a full-time, round-the-clock job, and it can be challenging to deal with some people. You've already had a taste of it."

True. When she returned from the service station, she found Odelia painstakingly climbing the stairs with Opal and Ruby St. Clair, a pair of elderly sisters who had just driven from Ohio in an enormous black car. Though hardly new to the guesthouse, they requested a tour of all the available rooms on the second and third floor. A lengthy discussion/argument ensued before they decided which one they wanted. Five minutes later, they emerged, having changed their mind. No sooner did they move to a different room than they opted to return to their first choice.

They were sweet, if slightly dotty.

But around here, who isn't? Bella thinks, having over-heard Odelia having a conversation with an invisible companion as she folded towels in the tiny laundry room off the kitchen while Bella made the sandwiches.

"I'm going to pay you," Odelia says firmly. "It's what Leona would want. Grant—if I could ever manage to get ahold of him—would agree. Besides, you do need the money."

Bella doesn't bother to argue with that or ask how she knows. Having spent so much time with chatty Max, Odelia is undoubtedly privy to their dire financial status and more.

"All right," she agrees. It does seem like a win-win prospect. How else would she possibly cover the car repair costs?

"Wonderful." Odelia leans back in her chair, smiling. "And you can use Leona's car, too, while you're here, as long as you know how to drive a stick shift."

"I don't."

"I can teach you, but until you learn, you can use my car. It's a bit of a jalopy, but at least it'll get you where you need to go."

She's making it sound as though this is long term. Bella wants to tell her they don't need to bother with stick shift driving lessons, but she can't figure out how to say it in a polite way.

"What if Grant hasn't shown up before I have to leave?" she asks instead, watching a monarch butterfly hovering above a petunia bed that could stand to be weeded.

"We'll cross that bridge when we come to it."

"Where does he live?"

"Where *doesn't* he live?" As always, Odelia's tone takes on an undercurrent of disapproval when discussing Grant Everard. "He's a bit of a vagabond."

Yeah, well, so are we right now, Bella thinks. The difference is that Grant has a job—he's a venture capitalist, according to Odelia. He was away at a prestigious college when Leona first moved here fifteen years ago and hasn't visited much since.

She's in the midst of telling Bella that it took her a couple of days to track down Grant to let him know about Leona's passing when Bella notices that Max and Jiffy are on the move. They're heading from the tree toward the water's edge—and the small wooden pier where Leona had her tragic accident. The cat has roused herself and is trailing along after them.

Bella sets aside her glass and plate, interrupting Odelia to call, "Guys! No! That's not a safe place to be!"

"We won't step in the goose poop. I just wanted to show Max something," Jiffy returns cheerfully.

Hardly worried about goose poop, Bella hurries toward them, weaving around the obstacle course on the grass.

The yard, like many around here, is heavily ornamented. There's plenty of outdoor furniture, along with a sundial, a couple of birdbaths, a birdhouse on a pole, and vine-covered trellises and arbors. Glass sun catchers and wind chimes dangle from tree branches and pinwheels randomly dot the grass—all motionless on this still afternoon.

Reaching the boys, Bella puts a hand on each of their shoulders before they can set foot on the pier.

In bright sunshine, there's nothing ominous about the timeworn wood structure jutting into calm, sparkly water. A small rowboat is tied to one of the two pilings that rise above the plank walkway.

That's where Leona hit her head.

An icy chill sweeps over Bella as she pictures the elderly woman out here alone in the dead of a stormy night.

"It was right there," Jiffy tells Max, pointing. "That's where he threw it."

"How can we get it?"

"Can you swim?"

"No!" Bella says sharply.

"I can swim, Mommy," protests Max, who learned to semi-dog-paddle courtesy of lessons last summer at day camp. He squirms out from beneath her grasp, as does Jiffy, who shields his eyes with his hand, gazing out at the water.

"How long can you hold your breath?" he asks her son. "Because, by the way, we have to dig under the water."

"I'm not sure. A long time."

"Like five minutes?"

"Probably."

"What are you two talking about, exactly?" Bella asks Jiffy as the cat sniffs the grass at the edge of the pier. It is, indeed, dotted with droppings courtesy of a small flock of geese floating on the water.

"Treasure," Jiffy says, as if that explains everything.

"Where? In the lake?"

He nods vigorously. "It's the sunken kind. And you have to hold your breath for, like, ten minutes to get it. I can do that, by the way. But I don't know about Max."

"I can! I can hold it even longer, by the way," he adds, inserting Jiffy's favorite catchphrase.

"Nobody can do that."

Bella, who—*by the way*—feels as though she's been holding her own breath for months, watches her son inhale deeply. Eyes closed, cheeks puffed out, he begins silently counting on his fingers.

"What's going on?" Odelia has limped over, huffing a little.

"The other night, in the middle of the night, I saw a pirate drop a big heavy treasure chest into the lake. Me and Max want to get it."

Determined to nip that plan in the bud, Bella says, "It was probably just a dream. Max has exciting dreams like that sometimes, right, Max?"

Still holding his breath and counting, Max nods.

"No. It was real," Jiffy insists. "I was wide awake. Well, I was sleeping, but the wind woke me up."

The wind . . .

"You were outside in the middle of the night?"

"No," he tells Odelia, as though that's the craziest thing he's ever heard. "I was *inside,* in my room. I was in bed, but then I got out of bed, and I sat on the window seat and I looked out the window and I saw the pirate."

"Which night was it?"

He shrugs. "The windy night."

The night Leona died, Bella realizes uneasily. Does Jiffy know about that?

She senses the wheels turning in Odelia's mind as she asks, "Which window was it, Jiff?"

He turns and points at the back of the yellow house on the far side of Odelia's. "The one in the corner."

It does look out in this direction.

"That's your bedroom. There's a window seat right there." Odelia turns to Bella with a nod. "I know the house well. That used to be my friend Ramona's niece Evangeline's room—she and my granddaughter Calla are like this." She lifts a hand and crosses her fingers.

Face red, cheeks bulging, Max lets out a sputtering breath.

"Thirty-two!" he announces triumphantly. "I can hold my breath for thirty-two minutes! Is that long enough to get the sunken treasure?"

"I don't think so. How deep is the water there, Odelia?"

Ignoring Jiffy's question, she asks him one of her own: "What, exactly, did you see out there on the windy night?"

"I saw a pirate walking on the dock. He was carrying a treasure."

"Do you mean . . . like, a big box or a chest?"

"Yeah. Maybe. I'm not sure. He was facing the other way, but it was heavy. I could tell by the way he was walking. And he threw it into the water and then he left."

The summer day goes arctic. Goosebumps prickle Bella's bare limbs and a chill slides down her spine.

"Jiffy? What did he look like?" Odelia's tone is gentle, almost casual, but her expression is intent.

"I don't know. I couldn't see him."

"How do you know he was a pirate?"

"Because he had on a long pirate coat, and it was blowing around his legs in the wind, and he was carrying treasure."

"Is there any way it wasn't a pirate? Maybe it was Mrs. Gatto you saw instead? Maybe she was carrying something out onto the pier?" Bella asks, hoping, praying she wasn't the object being carried, because that would mean . . .

"Mrs. Gatto?"

"Leona," Odelia clarifies. "Was Leona the person walking on the pier? Could it have been a woman? Maybe wearing a nightgown instead of a pirate coat?"

Jiffy shakes his head stubbornly. "No. It was a black pirate coat."

"So you're sure it was a man?"

"Pirates are men," he informs Odelia, as if everyone knows that. "Ladies are *wenches*."

Under different circumstances, Bella might have grinned at that comment. As it is, she can only edge a little closer to her son, again resting a protective hand on his shoulder.

"By the way, it wasn't Leona," Jiffy goes on. "My mom said Leona crossed over."

Odelia hesitates. "Did she tell you what happened to her?"

"She said she was probably sick. She was an old lady, you know. Older than you, even." Jiffy pauses and then glances down at Odelia's cast. "You're not going to die too, are you?"

"Not if I can help it." She ruffles Jiffy's hair. "Why don't you two run over to my house and get a couple of Popsicles from the freezer? The doors are unlocked."

"Yay! I get grape!" Jiffy is already making a run for it.

"I get cherry!"

"Wait," Bella squeezes Max's shoulder, holding him in place. "I don't know if that's a good idea."

"Yes! I want a Popsicle!" Her son—her sweet, obedient child—suddenly sounds like the petulant toddler he never was or the surly adolescent he may one day become.

"We can go with you," she offers, afraid to let him out of her sight.

"By the time I can make it past the apple tree, they'll have been to my kitchen and back and finished their Popsicles," Odelia points out. "They'll be fine. Truly. I promise."

She may be a psychic, Bella thinks, *but she's not a mother.*

Then again, maybe she is—or rather, was. She did mention a granddaughter.

But she's not Max's mother. In the wake of Jiffy's pirate tale, it's up to Bella to assess what is and isn't safe around here.

Still . . .

The house *is* right over there. And if the boys go, she and Odelia will have a chance to discuss what Jiffy told them. Which is the whole point of the Popsicle offer.

"Go ahead." She releases her hold on Max's shoulder, calling after him, "But come right back!"

As soon as the boys are beyond earshot, Odelia turns to her. "I'm sorry about that."

"It's okay. I'm just—I worry about him. It's a strange place." *And getting stranger by the second.*

As if to second the thought, Chance meows loudly, pacing restlessly along the grassy edge of the pier, staring out at the water.

"Like I said, it's safe."

"Except that there are pirates roaming around at night." Bella shakes her head, not daring to voice the terrible possibility flitting in her brain like the butterfly refusing to alight on a ruffly petunia. "What do you think that was all about?"

"I'm concerned. I thought it was about Chance the Cat."

At the sound of her name, the cat stops pacing and turns toward them with an expectant meow. Odelia bends and extends her hand. The cat comes over, nuzzling her face against Odelia's fingers and rubbing against her legs.

"You thought *what* was about Chance?" Bella asks, confused. "The pirate?"

"Leona's restlessness. I've been aware of it ever since she passed on, but I thought she was upset about the cat going missing. The disquiet should have subsided last night when you brought her back home, but it seems even stronger. And every time I look at that spot . . ."

Bella follows her gaze toward the pier and the placid waters beyond.

Somewhere, bells are tinkling, clanging . . .

She turns toward the wind chimes in the tree. They dangle motionlessly from the branch—not a hint of breeze to stir the silvery tubes or even rustle the leaves above.

"Do you hear that?" she asks Odelia.

"Hear what?"

Poised, Bella listens.

The chiming seems to have stopped abruptly. The only sound is the hum of a distant lawnmower and the faint splashing of kids in the lake. Then a screen door creaks and slams: Max and Jiffy heading into Odelia's house next door. They'll be back momentarily.

She frowns. "I don't know . . . I guess I was hearing things."

"It happens."

Unsettled by Odelia's knowing expression—along with everything else—Bella gets the conversation back on track. "What do you mean about Leona? About her being restless. Do you mean her ghost?"

"I prefer *Spirit,* but yes. Her energy is troubled. Some people are fretful in life, but that wasn't Leona. She was laid back during her time on this plane, but not where she is now. With her cat home safely and her guesthouse in good hands, I'd expect her to find peace."

"Can you ask her what's bothering her?"

Odelia offers a faint smile. "It doesn't quite work like that. It's not like picking up a phone and placing a call to whomever we want to speak to."

"How does it work, then?" she asks, thinking not just of Leona but of Sam. "I mean, when you contact the dead . . . or they contact you."

"That depends on the situation. We all have our own unique process. If you're interested in learning more about Spiritualism, there's a seminar tomor—"

"No, that's all right," she says quickly. "I was just wondering about Leona. Is she . . . here with us right now?"

"I don't feel her energy at the moment."

"When you do feel her, or when you did feel her, how did you know she was restless?"

"Because she allows me to feel what she feels. I receive her energy. That's what mediums do."

"Can you talk to them, then? To, you know . . ."

"Spirit."

"Right. To Spirit." The singular tense feels odd on her tongue. "Can they . . . can it—Spirit—tell you things?"

"Yes. Sometimes we hear directly from the soul in question. Sometimes we receive messages through our guides."

"Your spirit guides." Bella recalls her mentioning them last night. "Who are they, exactly? *What* are they?"

"They're highly evolved entities who offer enlightenment and protection."

"Is Leona a spirit guide, then?"

"Oh, no! At least not yet, and certainly not to me,"
Odelia explains—sort of.

"How do you know that?"

"Because I believe our guides exist on a higher realm,
and they're assigned to each of us before we're born. Their
job is to see us through our earthly mission. Some of my
guides never even existed in a physical form, and others
did, though not necessarily human form, and certainly not
in my lifetime."

Bella is trying to understand, really she is. But there's a
lot to grasp here, and she feels like Max, with his incessant
questions. "What do you mean, not human form?"

"One of my guides is a great white hawk. Another is a
Native American maiden. She tells me I was her husband
in another lifetime."

*Okay, so now we're talking about reincarnation. Perfect.
Next thing you know, she'll be telling me about dragons and
time travel.*

"You were a man?"

"According to my past-life regression, I've been a man,
a woman, and a number of different creatures."

Right. Here come the dragons.

"How many . . . past lives have you had?"

"Eight that I know about so far. It's fascinating stuff.
Some of it makes perfect sense. I've always been an astronomy buff, and I recently found out that I was once part
of Pickering's Harem. I don't suppose you know what
that is?"

"I do, actually." As a middle school science teacher,
she's created entire lesson plans based on the group of

women who collected astronomical data for the famous nineteenth-century physicist Edward Charles Pickering.

"I'm impressed," Odelia says. "Maybe we worked together at the Harvard Observatory. I was there from 1895 until just after the turn of the century?" She phrases it like a casual question—as if asking Bella whether they might have been simultaneously shopping at the local mall without having run into each other.

Bemused and amused, Bella shakes her head, and Odelia forges on.

"Some of my past lives make no sense at all, though. For example, I was once a doe. A mule would seem exactly right, but a doe?"

"What do you mean?"

"Let's face it, I'm not the most graceful gal around. And I'm very stubborn. My ex-husband may even have called me an ass now and then. Maybe *he* was the psychic. He was certainly an ass."

Bella can't help but laugh at that. Nor can she help but find Odelia as lovable as she is kooky. As much as she wants to believe the woman is off her rocker, she seems utterly earnest.

Not that that means anything, Bella reminds herself. *Just because she believes in all this crazy stuff doesn't mean it's real. She might as well be Max talking about the tooth fairy.*

"The thing is, Odelia . . ." She pauses, choosing her words carefully. "What if it wasn't an accident after all? Leona, I mean. What if Jiffy really did see someone out here on the pier that night?"

She waits for Odelia to assure her that wasn't the case, that the boy was merely dreaming or that he makes up stories all the time.

"He may have seen someone," Odelia says quietly, staring again over the water, "or he may have had a vision."

"Wait, is he . . . he's psychic, too? But . . . he's just a little kid."

"Children are often far more open to spiritual experiences. Unlike adults, they haven't yet fully learned what they're supposed to see and feel—and what they aren't," she adds with a wry smile. "His mother and his aunt are both mediums."

"So . . . you mean it runs in families?"

"It certainly runs in mine. I never realized until after she'd passed that my daughter Stephanie was gifted, but her daughter—my granddaughter, Calla—certainly is."

"She's a medium, too?" she asks, wondering what happened to Stephanie. Odelia's tone is matter-of-fact, but there's a hint of sorrow in her expression.

"It's not her career. She just published her first novel," she says proudly.

"But she's spiritually gifted, like you are?"

At Odelia's nod, she wonders how that works—especially for a young professional woman. Does Calla chat with dead people in her spare time, like a hobby, or . . . or more like a bizarre extension of her social life?

"Some of us may be more perceptive than others," Odelia tells her, "but anyone is capable of developing the ability to communicate with Spirit."

"What do you mean?"

"Think of it this way: Some people are born with extraordinary musical talent or natural athletic ability. We all can't be virtuosos or sports heroes, but just about anyone can learn to play the piano or catch a baseball, right? The key lies in willingness and practice."

"So you're saying. . . *I* can talk to the dead?" Seeing Odelia's expression, she amends, "Communicate with Spirit. I can do that?"

"Is it something you want to learn to do?"

Absolutely not.

Unless it's Sam, in which case . . .

"No," she tells Odelia, her thoughts still muddled from the crash course in mediumship. "I don't think I . . . no."

"Maybe you'll change your mind."

I won't.

Time to steer the subject back on track. "Can you ask your spirit guides about Leona if you can't reach Leona herself?"

"That depends. I can ask, but keep in mind that our questions aren't always answered in a way we might understand or expect. Spirit gives us what we need to know."

As Bella digests that, the screen door creaks and slams again. The boys are coming back.

"We'll talk about this later," Odelia tells her.

Later . . . after what? After she's asked Spirit?

Bella watches Max and Jiffy running toward them clutching Popsicles, carefree in the sunshine.

Forget Spirit. Forget later.

Forget everything for a change—everything but this moment and the fact that her son is smiling and he's made a new friend.

Chapter 7

After the Popsicle break, Odelia leaves to get ready for a Mediums' League meeting—whatever that is—and sends Jiffy home to check in with his mom.

Lost in thought, Bella heads inside with Max, accompanied by Chance.

Fate may have handed her a free place to stay and a way to pay for the car repair, but a few crucial details seem to have escaped her when she agreed to help run the guesthouse—or rather, to *run* the guesthouse . . .

Wow—what the heck am I doing running a guesthouse?

The more she mulls over the curious turn of events, the more conflicted she feels. One moment, it seems to make perfect sense; the next, it makes no sense whatsoever.

Stuck and outa luck.

Having her son share a roof with a houseful of strangers wouldn't be an appealing prospect under ordinary circumstances, but in the wake of Jiffy's pirate tale—

No. Don't even think about that.

The old pipes groan loudly as she turns the kitchen faucet so that Max can wash the red stickiness from his hands.

"It sounds like home," he says contentedly, stretching to reach the sink.

"Hmm?"

"The sink. It used to do that at home, too. I like it. This place smells like home, too, and it even kind of looks like it."

Yes. There's no denying that the house offers happy reminders of the one they left behind. If Bella could only set aside the nagging worry that something isn't quite right around here . . .

"Max, listen, I want you to sleep in the Rose Room tonight, okay?"

"No! That's your room. The Train Room is our room."

Our. He's referring, of course, to Chance.

"If we stay here through the weekend, you'll have to share with me. There's plenty of room."

"For all three of us?"

She eyes the cat, who eyes her right back, reclining on the mat in front of the sink beside her son's sneakered tiptoes.

"Sure," Bella agrees. After all, it's only a few nights.

"And the kittens, too?"

"Kittens?"

"Chance the Cat's. There's going to be seven of them. Maybe even eight."

"That's a lot of kittens," she points out with a smile, turning off the tap and handing Max a towel. "And they're not here yet, so . . ."

"They're coming tomorrow, and they'll need to sleep with their mommy, and she needs to sleep with me, so if I need to sleep with you . . ." Max shrugs, drying his hands. Clearly, it's a done deal.

"I don't know if they're coming that soon, sweetie."

"They are. Tomorrow."

"Well, then, we'll figure it out when they get here. For now, Chance can sleep with us. Okay?"

"As long as the kittens can stay, too."

She shrugs and agrees. Most likely, she and Max will be long gone by the time the kittens arrive, and if they're not, then . . .

Then it looks like I'll have a small boy and a large cat and seven or eight kittens in my bed.

"But you don't have to worry about the tooth fairy tomorrow or the next day. My tooth isn't even going to fall out until the Fourth of July."

"Well, that's good. The tooth fairy might push us over crowd capacity." She bends over and gives him a quick hug. His hair desperately needs a good trim, she notices. Millicent is bound to comment.

Sam was the one who always took Max to the barber. They'd go together, on Saturday mornings, and come back freshly shorn after a pit stop for burgers and French fries.

Since then, Bella has only had Max's hair cut once or twice, at her own seldom-visited salon. She couldn't bear to bring him alone to the barbershop, where they'd ask about Sam.

She pats Max's shaggy hair. "Thanks, kiddo."

"For what?"

"For always making me smile and for being resilient."

"What does—?"

"It means you're going with the flow. You know, not complaining about things."

"I like it here," he informs her with a shrug. "Don't you?"

"Sure."

Now that that's settled, she sends Max upstairs to move his things into the Rose Room. As she waits for a cup of tea to steep, she tries to talk herself into calling her mother-in-law but can't quite bring herself to pick up the phone just yet.

Instead, she turns her attention to the other detail
that escaped her when she said yes to running Valley View
Manor for a few days.

"This is for breakfast," Odelia had said earlier, handing her an envelope of cash.

"What do you mean?"

"For the guests. You'll have to feed them in the
morning."

"Feed them? You mean . . . I guess I didn't realize I'd
be cooking for them."

"Oh, you don't have to cook. It's just continental
breakfast—cereal, fruit, maybe some bagels or muffins if
you feel like baking."

She doesn't. She used to bake cakes and cookies when
Sam was alive. Max would help her, though his help mainly
consisted of asking questions and licking the bowl.

But it's no big deal, Bella assures herself as she surveys
the contents of the refrigerator and cabinets, making a list
of what she'll need to buy. Anyone can make coffee and
put out cereal and pastries, right?

But what kind of cereal? she wonders, dunking the tea
bag into the boiling water. *How many pastries? Where—*

Her thoughts are interrupted by a loud knocking on
the front door.

It must be another guest. According to Leona's painstakingly notated reservations file, another couple should be
checking in today. Their names are Karl and Helen Adabner, and they're from Iowa. There are a couple of check
marks by their names—whatever that signifies. Leona's
handwritten shorthand isn't always clear.

Earlier, Bella noted what looked like the word *frumpy*
or *fussy* or *prissy*—or maybe *hussy?*—jotted in the margin
beside another guest's name. When the exceedingly prim
woman, a bespectacled blonde named Bonnie Barrington,

checked into the Teacup Room, Bella realized the first three adjectives definitely applied. She entertained herself imagining that the unlikely fourth might, as well.

Prepared to welcome Karl and Helen Adabner, she reaches for the doorknob just as someone jiggles it from the other side. A female voice floats through the screen. "Bloody *hell!*"

Bella opens the door to a middle-aged woman wearing a flowered green-and-yellow dress, ballerina flats, and a straw sunhat. A pair of salt-and-peppery braids poke from beneath the brim, draped over her shoulders, with the tip of each wrapped in a bright scrunchy that exactly matches the fabric of her dress. The few stretches of skin she's allowed herself to expose are as pale as the porch trim and just as spindly.

"The door was locked," she announces.

Bella—who locked it—is taken aback by her accusatory expression. "Didn't you get a key when you checked in?"

"I'm not a guest, luv. I'm Pandora Feeney."

Judging by her tone—and expectant pause—that information should mean something to Bella.

It doesn't.

"It's nice to meet you. I'm Isabella Jordan."

Pandora extends her pasty hand—not to shake Bella's but to clasp it tightly. She closes her eyes and bows her head, murmuring something.

"Pardon?" Bella attempts to pull away, but the woman grasps her fingers.

"Shh! Shh!"

For a long moment, Bella stands awkwardly holding hands with her.

Then, abruptly, Pandora lets go. Her eyes snap open and she nods. "It's all right. You're supposed to be here."

Yes, I am. But what about you? Bella wants to ask as the stranger brushes past her, into the entry hall.

Spotting the mug in Bella's hand, she shakes her head in dismay.

"What's the matter?"

"For one thing, I'll have to teach you how to brew a proper cup of leaf tea. For another, Leona never locked that door during the day."

Maybe she should have.

Bella doesn't say that aloud, only, "The guests"— *which* you *are* not, *lady*—"get deadbolt keys when they arrive."

"Yes, and I'm quite certain I must have one somewhere. It's a good thing Leona never bothered to change the locks, isn't it?" Pandora strolls across the room to glance at the open guest register on the table with an almost proprietary air.

Apparently, Leona wasn't diligent about getting the keys back from prior visitors. Does that mean there are other strangers out there who can get past the deadbolt?

It's bad enough that a hotel in this day and age relies on metal keys in the first place. But Valley View Manor is, like the town itself, a throwback to an old-fashioned time when people couldn't pop into the nearest Home Depot and get a key copied.

Or when you trusted people enough that they wouldn't come in uninvited even if they had the means.

The thought is unsettling enough that Bella forgets, momentarily, to be irritated by Pandora Feeney as she helps herself to a handful of M&M's from the bowl beside the guest book.

She notices that it needs to be refilled—one more thing to add to the shopping list, as soon as this woman leaves, which . . .

When are you leaving? What are you doing here? Who are you, anyway?

"So you've stayed here before?" she asks Pandora, and the question is met with a buoyant chuckle.

"I 'stayed here' for years, luv. After all, it was my house."

"You owned it?"

"My ex-husband did—as much as one can 'own' anything here, anyway."

"What do you mean?"

"Oh, I'd forgotten—you've scarcely been in town twenty-four hours. I presume no one bothered to tell you how things work here?" Her smile isn't entirely condescending, but it's close.

"I'm pretty much in the dark"—*and probably better off that way*—"but I'm sure you wouldn't mind enlightening me."

As luck would have it—*go figure*—Pandora wouldn't mind at all.

She informs Bella that all the land in the Dale is owned by the Spiritualist Assembly, which, she painstakingly explains with the air of a benevolent guru addressing a dullard, is a religious organization made up of mediums and healers. Only their members can obtain property leaseholds.

"So you're saying that I couldn't buy a house in Lily Dale if I wanted to?" *And if I wasn't flat broke?*

"*Do* you want to?" Pandora's expression betrays a potent blend of surprise and dismay.

"No. It's a rhetorical question."

"Right, then . . . are you a Spiritualist, Isabella?"

She shakes her head, though Pandora already seems to know that—along with a lot of other details about her.

"Then you, my darling, cannot buy a house in the Dale," Pandora informs her tidily. "Just as *I* couldn't have bought this house back when I met my ex-husband. He bought it and left it to me to strip the ghastly old paint and wallpaper and tear out acres of frightful carpet. I was the one who sanded the bloody floors and restored the woodwork. Do you see that bay window in the parlor?"

Bella follows the direction where she's pointing.

"I made the cushions with my own two hands. The other ones as well. And the custom draperies in every room."

"That's a lot of work," Bella murmurs.

"It was a labor of love. I do love to sew—I made these," she adds, gesturing at her dress and hair accessories.

Bella politely compliments the ensemble but can't help wondering if she used leftover curtain fabric.

"The point is, I was the one who made this decrepit rooming house into a home. And for most of the marriage, I was the one who lived here. Quite alone, I might add." She pauses—for effect? For comment?

"I'm sorry." Bella watches her run her fingertips along the dark wooden molding framing the archway between the hall and the parlor.

"It was a long time ago, luv. Naturally, the wanker got the house in the divorce proceedings, then sold it off to someone who wanted to turn it back into a boarding house."

"Guesthouse." It's an important distinction, as far as she's concerned.

Pandora ignores her, obviously not sharing her regard for semantics. "He did it just to spite me. But I got the last laugh, didn't I? He's long gone."

"Did he . . ." Bella reaches for the proper Lily Dale lingo, settling on, "cross over?"

Pandora responds with a delighted laugh. "He 'crossed over' the continent to Hollywood. That's where he lives now, with his third wife. He's Orville Holmes," she adds.

Clearly, the name should mean something to Bella, who's growing weary of these significant pauses that make her feel as though she's missing something—weary of Pandora herself, really, who chatters on:

"It was a beastly divorce, but it doesn't matter in the end. I've a house of my very own right here in the Dale."

"Wait—so you *are* a Spiritualist?"

"I have been for years. But don't *you* go getting ideas about it, because it's not something just anyone can do."

Bella—who isn't by any means getting ideas—feels compelled to mention, "Odelia Lauder told me that anyone can learn to communicate with the dead."

"She did, did she?" Pandora's eyes narrow shrewdly. "Then you *are* considering—"

"No! We were just talking about how it works."

"Right. Just be aware that if you're going to become a medium registered here in Lily Dale—"

"I'm not."

"—you must be prepared to study for years and pass a series of tests. Which I did, with flying colors."

"That's great. Good for you."

Now that we've established that you're quite the sensation . . . why the heck are you in this house, and when are you going to leave?

As Pandora prattles on, telling her the entire history of the house, Bella makes a point of looking at her watch. Her visitor refuses to take the hint, telling her about the people who had died here a hundred years ago in the Spanish influenza epidemic and about a bootleg-running scandal a decade later.

"This is all fascinating," Bella finally manages to break in. "Thanks for sharing. It was so nice to meet you . . ."

"And you as well, love."

Making no move to go, Pandora wishes Bella luck getting the part for her car and mentions how lovely it is that her son has been playing with Jiffy Arden.

Disconcerted by how much this stranger knows about her, Bella merely smiles politely. Pandora Feeney may be clairvoyant, but Bella wouldn't rule out that her knowledge comes courtesy of good old-fashioned small-town gossip.

Finally, as a car pulls up out front, Pandora checks her own watch. "I must go, or I'll be late for my meeting."

"The Mediums' League?"

"How did you know?"

"I must be psychic," Bella tells her with a shrug, and Pandora graces the quip with a delighted smile.

The car stops in the unloading zone, and Bella realizes it's a taxi.

So much for Troy Valeri and his flying carpet comment. There are cabs around here after all. Why didn't he tell her that? He could have spared himself the drive here to drop her off. Then again, he's a nice guy, and he was probably trying to spare her the expense of a cab.

A man and woman climb out of the back seat. Both are pudgy, and both are wearing windbreakers, khaki shorts, and white sneakers with white crew socks.

"Ah, the Adabners have arrived," Pandora comments as the driver helps them retrieve luggage from the trunk.

"You know them?"

"They fly in every summer from Des Moines." She adds in a conspiratorial whisper, "Do be wary of the frisky old coot. I'm sure he'll find you rather fetching."

Terrific.

Pandora starts down the steps and then turns back. "I live in the little pink cottage over by the café, across Melrose Park. The one with the window boxes filled with red geraniums. Orville always said pink and red clash, but I find the combination quite smashing, don't you?"

Bella assures her that she does, and Pandora tells her that she must "come 'round for proper tea" while she's here over the weekend.

"Thank you. I'll try," she promises, with no intention whatsoever.

"Cheerio, then."

The woman pauses to briefly greet the newly arrived couple before making her way down the leafy lane, carrying on an animated conversation with an invisible companion.

Where Bella comes from, people tend to give a wide berth—and unflattering nicknames like Crazy Jane or Ned the Nutcase—to the neighborhood regulars who wander around talking to themselves. But here, she notices, pedestrians don't even give Pandora a second glance as they pass.

Karl and Helen Adabner pull their wheeled luggage toward the house. Bella descends the steps to offer a hand getting the bags up to the porch, but the man—a few inches shorter than his sturdy wife and a whole head shorter than Bella—insists on doing it himself.

"Heavy lifting isn't for beautiful young women like you," he tells her with a gleam in his eye. Thanks to Pandora's comment about him, she fights the urge to take a giant step backward as he brushes past her to follow his wife into the front hall.

Helen—remarkably spry for a woman of her heft—is already ringing the little silver bell on the registration desk.

"Oh, you don't need to do that. I can help you, Mrs. Adabner."

"You? But aren't you . . . staying here?"

"Where's Leona?" Karl asks.

Bella takes a deep breath and introduces herself before delivering the carefully worded and well-rehearsed news of Leona's demise. To her relief, the couple's shocked sorrow quickly gives way to acceptance. Like the others here, they seem comforted by the belief that death is merely a transitional phase.

"I was so looking forward to telling her that I finally figured out that the man with the glass eye—the one who kept talking about how much he loved me—was my grandfather," Helen says, shaking her hand. "She kept insisting I knew him, and I kept insisting I didn't. He passed when I was a little girl, and that eye was so realistic, I never knew it wasn't real."

"I thought it was a fine how-do-you-do that some other man was horning in on the reading I gave Helen as a Valentine's Day gift," her husband tells Bella.

"You were here for Valentine's Day?" she asks, remembering that she'd seen Helen's name followed by an asterisk in Leona's appointment book on that day.

"Oh, goodness, no. Lily Dale is buried in snow at that time of year. So is Iowa. We go to Florida for the winter. But Leona does phone readings. I was so looking forward to telling her that, as usual, she was dead on," she adds, without a hint of irony in her folksy midwestern accent.

"I'm sure you'll have plenty of opportunities to tell her anyway," Karl assures her. "Besides, it's not as though she doesn't already know."

As she shows them up to their room, Bella decides there's something to be said for treating a loved one's sudden passing almost as you would an unexpected road trip: with regret that you didn't get to say good-bye but confidence that they'll be in touch when they get to wherever they're going.

On the heels of Pandora's quirky self-importance, she finds the Adabners refreshingly unassuming and ordinary.

But she revises her opinion when they emerge ten minutes later wearing visors and fanny packs and inform her that they're heading out to hike the Fairy Trail.

"There's a ferry here?"

"There are *many* fairies here, my dear," Karl tells her.

"Where do they go?" she asks with a bittersweet pang, remembering that long-ago Saturday in Port Jefferson. "My son loves boats, and—"

The couple bursts out laughing.

"Not *ferries*," Helen says. "*Fairies!*"

She blinks. "As in . . . *tooth?*"

They laugh again. Then Helen earnestly tells her about the fairy population and the tiny homes the locals build for them along a woodland nature trail, and Bella wonders why she's the one who's feeling absurd in this topsy-turvy conversation.

As the Adabners head out in search of tiny winged creatures, Karl calls back, "Welcome to Lily Dale, Bella."

Yes. Wow.

Welcome to Lily Dale.

And this is only the first day.

Chapter 8

The rest of the day passes in a pleasant and relatively uneventful whirlwind, with nary a fairy to flit by and convince Bella that there might be some truth behind the little town's supernatural lore.

She borrows Odelia's car—which is, indeed, a jalopy, not unlike many other vehicles in the Dale. She and Max make the fifteen-minute journey to a supermarket in neighboring Dunkirk, where she's relieved to find that the Dale isn't as removed from modern civilization as it seems. There are plenty of familiar chain stores and fast food restaurants along this commercial strip adjacent to the Thruway.

She buys a cartload of groceries, including a few things Odelia said she needed—"zucchini, jalapeños, and limes so that I can bake cookies tomorrow."

"Using those ingredients? Together?"

"Oh, absolutely. They're delicious. You'll see."

Bella and Max make a stop at a busy Walmart to get a few other odds and ends and then wait nearly half an hour to be seated for dinner at Applebee's. Dinner out in a restaurant is a rare treat for both of them, but she's glad to return to the quaint serenity of Lily Dale.

They join the line of cars waiting to roll through the gate—the only way in or out of the Dale during the busy summer season.

"I hope Chance the Cat was okay without us," Max comments. The cat had gone into hiding before they left, and he was worried about leaving her behind.

"I'm sure she's fine. Cats know how to take care of themselves, and we left food out for her."

"I know, but she's getting ready to have her babies. I can't wait to see them. I already have eight names picked out."

"She may not have that many kittens," Bella reminds him, "and they may not get here before we have to leave for Chicago."

"There are seven or maybe eight. And they're coming tomorrow."

She sighs inwardly. Sometimes, when Max gets an idea into his head, it's best to let it go and deal with the inevitable disappointment later.

Inching the car toward the tiny gatehouse, she sees that a pretty brunette teenager has replaced the older woman who had been collecting the modest admission fee when they left. Odelia had promised to arrange a season pass for her. "In the meantime, when you're coming and going, just explain that you're working at the guesthouse."

"I don't need a season pass," Bella had protested. "Just one I can use for a few days."

"Oh, I know." Odelia smiled that mysterious smile as if she knew something Bella didn't.

Now rolling up to the gate, she leans out the car window and opens her mouth to introduce herself.

"You're Bella! And you must be Max." The girl's broad smile reveals a mouthful of braces.

Bella is again startled to hear her nickname on a stranger's lips.

The girl goes on, "I'm Roxi. It's great to meet you guys in person. Everyone thinks it's great that you've stepped up over at Valley View. We've been so upset about Leona, and I know her regulars would have been devastated if we'd had to turn them away today. You're doing a great thing."

"Yes, well . . . it's nice to be here." Bella smiles, feeling slightly guilty that if she didn't need some quick cash and a place to stay, she'd be halfway to Chicago right now. "Do I need some sort of ticket to get in?"

"We'll have your season pass ready tomorrow, so for now just drive on through. Oh, and if you ever need a babysitter for Max, just holler. I love kids."

"What about cats?" Max asks Roxi from the back seat. "Do you like cats, too? And kittens?"

"I do! I love them. How's Chance the Cat doing? She didn't have her litter yet, did she?"

"No, that's tomorrow," Max tells her, going on to explain that if there are seven kittens, they'll be named after the days of the week, and if there's an eighth, its name will be Spider.

"Why Spider?"

"Because Spiders have *eight* legs," he says, as though she should have known.

"Oh, of course." Roxi grins at Max, then at Bella. "He's adorable. Make sure you call me. I've got references if you need them."

"Thanks, but we're actually only here for a few days, so—"

"I heard. But you never know, right?"

Bella just waves and drives on, though pretty sure that she does know.

The streets are dappled in blue twilight shadows. The house is quiet, the cat still in hiding and the guests most likely down the street at the open-air auditorium. There's a speaker tonight, followed by the nightly message service.

Having forestalled the inevitable all day, she reaches for her cell phone and dials her mother-in-law.

"Jordan residence, Millicent speaking."

She always answers the phone that way regardless of the fact that she lives alone and that she has caller ID and knows very well who's on the other end of the line.

"Hi . . . it's Isabella," she says needlessly, inserting the awkward little pause, as always, instead of her mother-in-law's name.

When she and Sam were married, Millicent announced that she'd like her new daughter-in-law to call her "Mother."

Bella couldn't bring herself to do that. It isn't just that there's nothing maternal about the woman, but it would feel wrong, somehow. She already had a mother. Had beautiful, big-hearted Rosemary Angelo lived past Bella's toddler years, she'd undoubtedly have been "Mommy" or "Mama" rather than "Mother." But still.

Whenever Bella called Millicent by her first name after she and Sam were married, Millicent admonished her. "It's improper. All my friends' daughters-in-law call them Mother. It's what you do."

"It's not what I do," Bella said privately to Sam. "You don't mind, do you?"

He shrugged. "No, you can call her whatever you like."

Maleficent. A few times, Bella almost slipped and said it to her face. Better not to address the woman at all.

"Isabella. I've been expecting to hear from you." Her tone makes it clear that Bella has, yet again, disappointed her. "What time will you be arriving tomorrow?"

"Unfortunately, we won't be there until early next week. We're stranded in western New York."

"What do you mean, 'stranded'?"

She explains about the car repair and having to wait for the part.

"You should have had it fixed before you left home."

Her jaw clenches. "I would have if I'd known, but I didn't."

"Your regular service person should have caught it."

Yes, he might have. If she had one.

Reading into her pause, Millicent asks, "You do take the car in for regular service?"

She does not.

"So you set out on a thousand-mile drive without having had the car serviced in God knows how long?"

"Millicent, Sam always took care of that, and I've had my hands full just trying to get through the last six months. I've tried my best, but . . ." She pauses to swallow a lump in her throat.

Don't you dare cry.

Hearing Millicent's heavy sigh, she anticipates an apology. Instead, she says, "I don't know how many times I have to tell you to please call me Mother, Isabella."

Mother. If only she had a mother right now—someone warm and nurturing who would assure her that she's done a fine job picking up the pieces so far, someone who'd promise that everything is going to be all right—someone to *make* everything all right.

After her mother died, her mother's best friend— Bella's godmother, Aunt Sophie—did her best to fill that role. But she, too, is gone now. And so is Daddy. And Sam.

Everyone who ever took care of me. Everyone I could have turned to at a time like this.

She swallows hard. Clears her throat. Swallows again.

Don't you dare cry . . .

"I'm sorry, I—I have to hang up now. I'll let you know which day we're arriving."

"But I don't even know where you are or—"

"Good-bye, *Millicent.*" She disconnects the call and immediately turns off the phone.

Her throat is still clogged with emotion, and her blood simmers with anger. She's going to have to swallow it, along with her pride, between now and next week. Like it or not, she needs Millicent.

She should probably call and apologize for . . .

For what?

Her mother-in-law is the one who should be apologizing, for . . .

For being who she is? She can't help that any more than I can help who I am.

Bella and Millicent are oil and water. But they're stuck with each other, so . . .

Stuck and outa luck.

She picks up her phone to call back but thinks better of it. The call can wait until she's cooled off—literally. The kitchen feels hot and close. She leaves the phone on the counter and steps out onto the backyard to get some fresh air.

It's okay. It's going to be okay.

She watches the rim of sun slide into the lake against what Sam would have called a "sushi sky."

"What do you mean?" she'd asked the first time he referred to the sunset that way.

"All those streaks of red and pink and orange—it reminds me of the omakase platter at Oishii. You wait and wait for it, and it's absolutely beautiful when it gets there. But it lasts only a few seconds before it disappears."

"Are you talking about the sushi or the sunset?"

"With our appetites? Both."

"Very poetic. I think you really did miss your calling, there, Keats." Sam had passionately studied—and written—poetry in college.

"Nah. Poets are always broke," he said with the hubris of someone who had chosen a financial career and expected to always afford lavish dinners at their favorite Japanese restaurant.

Life was good back then. Good for a long time.

I have to figure out a way to make it good again, for Max's sake.

"Chance the Cat?" her son is calling, somewhere in the house. "Where are you, Chance the Cat?"

Staring at the sushi sky, Bella can feel her pulse slowing down and blessed tranquility seeping into her. She inhales deeply. The warm night air is scented with freshly mowed grass and mock orange blossoms. A firefly ballet begins to light the lawn. The lake is calm, barely lapping the tall grasses at the water's edge, where a chorus of croaks and chirps grows louder by the second.

Then, suddenly, something splashes up from the still water just beyond the dock.

It hovers, flailing in the air for a long moment before disappearing into the lake again, and it looked like . . .

A hand?

She could have sworn it was a hand, reaching, grasping.

Heart pounding, she stares at the spot, certain she must have imagined it.

But no—she can see radiating ripples in the water.

Something was there.

"Mommy! I found Chance the Cat upstairs!" Max's voice reaches her ears from a screened window above.

It couldn't have been a hand, because she'd have seen someone out there, or it would have surfaced again by now, unless . . .

It's Leona.

Is it her? Her ghost? Is she trying to tell me something?

Of course not. That's crazy.

It must have been a fish jumping out of the water.

They do that, don't they?

But do they hover in midair?

Enough. She's had enough.

It's been a long day, a *crazy* day, and . . .

And now I'm *crazy?*

No. She strides toward the lake, infuriated—with this place, mostly, but with herself, as well. She's lost many things over the past year, but her sanity is not among them. She may not always be in control of her emotions, but she prides herself on her strength, and she's certainly had a firm grip on reality . . .

Until now.

Did leaving Bedford trigger some kind of mental breakdown? Is she delusional?

Standing at the edge of the water with the reeds tickling her bare legs, she searches for some logical explanation for what she saw.

There is none. The water ripples and rolls the way lakes do, but there are no zombie hands out there.

Terrific. Does that mean that she isn't crazy? Or that she is?

"Mommy? Where are you?"

"Coming, Max," she calls, turning away from the darkening lake to hurry back inside.

She finds Max and his furry friend already snuggled into her bed in the Rose Room and kisses them both goodnight at her son's insistence.

"Chance the Cat misses her mom. Hugs and kisses make her feel better," he announces with the authority of one who knows only too well what it's like to miss a parent.

"Pretty soon she'll *be* a mom, kiddo." Any second now, judging by the cat's bulging stomach. "Then she'll have a family again."

"She wants us to be her family, too."

"How do you know that?"

"She told me."

Bella smiles, giving him—and the cat—one last kiss before grabbing the books she'd left on her nightstand.

Yes, she's tired. But she wants—*needs*—to know more about Lily Dale.

Maybe there's a chapter on . . .

On jumping fish that resemble floundering hands?

She shakes her head. What she saw—or rather, *thought* she saw—was merely a trick of the dying light reflected on the water.

Unless it wasn't.

Like the other bedroom doors along the hallway, this one locks—and unlocks—from both sides. She inserts the key into the interior knob so that Max can turn it and open the door if he needs to. Then she closes it and locks it from the outside using the duplicate from the master set Odelia gave her.

The large key ring weighs heavily in the back pocket of her shorts as she heads downstairs, but she's been carrying it around ever since the last guests checked in. The last thing she needs is to misplace it, as Odelia mentioned something about how the bedrooms' antique bit keys can no longer be copied.

For that matter, neither can the modern deadbolt keys, according to the *Do Not Duplicate* notice stamped on each of them.

Downstairs, she steps out onto the porch. Aglow with streetlights, the narrow, rutted road is deserted. The parking lot across the way is filled with cars, most with plates from New York or the neighboring Pennsylvania; Ohio; or Ontario, Canada. Noticing a few that are surprisingly far-flung, she wonders whether Lily Dale is a mere pit stop in a cross-country road trip or the final destination.

The auditorium service is still under way, and she should have the place to herself a while longer.

She finds a lighter conveniently sitting alongside a couple of jar candles on the porch rail and lights them. Then, kicking off her sandals, she settles on the swing to read.

According to the first book, the very ground here was charged with spiritual energy long before it was used as a picnic grove for mediums back in the mid-1800s. By the turn of the century, the Dale had evolved into a full-blown cottage colony whose illustrious visitors would later include Mae West, Harry Houdini, and even Eleanor Roosevelt.

Susan B. Anthony was a regular here, as were other prominent suffragettes, whose American movement had been born in the 1840s in a western New York lakeside community: Seneca Falls, 150 miles east of here. The ongoing campaign for women's equality found a fierce stronghold in Lily Dale.

A passage in the book jumps out at Bella: *As a female-centric society of freethinkers, the community remains a magnet for encumbered women seeking a safe haven in which to nurture budding independence. Surrounded by healing energy and support, many learn to draw upon the inner strength necessary to achieve emancipation.*

Bella looks out at the dusky landscape, pondering the words.

Odelia had told her that Leona found her way here after losing her husband. What she'd intended as a short visit became the rest of her life.

"You'd be surprised how often that happens, Bella," she said, so emphatically that Bella wanted to remind her—yet again—that it won't be happening to her.

Frowning, she snaps the book closed.

Then, after another long look at the view from the porch, she opens a map brochure to get her bearings. The lake runs behind the house and curves around the shadowy dead end to her left, where Friendship Park boasts a fishing pier, bandstand, and the beach where she saw people swimming this afternoon.

Again, she thinks of the hand she glimpsed out in the water.

Again, she tells herself it was a fish, a bird, anything.

But not a ghost.

Not a pirate, either.

She consults the map and then the view directly in front of the porch. Beyond the parking lot, stands of tall trees rise above low, gabled rooftops. Somewhere among them are the fire hall, a café or two, a few shops, and even a hotel. Judging by the skyline—or lack thereof—Bella assumes it's not a Marriott. Or even a Motel Six.

To the right, she can see the light spilling from the large auditorium. The post office and the Assembly offices are down around the bend, near the gated entrance.

The Fairy Trail lies on the opposite edge of town, as does Leolyn Wood, the most sacred spot in the Dale. The small, ancient forest is home to nature trails as well as a couple more local oddities: a pet cemetery and Inspiration Stump.

The pet cemetery—okay, she can understand that. People in the Dale love their pets enough to designate a special burial ground for their remains. But the Stump . . .

According to the book, it's all that remains of a legendary tree that once stood there, and it surges with some sort of mystical vortex. On that hallowed ground, mediums and visitors commune with nature, each other, and, of course, with Spirit.

So if Bella were to believe in any of that—which she doesn't—what might happen if she went to the Stump? Would Sam—

She tosses aside the map and glares at the carefree fireflies glinting in the dark like ethereal beacons.

This—this false hope isn't fair. Sam is gone.

Okay, he isn't *gone,* gone. But he sure as hell isn't hanging around a magical tree stump or chitchatting with Odelia Lauder or—God forbid—Pandora Feeney.

No, Sam is in heaven. Bella firmly believes in that. When she was a little girl and her father tucked her in at night, she always ended her prayers the way he taught her: ". . . and God bless Mommy in heaven."

She has no memory of her beautiful mother, but Rosemary Angelo lived vividly in Bella's imagination as a white-robed angel with gossamer wings and a divine glow, floating in a paradise filled with harp music and wisps of mist.

Maybe she can't quite picture her rugged father and Sam with robes and wings, but she knows in her heart that they're there in heaven with her mother and Aunt Sophie, too—all of them watching over Bella and Max.

Someday we'll all be together again. Together forever.

That's what her father promised her when she was little, and it's what Sam promised her in the hospital last winter.

If she's so willing to embrace that, then why not any of *this?* This Lily Dale stuff? If it makes sense that her lost loved ones are out there somewhere, wouldn't they want to communicate with her somehow? Wouldn't they let her know they hadn't disappeared forever?

If I were there and Sam were here, I'd be desperate to reach him.

And if Sam could find a way to reach me, he would, and . . .

And now, somehow, Bella finds herself *here?*

Not just here as in Earth. Here as in Lily Dale.

The town that talks to dead people.

She can't help but consider the billboard for the campground that doesn't exist, the cat on the doorstep back in Bedford, and the identical one in the road yesterday—the cat whose decidedly unusual full name Max had mysteriously known.

Pandora Feeney's cryptic words echo in her head: "You're supposed to be here."

She appeared to be talking to someone, Bella recalls. A ghost? Make that *Spirit.* Whose?

And what about Odelia? She claimed that anyone can learn to communicate with lost loved ones. What if Bella concentrates with all her might?

She closes her eyes and listens intently.

The night is alive with humming cicadas. Somewhere, a dog is barking. Faraway voices call to each other. In the distance, car doors slam and tires roll on gravel.

Then another sound reaches her ears: a creaking floorboard somewhere inside the house.

Max must be stirring. There's no one else around.

She turns to look expectantly at the screen door, waiting for her son to poke out his tousled head and ask for a glass of water. Yes, or tell her the cat just had kittens in her bed.

Another creak from inside the house. A long shadow falls across the porch floor. Someone is in the front hall.

"Max?" she calls, and the shadow moves away. "Max!"

No reply.

She gets up and looks into the house just in time to see someone disappearing through the archway that leads to the parlor. She only catches a fleeting glimpse, but she can see that it's not Max. It's an adult wearing a dark sweatshirt with the hood pulled up.

"Hello?" she calls.

There's no reply, though whoever it is had to hear her. Footsteps retreat to the back of the house and there's a faint, creaking click as the back door opens and closes.

Frightened, she isn't sure whether to chase after the person or run upstairs and check on Max.

Her child's safety takes priority. She hurries up the stairs and is relieved to find that he's sound asleep.

After closing the door and locking him in, she searches the first floor, looking for some clue as to who might have been there. Nothing is out of place.

She tries to convince herself that it might have been one of the guests. When the message service ends an hour later, she's sitting on the porch waiting for them as they trickle back to the house one by one or in pairs. First Jim and Kelly Tookler and Fritz Dunkle, the younger couple and middle-aged bachelor who had checked in with Odelia while Bella was gone. They're followed by Bonnie Barrington, the elderly St. Clair sisters, Karl and Helen Adabner, and Eleanor Pierson, though not accompanied by Steve, who arrives not long after, clutching a program from *Our Town* and raving about the performance.

Bella can't help noticing, with a tingling of apprehension, that not one of them is wearing—or even carrying—a dark hoodie.

Chapter 9

Waking to a rumble of thunder through the bedroom screens the next morning, Bella finds Max still snoring beside her. Snoring loudly. Much too loudly for such a small boy.

She stretches, allowing her sandpapery eyelids to close again just for a moment before forcing them open again. She's far from rested and refreshed, thanks to Max and Chance, whose furry heft was solidly wedged on her pillow for the first half of the night and on her feet for the second.

To be fair, it would have been a restless night regardless of her disruptive bedmates. After her guests had retired to their own rooms, she'd locked herself into this one with Pandora Feeney's comment ringing in her ears: *It's a good thing Leona never bothered to change the locks . . .*

Virtually anyone could have the key to the first-floor deadbolts. Not to this bedroom, though. Odelia said the old-fashioned room keys couldn't be duplicated. All the hardware in the century-old house is supposedly original.

But if there already are two copies of each key—with the apparent exception of the door to Leona's study—then at some point, even if it was a hundred years ago, someone made a second key for each bedroom. And if there's a second, is it so unlikely there might have been a third?

Last night, after locking the bedroom door from the inside, Bella removed the other key from the lock and slept with that and the master key ring under her pillow.

When she slept. The last time she looked at the bedside clock, it was nearly five o'clock in the morning. Now it's a quarter to seven.

Time to get up and brew the coffee. The posted hours in the breakfast room are seven to nine thirty, though Odelia had mentioned that Leona was pretty lax about sticking to that.

"She never minded if it was dawn or noon," she told Bella yesterday. "Leona always said, 'Whenever they get up, I'll feed and water 'em'—she ran a dude ranch, you know."

Bella didn't know that, or much else about her.

But now, as she climbs out of Leona's bed and glances around her bedroom, she can't help but feel connected to the woman—so to speak.

The dog-eared paperback novels stacked on the night-stand include several titles she herself read over the last year or so. The sandals sitting just inside the closet door fit her own feet perfectly—she knows because she mistook them for hers when she hurriedly got dressed yesterday morning. And Sam might have called her Bella Blue because of her eyes, but her favorite color has always been the radiant pinkish red in the Rose Room's décor. Everything about this room feels just right.

She gets out of bed and pads across the floor to find her toiletries bag. It's inside her suitcase, which sits atop one of those folding hotel suitcase racks inside the large closet.

Reaching for the doorknob, she pauses at the dresser beside the closet door. Like the one in the master bedroom she'd shared with Sam back in Bedford, its long wooden surface holds a jewelry box and a framed wedding portrait.

She leans in to get a better look. The groom is handsome, wearing a black cowboy hat, and the bride, Leona, she presumes, is . . . is . . .

Startled, she picks up the frame and gapes at the image.

The woman in the photo is much younger. Her hair isn't gray and her face isn't wrinkled, but it's the same one Bella glimpsed in the bathroom mirror in her disturbing dream yesterday morning. The dream where the wind chimes were ringing loudly—much too loudly, and she was brushing her hair, only it wasn't her hair, it was gray and it was . . .

Leona's?

She doesn't remember seeing these photos before she went to bed that night, but she must have. How else would this face have worked its way into her subconscious?

Unnerved, she turns away from the photo.

* * *

Half an hour later, as a pleasant rain patters into the shrub border beneath the wall of screened windows, Bella still has the breakfast room to herself. But as she sits at a café table sipping coffee and reading more about Lily Dale, she hears stirring overhead.

Time to greet the guests. She sets aside the brochure, with its list of tips for people preparing for a spiritual reading.

Receive information with an open mind.
Remember that you may not hear from the Spirit you expect.
Remember that free will impacts prophecy.

Helpful stuff for anyone who, unlike Bella, intends to visit a medium.

She goes to the kitchen to turn on the tea kettle. Odelia had mentioned that Leona always brewed a full pot in the mornings, but this gray, stormy morning is so muggy that Bella didn't want to steam up the kitchen before it was necessary.

The gas stove is as ancient as the one back in Bedford. Bella turns one knob after another, but none of the burners ignite, meaning the pilot light is out.

Sam was the one who relit theirs when that happened once. With a pang, she remembers that she spent an entire snow day without using the stove because she wasn't sure how to light it and she was afraid of blowing up the place. When Sam got home, she apologized for not making the pot roast she'd promised him. He laughed and showed her how to light the pilot and then suggested a snowy walk to the diner for dinner.

It's as if that happened to some other person, Bella marvels as she finds a book of matches in a drawer and kneels in front of the open oven door, peering inside. Some stranger who didn't know how to do much of anything on her own and didn't have to.

Now you have no choice.

She strikes a match and lifts it to the pilot hole inside the oven. It ignites instantly, singing her fingertips. She drops the match and hurries over to the sink. As she runs cold water over her hand, she hears a key in the back door. Turning, she sees Eleanor Pierson stepping over the threshold. Her face is flushed with exertion; her damp, dark brown hair is spiked with sweat and rain; and she's wearing jogging clothes.

"Good morning," Bella calls as Eleanor wipes her muddy sneakers on the mat.

Eleanor doesn't return the greeting, and Bella realizes she has on ear buds, listening to music.

Spotting her, Eleanor pulls them out of her ears and turns off her iPod. "Good morning," she says cheerfully. "It's really starting to come down. I had to stop. Steve is still out there, though. He's a lot hardier than I am."

"I didn't even realize you two were already up and out," Bella says, drying her still-stinging hand. "I'd have had the coffee ready earlier."

"Oh, I'm not a coffee drinker. Steve is, and he wanted to make some himself, but I told him it's not polite to go rummaging around someone else's kitchen."

"It would have been fine, but I'm sorry about that. Tomorrow I'll be up earlier. I'm still trying to get the hang of this." She turns the knob and this time the burner ignites beneath the tea kettle.

"No worries, you're doing a wonderful job. My husband gets up much too early, even on vacation, and he doesn't expect anyone to be at his beck and call at that hour, even though Leona always managed to be."

"So do you two run together every morning?"

"Steve runs every day, and I try to. We start out together, but I can only do four miles at the most on a good day. He does twice that, sometimes three times. He's very disciplined. He says it nurtures the heart *and* the soul. Are you a runner?"

"Me? No."

Not that her heart and soul couldn't stand a bit of nurturing.

Eleanor follows her into the breakfast room and puts a blueberry muffin and some fruit onto a plate, chatting the whole time. "I know you're just filling in here, so what do you ordinarily do?"

"I'm a teacher."

"So am I. Steve and I are both in education. That's why we always like to stay in the Apple Room," she adds with a smile. "What do you teach?"

"Middle school science, but . . . I just got laid off."

"So you're looking for a new position?"

I'm looking for a new everything.

Bella nods and asks about Eleanor's and her husband's careers.

"I'm a history teacher, and Steve taught English and drama for years, but now he's in administration. He's a superintendent, in fact, of a large district where we live in Massachusetts. I'm sure between the two of us, we can help you network, depending on where you live."

Not wanting to admit that she doesn't live any place at all, Bella thanks her and guides the subject away from careers. Eleanor lights up when she asks about family. She and Steve are celebrating their silver wedding anniversary next April, and she's convinced he's going to surprise her with a trip to Paris. They have three children—a son studying premed in college, another about to start law school, and a daughter who's expecting their first grandchild.

As Eleanor pulls out her cell phone to scroll through a montage of happy family photos, Bella murmurs all the right things. But it's difficult not to envy the other woman's life or to think about what might have been.

Max was supposed to have siblings. She and Sam were supposed to grow old together.

"For better, for worse, for richer, for poorer, in sickness and in health . . .'til death do us part . . ."

"Only 'til death? No, sir," she remembers quipping at the time. "You're not getting off that easily. I'm going to haunt you, Mister."

How easy it was back then to laugh about the future.

How unthinkable that all their vows would be tested within a few short years.

Two sets of footsteps descend the stairs, and the St. Clair sisters enter the room.

They're not the most attractive older women Bella has ever seen—not by a long shot. Mirror images of each other, they have sharp chins, sallow complexions, and smallish eyes set too close to their aquiline noses. They are fairly snappy dressers—she'll give them that. But octogenarians in matching outfits—navy-and-white polka dot cardigans, khaki pedal pushers, and blue espadrilles—is a bit much.

Bella introduces them to Eleanor as a pair, apologizing because she can't tell them apart.

"I'm Opal," one says, "and she's Ruby."

"We've met," Eleanor reminds them. "Last summer, and the summer before."

"We have? These days I scarcely remember yesterday," Ruby says, shaking her head.

"We met yesterday, too." Eleanor smiles gently. "We were talking about names, and I said that it was lovely that you're both named after gemstones."

"Oh, yes! Well, Papa was a jeweler, you know."

Eleanor nods. Clearly, she knows. "I was telling you that my own father was a history professor, and my twin sister Mamie and I were named for first ladies. Fortunately, we don't look like them," she adds.

"Look like whom, dear?" Ruby asks.

"Like Mamie Eisenhower and Eleanor Roosevelt."

"Where?" Opal looks around.

Bella fights a smile. "Eleanor was just saying that she and her twin sister were named after first ladies, just like you and your twin were named after gemstones, but that she's glad that they don't—"

"Oh, no, dear, we aren't twins at all." Ruby shakes her white bun. "People often make that mistake, though."

"I suspect it's because we look exactly alike," Opal tells her as though they've never before considered the prospect, "and we've always dressed exactly alike. Remember, no one could ever tell the three of us apart."

"The three of you? So . . . you're . . . you were . . . identical triplets?"

Bella's question is met with another shake of Ruby's white bun. "Oh, no. We aren't twins or triplets at all. Just sisters."

"I'm sorry, I thought you said there were three of you who looked alike and dressed alike . . ."

"Yes, three. Opal, me, and Mother." Ruby counts off on her fingers.

"And your mother is . . . here?"

"Where?" Opal looks around.

"I think Miss Jordan is asking whether Mother is alive," Ruby tells her sister.

"Goodness, no. She'd be a hundred and twenty years old."

"A hundred and twenty-two," Ruby contradicts.

"No, a hundred and twenty."

Eleanor diffuses the bickering. "I think it's sweet that you still dress alike."

"Well, it does get difficult at times, because Ruby is always much too warm, even in winter, and I'm always much too cold, even in summer. But Mother is always so pleased that we've continued the tradition."

"And she taught us to dress in layers regardless of the season," Ruby says. "Opal, I have a feeling that she'll scold you for leaving your windbreaker in the trunk of the car so that your teeth chattered all the way from Akron yesterday."

"Well, then, she'll scold you for running the air conditioning on high," Opal retorts.

"It was eighty-three degrees out!"

"It was eighty-one. And breezy."

Again, Eleanor deftly jumps in to redirect the squabbling sisters. "I'm at that age when I'm too warm one minute and too cold the next. It's all about the layers. Your mother is a wise woman," she adds, clearly unfazed that the sisters are still in touch with their dead mother.

Such is life—and death—here in Lily Dale.

I wonder if I'd ever get used to it.

Maybe, if Bella stuck around long enough, she'd go around talking about Sam—talking *to* Sam—as if he were still here.

Maybe she'd even believe that he is.

Which is exactly why you can't stay, she reminds herself.

It's hard enough to get over losing the love of your life. If she allowed herself to start imagining that Sam isn't really gone forever—or, even worse, if Max started to believe it . . .

Well, she doesn't need Doctor Lex or grief counseling to grasp that such delusional thinking would be a major setback in the healing process.

I have to get us out of here. The sooner, the better.

She'll make that phone call to Millicent, just as soon as it's a decent hour in Chicago. She'll start out by saying that she's sorry for last night, even though she can no longer recall exactly what she said or did that demands an apology. Does it matter? If Millicent feels slighted—and Millicent *always* feels slighted—then Bella will make amends, because right now, she's out of options.

If it comes down to either Millicent or Lily Dale, Millicent wins.

Or loses, as far as she'll be concerned.

But it's just until they can get back on their feet. It's not forever.

Nothing is forever . . .

Except, she reminds herself, for death.

* * *

It's long past nine o'clock Chicago time, but Bella's planned phone call to her mother-in-law still hasn't happened.

When she found a free moment to dial, she found two missed calls, both from western New York area codes.

There were two voice mails. The first was from Doctor Bailey, making sure she'd gotten the cat back where she belonged and asking her to call back to let him know.

That message was very short and straightforward.

The second one was anything but.

"Hi, Isabella, this is Troy. Troy Valeri. The mechanic? I'm just calling to let you know that I ordered the part, and it should be in first thing Monday morning, so I'll get it fixed right away, and you'll be all set, so . . . and if . . . um . . ."

She frowned, holding the phone against her ear, wondering why, if everything is on track with her car, he suddenly sounded so hesitant.

"If you need, uh, a ride anywhere this weekend while you're stuck without a car, or if . . . if you, um, want someone to show you around the area . . . or you need . . . anything . . . just give me a call. In fact, why don't you give me a call anyway, just so that I know you got this. Okay? Okay. Bye."

Taken aback, she listened to the message again.

There was no way she was going to call him back. He should just assume she got the message. That's what people do. They leave messages for people, and people listen to them. That's how it works.

Besides, she doesn't need to be shown around the area, she thought, irritated with Troy for no reason whatsoever. And if she needs a ride, she can just borrow Odelia's car again, right?

Of course.

Why is Troy Valeri going out of his way to be so nice? What's wrong with him?

Is he hoping to see her again for some reason? Is he . . . interested?

He might be, but you're not, she reminded herself firmly.

Pushing Troy—and Millicent, too—from her mind, she went back to refilling coffee cups, replenishing pastries, cutting up more fruit, and chatting with her guests.

She's pleasantly surprised to find that she actually enjoys her hostess duties. She certainly knows her way around a household, though she's never shared one with more than one other adult. Her greatest concern had been the social aspect, but somehow, it isn't difficult to find common ground even with this diverse bunch.

Jim and Kelly Tookler are about her age and live in the New York City suburbs not far from Bedford. Bonnie Barrington may be as straitlaced as they come, but like Bella, she grew up in the city itself. And Fritz Dunkle is another fellow teacher, a college English professor from Pennsylvania.

As she gets to know more about them, Bella finds herself wondering why they're here, the ones who seem so . . .

Normal is the word that keeps coming to mind, but *conventional* might be a better one.

Most of the guests are—on the surface, anyway—people you'd expect to find anywhere else.

There are exceptions, of course.

Certainly the St. Clair sisters—who with little coaxing perform an off-key but well-choreographed espadrille soft-shoe rendition of "Tea for Two"—are as dotty as their sweaters. And the Adabners, who are on their way to an early morning ectoplasm workshop, are more than a little wacky.

But the rest come across as utterly grounded and logical, which Bella finds simultaneously reassuring and disquieting.

She didn't have to wonder for very long how they all found their way to this strange little town.

Their paths stem from grief to new age curiosity to literary aspirations—Fritz is working on a book about Lily Dale. The others' stories have a common thread, though. They're searching. Searching for a connection, for healing, for answers . . .

Not unlike Bella herself.

Except I didn't realize that I was searching, and I didn't mean to find this place. It found me.

But Lily Dale, with its wide-eyed "the dead aren't really dead" philosophy, is no more likely to lift her burden of sorrow than the glass of ice water she's clasping will erase the angry red burn from her fingers. This serene little town and its residents are nothing more than a soothing, temporary balm—to her loneliness, not her grief.

"It's strange to be sitting here without Leona," Kelly Tookler muses, lingering with several others over yet another cup of coffee. She's tall, pudgy, and blonde; her husband is the exact opposite. Bella has noticed that she frequently punctuates her comments—as she does now—with, "Right, Jim?"

"Right." Jim barely glances up from his newspaper. He's a man of few words, *right* being one of his favorites.

"Well, Bella is doing a fantastic job picking up where Leona left off," Steve Pierson says pointedly, with a smile at Bella.

She smiles back. "Thanks for the vote of confidence."

Steve is a nice man. As soon as he found out she's an unemployed teacher, he asked if she'd consider moving to Boston—she said yes, because why not?—and he offered to look into openings in his district back home.

"Oh, I didn't mean it that way," Kelly says quickly. "I'm sorry, Bella. You've been great. It's just that I miss Leona."

"So do I," Bonnie says. "She always guides me in the right direction and makes me see things I've managed to miss even when they're right in front of me."

"We all do that," Eleanor says. "Sometimes I wonder if people like us are so focused on what we can't see that we forget to see what we can see."

There's a pause as her words sink in.

Then Steve puts his arm around his wife and gives her shoulder a squeeze. "I see. I think."

"You know what I mean," she says with a laugh.

"We all know what you mean," Bonnie tells her. "And Isabella, you're doing such a great job with the guesthouse—who knows? Maybe you can pick up where Leona left off with everything else, too."

"Wait, do you mean . . . ?" Bella falters. "I'm not . . . I'm just . . ."

"She's not a medium. She's just like the rest of us. Well, like *us,* anyway," Eleanor modifies, indicating her husband and herself. "I know that most of you are involved in mediumship training classes."

"I certainly am. And you are, too, aren't you . . . ?" Bonnie asks, looking at whichever of the elderly St. Clair sisters hasn't nodded off over her tea.

"Yes, we are," she says, nudging her sister. "Aren't we, Opal?"

She wakes with a start. "Aren't we what?"

"Learning to become mediums?"

"Oh, yes. We intend to speak with Mother directly. There are certain things we need to ask her that are rather . . ."

"Delicate," Ruby says. "And private."

After waiting a moment or two to let that provocative tidbit settle, Kelly announces, "We're taking a class too. Right, Jim?"

Nope—not this time. He says, "I haven't decided yet."

Until now, Fritz has been sitting at a corner table quietly listening. Stout and swarthy, with a receding hairline and a quiet voice, he's not the kind of man who commands much attention in a crowd.

Now, steepling his fingertips beneath his gray beard, he asks Jim what's holding him back.

"I'm just not sure it's something I want to do. Kelly wants me to, but—"

"It was your idea to come here in the first place."

"Yes, but that doesn't mean I—"

She talks over him, telling the others, "We were on our honeymoon in Niagara Falls—we were married at the end of October, so it was around Halloween, and Jim came across an article about Lily Dale in a local newspaper at the hotel."

"Was it one of those hokey pieces that make it sound like a cross between *Ghostbusters* and a haunted hay ride?" Bonnie asks her.

"How'd you guess?"

"Same thing every Halloween. Most reporters don't even try to help people understand what goes on here."

"No, but at least it inspired us to make a day trip to check it out. Even though it was off-season, a few of the mediums were in residence, so we decided to get readings. You know—as a lark. That's how we met Leona. She told us things she couldn't possibly have known, right, Jim?"

His *right* isn't quite as wholehearted this time.

Fritz seems to notice as well. "What kinds of things did she tell you, Jim?"

He opens his mouth to answer, but Kelly does it for him: "She gave him a message from his college roommate. He'd passed away a few months before our wedding. He was supposed to be our best man."

"What was the message, *Jim?*" Fritz emphasizes the name, and this time, Kelly takes the hint and lets her husband answer.

"She just said Barry—that's his name—wanted us to know that he was sorry he'd missed our special day."

"Did she mention him by name?"

"Not exactly."

Kelly jumps back in. "It was definitely Barry. Leona said the name might be Harold or maybe Harry and that he was young and he'd died suddenly and instantly. It was a car wreck. She was right."

"That happens all the time with names," Eleanor contributes. "Sometimes the medium just gets the first letter, sometimes a name that rhymes."

Fully awake now, Opal is nodding. "When Leona first connected with Mother, it wasn't by name, and it's a good thing."

"Why is that?" Bella asks.

She has a feeling, judging by their expressions, that the other regulars have all heard this before—if not last summer, then last night. The St. Clair sisters tend to repeat themselves.

"Mother's name was Ann and so was her mother's, and our other grandmother was Anna, and so were two cousins."

"All of them are in Spirit," Ruby says with a nod, "so we'd never have known it was Mother if Leona had just given us her name. Instead, she told us she could smell Mother's signature perfume, and we just knew it was her."

"What was it?"

"Jean Nate," Opal reports.

"It used to drive Papa wild," Ruby adds candidly.

Bella fights the urge to grin—and to point out that many women of a certain age wear the scent, which can be found on any drugstore shelf. If the sisters want to believe that Leona was channeling their mother, well then . . . where's the harm in that?

Fritz asks them, "So for you, hearing the medium mention your mother's perfume was a greater confirmation than her name would have been."

"Oh, yes. That and the Clark Gable business," Ruby adds.

Bonnie says, "Now *that* was really something," as the Piersons and Tooklers nod their agreement and Bella raises a curious eyebrow.

Fritz asks the obvious question: "*What* Clark Gable business?"

When Ruby responds with an utter non sequitur— "We're from Akron, you know"—Bella grasps that the sisters are merely senile. Obviously, the others are humoring them.

"Clark's hometown was a stone's throw away," Opal elaborates. "Mother had a torrid affair with him when she was young, before she met Father."

Hmm. Maybe they aren't senile. Or maybe they are—as it's difficult to imagine Clark Gable romancing a homely woman doused in Jean Nate.

"And Leona knew about that?" Fritz asks. "Did she mention Clark Gable by name?"

"Of course she did."

"That's some validation."

Yes. Much stronger validation than Jean Nate, Bella has to admit.

"I'll be interested in hearing all about your experiences, good and bad, if you're willing to go on record for my book," Fritz says, looking from the sisters to Bonnie, the Tooklers, the Piersons, and even Bella. "Without Leona's input, I'm going to have to start from scratch in some aspects of my research."

"She was helping you?" Bonnie looks surprised.

At his nod, Eleanor comments, "That's funny. In all the years I've been coming here, I've never heard her say one nice thing about the press."

"That's because when they write about Lily Dale, they don't get it right. I'm going to, and Leona knew it. She wanted to help me, and she gave me access to everything."

He may be writing about the Dale and trying to "get it right," but Bella notices that Fritz uses past tense when he speaks of Leona.

"When you say *everything*," Bonnie asks, "what do you mean?"

"We did hours of phone interviews, and she answered any questions I had. She even let me listen to recordings of her readings."

"She recorded them?" Bella is taken aback. "Do you mean . . . on a tape recorder?"

"No, she likes to say she's high tech. She has an audio recorder hooked up to her laptop. After the session, she'll e-mail you the file," Kelly explains.

"Did you have to sign a release, then, so that she could share those tapes with other people?"

"A release?" Kelly laughs. "It doesn't work that way. At least, not with Leona or any of the other mediums I've seen here."

Maybe it should, Bella thinks. This little refuge might consider itself immune to the litigious nature of the rest of the world, but it isn't hard to imagine someone—not Kelly Tookler—slapping Leona with a lawsuit for sharing an audiotape without permission.

"I can't tell you how many times I've gone back and listened to my readings," Kelly says. "Every time I do, I pick up on something new."

Bonnie nods. "Same here. It's so hard, when you're sitting there getting a reading, to keep track of every detail that comes through."

"I used to try to write it all down," Eleanor says, "but that can be distracting. It's much easier to just have the medium record the session for you. That's why so many of them do it. Sometimes, messages only make sense later, when you've had a chance to go back and listen and really think about it."

When you've had a chance to make the vagaries fit and convince yourself that your dead loved one came through after all?

Naturally, Bella doesn't say that aloud. They all seem so earnest, so trusting and naïve.

All but Fritz, the guileful fly on the wall, with a barely discernible glitter of doubt in his black eyes.

Fritz is an outsider, just like she is. It's obvious he doesn't buy any of this. But he's not letting them see his skepticism because he needs their cooperation for his book.

And Bella isn't letting them see hers, because . . .

Because in this moment, maybe I just need the companionship. I need them. All of them.

Who cares that they're an eclectic bunch of strangers or that she'll never see any of them again after the weekend? It's just nice, for a change, not to feel as though she and Max are all alone in the world. It's nice to feel as though they belong.

Even here.

Still, she squirms when the conversation meanders to the local dating scene—or lack thereof. Kelly asks whether Bonnie had seen a handsome man she'd spotted at last night's message service, and then again riding his bike past the house this morning. Bonnie doesn't seem interested, but that doesn't stop Kelly from speculating about whether he's available and who else around here might be.

The short answer, according to the others: no one. Apparently, there is a dearth of single, straight, available men in the Dale.

"What about you, Bella?" Kelly asks. "Do you date? Are you interested in—"

The doorbell rings.

"Be right back," Bella says, hoping the subject will have been dropped by then.

She hurries into the front hall, opens the door, and is startled to see Doctor Bailey standing on the porch.

He, too, looks surprised. "Isabella? What are you doing here?"

"Good question," she says. "I was just wondering the same thing."

He blinks. "I thought you were just passing through, returning the lost cat to the owner."

"I thought I was, too, but—it's a long story. I did get your message, by the way," she adds. "But I haven't had a chance to call back. Sorry."

"I just wanted to make sure the cat got to where she was supposed to go. After you left, I realized that it was irresponsible of me to give out that information and send you on your way with her. But I was worried about the puppy, and I hadn't slept in a few days, and . . . I guess I wasn't thinking straight."

"It's okay. I got Chance back here just fine."

"Good. I'm sure her owner was relieved. I thought I'd better come over here because I tried calling her, too, last night and today, but the voice mailbox was still full."

"Right. That's because she, um . . ."

Oddly, Bella's first instinct is to search for the right phrasing. But there's no need to mince words now, is there? Doctor Bailey isn't one of *them*—the Spiritualists who phrase conversations about the dearly departed as if they'd momentarily stepped into the next room.

Why mince words?

"The thing is . . . Leona died."

His dark eyebrows furrow. "I'm sorry to hear that."

"So was I. It sounds like she was a wonderful person."

"You never met her, though."

"No."

"And you'd never been to Lily Dale before. You'd never even heard of it."

She can't tell whether it's a statement or a question, but he pauses, waiting for her to acknowledge it.

"No," she says again, wondering if that's a gleam of suspicion in his brown eyes. "I was just passing through, remember?"

"I do, but . . . well, here you are in Lily Dale, answering Leona's door."

She laughs nervously. "Right, here I am. I know it must seem a little crazy to you."

And you're not the only one.

"A little," he agrees. "Is the cat . . . ?"

"Oh, she's fine. She's around here someplace. No kittens yet, but we're waiting."

"You're taking care of her, then?"

"Just for the weekend, because our car is in the repair shop."

"And Max?"

"*Not* in the repair shop," she quips, surprised that Doctor Bailey remembers her son's name—and her own, for that matter.

He chuckles. "That's good. So he's around here someplace, too?"

"Upstairs sleeping."

"Good for him. Everything is okay, then?"

Definitely a question.

She tilts her head, considering it. "I guess that depends on how you define okay."

"For me, *that* depends on the day. And sometimes, lately, the definition changes minute to minute."

"Same here," she says, and their eyes meet in a flash of empathy. "But right now, everything is okay."

"I'm glad. I just wanted to make sure. If you need me, you know where to find me."

"I do," she agrees, "and . . ."

She trails off, realizing she was about to tell him that he knows where to find her, too, if he needs her.

Why would he need you? You're not friends. You're barely acquaintances. He only said it because he's a vet, and you're . . .

As he sees it, she's a homeless stranger who found a pregnant stray, volunteered to return her to her owner on the way to a campground that doesn't exist, and then moved in. No wonder he's checking up on her. She's lucky he isn't calling the cops right now. Or the loony bin.

"Take care," he says, giving a little wave and then turning back. "Oh, and Isabella? Thanks for doing what you did."

"You mean the cat? No problem." Maybe he doesn't think she's crazy after all.

Again, he starts away, then turns back. "Tell Max that if I'd known he was here, I'd have brought him some chocolate chip ice cream."

She smiles. "I will."

"Not that he remembers me."

"Something tells me that he might."

Wearing a bemused smile, she closes the door and then finds herself watching through the window as he walks away.

Chapter 10

"Mommy?"

Alone in the kitchen washing out the coffee pot after the guests have dispersed, she looks up to see Max in the doorway.

"Good morning, sweetie." She turns off the water and goes over to hug him, but he pulls away. "What's wrong?"

"I can't find Chance the Cat."

"She was sleeping next to you when I left the bedroom." She'd locked the door from the outside with her key and left the duplicate sitting in the inside lock so that Max could let himself out.

"I just woke up and she was gone."

"Well, the door was locked, and I'm sure she can't turn a key with her paw, so she must be in there hiding somewhere. Under the bed or—"

"No, I looked everywhere. She's not there."

"Cats are really good at hiding. Sit down and eat your breakfast. After that, I'll help you look."

Max protests, but eventually agrees to have a bowl of cereal at the table. As he crunches his way through it, he winces.

"What's wrong, sweetie?"

"My tooth is wiggly. I don't want it to fall out and get swallowed. Then the tooth fairy won't come."

"Here, let me see." She tips his chin back gently, and he opens his mouth wide. The bottom tooth is crooked, nearly sideways in his mouth. No wonder he's having trouble eating. "Do you want me to get it out for you?"

"No! It has to fall out by itself or she won't come."

"The tooth fairy? I don't think that's the rule."

"That's what Jiffy said."

"Well, I say she'll come no matter what."

Clearly, Jiffy's opinion is all that counts. Max shakes his head, adamant, and clamps his mouth shut. Speaking like a bad ventriloquist, he says, "By the way, it's not falling out until the Fourth of July."

Bella smiles. "Whatever you say, kiddo."

She goes back to washing the rest of the breakfast dishes, still thinking about Doctor Bailey's visit, and Max goes back to his cereal and fretting about the cat. He's almost finished eating when they hear a rap on the back door.

Turning, Bella sees Odelia Lauder standing on the back steps, accompanied by a tall African American man who's holding a big umbrella over them both. He's handsome, with a square jaw and hair that's graying at the temples. Bella has only been here for a couple of days, but even she can tell that he's overdressed for Lily Dale in a dress shirt and slacks.

Both he and Odelia are wearing such serious expressions that she immediately tells Max to go back upstairs and check again for the cat.

"But you have to help me."

"I will. I'll be up in a few minutes. Just go look, Max. I think . . . I think I heard kitty footsteps in the closet," she improvises. "I bet that's where she is."

"I already looked there."

"Here . . ." She grabs a box of kibble from the counter. Last night, the cat heard it rattle and came running. "I bet if you go around up there shaking this, she'll find you instead of you finding her."

With her son safely on his way back upstairs, she unlocks the door and opens it.

"Sorry to barge in on you," Odelia says, "but it's pretty important."

"No problem, come on in."

"Bella, this is Luther Ragland. He's a good friend of mine, and he was a friend of Leona's, too."

His voice is a rich baritone, and his handshake is as fleeting as his smile. Propping the dripping, folded umbrella on the mat, he asks, "Can we have a word in private?"

Taken aback, she looks at Odelia, who leans in to say in a low voice, "Luther has some . . . questions."

"Questions?"

"About Leona. Let's talk in the study." Odelia limps in that direction, trailed by Luther and, after a moment, Bella.

Remembering last night's hooded visitor, she wishes she hadn't just sent Max back upstairs by himself.

In the parlor, Odelia is reaching for the knob on the closed French door. "That's strange."

"What is?"

"There's no key sticking out of the lock."

"Should there be?"

"Yes, just like the doors upstairs."

"There's one right here on the ring you gave me." Bella fishes for it in her pocket.

"Yes, that's the duplicate. But how did the door get locked in the first place?"

"Maybe Leona locked it," Luther says.

"She only did that when there were overnight guests in the house, which there weren't on the night she passed."

"Are you sure about that?"

"Pretty sure. And when she was home alone, she always left the key in the knob so that she wouldn't misplace it, because those keys can't be copied these days." She turns to look at Bella. "Other than Leona, no one but me has been here—until you."

"I didn't lock it," she protests nervously. "It was that way when I got here."

"No, I'm sure that it was. I'm just trying to figure out why." Odelia exchanges a long look with Luther before asking Bella for the master key ring.

She hands it over, and Odelia opens the French door without comment and motions them inside.

The room is exactly as Bella left it the other night. Noticing the appointment book on the table, she wonders if she should mention the missing page.

But it would mean admitting that she snooped around in here. In light of the key discussion they just had, she decides she'd better keep it to herself for the time being.

"It's funny," Odelia muses. "This room looks so much bigger to me now than it used to."

"What do you mean?"

"The walls were a deep shade of blue. But Leona spends so much time here that she decided to give it a makeover this spring and brighten things up. I'd forgotten all about that. I do love the yellow. It's much more cheerful, don't you think, Luther?"

Luther, who doesn't appear the least bit interested in décor, offers a monosyllabic agreement. He motions for the two of them to sit in the easy chairs.

Bella perches on the edge of one of them, conscious of his gaze and wondering if he can tell how anxious she is.

It's almost as if he's trying to be intimidating, sitting on the window seat, his spine held military-straight, not touching the three pillows along the back of the bench.

He wastes no time getting down to business. "Odelia has reason to believe that Leona's accident might not have been an accident. She's asked me to look into things."

"What do you mean? Did something else happen?" Bella asks, looking at Odelia in alarm.

"Something *else?*" Luther, too, looks at Odelia.

"I just meant . . ." Bella trails off, wondering what he knows—and *why* he knows. He seems like a no-nonsense kind of guy. Why would he be hanging around someone like Odelia? And Leona, too?

Unwilling to bring up the pirate story unless Odelia already has, she fumbles for the right thing to say.

Odelia bails her out: "I told Luther what Jiffy said about seeing someone carrying something on the pier the night she died. I couldn't stop thinking about it after he mentioned it."

"So you think Leona was . . ." She can't bring herself to say the word *murdered.*

"No, I just . . . I don't know."

"But if you think there's even a chance that . . . that someone deliberately did something to her, then shouldn't you call the police?"

"Luther *is* the police."

"Was," he corrects Odelia, and tells Bella, "I'm a retired officer—I live down in Dunkirk—but I do some private detective work now. Odelia and I met when she got in touch with me about a missing persons case I was on a few years back and—"

"And he thought I was off my rocker," Odelia cuts in.

"I wouldn't say that."

"You *did* say that. To my face." She shakes her frizzy orange head. "But you changed your mind pretty quickly when I led you right to the person you were looking for—in the last place you ever would have thought to look."

"I'll admit I was a skeptic," Luther agrees. "But I couldn't have solved that case without you."

"Since then, we've collaborated on quite a few others. But I never imagined that Leona . . ." Odelia shakes her head sadly at Bella. "Anyway, last night, I dreamed about it."

"About . . . the pirate?"

"About Leona."

"What about her?"

"She showed me that something happened to her that night. Luther already knows this, but . . . sometimes dreams are just dreams, and sometimes they aren't. You learn to tell the difference."

"What did she show you?"

"Just—"

Luther curtails Odelia's reply. "Before we get into that, Bella, can I ask you a couple of questions?"

She nods, looking uneasily toward the door, thinking about last night and about Max and wondering how long this is going to take.

He asks her some basic questions—her full name, her last address, that sort of thing. Then he asks one that makes her breath catch in her throat: "Can you tell me where you were on the night of June eighteenth?"

"June eighteenth?" she echoes. "Is that . . . ?"

"The night Leona died."

That date would have been included in the missing page from the appointment book.

Looking from the formidable Luther to Odelia, who avoids her gaze, Bella gulps. "I was back home in Bedford, same as every other night of my life since . . ."

Since Sam.

"Why are you asking?" As if she doesn't know. She swallows hard, trying to hold it together, to sound indignant, even. "Please tell me that you don't think that I—"

"Were you at home alone?"

"I was with my son."

Max. Again, she looks at the door, feeling trapped here. As worried about him upstairs alone as she is about the line of questioning, she chews her lip.

"Is there someone who can vouch for that?" Luther asks.

"Besides my five-year-old, you mean?" Of course there isn't. She never goes anywhere anymore, never sees anyone, never—"Wait a minute, did you say the eighteenth?"

"Yes."

Relief floods through her. What are the odds? That was the one night all year that she *wasn't* sitting home.

"I'm sorry, I didn't realize—I was out at a restaurant with some of the teachers that night."

"Are you sure about that?" Luther obviously suspects she'd conveniently changed her story.

"I'm positive, because it was the last day of classes. The women I work with had a little going away party for me, and one of them got her daughter to babysit Max. If you don't believe me, you can check online. My friend posted pictures on every conceivable social media site even though we all told her not to."

She shakes her head, thinking of Janice, a young and single library aide. She's one of those women who doesn't eat lunch, buy shoes, or see a movie without telling the entire world about it—the Internet world, anyway. She'd plastered the web with photos labeled "Girls' Night Out," much to the chagrin of Bella and her fellow teachers.

"I can show you," she tells Luther and Odelia, "if you want to see."

"I don't think we need to—"

"I'd like to see," Luther interrupts Odelia.

Bella pulls her phone from her pocket, presses a few buttons, and locates the incriminating—or rather, the opposite of incriminating—photos, which prominently feature not only the date but the time and the place where they were taken.

"You can talk to Janice—to anyone who was there that night—if you want to."

"Go ahead and give me the names and contact information." Luther hands back her phone and picks up a pad and pen from the table. After writing it all down, he tells her that he probably won't bother to talk to anyone.

"So you believe me?"

"It's hard not to, given the evidence." He seems softer now. "But you might want to tell your friend it's not a good idea to put stuff like that online."

Don't worry, Bella thinks, with a sudden pang for the life she left behind. *I'll probably never see her again anyway.*

Odelia is looking smug. "I told him you weren't involved in what happened to Leona. But sometimes, my guides aren't proof enough for Luther, so—"

"Your guides are *never* enough proof for me, Odelia. Ordinarily, online photos aren't, either. I learned to play by the rules when I was on the force. But in this case, I'm going to go with my gut. I don't want to waste any more time."

Bella nods, and he offers a hint of a smile—a one-man good cop/bad cop show.

She should tell him about the person who was lurking in the house last night. Although . . .

Lurking? That might be too strong a word. In broad daylight—even this gray, stormy daylight—it seems likely she just imagined that the person's behavior was furtive. Surely it was just one of the guests coming and going.

Going . . . fleeing? Out the back door? Ignoring her when she called out?

That's furtive. Lurking.

Then again, maybe he—she?—had on earbuds, listening to music, and didn't hear.

That makes sense. It just happened with Eleanor when she came in from her morning run.

That no guest had on a dark hooded jacket upon returning last night doesn't mean someone hadn't worn one earlier.

No, but why take it off? And if you did take it off—wouldn't you be carrying it?

Besides, the guests were all in the message service when she saw the person in the hoodie. She watched from the porch as they approached the house in dribs and drabs, all coming from the direction of the auditorium.

Was one of them carrying off a charade? Had he or she been prowling through the house and then doubled back to the auditorium and changed clothes?

Why?

It doesn't make sense.

Unless you throw in the fact that Leona might have been murdered. In that case . . .

In that case, I should get out of here right now, shouldn't I?

"I really think we should call the police," she says again. "Nothing against you, Mr. Ragland, but if—"

"Call me Luther," he says. "And we'll involve them just as soon as we know whether there's reason. Right now, we don't have much to go on."

"Not as far as they would be concerned, anyway," Odelia says. "Trust me. I've been there, done that too many times to count."

Bella grasps, then, what they're up against. Most law enforcement officials probably wouldn't consider a little boy's comment or a medium's dream-that-wasn't-a-dream— much less her contact with a restless spirit—sufficient evidence to open a murder investigation.

But what about the person I saw in the house last night?

She needs to tell Luther and Odelia about that and about the missing page in the appointment book. Then of course they'll agree to involve the police.

And the police will note that you're new in town, skittish, and utterly inexperienced at running a guesthouse, which is . . . well, it's not as if this is a private home. It's not as if you found someone ransacking the place or carrying a weapon.

Still, the person's furtive movements had made her uncomfortable. Her gut instinct told her something was wrong.

If *she* were the one to go to the police, they wouldn't lump her in with Odelia, who's probably always calling to report crimes based on psychic hunches.

She opens her mouth to point that out, but Luther's next comment stops her cold. "No law enforcement agency would be so quick to dismiss you as a suspect, Bella, if it turns out Leona's death was no accident. You'd have to be prepared to be front and center in a full-blown, dragged-out investigation, and I'm not sure you want to put yourself—or your son—through something like that."

She shakes her head, sickened by the thought of further upheaval for Max after all he's been through. What if they decided to detain her for questioning?

That happens all the time, doesn't it? People are falsely accused, arrested even, for crimes they didn't commit. She can't afford a lawyer and . . .

And who would take care of Max if she went to jail?

I'm all he has. I can't let that happen.

She swallows a rush of panic along with any intention of telling Luther and Odelia about last night's intruder. Not yet, anyway.

"Where did you find Leona's cat the other night?" Luther asks her, getting down to business. "Odelia mentioned that it was out on the highway. I understand that you're not from the area, and you probably can't tell me exactly, but . . ."

It's Luther Ragland's lucky day, because her answer isn't going to be nearly as vague as he might anticipate. She clearly remembers watching the odometer as she drove . . .

Yes, because you were following the directions on a billboard that doesn't exist to find a campsite that doesn't exist.

She can't tell him that, can she?

Maybe she can. It might sound nutty, but it's the truth.

Looking from Luther to Odelia and back again, she decides that he's used to nutty. Besides, every detail she can provide will take him one step closer to figuring out what happened to Leona—and will take the police, should they need to get involved, one step further from suspecting her.

So she tells Luther exactly what happened, and he nods and takes notes, writing down the mile marker location. She doesn't feel ridiculous; she feels smart and helpful . . .

And very glad she didn't mention the part about an identical pregnant gray tabby showing up on the doorstep back home. Because he might think that *she* thinks it was Chance, and of course it wasn't. It just looked like her.

Exactly like her.

Luther opens a map in his cell phone and checks the milepost number she gave him—the one she'd noticed right before she saw the cat in the road. "That's pretty far from here."

"Cats can wander miles away from home," Odelia points out, adding, for Bella's benefit, "Luther's a dog person."

"I have three," he says with a nod. "All rescues. An old guy, a middle-aged gal, and a pup."

Bella can't help but think again of Doctor Bailey. Maybe, since she's here for the weekend, she and Max should stop in to thank him again for helping Chance and see if the injured puppy pulled through. She forgot to ask him that when he was here this morning.

Then she reminds herself that she has no way of getting there without her car, and that the moment it's fixed, she and Max will be back on the road to Chicago. The thought fills her with nearly as much dread as she'd felt about leaving Bedford just days ago.

That was home, though. Lily Dale is just . . .

A nice place to visit, despite everything, but . . .

Luther and Odelia are back to discussing cats. "I understand that they can wander," he says, "but Chance was an indoor cat, right?"

"For the last year or so," Odelia confirms. "Except when she managed to escape."

"Did it happen a lot?"

"Often enough—or at least recently enough—for her to be expecting kittens." Odelia shakes her head. "I always told Leona she needed to get her fixed, because my Gert got pregnant when she was just a kitten herself, before I ever had a chance to spay her. But Leona wouldn't listen. She was used to barn cats, living out west—you know, letting nature take its course. Then a coyote got one of the neighbors' cats last summer, and she stopped letting Chance outside."

"So she got out and got pregnant . . ."

"Right. Again. This is her third litter. Maybe her fourth. But Leona loves having kittens around, and to her credit, she's always managed to find good homes for every last one of them."

"That's great." Luther patiently steers the conversation back to the topic at hand—a must, Bella has noticed, when you're dealing with Odelia. "You said earlier that you think the cat got out of the house the night Leona died?"

"She definitely did. She was inside that evening. I saw her from my porch, in her usual spot in the bay window. The next day, after . . . Leona was found . . . I was the first one who came into the house. I needed to find her nephew's phone number to give to the medical examiner. I was upset, but I do remember that the cat wasn't around. Normally, when I came over, she'd show up and rub against my legs because she smelled Gert."

"And you're sure you didn't inadvertently let her out when you came in?"

"Positive. She wasn't here. I filled her bowls and left them outside, because I figured she was hiding back under the porch and would come sniffing around for food. That's where she usually goes when she gets out."

"But not this time. I wonder why not."

"Maybe the pirate kidnapped her," Bella hears herself suggest, and they turn to look at her, apparently as surprised by the words as she is.

Where the heck did that *come from?*

"I don't mean an actual pirate," she says hastily. "Just . . . that's what Jiffy called him and—well, if there really was someone here that night, maybe he took the cat along and dumped her out on the way back down toward the interstate."

Luther is nodding. "That makes sense."

Does it?

Why would Leona's murderer—if she was, indeed, murdered—take a cat along in the getaway car?

"All I know," Odelia says thoughtfully, "is what my guides are telling me: if Chance hadn't wound up where she did, you and Max wouldn't have wound up in Lily Dale."

"What does that have to do with Leona?"

"Maybe nothing," she tells Bella. "It's not always about connecting the dots. It's like the night sky. Remember I mentioned that I'm an astronomy buff?"

Not only that, but she mentioned that she's the reincarnation of a nineteenth-century astronomer—which might strike Bella as amusing if she were in the mood.

Odelia talks on. "Think about how when you're in the planetarium, the patterns of the constellations are distinctly outlined. But when you're outside and the night sky isn't particularly clear, sometimes all you can see is a little pinprick of light here and there. You don't know if you're looking at part of Orion or just a couple of random, unrelated stars."

"I'm not sure I understand."

"Maybe we're trying to connect dots—these little glimmers of fact—that aren't part of the big picture."

"Do you mean Leona's death?"

"Not necessarily. Maybe the cat was *there* only because you were supposed to come *here*. Do you see?"

Confused, Bella looks at Luther, who shrugs.

"The message you should take from this is that you need to embrace it," Odelia tells her firmly.

"Embrace . . . what?"

"Being here. In the Dale."

"I *am* embracing it—for the weekend," she adds pointedly. "But as soon as the car is repaired, you know that I have to . . . Odelia, why are you shaking your head like that?"

"Because everything happens for a reason. There are no coincidences."

Now isn't the time to get sidetracked by Odelia's . . . by her psychobabble or her . . . her words of wisdom, if one chooses that viewpoint.

She takes a deep breath. *Focus.* "Odelia, you said you had a dream about Leona."

"Not a dream."

"A vision, then? What did you see?"

"She was standing in the bathroom brushing her hair, and someone came up behind her, someone she knew. And then . . ." She shakes her head. "And then she was trying to breathe, but she couldn't, and she was outside, and the wind was blowing, and the water was choppy . . ." She shudders.

She was standing in the bathroom brushing her hair . . .
The wind was blowing . . .

Bella's own dream comes back. The face in the mirror . . . the face, Leona's face . . .

"Were there wind chimes?" she asks, her pulse racing. "In the dream? Could you hear them?"

"I don't remember anything specific, but there are always wind chimes in the Dale. And there's usually wind." Odelia's tone is matter-of-fact, but her gaze is fixed on Bella's face. "Why?"

"I just . . ." She shrugs, not wanting to think . . . anything like *that.* "I dreamed about wind chimes, that's all. It reminded me—" She breaks off, looking expectantly at the closed French door as a floorboard creaks on the other side.

"Max!" Bella stands abruptly, realizing how much time has gone by. "Sorry, but my son was looking for the cat, and now he's probably looking for me."

She quickly crosses the small space and opens the door.

She fully expects to find Max standing there, with or without the cat. But the parlor is empty.

"Max?" Poised, she listens and hears nothing but the ticking clock. "Max!"

"What?" The reply is far off, coming from upstairs.

It wasn't him.

Then who was it?

Odelia and Luther are beside her, Luther's deep voice calling, "Hello? Is anyone there?"

Silence.

As Bella wonders if she—if all three of them—might have imagined the creaking sound, she looks down at the floor.

There, directly in front of the door, are the faint remnants of a wet, muddy footprint.

Someone was eavesdropping.

Chapter 11

"Wait here," Luther warns, holding up an arm to keep Bella and Odelia safely behind him, in the study.

Ignoring him, Bella pushes past and races to the stairs, frantic to get to her son. Her foot catches on a step halfway up, and she falls forward, slamming her knee. Heedless of the pain, she gets up and keeps going.

"Max! Where are you?"

"I'm in here," he calls from behind the closed door of the Rose Room.

Reaching it, she tries to turn the knob. It's locked. Of course it is—she'd told him to always keep it locked when he's inside, now that there are guests in the house. "Max!" She bangs on the door. "Max! Open the door!"

After a long, heart-stopping moment, he does. "Did you find Chance the Cat?"

"Chance? No, I—" She grabs him and gives him a swift, hard hug, relieved that he's okay.

Behind him, she can see papers scattered all over the floor in front of the closet, where the door is ajar. Before she can ask him what happened, she hears Luther calling from downstairs.

"Everything okay up there?"

"Yes," she calls back, and locks the Rose Room door before hustling Max back downstairs.

Luther and Odelia are in the parlor, Odelia sitting on the sofa with her injured leg propped on the coffee table beside the stack of photo albums.

"Did you find . . . anything?" Bella asks, resting a protective hand on Max's shoulder.

Luther shakes his head.

Max, assuming she's asking them about the missing cat, says, "I didn't know you were helping, too."

"Yes," Odelia says quickly, "and I'm sure Chance is just fine, wherever she is. She probably got out of the house and is hiding someplace dry until the rain lets up. She does that sometimes."

"But how did she get out of the house?" Max asks.

"She's a little escape artist, Max, believe me."

"But Mommy locked her into the bedroom with me, and she can't unlock doors."

Though the missing cat is the least of her concerns right now, that comment gives Bella pause.

Max is right. There's only one way the cat could have gotten out of the room: through the door. Certainly Chance couldn't have unlocked it, and Bella didn't unlock it, so . . .

Who did?

She shudders and pulls her son even closer.

"You know, cats like to hide indoors, too," Luther tells Max, pulling a small flashlight from his back pocket and clicking it on. "Why don't you take this and check underneath all the furniture?"

Max brightens along with the flashlight's narrow beam.

"Downstairs only, though," Bella says quickly.

"Yes, stay right with us for now." The avuncular Luther gives her son a pat on the head.

"Here, kitty, kitty," Max calls, crawling around the room, shining the light along the floor as, in a low voice, Luther tells Bella he'd swiftly and thoroughly searched the first floor. It was deserted with the exception of the St. Claire sisters, who are reading in the cozy library nook off the dining room.

"It must have been one of our own footprints outside the door," he concludes. "My feet were wet when I walked in. I guess I should have done a better job of wiping them."

As if to prove it, he aligns his own large loafer next to the barely visible traces of mud on the hardwood.

Finding it impossible to tell whether it's a match, Bella says, "But I didn't imagine that the floor creaked outside the door, did I? You guys heard it, too?"

They nod, but Luther says with a shrug, "Old houses settle. Mine makes all kinds of strange noises."

"So does mine," Odelia agrees, sinking onto the sofa with a wince, as though her leg is bothering her. She points at a meandering crack that runs along the plaster wall. "See that? It hasn't always been there. Even after all these years, the place is shifting on its foundation."

The walls and ceilings of the Bedford apartment were also marred by fault lines. She feels a little better.

Then Odelia adds, "And of course, sometimes, it's just Spirit."

"*Just* Spirit? Do you mean just a *ghost?*"

Cringing at Bella's reckless terminology, Odelia explains that Spirit energy can, on occasion, manipulate objects. "It's called psychokinesis. If you're interested in learning more about it, Patsy Metcalf is teaching a workshop on the subject this afternoon."

She most definitely is *not* interested. She's had her fill of Spiritualism for the moment, thank you very much.

Even Luther—seemingly sane, logical ex-cop Luther—doesn't seem to balk at the suggestion that the creaking sound might be attributed to something that isn't merely structural . . . or human.

He might not live here in the Dale, but he's accustomed to the way people think here. He respects their beliefs, whether or not he practices them.

"Look," he says, "I'm sure there wasn't anyone prowling around, other than those little old ladies. Maybe it was one of them, just looking for a quiet place to read."

"Then why didn't they answer when you called out?"

"Because they're hard of hearing."

"And why didn't they mention it when you asked them if they'd been in the parlor?"

"Because they forgot. In case you hadn't noticed, Bella, they're a little bit senile. It's a wonder they remember each other's names, let alone that they can tell themselves apart."

She has to smile at that, but it's fleeting.

She has to tell him. About last night.

She clears her throat and checks to make sure Max isn't listening before saying, "There's something you should know . . . it's probably nothing . . ."

But as she fills them in about the intruder, she isn't so sure.

"So it was a man?" Luther asks, pen poised.

"I don't know for sure. I'm sorry. I just didn't get a good look."

Predictably, Odelia says, "It could have been Spirit."

"Or one of the guests."

"I've been trying to convince myself of that," Bella tells Luther, "but the truth is, it could have been almost anyone." *Except Spirit.*

"Were the doors locked?"

"Both the front and back doors were, until I stepped out onto the porch. Then I left the front door open to let in fresh air through the screen. But I was sitting right there the whole time. It's not like someone walked past me."

"Are you sure? Maybe you dozed off."

She *was* tired last night.

But she shakes her head stubbornly, certain she'd been wide awake. "No, someone probably came in the back using the key. It seems as though everyone and his brother has one."

"Why do you say that?" Luther asks.

"Because Pandora Feeney—"

At the mention of the woman's name, Odelia makes an exasperated sound.

"What's the matter?" Bella asks. "Do you know her?"

Silly question. She learned last night that Lily Dale has a year-round population of a few hundred people at most.

"Pandora Feeney," Odelia says, shaking her head, "is easily the most meddling medium in town. I didn't realize you'd met."

"Yes, she stopped by yesterday. She said she has a key to the house, but she didn't bring it because Leona never locked the doors."

"That's not true. She locked them at night and whenever she wasn't home, just like anyone else with half a brain in her head. Which Pandora doesn't have. And by the way, she and Leona can't stand each other, so if she told you they were friends, she was lying, right, Luther?"

"They were not friends," he agrees. "What did she tell you about the keys, Bella?"

"She said that Leona wasn't very good about getting them back from guests when they checked out. And that she hadn't bothered to change the locks when she bought the place from Pandora."

"I doubt that." Odelia scowls. "She's a pathological liar."

"In case you hadn't noticed," Luther inserts wryly, "Odelia and Pandora aren't very fond of each other either."

"Pandora isn't fond of anyone in the Dale! Any female, anyway. She blames us—all of us—for her divorce."

"Why?" Bella asks.

"Because she thinks we welcomed the advances of her skirt-chasing ex-husband. Let me tell you, I wouldn't get involved with Orville Holmes if he had all the money in the world."

"At this point, he might," Luther says.

"Okay, Pandora told me he's her ex, but I feel like the name Orville Holmes is supposed to mean something to me. Why?"

"You've never heard of him?" Odelia grins at Bella. "Well, that's refreshing. Finally, someone who doesn't think he's the hottest thing to hit Hollywood since Rudy Valentino."

"Rudy Valentino—you call him *Rudy?* How *old* are you, anyway?" Luther asks.

"Older than I look. Rudy and I have been in touch lately. He visited the Dale once or twice back in the twenties. Stayed in this very house. The place was supposedly run by bootleggers at the time, if you want to believe Orville." She rolls her eyes. "After Rudy passed away, Mae West used to come to the Dale to try to make contact with him. She was convinced he was murdered."

"Was he?"

"No," she tells Luther decisively. "Anyway, poor Rudy's still trying to set the record straight."

"Do you mean about the murder or the bootleg rumor?"

"Neither. He's unhappy about the ongoing innuendo about his . . . masculinity. And let me tell you, there's nothing to it. He's quite the suave, seductive charmer, unlike the high and mighty Orville Holmes, who's just an ordinary medium just like the rest of us."

Just an ordinary medium?

Bella manages to keep a straight face as Odelia goes on. "The only difference between Orville and the rest of the registered mediums in the Dale is that he happened to have an available appointment the day Jillian Jessup came to town—you must know who *she* is, Bella?"

"Of course." Bella and Sam had seen *Wish Come True*—the romantic comedy that transformed Jillian Jessup into a huge movie star—on their first date.

They'd made an annual tradition of watching it on their anniversary, joking that the genie-in-a-bottle plot seemed cheesier and sappier every year. On their final viewing last year, they were snuggled together in Sam's hospital bed. He was too weak to crack a smile, much less a joke, and slept through most of it. She found herself surreptitiously wiping tears on the blanket during what she knew damn well was an overblown melodramatic denouement, envying the fictional couple's happily ever after and mourning the loss of her own.

"Jillian Jessup had a reading with Orville that day, and he connected her with her father," Odelia says, "and she was so impressed, she decided to make a film about the Dale and make him a consultant."

"There was a film about Lily Dale?" Bella asks.

"Pfft. After all that talk, they never even got that project off the ground. But that hasn't stopped Orville from acting as if he'll be winning an Oscar any moment now."

"He did make a big splash with the Hollywood crowd," Luther says. "You can't argue with that."

"Who's arguing? I'm just answering Bella's question."

She's uncharacteristically peevish. Clearly, neither Orville nor his ex-wife brings out the best in her. As she goes on with her story, Bella wonders whether there's any more to it than small-town dynamics and overbearing, egotistical neighbors who rub each other the wrong way.

"So the next thing you know, Orville's left Pandora—which was a long time coming. Now he's married to some bimbo starlet, and he calls himself the Psychic Guru to the Stars or some such nonsense. He thinks he's a big deal, and so do a lot of people around here who wouldn't have given him the time of day before."

"Does that answer your question, Bella?"

She smiles faintly. "I'm not sure I remember what it was."

Even Odelia has to grin at that.

Then Luther shifts the conversation back to speculation about how last night's visitor might have gotten into the house if it wasn't one of the guests. "Even if Leona had changed the locks, and even if she was careful to get the keys back from her guests, it wouldn't be hard for someone to have made a duplicate for whatever reason."

"They say *Do Not Duplicate*," Bella points out.

"Unfortunately, that doesn't mean *Can Not Duplicate*. In all my years as a police detective, I've never seen a key that can't be copied if you find the right locksmith."

"*Right,* as in someone who's willing to look the other way for a little extra cash?" Odelia asks, and he nods.

"What about the keys to the bedroom doors?" Bella asks, again thinking of the missing cat. "You said they're too old-fashioned to be copied."

"That's what Leona told me."

Luther just shakes his head. "Look, the truth is, if some lowlife wanted to get into this house—or any of the guest rooms—he'd find a way to copy a key, or he'd just break in. Burglars do it all the time."

"I know, but in this case, it doesn't seem like anyone broke in," Bella says, "and I don't think anything was stolen. The glassware in the dining room alone is worth tens of thousands of dollars."

"There are valuable antiques all over the house," Odelia confirms.

"So if someone was here who wasn't a guest, then we're looking at someone who wanted to go undetected."

Bella thinks of Leona and of the page she'd found ripped out of the appointment book, and her blood runs cold.

There's a long silence.

Luther looks at Odelia. "Do you have some kind of . . . feeling about any of this?"

"I can feel that Leona is troubled, but it's tricky when you're personally connected to someone who's crossed over so recently. Sometimes your own emotions create a block."

"Is there anyone you can think of who would want her dead?" he asks.

"No. Everyone here loves her. *Everyone.*"

"Pandora Feeney?"

"Not her. Everyone else."

"You're sure?"

Odelia's unkempt reddish brows furrow above the rim of her cat eye glasses. "No. I don't know."

"What about her nephew?"

"Grant? He's too fancy for my blood, but I only met him once or twice. And he was good to Leona. He always sent her a huge bouquet of flowers for Mother's Day, even though she wasn't his mother."

Bella gets that. She did the same for Aunt Sophie.

"And Grant was her only heir?"

"Yes—but he has plenty of money."

"How do you know?"

"He's a venture capitalist."

"Times are tough."

"Have you ever *seen* the guy? His watch costs more than I make in a year."

Luther shrugs. "I've never met him. Oh, and another thing I learned as a cop—rich people always want to be richer than they already are."

"Rich people, maybe. But not everyone. Besides, it's not as if Leona was worth a fortune. As far as I know, all she had was this house—and not even the land it sits on. It isn't worth much to anyone outside the Dale."

As they talk on, leaving Bella feeling as though she's sitting on the bench at a Ping-Pong match, she realizes that Leona, like Odelia, lived quite a modest lifestyle for someone who can—ostensibly—give people a priceless gift. And they're not the only ones.

Most of the cottages in the Dale are humble. Some could even be considered shabby. The cars parked on their weather-beaten driveways are typically as inconspicuous and unpretentious as the people who drive them.

There must be plenty of gazillionaires out there who would pay a fortune to contact their dearly departed. Orville Holmes is certainly cashing in.

But as far as she can tell, Odelia and most of the others remain committed to the Spiritualist camp's original mission: to bridge the gap between the living and the dead for the greater good rather than for personal gain. They receive only token payment in return for their service and consider it a donation that allows them to carry on spreading hope and enlightenment.

"If we rule out Grant Everard—not saying that I have—who else might benefit with Leona out of the picture?" Luther looks from Odelia, who shrugs, to Bella.

"I'm afraid I can't help. I never even met her."

"Pandora Feeney begrudged Leona this house from the moment she bought it," Odelia comments. "She thought it was a disgrace to turn it back into a 'boarding house'—that's what she calls it."

How far would she go to get it back? She was insufferable and eccentric, but she certainly didn't strike Bella as malevolent.

"It could have been anyone, even a total stranger—some random psycho who got angry with Leona and lashed out. Although," she adds, remembering how quiet the Dale was before the onslaught of summer visitors, "I'm guessing she didn't cross paths with very many strangers before the season started, right?"

Luther shakes his head. "Not likely. Good point."

"All of us who live here year-round have our regulars," Odelia comments. "I know all of Leona's, and they wouldn't hurt her in a million years."

"People do come around looking for readings during the off-season." Luther's next words send a chill down Bella's spine: "This is one of the few places in the world where it's not just acceptable to open your door to a total stranger and invite him into your home, but it's expected."

"That's true. But business has been slow lately for all of us. And I've spent a good part of the past month sitting on my porch, thanks to this." Odelia gestures at her leg in the cast. "I've seen just about everyone who's come and gone from Leona's place."

"What about on that last day?"

"Especially then. I remember because Jiffy only had half a day of school, and he'd come home with a big bag of colored chalk his teacher gave him. He was out there until dark, coloring a mural on the road. I wanted to keep an eye on him."

Bella bites her tongue to keep from calling their attention to the appointment book.

Luther writes something on his notepad. "You could have missed something. Someone."

"I could have. But Leona made digital recordings of every reading, and she kept meticulous written records."

"Where?"

"The audio files would be in her laptop, I imagine, and her notes must be around here someplace."

"Have you seen them?" he asks Bella. "The laptop, the notes."

She manages to keep her voice steady. "There's an appointment book on the table in her study. Is that what you mean?"

"There should be a notebook, too," Odelia says, shaking her head. "The appointment book just has her schedule."

"I didn't see a notebook. Or a laptop, either. Not since I got here. Do you want to take another look?"

Luther glances at his watch. "A quick one. I have to be someplace soon."

The two of them step back into the study. Luther takes a cursory look around and then picks up the appointment book. "I guess I'll take this with me."

He's going to discover that the page is missing. If Bella mentions it now, she might inadvertently incriminate herself. He'll wonder why she didn't bring it up before.

"Do you want to check the rest of the house for the other things?" she asks as they step back out into the parlor, in part hoping he'll forget the appointment book and in part wanting to reinforce that she's being cooperative.

"Unfortunately, I can't. I'm already running late."

"That's right, you said earlier that you have a hot date," Odelia says behind them as Bella locks the study door again and pockets the keys.

"Right now, I have a dentist appointment. I wouldn't call that a hot date. And then I have to go spend some time at the hospital with my mom."

"How is she feeling?"

"No better, no worse." Then Luther explains to Bella, "My mother has been ill."

"I'm sorry."

"Thanks. It isn't easy, watching your parents grow old."

Nor is it easy *not* getting to see them grow old. Or your spouse, either, for that matter.

"So your mom is your hot date?" Odelia asks Luther. "Because I distinctly remember your saying you had one today."

"That isn't until later tonight—and I don't recall saying *hot date*."

"I have a feeling it will be."

"I thought you were off your game, Odelia," he says, heading for the hall with the spiral appointment book tucked under his arm.

"Not about everything," she calls after him as Bella trails him out.

They find Max lying on his belly, shining the flashlight under the registration table.

"Still no cat?" Luther asks.

"Nope." He clicks off the flashlight and holds it out. "Thanks for letting me use this."

"You can keep it."

"Are you sure?" Max happily clicks it on again.

"Positive. I've got lots at home."

"Thanks!" Max shimmies across the floor on his stomach, flashlight once again in search mode.

"Good luck finding your furry friend, Max. If she got out, I'm sure she'll come back when she gets hungry enough."

"I just hope it's before the kittens are born." Max's top half disappears under the low edge of an antique console table, but his voice floats from beneath it. "They're coming today."

"Scheduled C-section?" Luther asks Bella dryly.

"More like wishful thinking. He wants the kittens to be born while we're here so that he can name them."

"Maybe they will be. And listen," he adds in a low voice, his hand on the doorknob, "if I thought you were in danger here, I'd tell you to get out right now."

"So you don't believe in this Lily Dale stuff?" she asks, now that Odelia is safely out of range.

She expects an ambiguous answer, but he nods. "I do believe it. Odelia's good. She's told me too many things she couldn't possibly have known. But mediums can only interpret the information they're given by Spirit. It's not a perfect science."

"Science? Is that what it is?"

"It's all about energy. Ever study quantum physics?"

"I teach it," she informs him, and enjoys the look of surprise on his face. "Well, I really just touch upon it. There's a lot to cover. I'm a science teacher. I mean, I *was*."

"Then you probably know what Einstein said."

"About what?"

Luther reaches into his pocket, pulls out his wallet, and takes a folded slip of paper from it. He hands it to her.

She reads the handwritten note aloud: "*Everyone who is seriously involved in the pursuit of science becomes convinced that a spirit is manifest in the laws of the Universe.*"

She looks up at him. "Einstein said that?"

Luther nods. "Odelia told me that when I met her. I didn't believe her, so I looked it up. After she'd helped me solve that first case, I wrote it down, and I've carried it with me ever since so that I won't forget."

She digests that as she refolds the paper along its well-worn crease and starts to hand it back to him.

"Keep it," he says. "I know it by heart. It might help you while you're here."

She tucks it into the back pocket of her shorts. "If you believe that there's something to this, why are you telling me that it's safe for us to stay here?"

"It's just like what Odelia said about connecting the dots. I don't immediately jump from one fact—*Leona died*—to another—*someone killed her*. There would have to be a lot of other facts for me to draw that conclusion, and right now, it's all too fuzzy."

"So are you humoring her, then? Is that why you came over here?"

"Absolutely not. Odelia's been right about this kind of thing before. But she's also been wrong." He chuckles a little bit, shaking his head. "Way wrong."

"Do you think she's wrong this time?"

"I hope so. All we have to go on is what she says might have happened—what she *feels* might have happened—and what a little boy thought he saw in the middle of the night."

"A pirate. I get it. I'm a mom." She nods her head toward all that's visible now of Max beneath the console: the rubber soles of his sneakers.

That, of course, brings her back to thinking about the muddy footprint and the creaking floorboard.

There are logical—and yes, illogical—explanations. It's all about how you connect the dots. She went from

point A—seeing someone in the house last night—to point
Z—that it might have been Leona's murderer.

"Here . . ." Luther takes a business card out of his wallet and hands it to her. *Luther Ragland, Private Investigator.*

"I'm going to look into a few things as soon as I
have time," he says, "but in the meantime, holler if you
need me."

"Thank you."

"Just please don't mention any of this to anyone."

"Don't worry. I won't."

She unlocks the door for him, and he steps outside.
Beyond the porch, the patchy lawn is pocked with marshy
puddles, and the furrows worn along the road have become
rushing streams that feed pothole ponds. A steady downpour falls from a contagiously monochromatic sky, washing away pretty pastels of the cottages, their vibrant garden
blooms and verdant foliage.

"It's still raining!" she exclaims.

Luther turns to shoot her an amused glance. "Better
get used to it."

"Oh, I'm used to rain. I just meant—it hasn't really let
up at all since I got out of bed. Usually, it comes and goes."

"Not here."

"You mean it rains like this a lot, then? Like . . .
all day?"

He nods. "But most of the year, it just snows all
day. All night."

"*Most* of the year?"

"All right, half the year—but that's no exaggeration.
This is blizzard country, Bella. We're buried in lake-effect
snow from October 'til April. Sometimes, it starts in September and lasts into May."

It snows back home in Bedford—though not as much
as here, by any means. But Chicago is blizzard country,

too. Sam told her about the legendary Great Lakes storms. She always thought it sounded like fun, being snowbound for days on end.

But with Sam.

Not with Millicent.

"I like rain," she says with a shrug, thinking that the drab weather suits her mood. "Not that it matters, since I'm only here a few more days."

"So you mentioned. A few times. Are you trying to convince me or yourself?"

"You forgot your umbrella by the back door. I'll go grab it for you."

"It's okay. Leave it for Odelia. I'm parked right over there." Pulling a key fob from his pocket, he aims it toward the parking lot across the street. A blue Jeep beeps and flashes its brake lights as he unlocks the doors remotely. "Oh, and Bella? Not an acceptable answer to my question, but I'll take it. For now."

Chapter 12

When Odelia invited Max to come back next door with her to bake her famous zucchini-jalapeño-lime cookies, Bella let him go. He was so worried about the still-missing cat that he needed a distraction.

But what about me?

All afternoon, try as she might to forget it, that muddy footprint has dogged her as effectively as if it had been an actual shoe—*pair* of shoes—with a relentless predator in them.

No matter how busy she's been around the house washing towels and making beds, no matter how eager she is to accept Luther's reassurance that there's nothing to worry about, she can't seem to forget that someone might have been eavesdropping at the study door.

Now, as she goes about her domestic duties, putting the guests' rooms back in order, Bella keeps an eye out for the cat.

There was no sign of her in the Rose Room, where she found that the papers scattered on the floor had apparently fallen from a box Max must have knocked off the closet shelf. How the heck did he reach it? He must have climbed on a chair.

He could have fallen and been seriously hurt.

I'm a lousy mother, she decided as she haphazardly collected the papers on the bureau.

She's had a couple of hours to reconsider.

Maybe she's not a *lousy* mother. Just an overwhelmed one.

Thank goodness for Odelia. Lifting the blinds on the window of the St. Clair sisters' third-floor, ballerina-themed guest room, Bella can see directly across the rainy yard into the kitchen next door. Her son is contentedly mixing cookie dough and appears to be chattering a mile a minute.

It's too bad her own mom isn't around or that Millicent isn't more like Odelia.

Millicent—Bella really has to call her just as soon as she finishes this last room.

She's not looking forward to the conversation, but she can't keep putting it off.

She turns to change the sheets on the queen-sized bed. Lifting one of the plump feather pillows, she finds a racy best-selling romance novel tucked beneath. She wonders which of the elderly spinsters is reading it and whether she intended to keep it hidden even from her sister.

Probably. If her journey through the guestrooms this afternoon has taught her anything, it's that everyone has secrets. *Everyone.*

For example, she never would have guessed that Bonnie Barrington's long blonde hair isn't her own, but there's an empty Styrofoam wig form sitting alongside the collection of bone china teacups on the bureau in her room. The staid Piersons seem to have quite the active love life, judging by the kinky black lace lingerie hanging on the back of the bathroom doorknob. And the Tooklers, well, they're in the opposite situation, judging by the self-help book and medication—prescribed for Jim by a urologist—on the nightstand.

Unaccustomed to glimpsing such intimate details in virtual strangers' lives, she's taken it all in with a twinge of voyeuristic guilt. It's not as if she's been snooping through drawers, though. She can't help but notice what's been left in plain sight.

As she finishes the hospital corners on the bed, she marvels that you never know what goes on behind closed doors, or even in people's private thoughts.

That doesn't mean Bella suspects any of the guests of having something to do with Leona's death. None of them were even here when it happened . . .

Unless someone had sneaked into town, killed her, and sneaked away again, only to show up two weeks later feigning shock at the terrible news.

She supposes that isn't out of the question, but why?

What if it was because—

"Hello?"

Startled by the voice behind her, Bella cries out. She whirls around to see a man standing in the doorway.

"Sorry," he says.

She's never seen him before, yet he looks very much at home, leaning against the doorjamb as though he belongs here and she's the interloper.

She knows the hammering in her rib cage is because he scared her and not—no, of course not—because he's incredibly good looking.

He is, though. Dark and slick and clean-shaven, he's wearing a well-cut suit and polished shoes. His devil-may-care elegance reminds her of the Gatsbyesque dandies she glimpsed the other night in the vintage photo albums.

He's quite the suave, seductive charmer . . .

What if Odelia's "Rudy" Valentino showed up at the wrong house this time?

Even as the thought crosses her mind, she acknowledges the utter ridiculousness of it.

She starts toward him and slams her thigh squarely into the bedpost. Ouch.

"Are you okay?" he asks mildly, watching her wince and rub the spot with her burnt fingers.

"I'm fine." *Just clumsy.* "Are you . . . ?"

She can't quite decide how to finish the sentence. *Are you . . .*

A ghost?

A crazy psycho killer?

Or maybe, *Are you . . . checking in?*

Or . . . *checking me out?*

Judging by the appreciative look in his black eyes, the last part is entirely true.

He completes the sentence for her: "Grant Everard."

"You're Grant Everard?" Her gaze shifts immediately to his wrist, but she can't see the fancy watch Odelia mentioned—the one that's a dead giveaway just how wealthy he is.

It's his turn to offer a fragmented question: "And you're . . . ?"

He obviously has no idea who she is, but he doesn't look as though he wonders whether she might be a ghost, a killer, or checking into the guesthouse. He may, however, believe she's checking him out.

Probably because you are.

"I'm Isabella."

"Nice to meet you, Isabella . . ."

"Jordan." She crosses over to shake his extended hand with her sore one. "I'm taking care of things around here for a few days."

His gaze flicks from her face to the erotic novel on the nightstand, waiting to be slipped back under the pillow when she finished making the bed.

He raises those decidedly masculine brows and flashes her a look that brings instant heat to her cheeks.

"That's not mine," she tells him quickly.

"That's what they all say." He flashes a lazy grin, and she resists the immediate urge to reach up and smooth her hair, wondering whether she remembered to brush it this morning—or her teeth, for that matter. Not that it matters, because she certainly isn't going to be kissing anyone, but . . .

Kissing? Since when is she thinking about kissing?

It's been a long time since she felt this kind of flustered.

No, he's not the first good-looking man to come along since Sam died. Not even the first one since she started her new life.

She thinks of Doctor Bailey, Troy, and Luther, too. She isn't blind; she's not immune to the opposite sex.

Grant, though, seems to have ignited a spark in the cool, dim place inside her where something warm and vibrant once glowed.

Yes, but look what happens when you play with fire, she reminds herself.

And for that matter, look at how you look.

She may never have been beautiful, regardless of what Sam called her.

My Bella Angelo.

No, but she'd been pretty enough, in a sporty, casual kind of way. Now whenever she looks in the mirror, all she sees are dark circles and worry lines and sad blue eyes.

My Bella Blue.

"How did you get in?" she asks Grant abruptly, determined to focus on the throbbing ache in her fingers and not the one in her heart.

"Sorry. I had a key."

Of course. Doesn't everyone?

"I probably shouldn't have let myself in. Sorry," he says again.

"It's okay. Odelia told me about you." *Warned* her, really.

"Oh yeah? What did she say? Wait, let me guess. She said I'm a ne'er-do-well?"

"Actually, she mentioned you're a . . . *do* well." Despite her effort at restraint, the quip escapes her lips with a flirtatious little smile and is met by a devilish grin.

"Well, I *ne'er* expected to hear that. I've always had the feeling Odelia doesn't think very highly of me."

"Why do you say that?"

"She may have mentioned it on the phone last week," he says with a laugh. "She doesn't mince words—and she doesn't take kindly to being awakened in the middle of the night, either. But I couldn't seem to keep my time zones straight."

"Where were you?"

"On a camel trek in Mongolia."

Bella starts to laugh but then sees his expression. "Wait—seriously?"

"Seriously."

"Why?"

"Why not?" he returns with a shrug. "Anyway, I had to fly back to New York and get my car. I got here as soon as I could, and it wasn't exactly easy to walk into this house just now without Leona waiting for me. She and Edgar were the closest thing I ever had to parents. They took me in when I was a kid in trouble with nowhere else to go."

"That's what family does."

"I wouldn't know about that. I never had any family—I mean other than Leona and Edgar, but they weren't blood relatives. Just a nice couple who couldn't have children of their own, and instead of pressing charges against the juvenile delinquent who broke into their house to rob them, they took him in and turned his life around."

Bella's mouth falls open.

"What's the matter? You can't believe I was a teenage thug? Come on, it's not so hard to imagine, is it?"

She doesn't know what to say to that.

He doesn't wait for a response. "I used to blame my bad behavior on being abandoned by my mother. It was a long time ago, though. And lousy luck doesn't give you license to live by your own set of rules. Leona and Edgar taught me that. I wish I'd met them sooner, but I owe them everything," he adds, bowing his head.

"I just . . . I thought you were Leona's nephew," Bella says lamely. "That's what Odelia told me."

"I guess that's what Leona told her. It probably made things easier. Although I have to say, I'm astounded that Odelia didn't figure out the truth, considering she's psychic." Judging by his tone, he's not astounded at all.

She doesn't respond to that comment either, feeling unexpectedly protective of Odelia—and of the others, and even of the wacky goings-on here in the Dale. Ironic, given her own newcomer status and blatant skepticism, not to mention the loss that ripped a gaping hole in her life.

If the people who inhabit this serene little village are convinced that they have all the answers and that you never really lose anyone you love, well then, more power to them. It must be nice to dwell in this luminescent little bubble, protected from the harsh realities of uncertainty and bereavement.

Bella gestures at the half-made bed. "I have to finish up in here," she tells Grant. "I made sure your room is vacant, though."

"Which room?"

"The one with the trains. Odelia said it's yours."

He smiles. "It is. I loved trains when I was a kid. Probably because I used to hitch a ride on a freight train out of town whenever I didn't like whichever foster home I happened to be in. Which was all of them, until I met Leona and Edgar."

"I'm sorry."

"It's the past." He shrugs. "Anyway, it'll be nice to sleep in a familiar bed for a change."

"I take it you've been on the road a lot?"

"On the road, the rails, the water, in the air . . . This has been one heck of a trip."

"You forgot the camels."

"Right—on camelback, too." His grin gives way to a yawn. "I'm so beat, I think I'll go to bed right now, if you don't mind."

"Why would I mind?" she asks defensively, wondering if he somehow thinks she'll miss the pleasure of his company this evening.

As if she imagined the two of them sitting together on the porch swing in the twilight . . .

"You know, the room. Is it ready?"

"My son slept in there the first night, but I changed the sheets, so it's all set for you."

"You have a son?"

She nods.

"How old?"

"Five."

"And your husband . . . ?"

"He died," she says flatly. No wide-eyed delusions here.

"I'm sorry."

Yeah. Me too.

She gives a little nod and turns away, staring at a print on the wall: lithe, carefree Parisian girls in frothy tutus lined up at the barre, not a care in the world.

She can feel Grant watching her for a long moment, as if he wants to say something else. But he doesn't.

She waits until he's back downstairs to exhale.

* * *

There's no fiery orange sunset to light the sky tonight. The rain hasn't let up all day, shrouding the lake in dense, gray mist.

For dinner, Bella and Max sit down to macaroni and cheese from a box, a far cry from the healthy, delicious dinners she used to cook for three in the cozy kitchen back in Bedford. Max picks at the gummy, orange pasta with his fork and leaves most of it untouched, still worried about Chance. There's been no sign of her all day.

Earlier, when Bella went next door to collect Max from Odelia, she speculated that the cat is probably still holed up somewhere staying out of the rain.

"I'm sure she'll be back when the sun comes out," Odelia assured Max as she packed several dozen surprisingly delicious cookies into a tin to take back next door.

"But she's going to have her babies today."

"Is she? That's nice." Odelia seemed preoccupied, probably because Bella had just filled her in about Grant's arrival.

She wanted to see him, but Bella told her he'd gone straight to bed.

"Well, tell him to come see me when he wakes up. I'm going to the message service, but I'll be home after that."

"He said he might sleep straight through until tomorrow."

"Oh, really? Well, good for him."

Now, other than Grant, still behind closed doors in the Train Room, the guests are all out at the evening message service. With Max fed—more or less—bathed, and moping in front of the parlor TV, Bella sits at the kitchen table and dials her mother-in-law's number again.

Millicent answers on the third ring. One more, Bella knows, and it would have gone to voice mail. She also knows her mother-in-law always has the phone close at hand, always checks caller ID, and always answers on the first ring.

This time, she waited to pick up on purpose.

She's making me sweat. Terrific.

"Jordan residence, Millicent speaking."

"Hello, M—" She breaks off. If she calls her Millicent, she'll be reprimanded. If she calls her Mother, she might gag. She settles on nothing, as usual. "It's Isabella. How are you?"

There's a pause. "Quite well. And you?"

"Quite well," Bella replies, though it isn't something she'd typically say, and it isn't the truth.

"And Max?"

"He's great." Another lie, followed by another. "Listen, I'm sorry about what happened last night."

There's a long pause on the other end of the line.

Then Millicent sighs deeply. "Lashing out at me that way—I just don't know what got into you, Isabella."

I do, she thinks, biting her lip. *Common sense.*

Millicent made her feel completely reckless and incompetent, as if it was her own fault the car broke down.

Somewhere in the back of her mind, Bella knows that if she'd had the car serviced, that might not have happened. She *couldn't* have it serviced, though, because she could barely afford gasoline, and the only reason she was driving halfway across the country in it was because she had nowhere else to go . . .

But now you do.

The thought flits into her head, and she pushes it right back out again.

No, she doesn't. She has Millicent and Chicago. That's all.

"I don't know what got into me either. I guess I was just frazzled and a little overwhelmed."

"All I was trying to explain to you is that a little foresight can go a long way."

Bella grits her teeth, staring at the gloomy dusk beyond the rain-spattered window.

"People who learn to take care of themselves can take care of others."

Did Millicent really just say that?

"I do take care of myself," she says tightly. "And my son."

"Well of course you're making an effort, and it isn't that I mind helping, but I just want you to be aware that if you had just—"

"Mom!" Max shouts from the parlor.

"I have to go!" she blurts into the phone, hanging up and tossing it aside.

"Max?" she calls, hurrying toward the front of the house. "Are you okay?"

"I am, but . . . look."

Reaching the parlor, she sees him pointing at the open bay windows above the cushioned bench.

Beyond the screen, flooded in porch light, Chance the Cat is looking in, a wee newborn kitten dangling from her mouth.

Chapter 13

Max hurries to open the door as Bella grabs a couple of towels from the laundry room. Spying a small wooden crate that holds a stack of tied newspapers waiting to be recycled, she hastily tosses the papers aside. Returning to the front hall, she sets the towel-lined crate on the floor just in time for Chance to drop in the kitten.

It's a fragile creature, no larger than Max's hand. It has straggly gray-and-black-ticked fur like its mother, a stub of a tail, and a rosy nose and paw pads. Its eyes are sealed tightly, ears closed and flattened to its head, and still-useless limbs splayed. It shimmies awkwardly on its belly, emitting a faint, high-pitched mew.

"What's wrong with it?" Max asks.

Bella has to swallow a hot surge of emotion before she can find her voice. "Nothing. Nothing at all. It's just a new baby. It can't see or hear or walk yet. It can't do anything without its mommy."

"But she's leaving!"

Sure enough, the cat is already marching straight back to the door, where she meows urgently until Bella opens it, then disappears into the night.

"Why did she go?" Max asks in dismay.

"Shh, it's okay. Just watch."

Moments later, Chance reappears with another wriggling kitten hanging by its scruff and deposits it into the crate beside its sibling.

This time, Bella and Max follow her outside to watch as she makes a beeline back to the shadows beneath the porch.

"That's where the babies are," Max realizes. "There are five more. Maybe six."

"Maybe. She was probably waiting for the rain to stop before she brought them inside."

The daylong deluge has finally ebbed. Bordered by dripping boughs and eaves, the narrow, muddy lane beyond the porch lamp is deserted, most of the houses dark. The wind chimes tinkle forlornly, stirred by a wet breeze. Dense fog still hangs over the Dale, drifting in a yellowish cast beneath widely scattered streetlamps.

The scene reminds Bella of a Jack the Ripper movie she'd seen years ago. This may not be nineteenth-century London, but it doesn't particularly look like twenty-first-century New York, and it isn't hard to imagine a cloaked man stepping out of the mist.

She hugs Max close to her as they watch Chance emerge from a hole in the porch lattice with another newborn clutched in her mouth. One by one, she transports her litter inside.

There are seven altogether—or so it seems at first.

Seven helpless, hungry, crying kittens, whom Max promptly names in order of appearance: Monday, Tuesday, Wednesday, Thursday, Friday, Saturday, and Sunday.

"I *told* you the kittens were coming today!" he crows. "And I told you there would be seven!"

"You sure did."

But how on earth did you know?

"Or maybe eight," he adds, as Chance makes one last trip outside, almost as an afterthought. But when she reappears a minute later, she's alone. She paces around the room, stopping below the window that faces the porch, then looks up at them and meows, almost as if she's asking a question.

"It's okay, sweetie," Bella says, leaning down to rub her head. "You did great. You can rest now."

As the cat settles into her makeshift nest to nurse her fuzzy little family, Max and Bella watch from a respectful distance, perched on the bottom stair.

"She keeps looking at the door, Mom. Do you think there's another baby out there?"

"No, she wouldn't leave any behind."

"How do you know?"

"The same way I knew she needed a box for them."

"Is it called psychic?"

"No. It's called maternal instinct."

"So that means moms just know stuff?"

"Exactly."

"Isn't that the same as psychic?"

"No, not at all," she says firmly. Psychics—so-called psychics—claim to rely on a sixth sense, while moms rely on . . .

Instinct.

Which is completely different. Of course it is.

One is supposedly supernatural, the other is . . . well, natural.

Don't all mothers, human and animal, possess the acute need to find a cozy place in which to protect their offspring from the big, bad world?

For now, this is ours, she thinks, looking around at the tawny wallpaper and rich woodwork swaddled in the golden glow of the etched glass ceiling pendant. The room is hushed, other than the ticking clock and the occasional peep of a wayward kitten momentarily losing its latch.

In this moment, the house belongs only to her, Max, Chance, and her babies. Unless you count Leona's nephew-who's-not-really-a-nephew, still presumably asleep upstairs.

Thinking of poor Grant, abandoned as a newborn, Bella acknowledges that not all females are natural mothers. She finds herself wondering about the story behind his tragic past—and then, for some reason, wondering if it's even true.

She's met men like him before. Smooth, self-assured, and, yes, seductive. Men who aren't above embellishing or even fabricating details to suit their needs.

To be fair, she doesn't know Grant well enough to assume that he fits that bill. But there's no denying that he's smooth and self-assured. Besides, Odelia has no use for him, and she—

Okay, she doesn't like *everybody*.

She has no use for Pandora Feeney. Nor for her ex-husband Orville.

But considering that she's psychic—or so she claims—she may have a sound basis for her . . . dislike? Mistrust?

A possibility occurs to Bella, so disturbing and frightening that she pushes it away.

No, that would be as preposterous as . . . as Jack the Ripper lurking in the mist that shrouds the Dale.

Still, she can't help but look over her shoulder, up the staircase. She half-expects to see someone looming there, but the hall above is dark and still.

"I have boy instinct," Max is saying.

"Hmm?"

"You have mom instinct, and I have boy instinct," Max tells her. "I told you the kittens would be born today, and I told you how many there would be."

Yes, he did.

Boy instinct . . . or prophecy?

"One, two, three, four, five, six, seven," Max counts, as if to make absolutely sure, and then he casts a fretful glance at the door. "I really think she forgot one."

"She didn't, Max," Bella assures him again. "Why do you keep saying that?"

"I don't know. I just do."

"What made you say the kittens were coming today?"

"*I* made me say it."

"Yes, but how did you know?"

He shrugs. "I just knew."

It could have been a lucky guess. Thinking back to their conversation at the animal hospital, she remembers that Doctor Bailey had said the kittens were due within the week and that there would be quite a few of them.

Maybe seven was another lucky guess. Anything between two and ten would have been sensible—though how would Max know that?

Then again, she reasons, he did say seven or possibly eight, giving him even greater odds of getting it right.

Good. See? All you have to do is take a step back from this mystical Lily Dale mentality and apply logical thinking.

She can probably come up with a rational explanation for most of the so-called psychic phenomena around here if she just—

"Mom! What is she doing?"

She looks up to see that Chance has left the crate and is staring at the door. Her ears standing straight up, twitching as if she's listening intently.

"I don't know. Maybe she heard something outside. An animal or something."

"It's her other kitten! She got lost and Chance the Cat couldn't find her in the dark, and now she's crying out there all alone."

"Did you hear her crying?"

"No, but her mommy did, because she has instinct and great hearing."

He may be right. Chance emits a sudden, agitated chirping sound and practically throws herself at the door.

Max hurries to open it. The cat scoots past him and is swallowed by the darkness, leaving seven crying kittens behind.

"It's okay, guys. Your mommy will be right back."

Bella certainly hopes Max is right. She peers outside, wondering what it was that lured the cat from the nest. Did she really drop one of her kittens?

Maybe she heard a bird out there, or a rodent, or . . .

What if she heard someone prowling around the house?

Oh, come on, Bella. She's a cat, not a guard dog.

"Hurry up, Chance the Cat!" Max calls. "Your babies are crying!"

After a brief rustling in the bushes near the porch, the cat springs up onto the porch, another kitten clasped in her mouth.

"It's Spider!" Max hollers.

Dumbfounded, Bella watches Chance trot calmly into the house and drop a wee black speck of a kitten into the nest with the others.

"Number eight! My boy instinct was right, Mommy, see?"

Bella nods as if she does. But she doesn't see anything at all, while her son somehow sees . . .

The future? Really?

What, exactly, did Odelia say about . . . wow. Was that only yesterday?

Entire seasons seem to have passed since Bella sat lounging in the sun-splashed yard, so new to all this, so naïve. Everything Odelia told her seemed farfetched.

And now . . . what? Now you believe it? You're an overnight convert to Spiritualism?

No. Of course not. It's just that things have happened since yesterday that she can't quite explain, including this latest experience with Max and the kittens.

So what was it Odelia had said about children and psychic experiences?

Unlike adults, they haven't yet fully learned what they're supposed to see and feel—and what they aren't.

She was talking about Jiffy, Bella reminds herself. His mother is a medium, and it runs in families. That's what Odelia claimed, and yet . . .

She also said anyone is capable, didn't she?

If anyone can do it, and if kids are more susceptible, then maybe Max is . . . one of *them.*

Bella abruptly closes the front door, as if that might somehow keep Lily Dale from seeping in.

"He's so tiny, Mommy."

"What?"

"Spider. He's really, really, really small. Like this big." Max presses his thumb and forefinger together.

"Let's see." Bella settles on the floor beside the crate to get her first good look at the brood. Most of the kittens are still prone and nursing, kneading their mama's soft fur with their tiny pink paws as they suckle. It's impossible to discern the tiny black latecomer from the wriggling, mewing heap of fur babies.

"I love them!" Max declares. "I want to keep them all."

"That would be nice, wouldn't it?" she murmurs, mulling the latest twist in their Lily Dale stay as her son talks on about all the fun he can have with "his" cat and kittens.

She's grateful when a key turns in the lock and Helen and Karl Adabner, in the midst of animated conversation, step into the house.

"I know you did, but I don't care. I just didn't think—" Karl breaks off, spotting Max. "Well, hello, young man. Isn't it past your bedtime?"

"No."

"Yes," Bella corrects her son, looking up at the clock. "Is the evening message service over already?"

"Not quite, but it's past our bedtime, too." Catching sight of the crate as she follows her husband toward the stairs, Helen stops short. "Oh, my! What do we have here?"

"We have here Chance the Cat and her eight babies," Max reports.

"What a neat surprise!"

"Don't get too close. Mom says we have to stay back here because they need privacy right now."

"Your mom is right. I just want to take a quick peek." Helen leans over the crate. "Oh! They're precious! Look, Karl. Oh, I want one!"

"I want them all," Max says.

"We can't have five cats, Helen."

And we can't have any at all, Bella thinks.

"You said we couldn't have three cats, either," Helen tells Karl. "Or four. And now look."

"Yes, now look," he says flatly, shaking his balding head.

"You have four cats?" Max is impressed. "Are they here?"

"No, our neighbor is taking care of them this week, which means I don't have to sleep with a cat on my head for a change." Karl yawns and walks toward the stairs.

"Mom and I are going to sleep with Chance the Cat and all her babies. Mom promised. Right, Mom?"

"What a nice mom. But what happened to your leg, Mom?" Karl asks, and she looks down to see her scraped knee and bruised thigh.

"Oh, that? I . . . I kind of fell up the stairs," she says with a laugh.

"*Up* the stairs? That's a twist."

"Yes, well . . . I like to shake things up a bit."

Karl grins again, yawns again, and looks at his wife. "Are you coming up to bed?"

"In a minute."

"I thought you were exhausted."

"I am." She kneels on the floor beside the crate. "I just want to see them for a second."

"Don't fall in love, Helen."

"Too late, Karl," she returns lightly.

Smiling, Bella moves aside to let him pass her on his way up the steps.

"Looks like you've got your hands full, there, Mom," he says, and winks at her. "Good night."

He seems sweet and harmless, though the wink gives her pause, and her good-night isn't as warm as it might have been if Pandora hadn't warned her about his friskiness.

Oh, come on. He's just being friendly, not flirtatious. Plenty of older men wink. Maybe not in New York, but Iowa . . .

Besides, look at you.

Checking her reflection in the mirror earlier, after Grant had retreated to his room, she'd noticed a purple grape juice stain on her T-shirt to match the circles under her eyes, the lovely scrape where she'd hurt her knee earlier on the stairway, and a fresh bruise where she'd bumped her thigh.

"Aren't you the sweetest little things?" Helen coos, and Bella turns to see her stroking the nursing kittens with a gentle fingertip.

Max is crouched beside her, boldly daring to get a better look now that Helen has breached Bella's safety perimeter.

"I love their markings. I see four gray tabbies like mama and a couple of black-and-white tuxedo kitties . . ."

"There's one that's only black, too, but he's getting smushed in there, see?"

A few of the kittens have formed a squealing little heap with a tufted tip of black tail barely poking from beneath.

"They're just trying to stay warm," Helen tells him. "It's okay. It's what they do."

"You must have mom instinct, too."

She smiles a sad smile and shakes her head. "I'm not a mom."

"Why not?"

"It just . . . it wasn't meant to be. But I did grow up on a farm, and I've been around plenty of newborn litters, so I guess I have . . . kitty instinct."

"I'm glad," Bella says, "because I'm new to this."

"In that case . . . be prepared to keep them all."

Predictably, Max says, "I *want* to keep them all."

"I wish we could, sweetie, but we can't."

"Then I'll just keep Spidey," Max decides. "And Chance the Cat, too."

"How do you know which one is Spidey?" Helen asks.

"He's the teeny tiny black one under there. His name is Spider, but I call him Spidey for short, because he's short. Extra short. He's a boy. There are four boys and four girls."

"Wow! You're not such novices if you can already tell what they are, because that's tricky when they're this little," Helen says.

"Oh, we can't tell. Max is guessing."

"I'm not guessing! Four boys and four girls. I'm not sure which is which, except Spidey is a boy. And I'm worried because his mommy dropped him outside and now he's the only one who's not eating."

"Let's have a look. Come here, Spidey." Helen gently reaches into the pile of kittens to extract the black one, and gasps. "Oh, my goodness. He's a true runt."

"What's a runt?"

"It's a baby that's much smaller and more fragile than his littermates." Cradling the mewing, writhing kitten in her hand, she tilts it so that they can get a better look.

Bella realizes Max wasn't exaggerating much when he indicated that Spider would fit into the fraction of space between his thumb and forefinger. The others may be tiny, but they're twice his size.

"This litter is too large for one poor tired mama cat to feed," Helen says, as a door creaks open upstairs followed by footsteps in the hall. "And this fellow is too weak and tiny to get his fair share. I don't want to alarm anyone, but he needs to see a vet right away. He needs nourishment immediately."

Max clutches Bella's arm. "We have to go to Doctor Bailey!"

"Max, we—"

"Please! Don't let him die!"

"Don't let *who* die?" a deep voice asks from the top of the stairs.

She looks up to see Grant Everard standing there. He's changed into a pair of jeans; sneakers; a T-shirt that reveals tanned, muscular forearms; and, indeed, a watch she can tell is expensive even from where she stands. A sweatshirt is slung over his arm, and there are keys in his hand. Even dressed down, he gives off an air of casual sophistication.

"Spidey needs to go to Doctor Bailey right now!" Max tells him. "It's an emergency!"

"It's going to be okay, Max." Bella puts a calming hand on his shoulder. "Come on, we'll go borrow Odelia's car and take her."

"You'll have to take them all," Helen tells her.

"What do you mean?"

"If you take her away from her mama, she might be rejected even if she survives. And the others are nursing nonstop, so mama can't leave them either," she continues, as Bella absorbs the seriousness of the situation. "But Odelia is at the service. She's not scheduled to read until the end, so she won't be done for a while, and you can't pull her away. You don't have a car?"

"It's in the repair shop." She remembers that the Adabners arrived in a cab, so they can't help her.

Grant walks down the stairs and peers at the kitten still cupped in Helen's hand. "What's going on?"

As Helen briefly explains the situation, Bella can see exactly where this is going.

Sure enough, he says, "I'll drive you to the vet. I was just going out to find some food."

"You don't have to do that."

"I'm afraid he does. You really need to get this kitten some help right away," Helen says anxiously, stroking the kitten's black fur with her forefinger.

Grant nods. "We're on our way. Let's go."

"Thank you, Mister . . . um . . ." Max hesitates. "What's your name?"

"It's Grant."

"Grant?" Helen raises her eyebrows, looking surprised. "Are you Leona's nephew?"

"I am."

No, you're not, Bella thinks, wondering why he doesn't bother to correct the mistaken assumption. True, Leona is the one who, for whatever reason, had told everyone she was his aunt rather than his foster mother, but it wouldn't be that big a deal for him to clear that up now, would it?

It's a white lie, and not even his own—or so he claims—but still, it doesn't sit well with her.

Even though you yourself called your godmother Aunt Sophie?

She wasn't Bella's aunt. She wasn't even a blood relative—just Mom's best friend and the person who stepped in to do all the things a mom would do: bake birthday cupcakes, make her a first communion veil, and help pick out a prom dress.

"I'd shake your hand, but I can see that it's full." Grant gives Helen an easy smile. "It's nice to meet you . . ."

"Helen. Helen Adabner. I'd heard about you from Leona. You're not quite what I pictured."

Wondering what she'd pictured, yet knowing now isn't the time to ask, Bella tells Grant, "You don't have to drive us to the vet. When Odelia gets out of the service, we'll borrow her car and go."

"Not to upset anyone," Helen speaks up, directing a meaningful glance at Max, "but I don't think you can afford to wait that long."

"I have to call the animal hospital to tell them we're coming."

"You can do it from the car." Grant jangles his keys—and alarm bells jangle in Bella's brain as she watches him pull on his sweatshirt: a dark-colored hoodie.

Chapter 14

"Drive faster, Mr. Grant! Please?" Max says, buckled into the back beside the crate containing the cat and kittens.

"You got it, buddy."

Undaunted by the winding road, inky black beyond the headlights' glow, he gives the luxury sports car a little more gas.

Sitting in the front beside him, Bella watches the speedometer edge even higher above the speed limit. She flexes her foot as if there's a brake beneath it and wishes she could tell him to slow down. But time is of the essence, according to Doctor Bailey, who told her to come right over with the kitten.

Besides, Grant isn't a reckless driver, just a confident one, and the car handles well.

Somehow, he seems to know exactly where he's going, even though he said he's never been to the animal hospital before. When she pulled it up on her phone and showed him the map, he glanced, nodded, and said he knows where it is.

She's been trying to convince herself that isn't unusual for someone who isn't from the area and supposedly doesn't visit very regularly.

Supposedly? So you don't believe him?

She isn't sure that she doesn't . . .

She just wishes she were sure that she does.

Her thoughts are muddled, and he seems lost in his own. He hasn't spoken much, other than to ask Max how the kitten is holding up.

Each time, the answer is the same: "He's sick. He's crying. Can you go faster?"

Of course he can. Bella has a feeling Grant would drive too fast even without an endangered newborn kitten on board.

Suddenly, though, he slows the car and makes a sharp left turn off the highway.

Startled by the abrupt move, she looks down at the map on her phone. They've just veered off course.

"What are you doing?" she asks, and her voice sounds too high-pitched. There goes that jackhammer in her chest again.

"I'm driving the car. What are *you* doing? Besides holding on for dear life and pressing your imaginary brake, I mean."

Under drastically different circumstances, that might have struck her as amusing. Right now, she's in no mood for banter.

"You were supposed to stay on the highway."

"I'm taking a shortcut. It'll shave off a few minutes. Trust me."

She doesn't.

I don't like this. Not at all.

The winding road, bordered closely by dense woods, is paved, but so pothole ridden that Grant has to weave into the other lane to miss one, and then another.

There's no oncoming traffic, yet she finds herself white knuckled. It isn't just the harrowing car ride, it's . . .

It's him.

What if . . .

Come on. How can you think such a thing?

Is it just because he's wearing a dark hoodie?

No. But that doesn't help matters.

Lots of people wear them, though. She herself had one on the other night. Sam's hoodie.

The weight that's constricted her chest for months has transformed into a crushing boulder, making it all but impossible for her to breathe.

How long can you hold your breath? Jiffy Arden had asked Max just the other day, outside in the sunshine. *How long?*

What she wouldn't give right now to be able to breathe again, safely back home in Bedford again with Sam and Max.

Sam is gone. Home is gone. Safe is gone.

And I am slowly suffocating.

And the answer to Jiffy's question is forever.

This is how it will always be: holding her breath, careening through the night, feeling helpless and afraid.

Right now, it's as if she's being tailgated by death itself, a stranger at the wheel and her frightened son in the backseat with a new mama cat and fragile babies, one of them barely clinging to life.

But what if . . .

Again Grant swerves, avoiding another gaping pothole, and her brain does the same to evade the awful thought. But it looms like glaring headlights on a blind curve, slamming her like an eighteen-wheeler.

What if he isn't who he claims to be?

There it is: the possibility that, when it first fluttered into her consciousness, had seemed as outrageous as . . . as believing in ghosts, fairies, or murderous pirates, for that matter.

Leona is dead.

What if he's just some . . . some strange man, posing as her next of kin?

As far as she knows, he's had no contact with anyone in the Dale other than her until the moment he emerged from his room tonight. Helen—who's been here many times before—didn't recognize him.

Why would she, though? She's never met him before.

Thank goodness her inner voice of reason is persistent. Almost as persistent as the absurdly paranoid part of her that conjured this idea in the first place.

Odelia herself mentioned that Grant comes and goes infrequently. It's possible that he's never crossed paths before with the Adabners or some of the other guests, but most likely, some of them have met Leona's "nephew" Grant. And certainly, Odelia would immediately know he's an imposter.

But she hasn't seen him yet. No one has.

Was he really sleeping behind closed doors? Or was he . . . hiding?

Bella fights back the urge to protest as he transports them deeper and deeper into the woods.

What if she's right about him?

Then it's better not to let on that she's suspicious, isn't it? Better to go along with this shortcut charade and wait for an opportunity to make an escape.

Right. Just bolt on the spur of the moment—with a kid, a cat, and eight kittens in tow.

That's not going to happen. Bella has to focus on the matter at hand: getting help for poor little Spider. She has to believe, for now, anyway, that Grant really is Grant. And that he's a good Samaritan rushing to save an innocent little life.

He brakes again and makes a right onto a road she didn't even notice was looming off to the side. *So how did he?*

He makes a left, and then another right, and they're driving deeper and deeper into dense woods, and then . . .

"There it is!" Max shouts, pointing to a sign. "That's it! Look, Mom!"

Lakeview Animal Hospital and Rescue

It's on the opposite side of the road this time; they came from a different direction. It was, indeed, faster. Much faster. The drive that had taken Bella nearly half an hour on that first night took about fifteen minutes, tops.

A shortcut, just like he said. Okay.

The boulder shifts. Not entirely, but enough so that she can catch her breath.

Grant doesn't seem to have lost sight of the kitten whose frail life is at stake. He jumps out of the driver's seat and opens the back door. "How's our little guy doing, Max?"

She's struck by the concern in his voice and the fact that he remembers her son's name—and used it.

I was wrong about him.

Well, of course she was, imagining that this man is some—some crazed killer, carrying out an elaborate masquerade.

How could she have entertained such a ridiculous notion?

It was just for a few moments. A few irrational, sleep-deprived moments.

"He's kind of quiet right now, Mr. Grant. He's not moving. Maybe he's sleeping."

At her son's hopeful words, Bella deflates. How is Max going to handle yet another heartbreak? This isn't anywhere near the catastrophic loss of Sam, and it doesn't even hold a candle to the loss of their home, but . . .

It isn't fair. She knows better than to think that life should be, but Max is just a little boy.

"Yeah, he's hanging in there," she hears Grant say. "I think he was just sleeping. Listen, he's crying again. He's feisty. Come on."

Fortified, Bella gets out of the car and hurries to catch up as Grant strides toward the building with the crate, Max running alongside.

The door opens before they even reach the porch. Doctor Bailey is waiting for them, wearing his lab coat and an expression of concern.

"That was fast," he says, flicking a curious glance at Grant.

"We need you to help Spidey," Max says. "Please! Can you save him?"

Bella is grateful that the vet doesn't even acknowledge the question as he reaches out to take the crate from Grant's arms. Silence is better than offering Max false hope or gloomy statistics.

She had already confirmed, courtesy of a quick Internet search on her phone when they first set out, that Helen wasn't being overly dramatic about the kitten's condition. It is dire.

"Should we come with you?" Bella asks as Doctor Bailey carries the crate toward an open examination room door.

He doesn't turn or stop walking. "Just one of you. The room is small."

She hesitates. The only thing that makes any sense is for her to go, but that would mean leaving Max alone in the waiting room with Grant.

Grant, who took on this rescue mission and delivered them here safely.

But is that just one side of him? Is there another side? A dark side?

Too muddled to remember exactly why she even thought that in the first place, she makes a snap decision. "I'll be right back," she says—a reassurance for Max and perhaps a warning for Grant.

In the examination room, Doctor Bailey is already handling the little black kitten with tenderness and efficiency. The crate is on a low counter next to the examining table. Chance lies inside nursing the rest of the litter, but her head is upright, eyes fixed warily on the vet as he places Spider on the table and shines a bright light on him.

"It's okay, little guy," he croons, gently checking over the mewing kitten.

"Have you dealt with many cases like this?"

He nods. "With a litter this size, the runt sometimes starves to death because there isn't enough milk to go around or because the siblings shut him out. Sometimes, the mother is overwhelmed and she rejects it altogether, and once in a while, she even kills it."

"Kills her own kitten?" she asks in horror. "Why?"

"Maternal instinct."

"That sounds like the exact opposite." Bella is nothing if not overwhelmed herself, but if anything, she's more protective of her child.

"Ever hear of a little thing called Darwin's Theory of Evolution?"

"Oh. Right." She nods. "I guess my emotions got the better of me for a moment there. I'm a science teacher, so—"

"So then you know all about nature and survival of the fittest." As he talks, he holds the kitten on the table with one hand and opens an adjacent cabinet and rummages around with his right. "If the mother senses a birth defect or an illness that threatens the rest of the litter, she might sacrifice one offspring to improve the odds for the others."

"Chance isn't going to hurt her baby," Bella says firmly. "I've seen how she is with him."

When they left the house, she was gently licking little Spider and keeping him warm beneath her arm, shielding him from the squirmy sibling fray.

"I hope that's the case, but you just never know," he says. "When were the kittens born?"

"I'm not sure what time, but it was today."

Again, she thinks about how Chance mysteriously vanished from the bedroom this morning. Obviously, she was seeking a private place in which to deliver her litter—but how on earth did she manage to get out of the room? And how did she get into the train room the first night?

Either she's a magical cat who can lock and unlock doors—or walk through walls—or someone let her in and out.

"The good news," Doctor Bailey lines up several items on the table and closes the cabinet, "is that this little guy he can be syringe-fed kitten formula through a feeding tube. I'm going to try that now, and we'll see how it goes."

She watches as he measures out a length of tube along the kitten's body, marks it with a Sharpie, and draws some liquid into a narrow syringe.

"It's so hard to listen to him crying."

"Crying is actually a good sign. It means he's hungry. If he weren't crying, I'd be worried."

Holding the kitten so that he's lying on his belly, Doctor Bailey gently places the tip of the tube into his mouth. Amid continued high-pitched wailing, he eases the tube inside, gradually getting it all the way down the kitten's throat and into its belly.

"The first time is always hard," he says, "but once they get used to it, they swallow the tube more easily, knowing food is coming."

With the tube inserted, he presses the syringe ever so slightly. As the first few nourishing drops hit the mark, the crying stops.

"There we go. That's it, little guy," Doctor Bailey says softly.

Bella leans over his shoulder to see. "He's eating?"

"Yes, he is. Like a champ," he adds with a laugh.

She swallows hard, so unexpectedly moved that it takes her a moment to find her voice. "Do you think he'll live?"

"I think he has a fighting chance."

For a few minutes, they watch in silence punctuated only by the squeaky cries from Spider's siblings in the crate.

Then she asks quietly, "What about the puppy?"

"Hmm?"

"The puppy. The one you were trying to save the other night, when we were here. He'd had surgery. Did he make it?"

He looks up. "So far. He's still here, out back, recovering."

"So you'll keep the kitten here, too?"

"Do you mean boarded, as a patient?" He shakes his head. "The queen hasn't rejected him, and we don't want that to happen, so he should continue to nest with her and the littermates."

"The queen?"

"The official name for a feline nursing mother."

"Queen Chance the Cat. I can't wait to tell Max she's royalty."

Doctor Bailey flashes a brief smile. "I'm going to give you everything you need to hand-raise him, and I can loan you a good book on the subject, too."

"Wait—hand-raise . . . ?"

"It just means you'll do the feeding, and the queen will do the rest—grooming, litter-box training, socializing. She'll instinctively handle everything he needs to become self-sufficient. But let's not get ahead of ourselves. For now, you'll have to feed him every two hours around the clock for the first week, then every three hours for the next—"

"Wait," she cuts in again, "I don't even live here. Max and I are leaving on Monday."

He frowns faintly, digesting this information. "I see. So the cat . . ."

"I don't know. I don't know who's going to take care of her, or the kittens."

She thinks of Grant, with his fancy watch and vagabond lifestyle.

And of Odelia, who already has her hands full—not to mention a lame leg.

And of Millicent, barely willing to take in her own daughter-in-law and grandson.

Somebody has to rescue Chance and her kittens.

But it isn't going to be me. I wish . . .

No matter how much she aches to keep a pet for Max, no matter how badly she wants to care for Chance and the kittens, no matter how desperately she wants to save this fragile newborn life . . .

She can't take the cats with her to Millicent's, and she has nowhere else to go.

You can stay.

And have Max surrounded with people who make a living by talking to the dead? A Spiritualist colony is no place to raise an impressionable child who's lost his father, and it's no place for a widow who needs to accept that the love of her life is gone forever.

"I can't," she says quietly. "I just . . ."

Choked up, she shakes her head and swallows hard, staring down at the miniscule kitten. He's once again huddled beside his siblings but cradled beneath his mother's protective paw.

Chance feels about her baby exactly the way Bella does about Max. She'll do anything to keep him safe.

She finds her voice. "I don't have any options. There's just no way I can help."

"All right. I understand."

"You do?"

"Believe me. I hear that a lot."

"What about you? Can't you keep him? And help him? Isn't this an animal rescue?"

Doctor Bailey's face is grim. "I'm overextended as it is. This time of year is kitten season. Do you know how many nursing queens and litters have come my way this week alone? It's hard enough to find foster homes for the healthy ones. If you're positive you can't take responsibility for them," he says, gesturing at the crate, "then the most humane thing to do might be—"

"No!" Bella hears herself shout as the awful insinuation hits her. "No, you can't do that."

"Isabella, my fosters are all tapped out. I can't hand-raise a kitten at the expense of all the other animals who need me."

"I thought you had other people on your staff?"

"Just my assistant. She lives in a one-room apartment with three cats of her own, and she's already fostering a stray queen and litter in her bathroom and a contagious stray in her closet."

"What about—don't you have a friend or relative, maybe, who can—"

He gives a bitter laugh. "Are you kidding? The ones who are willing to help are already above and beyond, and the others—believe me, after all these years, they run when they see me coming. Look, there's no one."

No one but me, Bella thinks, looking from Spider to his seven siblings to Chance, who meets her gaze with a long stare and then a slow blink.

She isn't begging, Bella realizes. She's . . .

Trusting. Trusting me with her own life and with her babies. Nine lives, all in my hands. What am I supposed to do? Throw them away?

No. No way. I've got this.

"It's okay," she tells Doctor Bailey. "I'll take care of them for now—all of them—until I can find someone else."

Surely Odelia will take on the challenge after she and Max leave for Chicago. Or Grant will. He, of all people, should understand the importance of stepping up to foster.

"I'm going to go talk to my son and my . . . friend," she tells Doctor Bailey as he removes the kitten from the crate again and puts him on the examining table. "I'll be right back."

He nods, again focused on tending to the kitten.

Bella steps out into the waiting room—and finds it empty.

The world skids to a halt. "Max? Max!"

She *knew* something was off about Grant! She should have known better than to—

Then through the screen, she hears, "We're out here, Mom."

Rushing for the door, she sees her son standing on the cement stoop. He's holding a pair of binoculars pointed at the filmy night sky, and Grant is beside him.

"What are you doing?"

"We're looking for Sirius. It's the brightest star in the sky," Max informs her, intent on the view through the lenses. "It's part of the dog constellation."

"Canis Major." That comes from Grant. "But you usually can't see it from here at this time of year."

Talk about a coincidence. Just this afternoon, Odelia was going on about constellations, about trying to connect the dots when you can't see anything but the occasional glimmer of light.

"There's a full moon tonight," Max says. "It keeps going behind the clouds, though."

"Where did you get the binoculars?"

"From Mr. Grant."

She doesn't allow herself to wonder why he might have a pair of binoculars handy.

"Here," he says, leaning over Max from behind and turning him a bit, adjusting his aim at the heavens. "Try looking that way."

"Nope. It isn't there tonight."

"It's always there. Sometimes, we just can't see it because the clouds get in the way." As he speaks, Grant turns to look at Bella over Max's head, raising a questioning brow and giving a slight nod toward the building.

Realizing he's wondering about the kitten, she says, "Hey, I have some great news about Spidey. He's eating."

Lowering the binoculars, Max asks, "Really? What is he eating?"

Grant answers before Bella can. "Probably a cheeseburger."

"Kittens can't eat cheeseburgers!" Max informs him. Then an afterthought: "Can they?"

"No. But I can, and I'll bet you can, too."

"And French fries," Max agrees, and turns to Bella. "Mr. Grant is taking me out to eat after this."

"Is that so?"

Sam used to take Max out for burgers and fries, she finds herself thinking. *That was their thing.*

"I told him that maybe we can swing by a diner later. I hope that's okay?" Grant asks.

No. It isn't okay at all.

She says to Max, "I don't think you can bite into a burger without knocking your tooth out and swallowing it."

"That's okay. The tooth fairy will come anyway."

"I thought you said—or was it Jiffy?—that was against the rules."

"Mr. Grant says it isn't. She'll come no matter what."

Jiffy's opinion might overrule Bella's, but clearly Grant's trumps all.

She turns to him. "I doubt anything would be open around here at that hour."

"You'd be surprised."

She sighs inwardly. Lately, she's been nothing *but* surprised at every turn.

Leaving Max and Grant to their celestial search, she heads back inside to learn how to hand-rear a newborn kitten.

Chapter 15

The wind is blowing again, and the wind chimes are chiming too loudly again, and . . .

And the alarm clock is bleating. Again.

Bella fumbles on the bedside table to silence it, wondering why it's so dark.

Slowly, it comes back to her: it isn't morning.

Well, technically, it *is:* four o'clock in the morning.

The last time she got up, it was two o'clock, only she hadn't slept more than ten or fifteen minutes before the alarm went off that time.

That's what happens when you go to bed at midnight with a troubled mind and a belly full of cheeseburger and most of Max's leftover French fries.

He had, indeed, managed to eat a burger without knocking out his loose tooth. And there is, indeed, an all-night diner around here. Grant had driven straight there—on back roads, of course—after they left Doctor Bailey's office. He even managed to convince her that the crateful of felines would be fine in the car for half an hour while they went inside to get a bite to eat.

How could she refuse? Max was beside himself with excitement at being out in a restaurant so late at night, especially when Grant told him to order anything he wanted.

"You, too," he said to Bella. "It's on me."

He wouldn't take no for an answer—about the money or the food. Anyway, she suddenly seemed to have a voracious appetite, as did Max. So she pushed aside her misgivings about her son eating burgers and fries with someone who wasn't Sam. She ordered a meal for herself, too, and she let Grant pay. She felt guilty, but she had no choice.

Lately, she doesn't seem to have a choice about anything, does she?

With a yawn, she gets out of bed quietly so as not to disturb Max and starts to feel her way across the room toward the crate.

Her bare foot slams into the post at the foot of the bed.

"Ouch!" She hops, rubbing her stubbed pinky toe.

Max stirs. "Mommy?"

"It's okay, kiddo. I'm just being clumsy as usual," she whispers. "Go back to sleep."

"What about the kitties?"

"They're fine. Don't worry. I'll take care of them."

And you. And everything.

I've got this.

Beyond the window, the sky has cleared, and the light of a fat full moon spills through the lace curtains, pooling on the floor where Chance lies nursing all but one of her kittens. Little Spidey, as she now affectionately calls him— "for short"—is nestled at his mother's furry side, his faint mews only audible when Bella is standing right over him.

She swiftly assembles the syringe, the tube, the formula, and a soft cloth on Leona's dresser top and measures two milliliters of formula into the syringe the way Doctor Bailey showed her. Then she gingerly extracts the runt from the nest, swaddles him in the cloth, and gently inserts the tube into his mouth. The veterinarian was right. He's learning to swallow it without as much of a struggle now, knowing that it will result in a comfortably full belly for a while.

For the third time since they left the animal hospital, she settles wearily into a chair to feed him.

Sitting there in the moonlight dutifully tending to a swaddled, famished newborn, she realizes that every part of her—save her throbbing toe—is numb with exhaustion. Tube and syringe aside, it all feels so familiar . . .

Just like the wee-hour feedings when Max was a baby.

Five years ago, he slept in a cradle on her side of the king-sized bed in a room very much like this one. She nursed him in a chair by the window.

At first, in a valiant show of parental solidarity, Sam insisted on getting up with her for every feeding. He would hover, perched on the arm of the chair, watching Max eat, making conversation when she would have preferred the quiet.

"I'm afraid that if I don't talk to you, you'll fall asleep," he'd say.

"Believe me, I won't."

"But I might." She can hear his laugh, hear him offering to burp the baby and singing silly songs to Max as he changed his diaper afterward.

Eventually, the novelty wore off, and Bella told him not to bother getting up. He had an early commuter train to catch, and anyway, she didn't mind when it was just her and Max. Just mother and son with the world all to themselves in those hushed hours.

Yawning deeply, lost in drowsy twilight, she can hear Sam's voice calling from the bed, "Are you two okay over there, Bella Blue?"

"We're okay," she whispers, and for a moment, before reality dawns, she expects a reply.

Why do memories of Sam seem to pop up more constantly here than they even did back home?

Not at first, of course. The first few months after she lost him, there was a constant ache. But as time went on, before she left Bedford, there were occasions when she almost forgot. There would be moments when she'd be going about her daily business—at work, at the grocery store, even, sometimes, at home—and she would feel like her old self again.

Here in Lily Dale, though . . .

It's like he's everywhere.

Maybe these people are rubbing off on her, with their philosophy that the dead are hanging around among, and interacting with, the living.

All the more reason to get out of here as soon as she can.

Chance's eyes glitter in the dark, keeping a protective watch over her kitten on Bella's lap.

"It's going to be okay," she whispers—one mom to another. "I promise. I'll figure it out."

It was too late when they returned to the Dale to talk to Odelia about taking on the cat and kittens, plus this special-needs one. And she didn't want to bring it up to Grant in front of Max.

The two of them seemed to have bonded over the binoculars while Bella was otherwise occupied in the hospital room. Over their late-night meal at the diner, Grant regaled her son with tales of his exotic travels. He'd dined with sultans, hunted big game, climbed the highest mountains, sailed the seven seas, and seen all seven wonders of the world—and then some.

At least, that's what he'd claimed. Maybe he was embellishing for Max's sake, or maybe every word of his story is true. Maybe he really is a venture capitalist with a penchant for adventure and a soft spot for kids, kittens, and his foster mother.

If not, well then at least she's no longer convinced, or even speculating, that he's a murderous pirate in a hoodie. She's too rational—or maybe just too busy, not to mention crippled by mind-numbing fatigue—to entertain outlandish notions.

She settles the sated Spidey back into the crook of his mother's arm and sets aside the feeding equipment on the dresser beside the stack of papers she'd found scattered on the floor this afternoon—make that yesterday afternoon. She never did have a chance to ask Max about them. Too much has gone on.

I'll ask him tomorrow—I mean today, she thinks as she climbs back into bed and resets the alarm for six o'clock.

Just as her eyes drift closed, she hears stealthy footsteps moving along the hall and then down the stairs.

One of the guests, no doubt. Maybe Steve Pierson, the early riser. For a moment, she wonders if she should go brew the coffee. Or at least investigate.

But she can't seem to muster the energy to open her eyes, much less lift her head from the pillow and her body from the bed.

It isn't long before sleep overtakes her, again bringing the wind chimes' foreboding knell and Leona's haunted face staring back at her in the bathroom mirror.

* * *

Too soon, Bella is once again startled awake. But this time, it isn't the alarm that jars her from the familiar dream.

It's a shrill, distant little scream in the night.

She sits up in bed, heart pounding.

Beside her in the dark, Max is snoring softly.

The cry must have come from the box of kittens. She must have slept through Spidey's next feeding.

No—according to the bedside clock, she's only been asleep for ten or fifteen minutes.

Straining her ears, she can hear muffled feline mews, but the sound that woke her was different.

She must have been dreaming.

Yes, that's right. She was. As she settles back against the pillow, it comes back to her—the recurring dream about Leona in the bathroom on the windy night right before she drowned in the lake.

She never gets to that point in the dream. It always cuts off right there in the bathroom, with the eerie wind chimes becoming louder and increasingly discordant. Somehow, she senses what's coming.

She—as in Leona.

Why does Bella morph into Leona in her dream? Why does she see things through the eyes of a woman she never met and feel whatever Leona was feeling that night?

She was so uneasy. Frightened, even.

Something must have lured her out into the storm to the water—or someone dragged her or carried her. She never would have ventured out on her own.

You don't know that, though. It was just a dream. You can't really think—

The thought is curtailed by a dull thud from somewhere below.

This time, it wasn't a dream.

For a long time, Bella listens for something more.

She hears nothing at all.

Logic tells her that it was just one of the guests moving around downstairs. A deep yawn overtakes her. And then another.

She rolls over, deciding she'd better get some sleep while she still can.

* * *

Beyond the lace curtains, the sun is coming up at last. Bella can hear birds chirping beyond the screen as she pulls a T-shirt over her head.

After forcing herself out of bed for baby Spidey's six o'clock feeding, she'd taken a quick, bracingly cold shower in an effort to revive herself and perhaps appear somewhat presentable.

It hasn't quite done the trick on either count.

Maybe some coffee will help.

Coffee and a hairbrush.

Looking into the bureau mirror, brushing the tangles out of her damp hair, she again remembers her dream.

But just like yesterday, the morning light brings reassurance. It seems silly to have lost even a moment's sleep fretting about something so insubstantial.

A dream is just a dream. It isn't evidence of foul play—regardless of what the medium next door might have to say about that.

Not even if the medium next door had precisely the same dream?

Choosing to ignore that, she reminds herself that there's no legitimate reason to conclude that Leona's demise was anything more than an accident.

You have more than enough real problems to waste any more time worrying about imaginary ones.

She sets aside the brush and finds the sheaf of papers she'd picked up from the floor. It's yet another violation of Leona's privacy, but curiosity gets the best of her. Especially when she comprehends that she's looking at a real estate contract.

Shuffling the pages into order, she sees that Leona sold a Wyoming dude ranch—also called Valley View Manor—to an upscale hotel chain. The contract is dated several years ago, and it lists an astronomical sum of money.

Which means that if Leona Gatto hung onto that money, she may have been worth far more than either Luther and Odelia seemed to realize—at least, according to yesterday's conversation. Either Leona chose not to tell them, or they chose not to mention it to each other—or to Bella.

Again, paranoia mingles with suspicion, and her mind flies through the possibilities.

Another if—big if, *huge* if: if Leona was murdered, could money have been the motive?

That would make Grant one of the most logical suspects. As Leona's trusted confidante and only heir, surely he had some inkling that her financial situation was hardly in keeping with her humble lifestyle.

But Pandora and her ex-husband Orville may also have been aware. According to another real estate contract in the stacked papers, Leona had purchased this place from Orville Holmes a few years after she'd sold her Wyoming property. Of course, Valley View Manor Guesthouse had cost her a mere fraction of what she'd made on Valley View Manor Ranch. But she'd paid in cash. That very well might have sent the message *There's more where that came from.*

What about Odelia, Leona's trusted friend? Had she really hurt her leg because she was clumsy? Or could she have hurt it in some kind of struggle . . . perhaps with Leona?

Is that any more implausible than anything else that's happened here?

Quickly looking through the rest of the documents she'd gathered from the floor, Bella sees that they mainly consist of financial paperwork: bank statements, investment accounts, legal contracts—that sort of thing. She can't go over it now—and maybe she should leave that to Luther. But it's too early to call him, and anyway, it's time to get moving.

She takes one last look in the mirror. With straggly hair and an outfit more suited to housework than playing hostess, she's not likely to set any hearts afire this morning. Not even Karl Adabner's.

Oh, well. At least I'm on my feet, she thinks, and shoves them into her sandals.

Oops—not hers at all. She takes one step in them, trips, and nearly falls.

Why do I keep trying to walk around in your shoes? she asks Leona silently. She could have sworn she'd put them away yesterday after this happened. She swaps out the sandals for her own pair. But the strap rubs so painfully against her pinky that she takes them right off again, remembering that she stubbed her toe on the bedpost in the middle of the night.

She's definitely overtired. Maybe deliriously so.

But it's worthwhile.

She looks down at the crate on the floor. Ever noble, Queen Chance reclines regally on the nest of towels. Most of her furry subjects are nursing, a couple of others are squirming around making pipsqueak sounds, and Spidey is snoozing contentedly beneath his mama's arm. Chance bestows a dignified stare upon Bella.

"That was a long night for both of us, wasn't it?" Bella whispers, reaching down to pet the *M* on her head. "But we made it through. Everything's going to be all right. I promise. I won't let you down. Any of you. I'll figure this out."

The promise is rewarded with a slow blink from those green eyes, leaving Bella feeling vaguely like Doctor Doolittle.

She turns toward the closet. Her suitcase sits within its shadows atop the tapestry straps of a folding wooden rack. Unwilling to wake Max by turning on the overhead light, she fumbles inside, feeling around for sneakers and a pair of socks.

She finds one sneaker, finds the socks, drops one as she looks for the other sneaker, and manages to drop the other as she crawls on the floor to feel around for the first one. As she blindly manages to retrieve both socks and shoves them into the back pocket of her shorts, she decides that unlike Grant, she doesn't enjoy living out of a suitcase.

Yet the thought of unpacking doesn't sit well, either. Is it because she doesn't want to bother, since she's only going to be here for a few days? Or because she wants to be able to make a quick getaway when it's time? Or because she's afraid she might be tempted to stay?

Where the heck is her other sneaker?

As frustrated with the search as with the flurry of questions in her mind, she gives up and puts on the sandals again—this time, the right ones. She'll have to suffer with the sore toe for now.

Just as she did yesterday morning, she leaves the key in the inside lock for Max, using the one on her key ring to lock the outside. The hallway is deserted, every door still closed.

Morning sunlight falls through the stairway's circular stained-glass windowpane, casting a fluid prism across the hardwood landing. The kitchen, too, is flooded with light, with a view of the sparkling, brilliant blue lake.

Yes, everything seems brighter today. Somehow, it's all going to be okay.

She hears the front door open and then close. Footsteps head into the breakfast room.

"Coffee's coming," she calls to whoever it is as she hastily scoops coffee grounds into a paper filter.

"It's okay." Grant appears in the doorway, fully dressed in jeans and a polo shirt, holding a newspaper and a paper hot cup. "Already got my caffeine fix, though this is gas station coffee, so I'll swap it for yours if it's on the way."

"It is. Sorry you had to go out for it."

"I was going out for the paper anyway. Do you know how far you have to drive around here to get a copy of the *Wall Street Journal?*"

"Can't you just access it online?"

"I like paper," he says with a shrug as she presses the button to start the brew cycle. "I'm an old-fashioned guy. And Internet access isn't always reliable around here. I learned that the hard way the first time I visited Leona here, when I couldn't check in for my flight and lost my seat. I was stuck here an extra day."

"Stuck, and out of luck, huh?"

"I thought so at the time. Now I'm grateful for every day I got to spend with Leona."

Seeing the genuine sorrow in his eyes, she wonders how she could have thought he was an imposter. Thank goodness she hadn't confronted him last night—or worse yet, tried to escape his clutches on the way to the animal hospital. Imagine if she had grabbed Max and the box of kitties and jumped out of the car at high speed?

Come on, you wouldn't have actually done it. You just wished you could, in a moment of panic.

What a difference a day—or rather, just daylight—makes.

She turns on the flame beneath the teakettle and wonders how to segue into asking him to take over with the kittens.

"So," she says casually, pouring half-and-half into a pitcher, "how long are you planning to stay here?"

"Only through the weekend. I have an important meeting next week in New York."

"Is that where you live?"

"I keep an apartment there."

Last night, he'd also mentioned a flat in London and a beach house in Southern California. Which of the three, she wonders, does he call home? Or are there other places as well?

"I thought you were here to settle Leona's affairs," she tells him, wanting to point out that those affairs now include a houseful of people—and felines.

"It's going to be a long, drawn-out process. I can't even meet with an attorney this trip because of the holiday weekend. I'll have to do a lot of back and forth. But that's fine with me, because I'm used to living out of a suitcase."

She nods, rummaging through the cupboard for a platter so that she won't have to make eye contact as she tells him, "I'm leaving on Monday, too."

"What? Monday? Why?"

"I think I mentioned that I'm just helping out for a few days because Odelia asked me to. I was never planning to stay." *Or even be here in the first place.*

She finds a platter, sets it on the counter, and reaches for yesterday's leftover pastries.

"Where are you going?" he asks as she starts setting muffins on the plate.

"Chicago."

"And you'll be back . . . ?"

She knows he's asking for a day or date.

But her answer is simply, "No."

She won't be back. Ever.

The guesthouse isn't her responsibility. It's his.

Still, the prospect of turning her back on this place is almost as hard to swallow as the thought of sticking around.

"That's too bad," Grant tells her, tucking the folded newspaper under his arm and depositing the paper cup into the garbage. Clearly, he changed his mind about waiting around for more coffee, telling her he'll be back down later.

Left alone in the kitchen, she assembles the tray of day-old pastries. They're still perfectly edible, but she'll have to get to the store again later—courtesy of Odelia's car and not Grant's, she promises herself.

Startled by a loud knocking at the back door, she turns to see Steve Pierson gesturing for her to open it.

She hurries toward him. He's holding his key in his hand, but it's trembling violently.

"I'm sorry," he says, panting, as she lets him in. He's wearing running clothes and sneakers, his face flushed and damp with sweat. "When I saw you, I had to—I just . . ."

"Are you okay?"

He shakes his head no, pressing a fist against his chest. Is he having a heart attack?

"Here, sit down." She hurriedly pulls out a chair at the table.

"Thanks," he manages to say, his breath still coming too fast and hard.

Noting the terrified look in his eyes, she grasps that something is terribly wrong. Something far more serious than overexertion. "Can you speak? Is it your heart?"

Again, he shakes his head.

She fills a glass with water and hands it to him. He sips and then wipes his damp forehead on one shoulder and then the other. Seeing a faint streak of pink on his red T-shirt, she realizes his face is bleeding.

"You have a couple of scratches on your forehead," she tells him, looking closer. "And on your chin, too. What happened? Did you fall?"

"No. Well . . . no."

What on earth is going on? Her mind flies through the possibilities.

"Where's Eleanor?" she asks, wondering if the couple might have gotten into some kind of . . . scuffle?

"She's . . . still sleeping, I think. I left her in bed."

"I'll go get her."

"Wait!"

She turns back.

"I don't want to . . . she'll get upset if she sees me like this." He takes a deep breath, exhales shakily. "Let me calm down first. I need a few minutes."

"But what happened?"

"I think . . ." He shakes his head. "I think someone just tried to kill me."

* * *

In the half hour it takes for Luther Ragland to reach the guesthouse after Bella's phone call, Steve Pierson has finally managed to regain his composure.

Bella, however, is just barely hanging onto hers.

Gone is her perception that everything is going to be all right. That newfound optimism vanished the moment Steve Pierson staggered into the kitchen, bleeding.

Only from superficial scratches, but still . . .

Someone tried to kill him.

Someone might have killed Leona.

Someone . . . someone . . .
Who?

Her initial—and dutiful—suggestion was that Steve call the police.

"Not just yet," he said. "I keep thinking I might have been wrong about what happened . . . but I don't think so. I just need to pull myself together so that I can think things through."

She'd persuaded Steve to allow her to summon Luther instead, explaining that he's a retired detective friend who stops to check on things now that Leona is gone.

It's a stretch but not an outright lie.

She'd called him from upstairs, having gone up to retrieve his business card. With Steve well out of earshot—and Max still snoring in the bed—she hurriedly explained the situation.

"I'm on my way," he said immediately.

Waiting for him, Bella paces the kitchen, trying to stay busy. She cuts up fruit and sets out utensils, cups, and plates for breakfast. Then she sets out even more utensils, cups, and plates—tall stacks of plates and too many cups nested in crazily tilting towers. One of them slips out of her hand, still tender from yesterday's burn, and breaks on the floor.

She finds a broom and dustpan. Sweeping up the shards, she remembers the vase she broke in her kitchen back in Bedford on the last day. The day she found a pregnant mackerel tabby with a red collar just sitting on her back step.

There are no coincidences.

Darn Odelia. Odelia and her . . . her hidden meanings.

There's a reason for everything.

Bella cuts her finger on a razor sharp triangle of broken pottery. "Ouch."

"Are you okay?" Still brooding at the table, Steve looks up in concern.

"Yes."

No.

Now they're both bleeding.

There are no coincidences.

The wound drips bright-red splotches into the white porcelain sink. She turns on the tap, running water over her finger, watching it dilute the blood. It fleetingly transforms into that brilliant beautiful color she's always loved, halfway between red and pink, like the wallpaper in the Rose Room, like . . .

Sushi sky.

The blood fades to pink and then translucent, swirled down the drain.

It lasts only a few seconds before it disappears.

Sam's voice.

Oh, Sam. What am I doing here?

She turns off the water, wraps her finger in a paper towel, and squeezes it tightly.

Everything happens for a reason.

Sam's voice? Or Odelia's?

Behind her, Steve is deep in thought, barely sipping the coffee she poured for him.

He said someone tried to kill him.

No coincidences.

There's a blast of sound, and Bella lets out a little scream as if someone has jumped out at her.

Oh.

The doorbell.

"That's Luther," she tells Steve, and hurries to the hall.

There he is, standing on the front porch. Sturdy, grounded, a welcome flash of *everything's going to be okay* . . .

Except that maybe it isn't.

"I had a court reserved for seven thirty." Luther gestures down at the tennis whites he's wearing. "You caught me on my way out the door."

"I'm sorry."

"Don't be. You did the right thing, calling me. Where's Mister . . . Pierson, is it?"

"Yes. Stephen Pierson. He's in the kitchen."

Stepping over the threshold, he asks in a low voice, "You didn't mention Leona?"

"No."

"Is anyone else around?"

"Not yet. It's still pretty early." She looks toward the stairway. It's empty, and all is silent above. Pretty soon, though, they'll be stirring.

She'd asked Steve if he wanted to go wake Eleanor or if he wanted her to do it. He did not.

"She'll just get nervous," he said.

Yeah. That happens. Most women get nervous when someone tries to kill their husband.

She leads Luther to the kitchen. Seeing him, Steve looks wobbly as he rises from his chair.

"You don't have to get up," Luther says, but Steve obviously isn't the kind of man who fails to stand and shake hands upon being introduced. Nor, she guesses, is Luther the kind of man who wouldn't expect him to, no matter what he says.

They're gentlemen, both of them. But one is in pristine tennis whites and quite used to this kind of thing, while the other is jittery, streaked with blood and sweat, and utterly out of his element.

After shaking Luther's hand, Steve sinks into the chair again.

Bella refills his cup with coffee, pours one for Luther, and finally refills her own.

"What happened to your hand?" Luther asks Bella, seeing the cone of paper towel, now stained with blood. "And your leg?" he adds, looking down and then up at her face in concern.

"Nothing," she says, suddenly conscious of the ache in her stubbed pinky toe. "I mean, I'm just . . . accident prone."

As soon as the words leave her mouth, she regrets the phrasing. Her own accidents really *are* accidents, thank goodness.

"Should I go into the other room?" she asks Luther.

"No, you should stay."

She's not sure whether she was afraid he'd say that or afraid that he wouldn't.

She doesn't have the energy for this right now. But she sits at the table with them and watches Luther take out a notebook and pen, in detective mode again.

"Okay. Tell me exactly what happened."

"I'm not sure, exactly." Steve hesitates, both hands cupped around his coffee as if to warm or steady them. "It doesn't make any sense at all. I keep going over it in my mind, and now . . . I don't know what to think."

"Okay. Just give me the details. Don't worry about why it might have happened or question whether it *did* happen. Just tell me what you remember."

Steve explains that he was out running along the shoulder of Bachellor Hill Road, on his way back from circling Bear Lake, which lies a few miles west of here. He describes how a car came up behind him, much too close to him, and he managed to jump out of the way just before he was sideswiped.

"Maybe the driver didn't see you?"

"That's what I figured. The sun hadn't been up for long, and it was in my eyes, so it must have been in his, too."

"So it was a man driving?"

"I couldn't tell."

Luther makes a note. "Did you get a description of the car? Make, model, color, plate?"

"No."

"But it was a car? Not an SUV or a truck, something like that?"

"No." Pause. "I'm not sure. It happened so fast."

"And you couldn't see the driver at all?"

"Not at all. Like I said, the sun was glaring."

"And what time was this?"

Steve guesses it must have been around six thirty. He'd left the house, he says, just after five.

Bella remembers the footsteps she'd heard in the hall before she stubbed her toe . . . or was it after?

Everything is muddled in her sleep-deprived brain.

But there were footsteps, definitely. She'd thought she'd heard a cry, too, and then a thud.

What time would that have occurred?

Her night had been neatly segmented into time slots for Spidey's feedings, but it's all fuzzy now.

Was it at two?

No.

Four, probably. After the four o'clock feeding. She remembers thinking the footsteps belonged to one of the guests and not caring that she wasn't downstairs to put on the coffee at that hour.

"What time did you get up?" she asks Steve Pierson.

"About a quarter to five. Maybe closer to ten of."

She'd put the kitten back and returned to bed long before that. She'd heard the footsteps earlier. And the cry, the thud . . .

If she'd heard those things at all. Maybe she'd been dreaming. Her dreams here have been so vivid. Leona in the mirror, the wind chimes . . .

Her eyes are burning. She closes them and rubs them.

Is it all in my head? Is this place getting to me? Is the exhaustion getting to me?

"After the car drove away, I started running again," Steve tells Luther. "But the next thing I knew . . . it was back. It was coming straight at me from the opposite direction. And then it swerved. It crossed over the line."

Just as Grant did last night when he was driving Bella and Max to the vet with the cat and kittens. Grant swerved around the potholes. He crossed over the line.

"So the car swerved to miss you? Is that what you mean?"

"No," Steve says flatly. "It swerved to *hit* me. I dove off the road into the bushes. I guess that's how I got scratched up."

"Let me get this straight." Luther puts down the pen and rests his chin on his fist. "A car passed you from behind, missed you, turned around immediately, came back, and aimed right at you?"

"Yes."

Luther's eyes briefly connect with Bella's. Clearly, he doesn't like this.

Yeah, well . . . join the club.

"Is there anyone you can think of who might have reason to harm you?" he asks Steve.

"You mean besides the president of the teacher's union back home?" Steve's staccato laugh is met by Luther's questioning brow.

"Look, Detective, I'm a school superintendent. There's a lot of strife between the union, the administration, and the board. I've made a few enemies, I'm sure."

"Has anyone ever threatened you?"

"Plenty of people have threatened to have me fired."

"How recently?"

"Recently. In fact, just last week."

"Why?"

"Because I'm not bowing to pressure from people who don't believe in diverting funding from other areas of the budget for our drama program. I've been involved in plenty of theatrical productions over the years, so yes, I'm a strong advocate for arts education. Stronger than most, maybe. But trust me—no one has ever tried to run me over because of that, and even if they wanted to, I can't imagine how they'd find me here."

"In Lily Dale?"

Steve nods.

Luther picks up his pen again. "So you didn't mention to anyone back home where you were headed on vacation?"

"Are you kidding?" He shakes his head. "No way. I told them I was going to Niagara Falls—which we did do, on the way here."

"Why *are* you here?"

"Because my wife insists. This is her thing. She used to come with her sister every summer, but then Mamie moved out west to be near her kids, so Eleanor talked me into coming with her. She doesn't like to travel alone."

"And you told people—your friends? your colleagues?— that you're on vacation in Niagara Falls? Why?"

"Why do you think? I'm in a position of authority, and I work with kids. The parents, the teachers—these days, everyone's a critic as it is. Do you think I want to jeopardize my job by having them buzzing about how Doctor Pierson hangs out with a bunch of Spiritualists?"

"In other words, you don't want to jeopardize your job."

"In this climate? Does anyone?"

Bella can answer that question: *definitely not.* Having been a victim of school budget cuts herself, she understands

Steve's point. Like most administrators, his head must perpetually be on the chopping block.

Steve steeples his fingers beneath his scraped-up chin. "I'm close to retirement with a nice pension and full health insurance coverage for me and Eleanor for the rest of our lives. There are plenty of taxpayers in the district who are looking for any possible way to trim the budget. Believe me, they'd jump at any opportunity to get rid of me and wriggle out of my benefits package."

"By 'get rid of,' you mean . . ."

"I mean fire me," he says with a jittery laugh. "Not . . . *kill* me."

"Are you sure about that?"

"I . . . I *thought* I was sure, but . . ." He breaks off and looks up at the ceiling as a floorboard creaks overhead.

Bella follows his gaze and then turns to glance at the stove clock. It's nearly a quarter to eight.

Time for the guests to start trickling down to breakfast. Almost time to feed Spidey again, too.

"Why don't we finish this conversation in the study?" Luther suggests.

"Study?" Steve echoes blankly, still looking shell-shocked at the notion that someone might be out to get him.

"Leona's . . . office. Whatever you want to call it."

The room that was locked when it shouldn't have been. The room with the missing key.

"We can talk privately in there," Luther tells Steve. "I just don't want to alarm anyone who's staying here. We don't want them to think there's any danger."

Unnerved, Bella gets to her feet, as do Steve and Luther. She pulls the key ring from her pocket as they head toward the study.

"I'll unlock the door for you. Then I have a few things to take care of . . . unless you need me?"

"No, it's fine," Luther tells her. "Go ahead. I'll connect with you afterward."

She nods. She has to tell him about Leona's financial situation. And about Grant.

Not that there's anything specific to tell, other than the fact that he's arrived. And that she's found herself suspicious of him one moment and convinced he's a great guy the next.

A great guy?

Hardly.

Sam was a great guy. No one else could ever compare.

Certainly not Grant. And not Doctor Bailey. Not Troy Valeri.

As she turns the key and opens the French door, she recalls that Troy mentioned he'd known Leona. He'd recently done some painting for her.

Odelia had mentioned Leona's springtime study makeover. Was it Troy who had given the walls their fresh coat of yellow paint?

For some reason, she's bothered by the notion of him hanging around this house—around this *room*.

This was Leona's sanctuary.

Yet Bella herself trespassed here just the other day. Who else did?

Has Luther had a chance to look over the appointment book? When he does, he'll notice the missing page. He'll ask her about it.

Or will he?

Not if he thinks I'm the one who tore it out.

Who knows? He might already have seen it, might already consider me a suspect. He wouldn't let on. He'd act as if nothing is wrong.

"Thanks, Bella," he says with a nod as she stands aside to let him cross the threshold, followed by Steve.

Yes, he'll act just like this.

Standing in the doorway, she finds herself staring at the empty spot on the table where she'd found the appointment book on her first night here. Hoping Luther didn't notice her gaze, she guiltily shifts it to the freshly painted walls.

That makes her wonder again about Troy, which leaves her feeling even more unsettled.

Then she notices the pillows.

There are three of them along the back of the window seat. Just yesterday, when she was in here with Luther and Odelia, they were perfectly aligned. She clearly remembers noticing that Luther, with his soldier-straight posture, didn't allow his back to touch them.

Now the pillows are askew, clustered on one end of the seat as though they were hastily tossed there.

But they couldn't have been. Not if they were straight before. Not if she hasn't returned to the room or let her key out of her possession ever since she locked the door yesterday after Luther looked around and grabbed the appointment book.

She hasn't. Of course she hasn't.

It's a classic locked-room mystery—and she alone has the key.

Except that I don't.

Someone else got into this room within the last twenty-four hours. Either that person has the missing key . . .

Or Chance the Cat isn't the only one around here who can walk through walls.

* * *

Looking for something out of the ordinary, Bella keeps a close eye on the other guests as they make their way to the sunlit breakfast room.

Everyone is eagerly anticipating this afternoon's guest speaker, a renowned medium who may not be a household name everywhere but certainly is in the Dale.

The doddering St. Clair sisters repeat themselves, squabble, and doze off between sentences. Fritz Dunkle reads his newspaper and occasionally expounds on some obscure topic. The Adabners chat animatedly about their upcoming aura identification seminar like it's an AARP bus to the casino. Kelly Tookler peppers the conversation with, "Right, Jim?" and Jim dutifully salts it with, "Right."

Meanwhile, Bella goes about her own business—brewing coffee, wiping crumbs, replenishing the pastry platter—as though nothing unusual happened. In some moments, she almost manages to convince herself that nothing has. Maybe Steve's near miss wasn't significant—or particularly threatening—to anyone but Steve himself.

But then either logic or sheer exhaustion grips her again, and she finds herself looking for signs that someone is hiding something. She shifts her gaze to the windows as if expecting to see an evil predator lurking in the mock orange shrubs with the crosshairs set on her.

Finally, she hears the study door open and footsteps cross the parlor, heading toward the front hall. She peeks in just in time to see Steve head up the stairs.

Luther is in the doorway. He waves her in.

"Close the door," he commands in a low voice. "We don't want anyone to panic and flee."

Panic and *flee* are some strong words. The latter is exactly what Bella herself longs to do. Just grab Max and get the hell out of here.

Max—plus Queen Chance the Cat and eight kittens?

"Maybe everyone *should* leave," she tells Luther as she closes the door. "Maybe it's not safe here."

He sits in one of the wingback chairs and gestures for her to take the other. The pillows are still heaped on the window seat, and she has to make an effort not to stare at them as he speaks.

"Nothing has happened inside of the house, Bella. Mr. Pierson wasn't even in the Dale. And what happened to him could very well have been an accident."

"What about Leona?"

"Accidents do happen." He gestures at her bandaged hand and battered leg.

He's right, of course. She shouldn't let her imagination carry her away.

Yet she has to ask, "Don't you think there's a chance that neither of those things were accidents? And that one might have something to do with the other?"

"It's a possibility. But if that's the case, then every single person under this roof is a potential suspect."

Including Bella herself. Yes, she gets that, loud and clear.

"If we let them scatter, we risk letting someone dangerous slip away," Luther goes on. "I think that the best thing to do right now is go on with business as usual."

Easy for him to say.

"I have a five-year-old child living under this roof, Detective Ragland."

"Call me Luther. I haven't forgotten that for a second, believe me . . . can I call you Bella?"

He might as well. The nickname is no longer reserved for Sam alone. Here in the Dale, for better or worse, she seems to have become Bella.

"I'm not asking you to stay indefinitely," Luther tells her. "Or even overnight. I just need a chance to look into a few things, and I'd rather you didn't mention Steve's incident to anyone else just yet. You haven't, have you?"

"No, but he just went upstairs. I'm sure he's told his wife what happened, and by now, maybe some of the others, too. And if he hasn't, Eleanor probably will."

"Don't be so sure. He doesn't want any of this getting out. They both want to protect his job and his retirement benefits. I'm guessing he's not going to tell anyone anything unless they ask. I hope you won't, either."

She hesitates before responding. "I won't. But—"

"I honestly don't think there's any immediate danger."

"So you don't think it's time to call the police?" she asks, even though she's pretty certain that there's no way to involve the authorities in Steve's brush with danger without potentially opening the door to an official investigation into Leona's death.

"Steve's not ready to do it at this point," Luther says. "He wants me to ask around, find out if maybe someone saw a speeding car this morning around Bear Lake."

"And you don't think we should report it?"

"We don't have any solid evidence that a crime occurred this morning."

"Just like with Leona's death."

"Exactly." Luther's comment is punctuated by his ringing cell phone.

"Sorry," he says, taking it out of his pocket and glancing at it. "I have to take this call."

He steps out of the room with the phone, leaving her alone to eye the bench beneath the window.

Does it, like the one in the living room, have a storage compartment beneath? Is that why the pillows were moved? Did someone open it, looking for something?

Maybe she should open it now.

But if Luther catches her, he might think she's hiding something.

So? I'm not.

But if she gives him even the slightest reason to think she's guilty, he might go to the police after all, behind her back. They'll come to question her. They might take her away for questioning, and that would mean leaving Max with . . .

Someone else.

I can't afford to trust anyone, Bella realizes. *Not right now. Not even Luther.*

He reappears in the doorway, looking harried.

"I have to get to the hospital. My mom isn't doing very well this morning."

"I'm sorry."

"So am I. I don't like to leave this way, but I've got to run. I'll be in touch as soon as I can. Think you can hang tight for now?"

She assures him that she can.

If "hang tight" means fighting off panic while continuing through the motions of an anything-but-ordinary day, then she's got it covered.

After seeing Luther to the door, she returns to the study. This time, she locks it behind her from the inside. Going over to the window seat, she tosses the pillows onto the floor and lifts the cushion, feeling around along the edges of the bench.

Sure enough, there's a concealed hinge and latch. The bench doubles as the lid of a storage area.

Tugging it open, Bella sees that it, like the other window seat compartment, is home to a mishmash of household clutter.

She sorts through it, looking for a torn-out page from the appointment book or the missing notebook or laptop.

They aren't here.

Either they never were or someone else got to them first.

Chapter 16

Just before ten o'clock, Bella trudges wearily up the stairs to feed Spidey again, wishing she were on her way back to bed instead.

This day has been plenty long enough, and it's still merely midmorning. How on earth is she going to stay upright for another twelve hours or so?

Even when she finally does finally get to climb under the covers tonight, she'll still have to set her alarm to wake her every other hour.

Yes, but at least she knows exactly what she has to do to keep the kitten alive.

When it comes to everything—*everyone*—else . . .

All bets are off.

Surely the driver who tried to run over Steve Pierson on Bachellor Hill Road this morning hadn't made a road trip from Massachusetts and wasn't motivated by overinflated school taxes. As disturbing as that scenario might be, it would, in the grand scheme of things, provide Bella some measure of comfort.

But it's simply too farfetched, isn't it? Especially when Steve Pierson's near miss happened so close—in timing and proximity—to Leona's death.

After replacing the window seat cushion, repositioning the pillows, and locking the study door behind her, she busied herself again with breakfast for her guests, who lingered in the breakfast room chatting and eating.

Still conspicuously missing were the Piersons and Grant Everard.

Less conspicuously: Bonnie Barrington.

Bella hadn't given her absence a second thought until Kelly Tookler asked if she'd seen her. "We had plans to go to the sweat lodge together. The ceremony starts at ten."

"Maybe she decided to sleep in instead."

"Bonnie never sleeps in. She hardly sleeps at all. She has insomnia. I knocked on her door. She wasn't in there."

Maybe she's hiding, Bella thought grumpily. *Maybe she just didn't feel like sweating or . . . or lodging. Or hearing, "Right, Bonnie?" all day long.*

Kelly was concerned, but Bella has too many other things on her mind to worry about whether one of the guests is going to be late for some bizarre ceremony.

Sweat lodge ceremonies, aura identification workshops . . .

Business as usual in a place where weird things happen all day—and all night.

Bella can pretend she's immune to the weirdness, and she can try to resist or ignore it.

But there's no denying that she herself has witnessed—and okay, experienced—some things she can't quite explain.

She first dreamed about Leona brushing her hair before she even knew what Leona looked like—and Odelia seemed to have almost the same dream minus the crazy wind chimes.

Wind chimes—just the other day, she witnessed the ones in the backyard moving, clanging, without the slightest gust of wind.

And almost in that very spot, she saw that hand—she swears it was a hand—in the lake.

And what about the identical pregnant cats four hundred miles apart and the nonexistent billboard for the nonexistent Summer Pines Campground?

And what about Max? What about his uncanny knowledge of Chance's full name and the fact that she'd have seven—or eight—kittens on the exact day?

It—all of it, every strange thing that's happened here—can be chalked up to lucky guesses or sheer imagination or coincidence, but . . .

There are no coincidences.

Darn you, Odelia.

The medium next door is getting to her.

At the top of the stairs, she notices that Grant's door is still closed. Is he in there, sound asleep? Is he awake? Is he there at all?

Was he walking down the hall at four thirty in the morning?

Was he speeding down Bachellor Hill Road two hours later?

But what could he possibly have against Steve Pierson?

What would Grant stand to gain from harming him?

The questions pelt like buckshot in her gut. Reeling, she unlocks the door to the Rose Room.

Stepping inside, she braces herself to find that something is off here, too.

But as she casts a wary eye around the room, her topsy-turvy world gradually rights itself again.

There's Max, snug and safe, asleep in the big bed. There's Chance, placidly licking one of her kittens—not Spidey—as the others suckle, wriggle, cry, and nap at her side.

The room is sun drenched and serene. A gentle breeze billows the lace curtains. Summer sounds seep through the screen: kids' voices calling out to each other, the hum of a

Jet Ski on the lake, cars passing on the road with the windows rolled down and music playing.

If only this—the sheer ordinariness of a warm July morning—could be Bella's real life.

If only this place were some other place, some mundane small town where people don't die under mysterious circumstances—and once they're dead, they stay dead. A place where the living talk only among themselves.

Then Max and I would be able to make our fresh start here.

The sudden longing doesn't make any more sense than anything else that's happened today. A minute or two ago, she wanted nothing more than to flee Lily Dale.

Now more than anything in the entire world, she wants to stay here?

It's only because she's not ready for more good-byes. Not even to people she's just met and a place she's just discovered.

She's tired of making difficult decisions and even more tired of having them made for her.

She pushes away the troubling thoughts and rubs the ache between her shoulder blades.

Surely once she's caught up on sleep and capable of rational thinking, she'll find herself looking forward to moving on again. And if not . . .

One thing at a time. First, feed the kitten. Then wake the kid. Then . . .

Catch the killer?

Sure. Something like that.

She wearily plucks Spidey from the litter and looks down at his precious little face.

Why, she wonders, did she, of all people, wind up with this little guy who needs so much more than she can possibly give? Why wasn't he born to some other stray cat? Why here? Why now?

Everything happens for a reason.

In Bella's lifetime—in the whole history of the world, for that matter—Odelia isn't the first person who ever said those words. But they keep coming back to her. She keeps looking for meaning in the smallest things.

"Why did Chance find her way to me? And why did you find your way to her?" she asks the little cat as she settles into the chair with him on her lap. "Is it because it's so much harder for me to walk away from someone who needs me so much?"

He only mews in response to her questions, as starved for nourishment as she is for some answers.

She swaddles him the way Doctor Bailey showed her, making him feel safe, and the kitten ingests the formula drop by drop, courageously determined to eat, to survive.

"Good job," she whispers, running a fingertip along his fragile little spine, stroking the downy black fur between his folded ears.

"Mom?"

Max has awakened at last.

"Good morning." She forces a jaunty note into her voice, but Max isn't fooled for a second.

"Why are you sad?" he asks.

"Sad? What makes you think I'm sad?"

"I just know."

Here we go again.

"Do you want me to cheer you up?"

"I'm fine, Max. Really. How'd you sleep?"

"I had a bad dream."

Her hand goes still on the kitten's toothpick of a spine. "What was it about?"

"I don't want to talk about it."

"That's okay."

I don't think I want to hear about it. Not right now.

"How's Chance the Cat? And the kittens? How's Spidey?"

"Everyone is doing great. Growing big and strong."

"Really?" Max gets out of bed and pads over.

His hair, in desperate need of a barber, is sticking straight up, his eyes are rimmed in dark circles, and his pajama top is on inside out. It's all testimony to the long, late night—and perhaps, Bella thinks with a pang, to bad mothering on her part.

"You're a good boy, Spidey," Max croons, gently stroking the kitten's head. "I'm so glad you're our kitty. Don't worry, Mom's going to take good care of you."

Bella swallows a hard lump of regret. She can't bring herself to tell Max that she can barely take good care of *him,* let alone this forlorn little creature.

"Hey," he says. "You cleaned up the mess."

"What do you mean?"

"The papers." He gestures at the stack on the dresser. "The ones that were on the floor."

"Where did you find them, Max?"

"On the floor."

"No, I mean before you dropped them on the floor. Where were they?"

"I didn't drop them on the floor. They were there."

"What do you mean?"

"Yesterday, when I came upstairs to look for Chance the Cat. There were papers all over the floor."

"So you didn't take them out of the closet? Off the shelf?"

"I can't reach that high."

"I thought you climbed on a chair."

"You said never to do that."

That doesn't necessarily mean he wouldn't. But something tells her that he didn't.

Who did?

* * *

"Boys! Slow down!" Bella calls, her stubbed pinky throbbing as she chases after Max and Jiffy, who roll along the bumpy road on a pair of scooters.

No surprise that the sleeker one is in the lead. It's red and belongs to Jiffy. Barefoot, he rides along with carefree abandon—as carefree as he can be, anyway, after grudgingly putting on the helmet Bella made him wear.

That helmet, like the one on Max's head, was found in the garage of the Ardens' rental house. So was the scooter Max is riding. It's a decidedly older model with faded blue paint, but he was thrilled when Jiffy brought it to the door at lunchtime and asked if he wanted to ride it.

"Can I, Mom?"

"Not outside by yourself."

"Don't worry. I'm going with him."

"I mean an adult," she told Jiffy. "I'll come, too."

"Is that okay?" Max asked Jiffy, who shrugged.

"You can't ride a scooter without a helmet," she added.

Jiffy shook his gingery head, his hair as badly in need of a haircut as Max's. "I don't think it's against the law."

"It's against mine. We'll have to pick one up at the store later on."

From the ever-resourceful—or just increasingly impatient—Jiffy: "I think there are some helmets in my garage. Odelia said some kids used to live there a long time ago. So let's go get one."

They did just that—although they got *two* helmets. Jiffy was slightly less accommodating when he discovered that Bella's law applies to him, too. But one of his finest qualities is that he's resilient.

That must come in handy in a place like this, with a life—and a mom—like his. When Bella suggested that Jiffy tell her they were off to ride scooters, he explained that she was behind closed doors with a client.

"I'm not s'posed to disturb her unless I'm bleeding," he said cheerfully.

That comment reminded Bella of the morning's stressful events, but she was determined to put it all aside for a little while. Steve and Eleanor had yet to reemerge from behind their closed bedroom door when she left. Nor, for that matter, had Grant.

She was glad for an excuse to get out of the house with Max. It was starting to feel claustrophobic as the day wore on. She'd gone over to Odelia's earlier, planning to ask to borrow her car to make a quick supermarket trip, but a sign was hanging on the door:

Do Not Disturb. Reading in Session.

It was just as well. She was afraid she might slip and mention what had happened to Steve or that she'd seen Luther this morning. She isn't sure that it's a good idea to tell even Odelia about that—if she doesn't already know.

The cold shower and coffee overload might not have banished her exhaustion, but this fresh air and exercise have done her a world of good.

In an effort to avoid the pedestrians and traffic streaming toward the auditorium for the much-anticipated afternoon speaker, she'd initially guided the boys and their scooters to a playground at the end of Fourth Street. They played for a while on the swings and slide and then hunted for signs of buried treasure in an adjacent field bordered by woodland.

Watching them—kids acting like kids—she almost managed to forget about all the drama back at the house. But now it's time to head back, with only another twenty minutes to go until the next kitten feeding. At least the crowd has thinned considerably along these sun-dappled streets—many of which are little more than narrow pathways between abbreviated rows of cottages.

She catches up with the boys at the corner as they're studying a sign outside a small café. It shows a double-scoop waffle cone emblazoned with the words "Perry's Ice Cream."

"Can we get some, Mom?" Max asks.

"I don't know if I even have money with me."

"Don't worry, I have some." Jiffy fishes in the pocket of his shorts and comes up with a dime and a couple of pennies.

Bella feels around in her own pockets. Along with her cell phone and key ring, she finds evidence of her chaotic morning: Luther's business card, the crumpled bloody paper towel from her cut finger, and the socks she didn't need after all. She also comes up with a couple of dollars and some loose change, which Jiffy, who seems to be a regular at the café, assures her is enough to buy two ice cream cones.

One nice thing about Lily Dale is that he's probably right. After living in one of the costliest areas in the country, Bella is noticing that she'd be able to afford a much nicer lifestyle here than she ever could back in Bedford. *If* she had a job, that is. And *if* she could possibly live here.

One nice thing . . .

There are other nice things, she notices as she stands around beside the parked scooters, holding the two helmets and waiting for the boys to emerge with their ice cream.

Like the weather—today, anyway—and the easy, indoor-outdoor lifestyle. Open windows, screen doors. When it's this warm back in the New York City suburbs, you seal off the house and turn on the air conditioning. Here, nobody seems to bother with it, thanks to a perpetual breeze off the lake.

Okay, maybe not perpetual.

It wasn't blowing the other day in the yard when you heard the wind chimes clanging.

Bathed in golden light, the rows of Victorian cottages that seemed so foreboding in the rainy fog the other night now look like a perky storybook village. Everywhere she looks, there are vivid splashes of color, from the bright exterior paint palettes to the lush foliage and flamboyant blooms that fill garden beds and borders, pots, planters, and window boxes.

Her gaze lands on the red geraniums that fill the scalloped white window boxes of a cozy pink cottage.

Pandora Feeney's place?

As if summoned by the mere thought of her name, the woman emerges from the front door in that very instant. As before, a straw sunhat sits atop her head, and a flowing floral dress does little to enhance her bony frame. She has a canvas tote bag over her shoulder and is holding a large key ring similar to the one in Bella's pocket.

As she watches Pandora insert one of the keys to lock her front door, Bella can't help but wonder about the others. Pandora had mentioned she still has a key to the front door of the guesthouse. What if she'd kept all the rest as well?

She turns away from the house and looks squarely at Bella, as if she'd had a preternatural awareness of her presence.

Maybe that isn't the case. Or maybe Pandora simply spotted her from inside.

She beckons to Bella, who reluctantly walks over.

Pandora greets her with an air kiss. "How delightful that you've accepted my invitation to come 'round for tea!"

"Actually, I'm just waiting for my son." She holds up the pair of helmets. "He's in the café getting ice cream with his friend."

"Jiffy Arden."

Bella nods, though it was hardly a question. No secrets in Lily Dale.

"I do wish you'd stay for a short visit."

"Thanks, but I really can't right now." She glances at her watch.

"Keeping a tight schedule, are we?"

She finds herself irritated that Pandora pronounces the word with a *sh* sound instead of a *sk*, even though she knows that's the British way.

It's the attitude, not the accent. It's as if she's questioning that Bella might actually have something better to do than sit around sipping tea in the little pink house.

"I'm sorry," she says tautly, "but it's been a crazy day."

"I can imagine."

"Anyway, you seem to be on your way out," she tells Pandora. "Are you going to the speaking event at the auditorium? Everyone else seems to be."

"I was just about to stroll over, yes. But now I've thought better of it. It's bad form to show up late for these things. People do talk around here."

Oh, really? People other than Pandora herself?

"You should go," Bella tells her, but she's shaking her head, her mind made up.

"I rather don't feel like it. My timing is simply off today. I'm afraid I was so knackered this morning that I didn't get up until noon."

Why, Bella wonders, *would she bother to share that bit of information?* Why mention where she was all morning unless she's attempting to subtly let Bella know where she was *not*?

As in driving down Bachellor Hill Road in the car that's parked in her driveway.

She dismisses the notion as farfetched the moment it enters her mind.

Pandora is simply the kind of conversationalist who overshares everything. She chats on about having eaten eggs for lunch and the delightful weather and invites Bella to admire her geraniums and various delights in her yard. An avid gardener, she insists on identifying flowers by their botanical names, presuming that Bella will appreciate them because she's a science teacher.

Did I tell her that? she wonders. *Or did she find out on her own?*

Why would she care?

For that matter, why is Bella bothered by it? She's met plenty of people like Pandora, who have nothing better to do than concern themselves with other people's lives. Irksome but harmless.

As Pandora chatters on, she casually twirls one of her braids. Both are once again accessorized with a pair of scrunchies that match her dress.

Bella keeps an eye on the screen door of the café and is grateful when the boys emerge at last.

"Max!" she calls. "Jiffy! Over here!"

They come toward her, licking their ice cream cones and chatting as if they've known each other all their lives. Max is starting to fit right in with his ragamuffin pal, from his unkempt hair to knees that are dirty and scraped from a few early falls off the scooter. He's hardly become proficient at steering, but at least he's no longer crashing to the ground after managing to hit every pothole on his way over.

And he's wearing shoes She insisted on that. When she suggested that Jiffy do the same, lest he step on broken glass or a yellow jacket, he proudly showed her the scars on the bottoms of his filthy feet from having done both.

"Pandora, this is my son, Max, and this is Jiffy."

"Oh, I know Jiffy. It's good to see you again, young man. And it's lovely to meet you, Max." She shakes their sticky hands, which wins her a slight reprieve from Bella.

Still, however, eager to escape, she says, "Well, it's been nice talking to you, Pandora, but we'd better get going."

Max looks at the helmet she holds out to him. "Don't we have to finish our ice cream first?"

"Of course you must," Pandora tells him. "One cannot eat ice cream in a helmet, much less ride a scooter."

She's right, of course. Max can barely maneuver the scooter without an ice cream cone in his hand.

Bella reluctantly accepts Pandora's invitation to sit on her porch swing for a few minutes.

"The lads can explore the garden," she says.

"But stay where I can see you," Bella cautions them as they head across the lawn. "And don't trample anything!"

"No worries. I'm sure they'll be very careful." Yet Pandora, too, keeps a watchful eye on Max and Jiffy as they poke around the yard speculating about buried treasure.

Meanwhile, Pandora herself pokes around Bella's business and speculates about everything from her love life to her future plans.

"I heard Grant Everard is back in town," she says, after prying into whether Bella has dated anyone since losing her husband and whether she's reconsidering staying in Lily Dale after all—for the summer or permanently.

The answer to both questions is a decided no, of course. As for Grant . . .

Pandora didn't ask a question, but Bella decides it's her turn to pose one. "Do you know him?"

"We've met a few times. Rather handsome bloke, isn't he?"

Ignoring that, Bella asks Pandora how she knew Grant is here. "Have you seen him?"

"I haven't, but someone mentioned that he was here."

"Who was it?"

"Oh, I don't know," she says off-handedly. "Maybe Roxi, the girl who works the gate. Does it matter?"

It does if she heard it from someone who would recognize Grant on sight. That would confirm that the man who checked into the guesthouse is, indeed, Leona's vagabond so-called nephew.

Hearing sirens in the distance, she automatically glances over at Max. He's fine, of course, still holding the cone in one hand and a stick in the other, using it to gently prod into a clump of pachysandra.

Jiffy, too, is accounted for.

But the sirens are a reminder that somewhere, someone is in trouble.

"We really should go," she tells Pandora, looking at her watch. "Boys? Come on. Finish up!"

"There's no need to hurry, love."

"There is. I have something I need to do in a few minutes."

"Oh? What is it?"

Something in Pandora's tone bothers Bella. For one thing, she's tired of the questions. For another, she can't help but wonder if Pandora already knows about the kittens and the feedings. She seems to know everything else about Bella's life, past and present.

Is she a harmless snoop or a dangerous one?

The sirens aren't fading. They're coming closer, making her tense.

"Boys!" She stands abruptly. "Let's go."

"Coming!" Max calls.

Pandora, too, is on her feet. "I'll walk you home. I was about to take a stroll anyway."

"Oh, it's . . . it wouldn't really be a stroll, with the kids and the scooters."

"I don't mind. I rather want to ensure that you get there safely."

Halfway down the porch steps, Bella turns back. "I'm sure we'll be safe," she says with a nervous little laugh. "I mean, why wouldn't we be?"

"Oh, I didn't mean it like that." Pandora offers what she surely intends to be a reassuring smile.

But there seems to be something more to it—a sharpness, or maybe an awareness, in her eyes.

Maybe she's picking up on Bella's anxiety. She probably wouldn't have to be psychic to do that.

But she *is*—supposedly—psychic. Maybe she does know something.

"Mom, look! This will cheer you up!"

"Hmm?"

"Remember this morning when you were sad? Here. This will cheer you up."

She turns to see Max holding out a flower. It has a long, slender stem topped by a well-spaced row of deep-blue, ruffle-tipped petals shaped like miniature upside-down lilies.

"Where did you get that?" Pandora asks, behind her.

"Over there." Max points to the pachysandra.

"I'm so sorry," Bella tells Pandora. "Max, I told you not to disturb Ms. Feeney's garden."

"You said not to trample. I didn't trample. I picked. Right, Jiffy?"

"Right."

"Max, may I see it, please?" Pandora is beside Bella, holding out her hand.

"It's for my mom."

"Max!"

He hands it over to Pandora, who doesn't even have the grace to smile.

Bella bristles. Yes, Max was wrong to pick the flower. But Pandora is the one who invited him to explore the yard. If it weren't for her meddlesome attitude, they wouldn't be here in the first place.

"Max, please apologize," she says. "Pandora, I'll replace the plant if you'll just tell me what it is. I'm going to the store this afternoon."

"*Hyacinthoides non-scripta*. Back in England, it's our national flower. It's my favorite. I planted it here, just as I did at the guesthouse."

"Oh! Odelia said something about that."

"About what?"

"She said that Chance—Leona's cat—was born outside in a bed of blooming Wood Hyacinths."

Pandora shakes her head, irked. "Wood Hyacinths are something else entirely. Those are *Hyacinthoides non-scripta*. I do wish Odelia would get her facts straight. But it's the most peculiar thing . . ." Staring at the blossom, Pandora shakes her head, and then she looks intently at Bella.

"Maybe you can write it down for me so that I don't get confused," Bella suggests. "I'll try to find it at a nursery, and if I can't—"

"No, I don't give a fig about replacing the flower. It's a perennial. In the spring, there are scads of them." She gestures at the pachysandra. "But not this late."

"What do you mean?"

"Max, why did you pick this flower for your mum?" Pandora asks.

"Because she needs to be cheered up."

"But why *this* flower?"

"Because it was the only one."

Bella follows Pandora's gaze to the riot of blooms cascading over the yard.

"But that isn't true. There are lots of other flowers," she tells her son, "and anyway, you weren't supposed to pick any of them."

His brown eyes fill with tears. "I wanted to cheer you up."

"Sweetie, I know, but I wasn't sad. I'm okay."

"You're *always* sad. It makes me sad."

"And your dad, too, by the way."

At that comment from Jiffy, Bella widens her eyes.

"That's what Max said," he goes on. "Right, Max?"

"Max, what did you say?"

He shuffles his feet under her gaze. "I just said we miss Dad, so we get sad."

"And you said so does he," Jiffy says matter-of-factly. "You said he doesn't want you to cry."

"He wouldn't want us to cry," Bella agrees, watching Max stare at his sneakers, "but he can't *say* that to us. We

just know it in our hearts, because he loved us, and . . ."
She swallows hard.

"Plus, boys don't cry, mostly." That comes from Jiffy.

"Did your dad tell you to pick that flower for your
mum?" Pandora asks Max, watching him intently.

"Pandora!" Bella says sharply, putting a protective
hand on his shoulder.

"I don't know why I picked it."

"'Cause your dad said it would cheer up your mom,"
Jiffy says. "Remember?"

Bella's heart lurches.

She sees Pandora give a slight nod and realizes that
she's no longer looking at Max. She's staring at something beside him, in a spot where there's nothing but
thin air.

It's just like the first day Bella met her, when she was
conversing with an invisible someone and informed Bella
that she's supposed to be here.

Really? Because right now, she'd rather be just about
anyplace else on the face of the earth. Enough already.
She's got enough problems wrangling the living. The last
thing she needs to do is worry about the dead.

"We have to go," she says firmly. "Right now."

"Bella, wait. *Hyacinthoides non-scripta* doesn't
bloom in July," Pandora tells her as she hands the helmets to the boys and starts propelling them away with
one hand on each of their shoulders. "It only blooms in
springtime."

Bella whirls on her. "Stop! I don't want any more
botany lessons! Can't you see I don't care? You're out of
line! How can you get so upset with a little boy for picking a stupid flower? And then to insist on talking to him
about . . . about . . ."

"Oh, darling, I wasn't angry that he picked a bloody flower! Children have been doing it for centuries. Especially those."

"What do you mean, especially those?"

Pandora recites, "'*That such fair clusters should be rudely torn from their fresh beds, and scattered thoughtlessly by infant hands, left on the path to die.*' At least Max left the petals intact," she adds with a rueful smile.

He turns around to look at her. "Hey, is that a poem?"

"Yes. It's about England, and it's called 'I Stood Tip-Toe Upon a Little Hill.' It's by Keats."

The name hits Bella like a splash of ice water.

Pandora takes a few steps toward her, as if approaching a skittish animal. After a moment, she cautiously holds out the flower. "Here, love. Please take it. You're supposed to have it."

"What . . . what do you mean?"

"I'm sorry. I wasn't trying to give you a botany lesson. I just thought it might have special meaning for you. It must be blooming out of season for a reason."

"That's a poem, too, by the way," Jiffy observes. "*Season* rhymes with *reason.*"

Everything happens for a reason . . .

"My dad liked poems."

Oh, Max. Your dad especially liked Keats.

But he wouldn't know that.

"We have to go," Bella says again, and her voice comes out choked.

"Right, then." Pandora reaches for her hand, pressing the flower into it. "Just take the bluebell."

Bluebell?

"I thought you said it was a . . . some sort of hyacinth."

"*Hyacinthoides non-scripta* is the botanical name. Back in Britain—and here, too—we just call them bluebells."

Bella stares down at the flower.

Bluebell.

Bella Blue.

As she wipes at her stinging eyes with her hand, she hears Jiffy tell Max, "I don't think that flower cheered her up very good."

She hears something else, too.

Sirens. Louder now, wailing closer by the second.

"Mom?" Max shrinks a little closer to her. "Is there a fire?"

"It isn't a fire truck," Pandora says, and Bella follows her gaze across the park.

Now she sees it too. It isn't a fire truck. It's an ambulance. And it's heading down Cottage Row toward Valley View Manor.

* * *

Less than ten minutes later, Bella closes the Rose Room door behind her and exhales at last.

She hustled the boys away from Pandora's and was relieved when she saw that the ambulance had gone on past Valley View Manor. Down in the grassy common at the end of the lane, she could see the spinning red lights. Paramedics were kneeling there, nearly obscuring a prone figure on the grass at the water's edge.

There were a few rubberneckers, but not many. Most everyone was still in the auditorium.

"What happened?" Max asked.

She managed to find her voice. "I don't know. Let's go inside."

Jiffy wanted to investigate, but Bella told him to come along with them.

"Come on," she coaxed, "you can have cookies and watch TV."

"It's the middle of the afternoon," Max reminded her. "And we had ice cream."

"I know, but it's a special treat because Jiffy is a guest. The cookies will be your dessert."

Giggling at the hilarious notion of dessert after dessert, they accompanied her into the house. She turned on the television and filled a plate with Odelia's zucchini-jalapeño-lime cookies and told them to stay put while she fed the kitten.

As she enters the room, Chance looks up expectantly, almost reproachfully, as if to say, *You're late.*

Well aware that there's no time to waste getting food into little Spidey, Bella walks over to the dresser and looks down at the flower in her hand. She'd squeezed it so tightly all the way home that its petals are drooping a bit. They aren't just shaped like upside down lilies. They're shaped like bells. Little blue bells.

Bella Blue.

"Sam?" she whispers, staring at it, trying to focus, trying to hear him, just like Odelia had said. "Sam, are you here?"

All she can hear are the kittens' faint mews and more sirens.

"Sam? Please. I think they've pulled someone out of the lake, and I don't know who it was, and I . . . I'm afraid. I try to be strong, but . . . I need you. Please."

No reply.

She tosses the flower onto the dresser. It lands on the pile of Leona's financial papers. None of that seems to matter now.

As she turns toward the box of kittens, she remembers what Odelia said about Chance—that she was born in the spring, in a bed of blooming Wood Hyacinths that weren't Wood Hyacinths at all. No, Chance, the cat who crossed her path and led her here to Lily Dale, was born in a bed of bluebells.

"You sent her, Sam, didn't you? You sent her to me. You knew I'd figure it out sooner or later. Bluebells. Bella Blue."

Once again, her eyes are filling with tears. She wipes at them with her hand, but they keep coming.

"Can't you just say something, Sam? Can't you let me hear you, or see you?"

She reaches into her pocket for the crumpled paper towel that was there a few minutes ago, entangled with the keys when she went to unlock the front door.

She must have dropped it. But she feels the socks she'd stashed there and pulls one out, not caring if she gets it soggy with tears or even blows her nose on it.

As she lifts it to her face, though, she realizes it isn't a sock at all.

It's a floral-print scrunchy. Not the same print as the dress Pandora had on this afternoon, but the green-and-yellow one she'd worn the other day.

How did this get into her pocket?

Frowning, she reaches back in for her socks. She finds one.

Only one.

But she'd dropped two on the closet floor this morning while she was looking in her bag for her other sneaker. She'd picked them up, one right after the other, and put them into her pocket.

Frowning, she hastily wipes her eyes on the sock and walks over to where her open suitcase sits on the low mahogany rack just inside the closet door. She pulls a chain to illuminate the overhead light.

Beneath the crisscross of the rack's wooden legs, on the closet floor, sits the other sock she'd dropped and thought she'd picked up.

Pulse racing, she looks again at the stack of papers on the dresser. The ones Max had said he'd found scattered on the floor.

All at once, they matter again.

I have to tell Luther.

He's at the hospital with his sick mother. He said he'd be back as soon as possible. She shouldn't call him in the midst of a personal crisis.

But what if she just sends him a text? That wouldn't be as intrusive as a phone call, would it?

He said to holler if I need help. And I need . . .

She looks back at the wilting bluebell lying beside the papers.

Sam.

He's what she needs. But he isn't answering her plea. Luther might.

She grabs his business card and her phone, wondering if he can even receive texts. Oh, well. She'll soon find out.

She starts typing with trembling fingers: *Sorry to bother you, but I figured out who did it. It's—*

She pauses, realizing that her heart isn't the only thing that's pounding.

There's a burst of loud knocking—banging—on the front door.

"Mom!" Max calls. "Someone's here!"

Still clutching the scrunchy and her cell phone, she scurries out into the hall and down the stairs. Through the glass, she can see the outline of a man.

Has Luther, like Pandora Feeney, materialized at the mere thought of his name? Is that how it works here in Lily Dale?

For a fleeting instant, in her overworked, over-tired brain, it seems entirely possible. Anything seems possible.

Then she opens the door and sees that it isn't Luther at all. It's a uniformed police officer.

Chapter 17

For the second time today, Bella sits at the kitchen table with an authoritative man.

But John Grange isn't the least bit avuncular, there's no warmth in his blue eyes, and he isn't retired law enforcement. He's a police lieutenant. And she's pretty sure he's not trying to determine whether there's been a crime. More likely, he's investigating one that brought him to Bella's doorstep.

Her legs had nearly given way when she saw him standing there.

He flashed his badge, asked if she's the woman who's taken over for Leona Gatto, and said he needed to speak to her.

Her voice quaked as she invited him in.

Conscious of Max and Jiffy watching, wide-eyed, from the parlor, she led him straight to the kitchen.

Now they face each other. He has a body builder's physique, a blond buzz cut, and a hint of sunburn on his clean-shaven cheeks.

He reaches into his pocket.

Is he going to take out a gun? Handcuffs?

Pandora Feeney's matching scrunchy?

Possibilities fly through her head as she steels herself for whatever is about to happen.

A pen. He takes out a pen. And a small notepad.

She attempts to resume breathing, but the boulder has rolled over her ribcage again, as if nudged into place by a barrage of questions.

Did Luther determine that Leona was murdered?

Or did Odelia go to the police?

Had the two of them been conspiring against Bella?

Has she been a suspect all along?

Is she going to need a lawyer?

Millicent—she'll have to call Millicent. Her mother-in-law can afford to help, but at what price? She already seems to have concluded Bella is an unfit mother. What if she takes Max away, regardless of whether Bella is convicted for a crime she didn't commit?

Convicted? Stop getting ahead of yourself.

She doesn't even know why Lieutenant Grange is here.

He's asking her questions, writing down the answers: her full name, date of birth, address . . .

She falters.

The cop rephrases the question. "Where do you live?"

Aware that stumbling this early in the game doesn't bode well, she explains, "I'm actually on the move."

She immediately regrets her phrasing. Does *on the move* sound too much like *on the lam?*

"That is, we're moving," she amends. "My son and I are moving. From New York to Chicago. We just stopped here for a few days when our car broke down."

He asks her about that and for her last address and the one in Chicago. Her heart sinks as she provides it. Now Millicent is irrevocably involved.

After a few final questions, she works up the courage to ask him what's going on.

"A woman was found a short time ago lying unconscious in the reeds at the edge of the lake."

Her breath catches in her throat.

"Unconscious? So she's not . . . ?"

"She's alive, but barely. She'd been in the water, and it looks like she nearly drowned but managed to get to shore."

"Who is she?" Bella asks. "The woman, I mean."

"We don't know. She had no identification. But we found this in her pocket." He holds up a key ring that contains an old-fashioned bit key, a deadbolt key, and a silver heart-shaped disk inscribed with *VVM*. One of the sets Leona had engraved for this season.

That explains his presence. Wanting to believe that this has nothing to do with Leona's drowning, Bella's mind flies through the catalogue of female guests: Eleanor Pierson, Helen Adabner, the St. Clair sisters, Kelly Tookler, Bonnie Barrington . . .

Bonnie was nowhere to be found earlier.

"What does she look like?" she asks Lieutenant Grange. "Is she young?"

"Older."

"Elderly?"

"No. Middle-aged. Short, dark hair."

That description narrows it to Helen or Eleanor.

"What kind of build does she have?" Bella asks, her heart sinking. She likes them both. "Is she more athletic or heavyset?"

"Neither. She isn't heavyset—but I wouldn't say athletic, either."

Eyeing his muscular body, she considers his perspective. A man as fit as he is might not describe very many people as athletic—not even a fifty-something woman who jogs most mornings.

With a stab of sorrow, she says, "I think I know who it is."

Eleanor.

He writes down the woman's name.

"When was the last time you saw her?"

She thinks back. "Last night, around dinner time, when she and her husband left for the message service."

"So she's here with her husband? What's his name?"

He writes it down and then asks Bella when she last saw Steve.

"This morning." She hesitates, not sure whether to mention what had happened to him while he was out running.

Before she can decide, the officer asks again about Eleanor—about where she might have been this morning and whether Steve had mentioned her.

"He said she was still sleeping."

But Eleanor, too, runs in the mornings. What if she wasn't there when Steve went upstairs after Luther left?

If she were missing, though, wouldn't Steve have come looking for her?

He would . . . unless he hadn't told the truth about having left her in bed this morning.

He hadn't wanted to call the police.

Bella presses a hand to her forehead, wishing it could steady her whirling thoughts.

"Where is Mr. Pierson right now?" Lieutenant Grange asks.

"Last I knew, he was upstairs in his room, but I haven't seen him in a few hours."

"Mind if we go take a look?"

She shakes her head and forces herself to her feet. Max and Jiffy are so absorbed in their program again that they don't even look up as Bella and Lieutenant Grange pass by on the way upstairs.

In her haste to answer the officer's knock, Bella left the door to the Rose Room ajar. Beyond the threshold, she knows, Chance is tending to seven of her kittens, as the eighth goes hungry.

She's counting on me.

Yes, just like Bella's own mother had long ago asked Aunt Sophie to step in for her. It's just what moms do—take care of other moms' children when they can't do it themselves.

Can't—or just don't, she thinks as she passes Grant's closed door, thinking of him—and of Jiffy, too. And of Leona and Odelia and Odelia's medium friend Ramona, all of whom have tended to the orphaned, abandoned, or wayward offspring of other women.

I guess it really does take a village.

Even Lily Dale, which is perhaps the oddest village in the world, is just like any other caring community when you look beyond its mystical façade.

Bella leads the police officer down the hall to the Apple Room and steels herself as she knocks on the door. Hearing no movement on the other side, she turns to the officer. He holds up the key ring with a questioning look, and she nods.

Just as he's about to insert it into the lock, the door opens.

Eleanor Pierson looks back at them with red-rimmed eyes that widen when she sees the police officer.

Hearing a gasp, Bella is uncertain whether it came from Eleanor or herself. Perhaps both.

She's startled—albeit relieved—to see Eleanor.

Eleanor appears equally startled—and anything *but* relieved—to see a uniformed officer. She braces herself against the doorframe. "Did something happen to Steve?"

"No," Bella says, laying a hand on the woman's arm to steady her.

Nothing happened to Eleanor, either. So who is the woman barely clinging to life down by the lake?

"Are you Eleanor Pierson?" Lieutenant Grange asks.

"Yes. Is it Steve? Did something happen to him?"

The police officer assures her that's not why he's here and asks where her husband is.

"He went to fill up the car with gas and get a few things from the store."

Bella notices an open suitcase and a pile of clothing behind her on the bed. "Are you leaving?"

Eleanor's gaze flicks to the police officer and then back to Bella.

She nods. "Our daughter called. She's in labor. We have to get back to Boston."

Bella would be certain she's lying if she didn't sound so earnest—and if she hadn't mentioned just yesterday that their daughter is expecting their first grandchild. Besides, how could a fine, upstanding woman like Eleanor Pierson lie to a police officer?

But she does look upset, Bella realizes, as if she's been crying.

Is it just because Steve told her what happened to him this morning, or has there since been another threat?

Should Bella bring up any of that here and now, in front of a police officer trying to identify a nearly drowned woman?

Can the victim be Helen Adabner after all? She, too, has short, dark hair. Maybe Lieutenant Grange interpreted *heavyset* to mean something more drastic. Helen Adabner isn't morbidly obese; she's just . . . pleasingly plump.

Or maybe the woman at the lake isn't someone who's even currently staying here.

"We'll leave you to your packing, ma'am," Lieutenant Grange tells Eleanor Pierson. "Have a safe trip."

"Thank you." She closes the door.

As Bella and the police officer step away, she hears, after a moment, the distinct click of the lock being turned.

Pushing back her growing trepidation and trying not to think of the starving newborn kitten, she leads the police officer up another flight to the third-floor room Helen and Karl Adabner share. There's no answer to their knock on the door.

After a lengthy wait, just in case, Lieutenant Grange inserts the key into the lock.

It doesn't turn.

Bella exhales, again relieved.

"I can't think of any other guest who fits your description," she says.

"But the key is all I have to go on. It must fit one of the doors in this guesthouse. Let's find out which one," the police officer decides.

They work their way from the third floor back to the second, knocking on every door. The afternoon sessions are under way. No one is here. The house feels empty.

Lieutenant Grange inserts the key into one lock after another, but it won't turn.

Bella is now certain she knows which door it opens— and it isn't any of the three they have yet to try on the second floor.

The Teacup Room. The Train Room. The Rose Room.

As Lieutenant Grange inserts his key into the first of the final three locks, Bella wants to tell him not to bother. She has to take him back downstairs. And when that key opens the lock to Leona's study, it might also open the door to more trouble than she can possibly handle.

"Lieutenant Grange . . ."

She breaks off.

The key turns in the lock.

The door opens.

The pink-and-white-wallpapered room is hushed and empty. And the first thing she sees, beside the bone china cup collection on the white bureau, is a Styrofoam wig form.

It had entirely slipped her mind amid the exhaustion and confusion.

Bonnie Barrington, she realizes, might have short, dark hair after all. And Kelly Tookler had been worried about her this morning.

As she tells Lieutenant Grange about that, she finds herself wondering whether the blond wig was some kind of disguise. She doesn't mention that, though. She just volunteers to see if Bonnie left any photo ID behind in the room.

Finding her driver's license in her purse, Bella sees that the photo is indeed of a brunette—but with long hair, not cropped, as the officer described.

Still, the moment he glances at the photo, he offers a grim nod. "That's her. I'll need to take this with me. The wallet, too."

Is he supposed to have some kind of search warrant? Or are they lax about such things around here?

As she hands it over, she realizes that she never even looked closely at his badge when he flashed it. Walking him back downstairs to the door, she wonders if she should ask to see it again.

Then she notices Max and Jiffy hovering in the archway.

"Is that a real gun?" Jiffy asks, pointing at the officer's holster.

He doesn't answer the question, just thanks Bella and tells her that he'll be in touch shortly.

"Thank you. And tell Bonnie . . . tell her we'll all be thinking good thoughts for her."

"I will," he says, but something in his expression tells her that he doesn't expect to be having a conversation with Bonnie Barrington anytime soon.

As he steps out onto the porch, she notices that the sun has slid behind a cloud and the air feels cooler.

He gives a wave and is gone, leaving her to deal with two curious little boys.

"Why was the policeman here?" Max asks worriedly.

Jiffy answers before Bella can come up with a reasonable explanation. "Because he's looking for the bad guy."

That gives her pause. "Which bad guy?"

"The bad guy. You know."

"I'm not sure who you mean." She holds her breath, waiting for him to say it.

When he merely shrugs, she hears herself ask, "Do you mean the pirate? Was there a pirate?"

"I guess. By the way, can we have more cookies?"

"You forgot to say please," Max hisses into his ear. "Remember? I said she doesn't give things to people unless they say please."

"Can we please have more cookies?" Jiffy amends.

"Guests need extra treats sometimes," Max tells her.

She can't help but smile at their little cookie conspiracy as she tells them that unfortunately, there aren't any left.

"Odelia has a lot more. We can go get some."

"No!" Bella says, a little too sharply.

"But—"

"Max, no means no," she tells him.

"I can go." Jiffy takes a step toward the door.

Her first thought is that she can't very well stop him. Her next is that she has to. It isn't a good idea to let him wander, given what's going on down by the water . . .

Or overall.

"I'll tell you what, boys. We'll borrow Odelia's car and go to the store and buy lots of treats."

"Can Jiffy come?"

"If his mom lets him."

"She'll let me."

"We'll have to check."

"Okay, let's go."

"First, I have to feed the kitten."

"You already did that," Max says.

No, she didn't. She was about to, but she was delayed trying to communicate with her dead husband after he sent her the bluebell. Then she found Pandora Feeney's hair scrunchy in her pocket. Then the cop showed up.

Never a dull moment.

"Spidey's still pretty hungry," she tells the boys. "Maybe he needs some dessert. I'll go give it to him, and then we'll go. You two can watch TV until I'm ready."

They nod agreeably and head into the next room as she goes back upstairs.

Stepping back into the Rose Room, she hears the litter's familiar pipsqueak sounds. Bending over the crate, she's reassured to find that pipsqueak Spidey is mewing heartily along with his siblings.

"I'm so sorry, little fellow," she says as she inserts the tube and begins feeding him right there on the floor, not wanting to waste time getting situated on the chair. "I didn't mean to make you wait so long. I promise it won't happen again."

As he ingests the kitten formula drop by painstaking drop, she looks over at the closet. Again, she wonders how Pandora Feeney's hair scrunchy wound up there.

She *did* live in this house at one time.

But she hasn't in years. Her belongings shouldn't be lying around here as if she still comes and goes freely . . .

Unless she does.

The door is open, the light still on. From this angle, she can see all the way to the back wall of the closet, beneath the row of hanging garments that are neatly arranged in order of length.

There, beneath the hems of Leona Gatto's skirts and dresses, she can see a crack in the closet wall. Not a snaking fissure in the plaster like the one that runs along the ceiling above the bed and elsewhere in this house—in all old houses.

This is a perfect straight edge, perpendicular to the floor.

Somehow, Bella refrains from jumping up and jarring the swaddled, still-feeding kitten on her knees. Somehow, under Chance the Cat's maternal gaze, she manages to carry on as if nothing has happened. She croons patiently to Spidey and strokes his head with her fingertip, hoping he doesn't pick up on her tension as she gapes at the closet wall.

"Take your time, little guy. You deserve it. I sure took my time getting back here to you, didn't I?"

At last, he's ingested two milliliters of formula. She removes the tube and settles him back into the nest with the others. Chance the Cat gives her a slow, appreciative blink before busying herself grooming Spidey as his siblings continue to nurse and knead at her.

Bella pauses to pet Chance's head as she dutifully licks her kitten's fur. "After all you've been through, you're such a good mommy."

Everyone needs to hear that once in a while.

Sam used to say it, and often.

You're such a good mommy . . .

She doesn't suppose she's ever going to hear those words again. Certainly not from her mother-in-law.

Again, she feels a prickle of dread when she thinks about leaving for Chicago. Again, she warns herself to focus on the moment at hand. Max and Jiffy must be growing restless downstairs.

She quickly goes over to the nightstand and opens the drawer where Max stashed Luther's flashlight.

She takes it out, turns it on, and hesitates before going over to lock the Rose Room door from the inside. Just in case.

Then she hurries back over to the closet. Crouched down beneath the row of hanging clothes, she trains the beam along the geometric crack in the wall.

It's definitely not due to a settling foundation. It isn't a crack. And the back wall isn't made of plaster. When she reaches out to knock on it, she hears a hollow sound.

For the second time today, her trembling fingers feel their way to a hidden latch. Yes, there it is, a raised ridge in the corner where the hollow wall meets the plaster one. She presses it and gasps as a piece of the back wall swings away from the back of the closet.

Okay.

Okay.

What now?

She leans out of the closet, listening for Max and Jiffy.

Instead, she hears the faint sound of the front door opening and closing downstairs, signaling the return of one or more of the guests.

Maybe it's Steve Pierson. She wants to see him and Eleanor before they leave. She needs to know whether their daughter really is in labor or if they're frightened, fleeing.

She thinks of Pandora and again looks into the closet.

She has to know. Before she does anything else, before anything else *happens,* she has to find out what's hidden behind that wall.

She reaches past the hanging clothes and pulls the door open until it brushes against them. Then she crawls in and shines the flashlight into the wedge of opening.

The rectangular space that lies beyond isn't a storage niche like the ones downstairs beneath the window seats.

Strips of loosely peeling floral wallpaper in shades of peach and gold cover the back and one sidewall, indicating that they must once have been part of the bedroom itself. Shining the light upward to where those walls meet the ceiling, she sees a carved right angle of wood that matches the painted crown molding in the room. Eerily shrouded in spun webbing, a curved metal bracket extends from the wall to a frosted glass shade with a gaslight key. The fixture is identical to the electric-converted sconce on the bedroom wall just outside the closet door.

This nook, and possibly the closet, too, must have been added long after the house was built. Angling the beam downward, she sees that the hardwood floors, which extend seamlessly from the bedroom into the closet, are abruptly curtailed at the edge of a yawning chasm.

So then, this isn't a secret hiding place.

It's a secret . . .

Portal.

Chapter 18

Bella leans further into the secret doorway, shining the flashlight's beam down into the hole in the floor, into a vertical tunnel. A crude wooden ladder is built into wall, appearing to extend well beyond fifteen, maybe twenty feet—down past the first floor and into the bowels of the house.

She reaches into her pocket and feels around for the change from the ice cream cones. The key ring is there, and her phone, and Pandora's scrunchy, and—

Some coins. She pulls one out, not caring whether it's a penny or a quarter. She drops it into the hole and then listens for a sound.

It hits solid ground with a clank. So then this isn't a hidden well. Nor is it a bottomless pit. It sounded like metal on stone—the basement floor?

The coin drop is immediately followed by a rustling sound that makes her skin crawl. As she leans forward, training the beam in search of glittering rodent eyes and wondering whether she can possibly force herself to climb down that ladder, something furry brushes against the back of Bella's bare leg.

She cries out, nearly toppling into the pit, catching herself on the roughly sawed-off edge of the floor.

It's only Chance the Cat, who for the first time in two days has left the crate with her babies.

Shaken, Bella watches the cat walk calmly past her and hop onto the ladder's top rung. For a moment, she peers into the darkness, whiskers twitching. Then she deftly descends into the hole as if she's done it thousands of times before.

She probably has, Bella realizes. It would explain how she manages to come and go without opening a locked bedroom door. Even a cat's paw could probably depress the secret latch.

But where does the tunnel lead?

There's only one way to find out.

Watching Chance stealthily slink into the darkness beyond the flashlight's glow, Bella tries to convince herself to follow. Only the thought of Max and Jiffy stops her.

Well, not *only* that.

It would be stupid, perhaps even dangerous, to go down there alone.

This, too, will have to wait for Luther.

She clicks off the flashlight and crawls backward out of the closet, leaving the door ajar for the cat.

"Don't worry, guys. She'll be back soon," she assures the mewing litter.

Having promised the same thing to her own offspring, she returns the flashlight to the nightstand drawer and steps out into the hall, locking the door behind her.

A glance down the hall shows that the door to the Piersons' room remains closed, indicating that they haven't left yet.

Sure enough, as she goes downstairs and is about to step into the parlor, she walks right into Steve coming around the corner from the opposite direction.

"Oops, sorry, there," he says, reaching out to steady her. "Are you okay?"

"Yes—are you?"

"Still a little jumpy, I guess."

She looks him in the eye. "Is that why you're leaving?"

He seems taken aback. "Eleanor told you?"

"Yes. She's upstairs, packing. She said your daughter is in labor back in Boston, but I'm guessing that might not exactly be the case. Did something else happen?" she asks. "To you or to her?"

He looks away and then back at her, and she realizes she's hit the nail on the head. "You know, running scared isn't something I've ever done in all my years on the job. I've had to deal with some tough issues. Unions, the community, state mandates, budget problems—I've always prided myself on facing them head on."

"But now?" she prompts when he stops talking and fidgets.

"But now I'm out of my element. If someone tries to kill me or . . . or hurt my wife, then . . . then I may be tough, but I'm no fool. We're not going to stick around here like sitting ducks."

"What happened to Eleanor?"

"What did she say?"

"She didn't say anything at all. Only that you were leaving because of your daughter."

"And you didn't believe her."

"I wasn't sure. What hap—" she starts to ask again.

And then it hits her.

The house is too still.

She'd left the boys in front of the television, but . . .

But now the TV is off.

And the boys . . .

"Max?" she calls abruptly. "Max!"

"He left," Steve tells her. "He and his friend."

"*What?*"

"They were just leaving when I came in."

"What?" she says again and rushes toward the front door with Steve hurrying behind her. "Where were they going?"

"I'm not sure."

"Did they say anything about the playground?" she asks. "We were there earlier. They were looking for buried treasure."

"That must be what they were talking about. I heard one of them mention treasure."

Darn that Jiffy Arden. He might be a sweet kid, but he's a terrible influence. Max would never have wandered outside alone before meeting him.

She pushes out onto the porch, hoping she'll see the boys riding recklessly, perhaps even helmetless, on the street. As long as they're here and in one piece . . .

But the scooters are right where they left them at the foot of the steps, helmets dangling from the handlebars.

The weather has, indeed, changed. Rain wasn't in the forecast, but Odelia isn't the only one around here who pays little attention to meteorologists. When Fritz Dunkle mentioned over breakfast that the newspaper's weather report was calling for a picture-perfect Fourth of July weekend, several of the regulars shook their heads knowingly.

"The weather around here changes on a dime," Kelly Tookler said. "There's really no use trying to predict it."

At the time, Bella found that ironic, since Kelly had just finished talking about a psychic development seminar she'd attended yesterday.

She darts a worried look up and down the lane, gloomy and deserted beneath the darkening sky.

Down in Friendship Park, the ambulance is gone and so are the paramedics, the bystanders, and the victim. Bonnie.

"Max!" she calls. "Max!"

Silence, and then a smattering of applause from the auditorium where the speaking event is still in progress. Across the way, the parking lot is still jammed with cars. A silver sedan with Massachusetts plates sits parked in front of the house.

She takes it all in, searching, but there's no sign of Max.

Panic edges in. She turns to Steve.

"How long ago was it?"

How long has it been, she wonders, since she heard the front door open and close? How long was she upstairs poking around in the closet while her son was . . . he was . . .

A sudden gust off the lake stirs the wind chimes that hang from the porch eaves. They sound louder than they should. Discordant.

Like the wind chimes in her dream.

Startled, she looks up at them.

"It may have been five minutes," Steve is telling her. "Ten, maybe?"

Even one minute is much too long for a boy to be out on his own here, among so many strangers, with the lake . . .

"I wasn't paying much attention," Steve says. "I'm sorry. I didn't realize—"

"Max!" Bella starts to run, limping on her sore toe. "Max! M—"

Steve chases after her, jangling car keys. "Wait, Bella, I'm parked right there at the curb. Come on, I'll drive you over to the playground. I know where it is. I run near there every morning."

Grateful, she hurries with him to the car. He removes a plastic shopping bag from the front seat and tosses it to the floor. Looking down, she sees that it contains bottled water and snacks, all set for the long drive home.

If sensible Steve and Eleanor Pierson are leaving town, then so should Bella and Max. Yes, as soon as she finds him, she decides, they're out of here. They'll take the cat and kittens and . . . and just figure something out.

Like what? Stealing a car? Asking Troy Valeri for a ride to Chicago?

She buckles her seatbelt as Steve climbs behind the wheel and inserts the key into the ignition. Noticing his keychain with its dangling drama masks, she's reminded of the *VVM*-engraved keychain, a troubling thought that leads her right back to poor Bonnie Barrington.

How did she wind up in the lake?

Pushing aside thoughts of menacing pirates, Bella keeps an eye on the road as they bump along. Surely they'll come across Max and Jiffy, or at least people out walking. They can ask if anyone has seen the boys.

But with a big-name draw in the auditorium and a storm brewing, the Dale is a proverbial ghost town. A couple of cats prowl the streets, as always. One—a black one—walks in front of the car as Steve brakes at a corner. She chooses not to interpret that as a sign—not even here.

"We need to stop and ask whoever is working at the gate if the boys have come by," she tells Steve anxiously, looking down the street toward the little hut beside the entrance.

"I'm sure they wouldn't leave town. They must know better."

"Max knows better than to leave the house at all without permission," she blurts. "But that doesn't seem to have stopped him!"

"Hang in there, Bella. Let's just get to the playground. It's going to be okay. I know they were talking about a treasure. They were caught up in an adventure. That's how kids are. I'm a dad, remember?"

She says nothing. If the boys aren't by the playground, she'll ask Steve to drive back over to the gatehouse. No one can come or go without passing that way.

Not officially, anyway. It's not as if the town is an impermeable fortress surrounded by high walls and a moat.

A raindrop splats on the windshield as she spots the swing sets at the end of the road, beside the Lyceum— the Spiritualist Sunday school.

Steve accelerates toward the little patch of gravel near the playground.

She scans the wide field, not wanting to even consider the forested acres that wrap around it. Even earlier, in the sunshine, the dense thicket of trees felt ominous. Now it's downright sinister.

She's aware that this land backs up to Leolyn Wood, with its mysterious Stump and spirit vortexes. She'd said no earlier when Jiffy asked if they could go there so he could show Max the pet cemetery.

Maybe that's where they are now. At least there's no drowning danger there. The lake is back in the other direction, and—

And Jiffy was convinced there might be treasure in the water, she remembers. Sunken, not buried.

Steve has driven beyond the gravel lot and out across the grass, rolling the car to a stop at the edge of the tree line. "Let's go take a look."

Bella sits motionless in the passenger's seat, her mind flying through the possibilities. Searching the woods is going to take a long time. Precious time wasted if the boys don't turn up.

But if they are, and they're in trouble . . .

What do I do?

Sam would know. If he were here, he'd know exactly what to do.

Useless thinking. Sam isn't here, despite what the residents of the Dale would like her to believe. Despite the bluebell, even. She has no one to count on but herself.

And in this particular moment, Steve Pierson. She turns to him, grateful she isn't alone out here. "What if they didn't come this way?"

"Then they went somewhere else, and we'll find them there," he says logically, turning off the car and removing the keys. "But right now, we're *here,* and hopefully so are the kids. Come on."

A soft summer rain is falling in earnest as she steps out into the field and follows him toward the edge of the field. The tall grass, wildflowers, and shrubby undergrowth are broken in a few places. If the boys had entered the woods, they'd have taken one of those paths.

"Max!" she shouts as they circle the perimeter of the field. "Jiffy!"

Steve calls, too. No reply.

Her hair is plastered to her head, and her shoes are thick with mud. But at least there's no thunder or lightning. Max won't like being out in this, though. He'll be wishing he'd stayed home.

Oh, Max. Why would you leave without telling me?

"They must have gone down one of the trails," Steve says when they've circled all the way around to the other side of the field near the car. "Let's start with this one and work our way back." He points at a barely visible break in the foliage.

She hesitates. "If they're in there, they can't have gotten very far. Wouldn't they have heard us calling?"

"Probably. But they might be hiding."

"Max would never do that." Jiffy very well might, though.

They shoulder their way into the woods, Steve walking ahead and holding the boughs so that they won't snap back in her face. High overhead, the leafy canopy does little to shield them from the pattering rain. A few spots are slick with moss. She peers into the dense undergrowth on both sides of the trail, trying to imagine Max willingly venturing this far.

If he came, he was trying to impress Jiffy. Slightly older, far more worldly Jiffy. Anger stabs Bella's gut as she thinks of him. Anger and guilt. He's only a child. He isn't to blame for Max's actions or, really, even for his own.

It's his mother's fault. What is she thinking, letting him roam around unsupervised?

She's to blame. So are the rest of them, these so-called mediums who are so focused on contacting the dead that they seem to have lost touch with the living.

It's what Bella wants to believe, and yet . . .

That isn't entirely true, is it? Maybe it's not true at all.

Look at Odelia. She may be unconventional, but her heart certainly seems to be in the right place.

Then again, Bella doesn't really know her, does she? She's not a surrogate mother, a close friend, or a godmother.

Maybe I just wanted her to be those things. And more.

Maybe I just wanted this to be . . . home.

"Max!" she screams, hating her vulnerability almost as much as she hates this place and those people. "Jiffy! Max!"

What if they're not here? What if they are and can't respond?

Are they injured? Has someone taken them?

"What if somebody got to them?" she asks Steve, clutching the sleeve of his polo shirt.

"What do you mean? Why would somebody—who?"

"Leona might have been murdered," she blurts. "And Bonnie Barrington was pulled out of the lake this afternoon."

Something flickers in his eyes. "I'm sure Max is fine," he says, but he's lying. She can feel it. He's trying to protect her from the truth.

And the truth is . . .

Whoever got to Leona and perhaps to Bonnie, too, could have gotten to Max.

Whoever?

She thinks of Pandora's scrunchy lying on the floor of the closet and of the secret tunnel buried within.

Max wouldn't consider Pandora a stranger. He met her this afternoon. She shook his hand.

If she . . .

"I know who it is," she tells Steve in a rush.

"What are you talking about?"

"Pandora Feeney. She did it. She killed Leona."

"How do you know that?"

Quickly, she tells him about the tunnel.

They're not walking anymore. Steve stands listening to her, clutching his keys in his hands.

His keys with the hanging medallion that shows the drama masks.

"But why do you think Leona was murdered?" he asks.

"I . . . I just . . . Please, I have to find my son."

It's pouring now. The wet breeze is turning the leaves overhead, and somewhere, she can hear wind chimes.

They're everywhere in the Dale. But this deep in the woods? There aren't any houses nearby.

And these chimes aren't pleasantly melodious. They're harsh, like the ones in her dream about Leona. They seem to grow louder as she looks at the masks on Steve's key chain.

Chapter 19

"What's the matter?" Steve glances down at his keychain and then up at Bella. "Why are you staring at my keys?"

"Because I was just . . . thinking we should go." She edges away from him, one step, and then another, back toward the field.

"What about the boys?"

"I'll look by the lake. I bet they went to the lake."

"Why do you think that?"

"Because . . . it makes sense, doesn't it?"

No. Nothing makes sense. Nothing.

Or is it the opposite? Does everything make sense now? A terrible, frightening kind of sense?

He's a theater buff, she reminds herself. *That's why he has the drama masks.*

That thought, as it sinks in, only makes it worse. He's done some stage work. Actors are adept at pretending to be someone they're not.

"But why the lake? I heard them say they were looking for buried treasure."

She fights to keep her voice from quavering. "I bet they said *sunken* treasure. That's what they were—"

"Wait—did you hear that?"

"Hear what?"

He stands with his head tilted, listening intently. She holds her breath, listening to the dissonant wind chimes. So he, too, hears them? They're real and not some kind of . . . ghostly harbinger?

"I thought I heard someone shout 'Mom.' It sounded like a child."

"What? I didn't hear it!" No, she was too busy listening for things that aren't there or reading into things that are. "Where did it come from?"

"That way." He points ahead on the trail, using the hand that's still holding the car keys.

Again, she looks at the keychain depicting flip sides of human nature.

Is Steve himself wearing a mask? Is he hiding a dark side?

"Come on, let's go." He starts to push forward.

If she stands her ground, he'll be suspicious. Which is fine, if he's the man he claims to be. But if he isn't . . .

She starts walking again behind him but reaches into her back pocket, feeling around for her cell phone. Surreptitiously, she takes it out. Just in case . . .

In case you need to call for help?

If Steve Pierson is some kind of criminal, then he's hardly going to stand by while she dials 9-1-1.

If he's a criminal, then was he lying about having seen Max and Jiffy? Did he do something to them?

No. No, she can't even allow herself to think that way. If she does, she'll . . . she'll go crazy. Right here and now.

She has to remain rational.

If Steve can be trusted, he's trying to help her.

If he can't, he's trying to lure her deeper into the woods so that he can hurt her.

It's that simple.

Is this what happened to Bonnie Barrington? And to Leona?

But they were both in the lake.

This has nothing to do with that.

If it weren't for that keychain of his, she wouldn't be suspicious of him in the first place, except . . .

Except that she was, she remembers. This morning. When she felt as though his story wasn't adding up. And when he was so reluctant to call the police.

What if he'd made it all up?

Why would he do that, though?

She trips over a vine stretched across the path and topples forward. Steve turns as she cries out, just in time to see her phone flying out of her hand. It lands on the trail by his shoe. Seeing it, he narrows his eyes just slightly and starts to reach for it.

She grabs it before he can and gets to her feet.

"Are you all right?" he asks as she brushes herself off with shaking hands.

"I am. I'm fine. Sorry."

Again, he looks at the cell phone.

She thinks quickly. "I was just getting a text. It startled me when it buzzed in my pocket."

"From whom?"

"What?"

"The text. Who was it from?"

"Oh." Casually holding it so that he can't see it, she activates the screen.

There really is a text, but it's not incoming. It's the unsent one she'd started typing to Luther.

Sorry to bother you, but I figured out who did it. It's—

She was going to write Pandora's name.

"Who sent the text?" Steve asks again, more forcefully.

No actress, she attempts to feign happy surprise. "Max!" The word squeaks out of her mouth. "It says he's back at the house."

"He texts you? I thought he can't even read yet."

Is he guessing, based on Max's age? Or does he know it for a fact?

Not wanting to be caught in a lie, she says, "Oh, he can't. He just . . . he uses voice texting."

As she speaks, she's hastily typing *Steve Pierson* into the text she'd meant for Luther, followed by, *I think I'm in danger.*

"What are you doing, Bella?"

"I'm just responding to him, letting him know I'm on my way back." She resorts to shorthand, hoping Luther will be able to decipher it, praying he can even get a text in the first place: *in wds by plygrnd snd hlp pls hrry.*

"Let's see." Steve stretches out his hand for the phone.

She presses Send and shoves it back into her pocket. "There. All set."

"Can I see it?"

Ignoring the request, she turns and begins to backtrack along the path. "I really want to get back to the house. He's alone, and he's scared."

"Bella, you didn't just text your son."

Trepidation prickles the back of her neck, but she forces herself to keep moving. "Why would you say that?"

"Isn't it obvious?"

Dear God. He knows that Max can't possibly be texting her because . . . because . . .

She tries to shut out the thought, but it comes at her, smothers her.

If anything has happened to Max . . .

I'll die.

Not "cross over," "pass on," "be called home," or any of those innocuous-sounding things the locals refer to. Not merely feel as though she's stopped breathing. No, she actually will stop. She'll cease to exist.

She. Will. *Die.*

Please let him be okay. Please.

"You just told me he can't read, Bella. So how can you text him?"

"We voice text! I told you!"

Realizing she sounds shrill, she turns to look at him. Something has hardened in his eyes.

She whirls again to face the top of the path.

"No," he says behind her as she takes a step in that direction. "Stop."

It isn't a suggestion. It's a command.

She ignores it, breaking into a run.

"Stop!"

He's running, too. Chasing her.

"Help!" she shrieks. "Help me! Someone help me!"

She trips over another vine but manages to stay upright. He hits the same vine but isn't as lucky, and she hears him fall with a curse. That buys her a little time, but not enough. He's gaining on her.

"Help me! Please help me!" She screams as though there's someone, anyone, around to hear.

She hits a patch of moss as slick as an ice skating rink. Her feet skid and arms flail. This time, she can't keep her balance. She sprawls face down on the path, her foot twisting at an unnatural angle.

He's right behind her, standing over her.

"Get up."

She tries to scramble away, clawing at the ground, ignoring the fierce pain in her ankle.

"I said get up!"

She sees it then. Sees his hand.

Sees the gun.

"My son. Did you—"

"Max is fine. Do you think I'm a monster? I have a little girl the same age. I would never hurt a child, Bella. Never."

Panic is surging, making it difficult to form coherent thoughts, let alone words. "Why—why should I believe you?"

"Because this isn't about Max."

"Then what? What is it about?"

"Shut up. *Move*."

She shuts up and moves.

"Walk."

"I'm trying." She tests her weight on her right foot. "My ankle . . . I think it might be broken."

"Walk anyway."

She limps, just like . . .

Oh, Odelia. I can't believe there were moments when I didn't trust you.

Please watch over Max for me. Please . . .

I wish you could be the one to raise him.

The wayward thought catches her off guard, but it's utterly right. So right that she's filled with a deep sense of regret that it won't possibly happen.

He should have had his parents. It's not right. It isn't fair.

Prodded through the forest with a gun in her back, she feels tears mixing with the rain on her face. "Why are you doing this?"

"Doing what? You mean helping you look for your son? This was your idea," Steve Pierson says. "Don't you remember? You said he was at the playground looking for treasure in the woods."

"*You* said that."

"Did I?" he asks mildly. "I think that anyone who might have overheard our conversation would agree that you were the one who thought the boys might be in the woods. I was being helpful, driving you here and helping you search."

"You weren't helping." Her words are laced with venom, and she doesn't care. "You were plotting."

"Oh, I don't think so. We split up when we got here, of course, to cover more ground. And then I heard you screaming for help. I searched until I found you . . . but it was too late."

"What are you talking about?"

"You'd fallen down a steep slope and hit your head so hard that you'll never wake up. It will be a terrible accident. Such a shame. Eleanor and I will be so sorry to hear about it, but of course we'll probably be long gone by the time they find your body. Funny how things work out."

His matter-of-fact tone is as chilling as the awful things he's saying—a blow-by-blow recap of something that hasn't happened yet. But he's no psychic. He's a psychopath.

"You made it up," she says in wonder. "What happened this morning, out on the road—you made it up."

"You can't prove that. Nobody can."

"But why? Why would you do it?"

Her mind is cluttered with puzzle pieces, arranging and rearranging them. As they begin to fall into place, she desperately looks from side to side along the trail, instinctively searching for a path to freedom.

It's just like last night, on that dark road with Grant. Except this time, her instincts are dead on. And this time, she doesn't have to worry about making a break for it with her son in tow. This time, it's only her.

Her ankle is hurting, but it's not broken. She's walking on it. She can run on it if she has to.

You can do this. Just look for an opening. Keep walking, keep him talking.

"You were the one I saw in the house that night in the hoodie. You told your wife you'd gone to see *Our Town* at Chautauqua, but you didn't."

"Oh? I had the program. Didn't I show you?"

"Maybe you went just long enough to get that. And then you came back, and you were prowling around the house, looking for something. What was it? Leona's notebook?"

"Oh, please, that's useless. I've had it ever since—" He breaks off, tellingly.

Since the night Leona died.

The night he killed her.

"There's nothing of interest in that notebook," he says. "Even if there was, who could tell? Her handwriting is chicken scratch."

"You're the one who's been coming and going through the tunnel in the closet."

"Tunnel in the closet?" he echoes, sounding as if he has no idea what she's talking about.

He's just playing a role, she reminds herself. She goes on: "You're the one who went through her papers, and you've been looking for her laptop because . . . because . . ."

Why?

Steve stops short, puts a hard hand on her shoulder, and jerks her around to face him. "Do you have it?"

"Why do you want it so badly, Steve? And why did you tear a page from Leona's appointment book?"

The questions are met with a staccato laugh. "You expect me to tell you that?"

"Oh, come on. What do you have to lose?"

Another laugh, humorless. "I have everything to lose. But I'm not going to. I've worked hard all my life to make sure that doesn't happen. I'm going to get what I deserve. And so are you. Now let's go." He nudges her in the back to make her walk again.

The trail narrows ahead, growing steep. But she isn't going to let him march her to her death. There must be a way out of this.

But there isn't. There's only Steve, and woods, and rain, and that gun . . .

Can she get it away from him somehow?

She'd have to catch him by surprise.

Make him think she's given up, resigned to her fate.

As if.

"You know, I'm not afraid of dying," she hears herself say as they continue pushing up the narrow trail, branches snapping back against her now, sharp twigs and wet leaves slapping her in the face.

"Yeah. Sure you're not."

"I'm not," she insists. "I mean, it's just crossing over. Like stepping into the next room. I'll still be here."

He snorts. "That's a load of bull."

"You really think so?"

"You don't believe in any of that stuff. I could tell from the moment I met you."

But something tells her he may not be as certain as he sounds. About her beliefs . . . or about his own?

Both, she realizes, hearing the slightest hint of doubt as he talks on. "No one in their right mind would buy into these parlor tricks. People around here might *know* things, but it's not because 'Spirit' tells them. It's because they snoop."

She can't help but thinks of Pandora Feeney. "Why do you say that?"

"I've seen it time and again. No matter how careful you are, they'll find out your secrets and use them against you."

A burst of clarity. There it is.

"That's what happened with Leona, isn't it? She found out your secrets. So you . . . you killed her and made it look like an accident."

Just as he said he's about to do to me.

"She was brushing her hair that night, and the wind was blowing." Her voice is deceptively steady. "And you sneaked up on her and hit her in the head and made it look like she'd fallen. And then you walked out onto the fishing pier and threw her into the lake."

"How the hell do you know any of that?"

Her gut churns. So it's true. "Like you said, we find out your secrets. No matter how careful you are."

"*We?*" He gives a scoffing laugh. "You're not one of them. How do you know all this?"

Common sense. Educated guesses.

Nothing more. It *can't* be anything more than that.

Stay focused.

"Everyone has secrets, Steve. Even me." She stops walking and turns to face him.

Their eyes meet.

He recoils as if from a physical collision.

In that moment, seeing him falter, she makes her move.

She leaps on him, grappling for the gun. They fall to the ground and roll into the moss and mud, entangled in weeds and wet ferns. Fighting for her life, she claws at his hand and the gun.

Wrangling it from his hand into her own, she rolls away and gets to her feet, panting hard.

She's never touched a gun before in her life, let alone shot one. As she holds it in shaking hands, arms outstretched in front of her, she isn't sure she's capable.

He clearly doesn't think so.

Lying at her feet with the barrel aimed squarely at his chest, he laughs.

"Don't move!" Her thumb clumsily searches for a way to cock the weapon, like in the movies. "Don't move, or I swear I'll shoot!"

"Ladies shouldn't swear." With a chuckle, he gets to his feet.

"I said don't move!"

He reaches out in an attempt to pluck the pistol from her hand, but she holds on tightly.

"I'll shoot you! I will!"

"Not with that, you won't. It's a prop, Bella. We used it in a production of *Arsenic and Old Lace* years ago. I'm a theater buff, remember?" He holds out a hand. "Give it to me."

Her fingers tremble. She doesn't believe him. She doesn't believe a word he says. He's pathological. He lies about everything.

I have a little girl the same age . . .

He does have a daughter. Bella saw photos of her on Eleanor's phone. She's grown, though, expecting a baby of her own.

Why claim she's a little girl Max's age?

But it doesn't matter. All that matters is Bella's little boy.

He needs me. I have to get back to him.

She struggles to keep her aim steady. Focus. Focus.

She's no longer relying on Spirit to bail her out of this.

I can do it myself. I'm doing it now.

"All right," he says. "If you don't want to hand it over, then just drop it."

"Step back! Right now!"

"Don't drop it, then. Don't hand it over either. Go ahead and shoot me." He raises both hands. This time when he looks her in the eye, she sees not a hint of misgiving.

She keeps the gun pointed squarely at his chest, but she knows it's over. The gun is useless. A prop.

Again, he reaches for it.

Again, they wrestle for it.

This time, though, he wins. The moment he grabs the gun, he turns around, takes aim at a nearby tree, and fires.

The sound is deafening. Birds lift from overhead boughs, flapping and squawking.

And Bella spots, with alarm, a splintered bullet hole ripped into the bark.

Chapter 20

"Guess I lied." Steve Pierson gestures at the tree and then at the gun, grinning at Bella. "I've never even seen *Arsenic and Old Lace.*"

A strangled, frustrated sound escapes her throat.

"Let's go. Walk."

He jabs the gun into her back and pushes her along the path into the woods.

Her ankle throbs as she picks her way along.

"Faster," he says. "Faster!"

She trips.

Falls.

He bends over, nudging her with the nose of the pistol. "Get up."

Fury darts through her. "No."

"I said, get up."

"No."

"I'll shoot you."

"So shoot me."

Two, she thinks, *can play at this game.*

He doesn't want to shoot her. She's taking a chance—a huge chance—that he won't.

He's already told her that he intends to make this look like an accident. If it doesn't, if she's found with a bullet in her head in the woods, the cops will leave no stone unturned to find out who did it.

It's not as if he can go into hiding when he leaves here. He wants to take his wife back to their cushy, respectable, happy life in Boston. He wants to retire with full benefits and a nice salary so that he can travel to places that aren't Lily Dale and go to the theater and run miles every morning.

That's exactly what he's doing now: preparing to run. He's been poised to break away from the moment he and Eleanor arrived.

He'd gone through the motions of arriving for their annual vacation, but it was a ruse. He didn't expect to have to stay here. Even if Eleanor wanted to, he knew they wouldn't be able to. Not with Leona gone.

He didn't bargain on my being here to run the place. I put a hitch in his plan. And I'm doing it again right now.

"Nothing happened to you on Bachellor Hill Road this morning," Bella says boldly. "You made up that story because . . . because you did something to Bonnie Barrington this morning, and then you panicked."

Again, his eyes widen just enough to let her know she's on the right track.

"You realized there was only one way to make sure no one suspected you, and that was to make them think you were almost a victim, too. You told Eleanor that someone had tried to run you down, and God knows what else you said, but you scared the living daylights out of her. She thinks the two of you are leaving today because your lives are in danger. The truth is, you're leaving because you killed Leona. I'm just trying to figure out why."

"Why do you think?" He gives a brittle laugh. "Oh, wait, I'll tell you. It's because I'm sick of coming to Silly Dale. So I killed off our hostess. *That* makes perfect sense."

"No. You were trying to keep Leona quiet about something."

Bingo. She's right. She can see it in his eyes. Slowly, aware of the gun, she gets to her feet.

"It's why you tore out the page in her appointment book right before she died, isn't it? Because your name was on it."

"Nope. Sorry, Nancy Drew. You're wrong. *My* name wasn't on it."

This time, he isn't lying. The way he says it, with the emphasis on the *My,* drives home the truth.

"Oh, that's right. You don't believe in this stuff. But your wife does. Eleanor had the appointment. And Leona told her something she didn't want to hear . . . or was it something you didn't want her to know?"

He laughs. "You can think whatever you want. I don't care."

"Sure, you do. Because it's all true. And if I know what really happened, then who else does?" She shrugs. "You can get rid of me, but what about everyone else?"

He glares at her.

She's getting to him.

"This town is filled with people who somehow know things, Steve. It doesn't matter how they know—parlor tricks, magic, spirit guides. But they know. You can run—you're always running, aren't you? You love to run. Every single day. But sooner or later, the truth is going to catch up to you. And when it does . . ." She shakes her head sadly. "I just feel sorry for your family."

"You know nothing about my family."

"I know that your wife loves you. Eleanor believes in you, no matter what you've done to her."

"What are you saying?"

She isn't quite sure—but obviously, she's struck some kind of chord with him.

"Your wife and I had a nice little chat about you." She almost added *the other morning* but thought better of it. Why pinpoint the time? Why not pull the rug out from under him and let him think it transpired since he last saw Eleanor? If he needs information Bella alone can provide—if only to know what to expect when he returns to the guesthouse—then he'll have to keep her alive. At least, for now.

"What did she say?"

"What do you *think* she said?" Bella returns.

"So she knows? Is that it?" Panic is creeping over him.

"Did you really think you could keep secrets from her, Steve? After more than twenty-five years of marriage?"

He rakes a hand through his hair. "How much does she know?"

"Everything," she says simply. "Leona, Bonnie . . ."

He shakes his head impatiently. He knows she's bluffing.

But somehow, she has to keep him talking, keep him convinced that she knows what they're talking about when it's all she can do to maintain her own composure facing a loaded weapon.

"Do you mean your other secrets?" she asks, her thoughts careening through possibilities. "Are you talking about what Leona told her in that last reading, back in June?"

"Of course not. She didn't tell her 'everything.' She barely told her anything. I was sitting right there the whole time."

"Wait—are we talking about the same thing? When you were in Lily Dale, in June?"

"We weren't here in June."

"No, I know, I meant . . . I meant the *phone* reading. In June."

Bingo.

"I heard Eleanor's side of the conversation," he says. "Leona kept talking to her about Paris and April—and of course Eleanor thought she meant the city and the month."

Paris. April.

Bella remembers now that Eleanor had told her about the trip she was so certain her husband was planning to surprise her for their silver wedding anniversary next spring.

"All that time—six years—Leona never brought them up in a reading. Don't think I wasn't worried that she would. Don't think I didn't do everything in my power to keep Eleanor away from her—from Lily Dale. But my wife has a mind of her own."

Good for her. She's going to need it, Bella thinks as he talks on.

"And then out of the blue—bang. There they were: Paris. April. Maybe it was because I'd just seen them the night before. Who knows? But how long do you think it would have been before Leona brought them up again? And next time, she might have figured out who they are."

Who they are. Not what.

Paris and April are people.

Six years . . .

I have a little girl the same age . . .

One of them is his daughter, she realizes. Her name is Paris. Or April. The other must be his mistress.

A secret like that could destroy a man like Steve Pierson if it ever got out. If his job—his reputation, his livelihood, his future—is on the line because the taxpayers don't agree with him over the school budget, imagine what they'd do if they discovered he has a love child with another woman.

"It was only a matter of time before Leona figured it out and told Eleanor. That's why . . . that's why I had to make sure that wouldn't happen."

"Eleanor knows anyway, Steve," Bella tells him. "About April and Paris."

"Who else knows?"

"You mean besides me? And poor Bonnie?"

"Not *poor* Bonnie," he snaps. "The woman was a nuisance. She should have known better. At that hour, all I wanted to do was drink my coffee in peace and then go for my run. And then *she* shows up and starts telling me that she'd been channeling Leona's spirit and that she thinks she was murdered. She was insisting that we call the cops. And the more I say that's crazy—*she's* crazy—and tell her to shut up, the more she badgers me. And then I see the way she's looking at me and I know . . ."

He trails off, shaking his head, and Bella absorbs the terrible truth. Bonnie had perceived that Steve was Leona's killer.

"So you decided to get her out of the way, too," she says quietly. "You decided she should die to suit your selfish purposes."

"I'm not the one who gave her the death sentence."

"What are you talking about?"

Seeing her startled expression, he attempts to gloat. "So there's actually something Miss Know-It-All didn't know?"

"There are plenty of things I don't know," she tells him. "Like how you could have hurt an innocent woman."

"Innocent, maybe. But she didn't have much time left anyway. She told Eleanor yesterday about how she just finished another round of chemo and the doctors are running out of options."

Bella remembers the wig. To think she'd suspected Bonnie might be using it as a disguise when, in reality, she'd been ravaged by treatments in a fight for her life.

"She's going to pull through this," Bella snaps. "And she's going to 'go on and on' about you when she gets to the witness stand."

"What are you talking about?"

So he doesn't know.

She'd only told him Bonnie had been pulled out of the lake, not that she was still alive.

"She's a fighter, Steve. If she wasn't going to let cancer steal her life away, then she sure wasn't going to let you do it."

A shadow slides across his face, nudging the mask out of place. He's wild-eyed, starting to lose his grip—on his emotions, not on the gun.

"You must know this is it," she tells him. "You can do whatever you want to me, but it's not going to change what's going to happen to you. A lot of people are going to be devastated when they find out who you really are."

For a long moment, he just stares at her. Then he cocks the trigger and raises the gun.

This is it.

She braces herself.

This is where it happens. This is where it ends.

She fervently hopes Odelia and the others are right, that it is just crossing over. That she won't just cease to exist. That she'll still be . . . somewhere. Either on the Other Side with Sam or here on earth with their son . . .

Max. I'm so sorry I have to leave you. I love you so much, and I—

But Steve isn't pointing the weapon at her.

Wild-eyed, violently shaking, he's pointing it at his own temple.

Her jaw drops. A word forms on her lips.

"Stop!"

It didn't come from her own mouth. And the resounding shot didn't come from the pistol in Steve's hand. It skitters into the undergrowth as he drops to the ground, bleeding not from the skull but from his shin.

Suddenly, someone is there with them.

"Luther?"

"You okay?" Luther clutches a gun in his right hand and a phone in his left, thumb dialing it as he gives her a quick once-over.

Unable to answer, still trying to catch her breath, she just nods. She may not be okay in this particular moment, but she will be in the next—or the one after that. Soon she'll be able to speak, able to *breathe* again.

"Yeah, send medics up here, too," Luther barks into the phone, bending over Steve as he writhes and moans on the ground. "Tell them they'll see a path right next to my Jeep and to follow it up. Yes, but it's a superficial wound. Bullet nicked him in the leg. What's that? No, she's right here with me. She's safe."

He hangs up and pulls a handkerchief from his pocket. He tosses it onto the ground beside Steve, who grabs it and presses it against his bloody leg. Blood smears on the white linen.

Incredulous that he's actually here, Bella manages to ask him how he found her.

"I heard a gunshot. Saw the maple he hit down there. If he was aiming for you, he's a lousy shot."

She cringes. "He was aiming for the tree. He's an excellent shot. But . . . you couldn't have heard it from the hospital."

"I didn't." He holds up his phone, a twinkle in his kind, brown eyes. "I got your text."

"But . . . how did you make it here so fast?"

"Magic." He winks at her. "This is Lily Dale, after all."

"You might just have made me into a believer." She manages a faint smile, shaking her head, and he laughs.

"I was already back here in the Dale when you texted. I got to the house right after you left. Max and Jiffy had heard you leave, and they didn't know where you were, but—"

"Max and Jiffy? They were *there?* In the house? But I looked for them, and I couldn't find them."

"They were locked in the basement with the cat."

"In the *basement?*"

"They were playing hide-and-seek—with *him.*" He flicks a look of disgust at the man on the ground. "When I got there, I found the front door standing wide open, and I thought something might be wrong."

Yes. She hadn't locked or even closed it in her haste to go find Max, never thinking to question Steve when he said the boys had left the house.

He'd sent them to the basement under the pretext of a game, to get them out of the way.

I would never hurt a child.

Thank goodness. Thank goodness he'd told the truth about something.

"I heard them shouting," Luther says, "and they said they didn't know how the door got locked behind them."

She shudders at the thought of her skittish son trapped in the dank, old cellar, but it could have been worse. Much, much worse.

Then she realizes something. "Wait a minute—you said the cat was down there with them?"

"Right. When I opened the door, all three of them came running out. Max brought her right back upstairs to her kittens, though. He was worried they were hungry. And speaking of magic . . . he told me that the cat can walk through walls."

"I was almost starting to believe the same thing," she says, knowing that the tunnel must open into the basement. "But I was wrong."

About so many things.

"I have to get back home, Luther. I can't leave Max alone."

"He isn't. Pandora Feeney is with him and Jiffy."

Well, speak of the devil. Except she isn't the devil after all. She's just a gossipy local biddy.

Maybe even a magical one, Bella thinks, remembering the bluebell.

"Why is *she* there?" she asks Luther, unsure whether to be dismayed or relieved at the news.

"You'll have to ask her that. She's the one who called me at the hospital and asked me to meet her at the house as soon as possible. She showed up just as your text came in, and I told her to stay so that—what's the matter?" he asks, seeing the look on her face.

"It's just . . . until we got up here and this happened," she says as she gestures at Steve Pierson, "I thought Pandora was behind all this."

"Why would you think that?"

"Because I found this in my closet." She pulls the distinctive floral print hair accessory from her pocket and shows it to him. He listens thoughtfully as she tells him about the secret passageway in her closet.

Two-faced Steve might have been guilty of one crime, but that doesn't mean Pandora Feeney isn't guilty of another.

"And now you're telling me that she's alone with my son, Luther. Just tell me whether she's dangerous."

He shakes his head vehemently. "Not the way you're thinking, no."

"What do you mean?"

"Look, I may not always buy into this Spiritualism stuff, but . . . after all these years on the job, I'm pretty good at reading people. Especially around here. Some of them are the real deal. They really do know things they shouldn't know, and they see things no one else can see."

Yes. Leona did. And Bonnie, too.

"So you're saying that Pandora knows things . . ."

And she sees things.

Sam. She's seen Sam.

"That's what I'm saying, Bella. And that knowing, and seeing, can be dangerous."

He's right about that. But sometimes, it can save your life.

"Pandora had a premonition about Leona's death months ago," Luther tells her. "She tried to warn her, but like Odelia, Leona had no use for her. And likewise, I'm sure. Sometimes, living in such close quarters and isolated for so many months of the year, things can get a little bit dicey among the full-time residents around here. You know—typical small-town life."

Yes. In a town that's anything but typical.

"Anyway, when it happened, Pandora immediately suspected it wasn't an accident. She knew better than to go to the police."

"Because they wouldn't take her seriously, or because they'd suspect her?"

"Both. She took it upon herself to investigate."

"She's been coming and going, then?"

"Yes. She told me about the secret stairway. There are a few of them, actually. She uncovered them when she was doing renovations years ago. They were built into the house during Prohibition."

Ah—so Pandora's bootleggers were authentic after all. And Pandora herself . . .

"Why?" Bella asks. "Why was she sneaking around the house?"

"She knew no one would believe her without evidence. She was trying to figure out motive and pinpoint a suspect."

"You mean, her spirit guides didn't give her that information?"

Luther matches Bella's wry tone. "Sometimes, everyone has to rely on good old-fashioned investigation tactics. Even mediums."

"Why did she call you over today, then? Had she figured out the truth about Steve?"

"No. She'd had a premonition about you. She thought you were in danger."

"She was right." She digests that for a long moment.

Hearing sirens and knowing they're headed this way, she asks, "Can I go now? Or do you need me here?"

"The police will want to talk to you."

"Is it going to take long?"

"Absolutely."

"Then can I go home quickly first? I really need to hug my son."

Luther hesitates, and his eyes are a little bright as he says, "Sure. It's not as if we don't know where to find you. Go hug your son."

He's thinking of his own mother, she knows. A mother who's slipping away from her son moment by moment.

Poised to go, Bella asks one last question. "How's your mom, Luther?"

"She's hanging on."

As is he, Bella knows. Even at his age, even after so many years together, he's not ready to say good-bye.

That's how it is when you're losing someone you love. You hang on tightly for as long as you can. Even when it's time to let go.

"Oh, and Bella? Don't say anything to Eleanor Pierson. They're on their way to the house to talk to her."

"I won't."

"Good. Go ahead. Go home."

She takes off down the trail, his last words dogging her.

She wants to go home so badly that she's almost running, despite her aching ankle.

Running . . .

It nurtures the heart and *the soul*.

So said Eleanor Pierson, quoting her husband, who possesses neither of those things. What if Bella hadn't grasped the truth about heartless, soulless Steve Pierson?

What if she hadn't interpreted that keychain as a sign?

Then I would have been blindsided. I wouldn't have survived.

Just this morning, she'd been wondering how, if everything happens for a reason, that rare kitten had managed to wind up in her care. Now she knows.

Really? So you think it all comes down to something mystical?

What about instinct?

She's a mother. She's been relying on instinct from the moment Max was born.

Luther relies on it as a detective, along with good old-fashioned investigation.

Where is the line between instinct and magic?

One is based in science, and the other is . . .

I don't know. Right now, I don't know, and I don't care.

She bursts out of the woods onto the field and sees Luther's blue Jeep parked nearby. She should have asked him for the keys.

She'll just have to keep going on foot.

Going home.

Chapter 21

Bella can hear the sirens falling away behind her as she races down narrow, muddy lanes, past rainbow houses washed clean beneath a chalky sky. She weaves around cars and pedestrians, splashes heedlessly into pothole puddles. The rain has stopped. The cool lake breeze is in her face and wind chimes tinkle pleasantly, dangling from gingerbread porches and leafy boughs in overcrowded gardens.

She reaches the auditorium. Its doors are propped open, people spilling forth to wander the streets once again. The ghost town has given way once again to the land of the living . . .

The living in search of the dead.

Bella, too, was searching when she arrived in Lily Dale.

But it wasn't for someone she's lost. She knows Sam is gone. He isn't coming back. She'd like to believe he's still out there somewhere. That he sent her that bluebell to let her know she isn't alone. That he might even pop in sometime to say hello. But . . .

I won't hold my breath for that.

It's time to start breathing again. Time to let go.

She did come here searching for something she really can believe in. Something she's lost, yes . . . but not *someone.*

She rounds the corner and sees the big lavender house.

Home.

Where, if not here? If not this house, this town . . . with these people?

They're all there on the front steps: Max, Jiffy, Odelia, Pandora, even Grant, and . . . Doctor Bailey?

Max spots her. "Mom! Where did you go?"

She swallows hard and shakes her head mutely, aware that everyone's eyes are on her. She grabs Max and hugs him.

"You're squishing me, by the way!"

At last, she's able to make a sound. Laughter.

She lets Max go and looks around at the others. "What are you guys doing here?"

"I was just stopping by for a spot of tea," Pandora says.

Yeah. Sure she was.

Odelia is nodding. "And I saw her through the window and thought I'd come over and join you."

No, she was keeping an eye on things, wary of Pandora.

As for Doctor Bailey—"I just wanted to check on the kittens and drop off more formula. I thought maybe you could use it. And I brought over that book about hand-rearing kittens. I forgot to give it to you. Oh, and a scale so that I can weigh them and make sure they're eating enough. Especially our boy Spidey."

"I didn't realize you made house calls."

"I don't, usually. But I figured you might have your hands pretty full around here."

"I do," she admits, knowing he has his hands full as well. But today, dressed casually in jeans and a chambray button-down shirt, he seems much more relaxed than he did in his office.

She points him up the stairs to the Rose Room, telling him she'll join him up there shortly. It's almost time to feed the kitten again.

"Isn't he a splendid chap?" Pandora asks when he's gone.

They all agree that he is—even Odelia, who isn't particularly prone to agree with anything Pandora says.

Grant merely fiddles with his car keys and says, "He's all right."

"Are you on your way out?" Bella asks him.

"I was just about to take my car through the car wash now that the rain has stopped."

"Which seems like a waste of time and money to me," Odelia puts in, "since the rain washes the car."

"Haven't you ever heard of acid rain?" Grant asks her. "The residue is bad for the finish. You should always wash your car after the rain."

"My car? Have you *seen* my car?" She cracks a smile. "I think residue is all that's holding it together."

"Mom, Mr. Grant wants me and Jiffy to go to the car wash with him. Can we?"

"Oh, I don't think he needs company to go to the car wash, Max."

"Yes, he does. He invited us!"

"I really did invite them," Grant says with a smile. "But Max told me he couldn't go without permission, and he didn't know where you were."

"I thought maybe you were playing hide-and-seek with us," Max tells her. "I *hate* that game, by the way. And I hate the basement."

"Me, too," Jiffy agrees. "Except we have to go back down there to get the laptop, because mine is broken and I need one."

"Laptop?" Bella asks. "There's a laptop in the basement?"

"Yes, and I hate the basement, but I need to go get it. Oh, and I hate that guy, too, by the way," Jiffy adds.

"Which guy?" Grant looks around. "Doctor Bailey?"

"No! The hide-and-seek guy!"

"I hate him, too. But I love Doctor Bailey!" Max speaks up. "He saves puppies and kittens."

"I love him, too," Jiffy agrees. "And I love puppies and kittens. I'm getting a puppy this summer. My mom said I can, to keep me out of trouble while she's working."

"Can we get a puppy, too, Mom? To keep me out of trouble?"

Bella smiles wearily. "Don't you think a cat and eight kittens are enough?"

"I need a puppy, too. And I need to go with Mr. Grant to the car wash. Can I?"

Knowing it's best to get him away from the house for a while, Bella agrees.

"Yay! Let's go!" Jiffy says, eager to hop into the red sports car.

"First, you need to go ask your mom, too," Odelia tells him.

"She won't care. She lets me do whatever I want."

That seems to strike a chord with Grant, who rests a hand on the boy's shoulder. "No one gets to do whatever they want. Come on, let's go talk to her."

As they disappear down the street, Bella sees a police car turn the corner. It rolls slowly toward them, crunching on gravel.

Pandora, too, sees it coming. "I think I'll go inside and brew some tea. I'm sure there must be some Yorkshire Gold Leaf in the pantry."

Predictably, Odelia trails her into the house, saying, "I'm sure there isn't."

The door closes behind them, and Bella turns back to Max, wondering whether he's noticed the approaching police car.

He hasn't. He's facing the park at the opposite end of the street.

"Mom, look!" He points. "Do you see it?"

"The lake?"

"No, the rainbow."

She searches the gray sky above the water. There are a few breaks in the clouds where patches of blue are starting to burst through the gloom, but no rainbow.

"I don't see it, Max."

"Well, it's there."

Somehow, she doesn't doubt that for a moment.

Epilogue

July 4

Standing in the kitchen window washing the last of the breakfast things, Bella can see the sun valiantly attempting to peek through the low lake sky.

At the table behind her, Max and Jiffy are in the midst of a surprisingly rousing game of Candyland with the St. Clair sisters, who showed up just as the boys were begging Bella to join in.

"Candyland?" Ruby exclaimed. "It's our favorite game!"

"Candyland was around when you were kids?" Max asked in surprise.

"Oh, my, no. Not until we were grown."

"But we play it nearly every night back home," Opal added. "It's great fun. Do you mind if we join you?"

"Only four people can play," Jiffy told her. "We already have three."

"You can take my place," Bella said quickly, and after a short argument between the elderly women—both of whom wanted to be the red piece—the game was under way.

That freed up Bella to put the breakfast room and kitchen back in order and mull over all that's happened since Lieutenant Grange showed up yesterday to escort Eleanor Pierson away.

As they left, Bella could hear her asking, "It's Steve, isn't it? Something terrible has happened to Steve."

She was right, of course. Perhaps something more terrible than her wildest imagination could fathom. It's going to be a long road back for her.

Eleanor has since been told about April, her husband's longtime mistress, and Paris, his five-year-old daughter with her. He'd set them up in an apartment in Boston and had been living a double life for years—all the more reason he was worried about his financial situation.

Last night at the precinct, after lengthy hours of being questioned by the police—as a witness, not a suspect—Bella was able to hear the audio recording of Eleanor's last telephone reading with Leona. It was discovered on Leona's laptop, which, thanks to Max and Jiffy, Bella had found stashed on a cobwebby shelf in the basement and handed over to the authorities.

They didn't have to let her hear it, she knows. It was a courtesy they'd extended via Luther.

The reading didn't just bring closure but gave her a glimpse into how the Lily Dale mediums communicate with their clients—and, if you choose to believe, with the dead.

Do I believe that's what they're doing?

Or do I believe in coincidences?

Those are the questions Bella has been asking herself since yesterday.

It's not as though she's seen any hard evidence. If she searches hard enough, she may very well find logical explanations for all the strange things that have been happened since she arrived here. For the moment, though, she's suspended the search.

She was astounded by accuracy with which Leona delivered the information. It came at the end of a long reading that was filled with information about personal things Eleanor may or may not have previously shared with Leona.

The medium knew, for example, that there was a baby on the way and was feeling "female energy attached to it." Whether that's accurate remains to be seen. She talked about the importance of taking some time off—which most teachers do in the summer. She repeatedly stressed the importance of Eleanor getting plenty of rest, because "Spirit is showing me that you're overextended."

Who isn't? Bella found herself thinking, unimpressed with the reading at that point, feeling a familiar tide of skepticism washing over her.

Then it came.

"I'm getting something about Paris," Leona's voice said. "It's very important. I don't know if you've been to Paris recently, or maybe you have plans?"

"No," Eleanor replied. "Not at all."

"Europe, then?"

"No. I've never been to Europe. I've always wanted to go, but it's too expensive. We can't afford it. Anyway, I've heard that they don't like Americans in Paris, so that's not even at the top of my list. Maybe they mean Rome? Or Venice? That's where I'd really love to go."

"No. It's Paris. Spirit is very persistent." Long pause. "Paris. And something about the spring? April and Paris."

"Paris in April . . . isn't that a song?" Eleanor asked. "Steve will know. He's right here. Do you know—"

She was cut off by a rumble of male voice in the background.

"Steve says it's a song. But it doesn't mean anything to me."

"That's what I'm getting. Paris. April." Leona sounded like she was listening to someone and relaying their messages. "April. April. Eleanor, Spirit just won't let go of this. Does the month of April have any significance to you?"

"Other than my twenty-fifth wedding anniversary?" Eleanor's voice laughed. "Honey? I think Spirit just blew your surprise. Are you planning to take me to Paris in April?"

Again, the male voice.

Steve, denying it.

Was that the moment when he'd realized Leona was a threat?

From his hospital bed, recovering from the superficial bullet wound to his leg, he'd confessed to killing her. He'd sneaked into the bathroom and knocked her unconscious, then carried her out to the lake and dropped her in.

He was Jiffy's pirate.

I saw it, too, Bella knows now. *The first part, in the bathroom. I saw how it happened, what she was doing, how she felt.*

Was she channeling Leona's spirit?

Someday, she might get the chance to speak to Bonnie Barrington for more details about her own experience with that. Bonnie has yet to regain consciousness, but her condition has been upgraded from critical, and she's expected to pull through. She can't have visitors yet, but whenever she can, Bella will be there.

Last night, she called Millicent to say that she and Max won't be spending the summer in Chicago after all.

"I've found a temporary job here in western New York," she told her mother-in-law.

"Doing what?"

"Managing an inn."

There was a long silence as Millicent digested the news. "That's great, Isabella. Will it lead to something full time?"

"It's just for the summer." Grant had told her this morning that he'll pay her—very well—if she'll keep the place up and running for the rest of the season. She'd be a fool not to take him up on the offer.

He didn't mention September. Neither did she, no longer concerned with what the future might bring. Not the distant future, anyway.

Right now, the only prediction she cares about is the weather.

In keeping with the meteorological forecast of a dazzling Fourth of July, the day had dawned with golden promise. Now, however, the morning sunshine has turned thin and filmy.

It doesn't bode well for Odelia's barbecue this afternoon. Yesterday, she'd invited everyone at the guesthouse to join the party, and they'd all said yes. Even Grant.

She'd included Pandora, who had agreed to come, too, but only after mentioning that it's hardly her favorite holiday.

"Still loyal to the crown?" Odelia had asked. "Or do you have something against sparklers and hot dogs?"

"I *adore* sparklers and hot dogs," she returned, and launched into a diatribe against the American Revolution.

Odelia nipped it in the bud. "Let's put it to rest, Pandora. The war ended hundreds of years ago."

Bella half expected Odelia to add that she was there when it happened, but for once, she refrained from bringing up her past lives.

"Just join us, Pandora. It's going to be a spectacular day."

"I never pay attention to weather forecasts."

"I'm not talking about the weather. Rain or shine, we'll be celebrating freedom," Odelia said firmly, with a meaningful nod at Bella.

How about rain *and* shine? At the moment, the sun is still peeking out, but it's started to sprinkle.

Rainbow weather.

Max insisted he saw one yesterday, but it eluded her. Now finishing up with the dishes, she finds herself searching the sky above the lake. Nope. Nothing but clouds and sun. Rain and shine.

That's okay. I'll take it.

"Oh, no! Mom!"

Bella turns to see Max, wide-eyed, clutching a crimson-stained napkin against his mouth.

"What happened?"

"My tooth!"

His tooth.

Thank goodness. Thank goodness.

Bella hurries to his side and gently tips his head back. "Here, open your mouth. Let's see."

"But I swallowed it."

"Just like you said," Jiffy tells him admiringly. "On the Fourth of July."

That gives Bella pause.

Do I believe in coincidences?

"No, that's mine!" Opal St. Clair is insisting to her sister. "Bella, dear, tell Ruby that it's mine."

"Your what?"

"My red piece, right there in the Lollipop Woods. She thinks it's hers."

"I'm red, because it matches my name."

"No, you're yellow."

"Yellow doesn't match. My name isn't yellow."

"It isn't red, either."

"If I'm not in the Lollipop Woods," Ruby says, "then where am I?"

"But by the way," Jiffy tells Max, "the tooth fairy won't come if you swallow your tooth."

"Yes, she will. My mom says. Right, Mom?"

"The tooth fairy will come no matter what," she assures Max.

"Are you sure?"

"I'm positive. She pops in here all the time to, you know, hike the Fairy Trail."

"The Fairy Trail! That's it." Ruby studies the game board and then looks up, confused. "Where is the Fairy Trail, dear?"

"I think you're still back there in the Peppermint Forest," Max tells Ruby.

Noting that it's time to feed little Spidey again, Bella leaves her son grinning a happy, gappy grin and makes her way back through the quiet house.

Doctor Bailey had been pleased yesterday to see that the little kitten is thriving and that Chance hasn't rejected him.

"She's an unusual cat," he commented as he packed up his scale and instruments.

"You don't know the half of it," Bella replied.

But at least she doesn't walk through walls.

Doctor Bailey promised he'd be back to check on the kittens again later today.

"On a holiday? Is that necessary?" she asked, worried that the kitten might not be doing quite as well as he'd implied.

When he assured her that it *is* necessary—and that he doesn't have other plans anyway—she found herself wondering whether he's simply the most conscientious veterinarian in the world or looking for something to do on this first holiday of summer.

Maybe a little bit of both. Maybe something more, too.

Before he left, Odelia managed to invite him to the barbecue.

He accepted immediately.

Doctor Bailey . . .

Grant . . .

Bella isn't sure how she feels about that.

As she starts up the stairs, she sees that sunlight is falling through the stained-glass window. Multicolored light arcs across the landing.

There. She got her rainbow after all.

Maybe it's a sign. Maybe it means that everything is going to be—

Her foot catches a stair tread.

She falls forward.

So much for signs, Bella thinks wryly, sprawled on her hands and knees. *I really hope that wasn't—*

Wait a minute.

The landing's hardwood floor, now just inches from her face, is . . .

Off.

One of the cracks between the floorboards is a little too wide.

Heart pounding, she looks for evidence of a hidden latch or hinge. Finding nothing, she feels her way along both sides of the crack, pressing, probing. Nothing happens.

She hurries back to the kitchen.

"What are you doing, Mom?" Max looks up from the game as she jerks open a drawer and fumbles around inside. "What's wrong?"

"Nothing. Nothing's wrong. It's fine. I'm fine."

Grabbing a butter knife, she races back to the landing. With a trembling hand, she slides the tip into the space between the floorboards. She runs it along the length of the crack, jiggling it back and forth.

Nothing happens.

This isn't like the closet. No hidden panel swings open or springs toward her.

Maybe she was wrong.

As she pulls the knife out of the slot between the floorboards, she sees one of them rise. Just a little—but enough.

She jams the knife back into the crack and begins to pry.

It isn't easy. She has to wiggle and tug for a long time before anything happens.

At last, it comes free: a rectangular wedge of wood camouflaged as floorboards.

Beneath lies a shallow hidden compartment.

Probably empty, she thinks, as she pokes her hand into the shadows. Or maybe she'll find a ninety-year-old bootleg stash.

But there's a box inside.

A small box that fits into the palm of her hand. It's wrapped in white paper imprinted with golden angels and tied with a blue ribbon.

Slowly, she tears it away and lifts the cardboard lid.

Inside, on a rectangle of cotton, is a necklace.

A delicate tourmaline pendant that exactly matches the color of her eyes.

There is no wilted bluebell tucked beneath the ribbon.

It doesn't come with a note from Sam.

It isn't even a Christmas present. Not really.

No, she thinks as she fastens the chain around her neck, *it's an Independence Day present.*

She smiles through a flood of tears, tilting her face upward, bathed in rainbow light falling through the circular window.

"Thanks, Sam."

Acknowledgments

This series would not have come to fruition without my editor, Matt Martz, who may not be able to communicate with the Other Side but makes incredible things happen on This Side, and my agent, Laura Blake Peterson of Curtis Brown, who's held my hand, picked up the pieces, hit me over the head, and carried me through for over twenty years now. I also extend deepest gratitude to Laura's assistant, Marnie Zoldessy, and to my film agent, Holly Frederick, at Curtis Brown; to Dan Weiss, who published my first novel back in 1993 (we've come full circle twenty-two years later!); to John Lippman for this fantastic opportunity, Nike Power for wrangling and wrestling many Wendy things, and to the rest of the gang at Crooked Lane; to PR powerhouse Dana Kaye; to Carol Fitzgerald and the gang at the Book Report Network; to Peter Meluso; to the Atwell/Cody family—Laura, Todd, Diana, and John—who lovingly fostered Chance and her six newborn kittens while I was away on my summer book tour; to Penelope Smith-Berk and her Community Cats Rescue Organization in Bedford, New York, who help save the lives of hundreds of strays every year (Chance and her babies included); to Doug Halsey and Ready For Rescue, for pulling my fosters Frenchy and Cha Cha and Sunday and more from the kill shelter; to my husband, Mark, who read, reread, and reread again. And again. And—you get it. Finally, to my readers, who can never get enough Lily Dale. If it weren't for you, I wouldn't have been inspired to make this mystical place come alive again in my work. Thank you for believing in me and in Lily Dale. Stay tuned!